Against a background that moves from the desolation of Newstead Abbey, through a Europe still torn by the aftermath of the Napoleonic Wars, to the final desperate struggle for freedom in Greece, this novel tells the story of the battle for the possession of Lord Byron's soul.

Lord Ruthven, his friend, mentor and evil genius, fascinates Byron with his apparent mastery of the world of evil and darkness which holds such fatal attraction for him. Ruthven's dominance is threatened only by Lucy Emerton's passionate love for the crippled poet, a love that endures humiliation and apparent defeat when she becomes Ruthven's unwilling bride.

It is, however, only the beginning of a lifelong battle, for Lucy is determined to save Byron from the darker side of his own nature, which draws him back to Ruthven. In defiance of Ruthven she follows Byron to London, where she is befriended by Shelley and other revolutionary romantics, and later to Europe — but always the sinister shadow of Ruthven falls across their path, haunting their lives and Byron's poetry . . .

> 'Though thou seest me not pass by,
> Thou shalt feel me with thine eye
> As a thing that, though unseen,
> Must be near thee, and hath been . . .'
>
> MANFRED by Byron

Miranda Seymour

COUNT MANFRED

HUTCHINSON OF LONDON

Hutchinson & Co (Publishers) Ltd
3 Fitzroy Square, London W1

London Melbourne Sydney Auckland
Wellington Johannesburg and agencies
throughout the world

First published 1976
© Miranda Seymour 1976

Set in Monotype Baskerville

Printed in Great Britain by The Anchor Press Ltd
and bound by Wm Brendon & Son Ltd
both of Tiptree, Essex

ISBN 0 09 126370 0

For Andrew

Manfred

'Though thou seest me not pass by,
Thou shalt feel me with thine eye
As a thing that, though unseen,
Must be near thee, and hath been;
And when in that secret dread
Thou hast turn'd around thy head,
Thou shalt marvel I am not
As thy shadow on the spot,
And the power which thou dost feel
Shall be what thou must conceal.'

BYRON

Count Manfred

Part One
COUNTRY

I

I sat up with a start as the London mailcoach rattled into the cobbled streets of Nottingham. The carriage heaved with the gentle snores of my fellow-passengers as I pressed my face to the misted window. Ten more minutes and we would be at the coach-house: I began counting off the passing landmarks of the town.

I was coming home, never thank heaven, to return again to Mrs Quentin's Academy for Young Ladies, 22 Hans Place, Knights Bridge. I had spent the last five years at this establishment without, I am afraid, any remarkable results to show for it. My desire for education had ended on the day I discovered the shelf of Gothic novels in the circulating library.

It had been, I heard, a dramatic moment in the history of the Academy when it was reported that Miss Emerton had been secretly supplying her fellow-pupils with the novels of Mrs Radcliffe and that she had actually taken payment for this service. I was summoned to Mrs Quentin's room and told that I was a disgrace to the name of Emerton and the cause of grief and despair to the Academy. My tears were abundant – but unconvincing. In the eyes of Mrs Quentin, a fervent admirer of the works of Dr Johnson, I had committed a cardinal sin. Hence my departure.

I was not in the least repentant. Nothing seemed more delightful than the prospect of returning home to Alvedon, the rambling manorhouse which had belonged to the Emertons since the time of Charles II and which was now owned by my uncle, Mr John Emerton.

As to my history before I came to Alvedon, it's soon told and will be done before I reach the coach-house.

11

I have no memories of my father. He died when I was two, and Harry and I were brought up by our mother. Money was always short and my mother was proud. She would have starved rather than beg off the Emertons, who thought my father had married beneath him. For eight years, she waged a silent battle for a respectability which we could not afford. Newspapers patched up the cracks in the walls and Harry went out, shame-faced, in my father's old shoes and breeches twenty years out of fashion, while I got my new dresses from the drawing-room curtains.

People often said that I looked like my mother when she was young, having the same mass of copper-brown hair, narrow face and green eyes set at a slant. Whether it was true, I do not know. I only remember her as a tired, angry woman in black, who would hit us for no reason and then burst into tears and say we were the devil's children. Harry stayed out of her way when she was in that mood and I soon learned to do the same.

I was eight when one of the village women told me my mother ought to be in Bedlam. Not knowing what Bedlam was, I laughed. But Harry knew.

'Mad?' I whispered, as we sat side by side on my bed in the dark. 'But how can she be?'

'You'll see,' Harry said. 'Everybody says so. They'll come and take her away soon. Then we can go and live with Uncle John at Alvedon. I wish they'd hurry.'

I looked at him with my mouth open. 'How can you say such things? Anyway, I don't believe you.'

'That's because you're such a baby,' said Harry, who was four years older than me. 'That's why she's always hitting us and screaming. Other mothers aren't like that. I've seen them.' He patted my hand. 'Don't worry, Lucy. I'll look after you.'

Two years passed and the village were openly saying what they had once only dared to whisper. They pointed at us in church and shook their heads. They drew back when my mother made one of her rare excursions into the village, staring straight ahead of her, her grey plaits flapping against her shoulders. She hardly spoke to us now. I don't think she even noticed us. She spent all day in her room, staring out of the window while Harry and I ran wild with no one to gainsay us.

12

I was ten when the carriage with black blinds came and took her away. I never discovered who had arranged it. Uncle John arrived the same morning and told us we were going to come and live with him. I began to cry and when he asked me why, I said I was afraid they would come and take me away too, for everybody said that I was like my mother. Harry laughed, but my uncle shook his head and said I must never think of such things. But I have, ever since. I can't help but think of it, when everyone says that madness runs in families.

So Alvedon became our home and after a year I was sent to Mrs Quentin's Academy to learn to be a young lady – which brings me back to the present.

The stagecoach drew up with a great blowing of horns and clamour of voices. I climbed down behind two stout farmers' wives and looked round eagerly for Harry. Instead, I saw my uncle's coachman, Jackson, waiting on the edge of the crowd. Slowly, I made my way towards him.

'Why didn't Harry come? He *always* has, every year.'

'You'd best ask your uncle about Mr Harry,' the coachman said. 'It's not for me to tell you.'

'Why, what . . . ?' But the carriage door closed, preventing any further questions. I sat back with an angry shrug and only began to smile again as we turned into the avenue of limes leading to Alvedon.

We came at a smart trot round the turning into the village and were brought to a halt by such a crowd as I had only seen on election days. A regiment from the Nottinghamshire Yeomanry had come to look for volunteers to fight against Boney and every boy in the village had turned out on the green. You never saw such a shouting and waving of the swords which had lain, cloth-covered in the parlour-cupboards since the last war-scare in '98. The sun glittered down on the gold braid and the soldiers stared ahead, scornful as princes, while their horses stamped and tossed their heads in the heat.

A shadow fell across my dress as Jackson leapt down and elbowed his way into the foray to seize his son by the shoulder, cuff him and dash his hand from the captain's reins. 'I shall go, I shall!' The boy stormed and struggled against his burly father's grasp, while the mothers laughed and cheered. 'Next time, sonny,' I heard the captain say, and Jackson's son slunk back through the ranks, low as a whipped puppy, while others pressed forward to take his place.

'You should have let him go,' I said as Jackson came slowly back, brushing the dust off his broad shoulders. 'To be known as the only boy in the village who didn't fight the French!'

'Aye, and maybe the only boy who lives to say so,' he answered placidly, flicking his whip across the horse's back. 'He's been in enough trouble already in the town.'

'The riots are still going on in Nottingham, then?'

He looked back at me and shook his head. 'Don't call them riots, Miss Lucy. They've got cause to fight for their rights when they're starving. I know them.'

'And I don't, I suppose?' I said, flushing with annoyance. I was not used to being contradicted. He pulled up the horse and looked down at me bleakly. 'Listen, Miss,' he said. 'Things have changed. Look over there.' He pointed the whip towards the stretch of common land where the villagers had once grazed their cattle, sent their children to play, from which they had fuelled their fires and filled their cooking pots. I looked. A neat hedge surrounded it, cutting it off from the village and joining it to my uncle's land. I turned to find Jackson watching me. He nodded slowly. 'Things have changed, Miss,' he repeated and turned his back on me.

Round the curve of the hill we came, past the square grey church and the long grass sighing on the graves, down to the end of the neat street and into the dusty avenue through the park.

'I'll walk down to the house,' I said, opening the door. 'And Jackson – don't tell Mr Emerton that I'm here.'

The coach rolled on past me, bumping and turning on the uneven ground as I walked aside into the field of feather-tipped grass and buttercups, too hot for the sleek cows who raised their heads to stare at me from the shadowed coolness beneath the poplars. Through the branches the soft red brick of Alvedon smouldered, the curving gables and high chimneys sharp against the bright sky. I looked up at it, smiling, then picked up my skirt and hurried through the kissing gate, with a hand to my mouth for luck, running down the close-cropped lawn to the low stone-stepped flower garden where bees hummed through a sea of yellow and rose.

In the yellow-curtained half-light of the library, I found Mr Emerton in his usual attitude, sprawled back in the high-backed leather corner chair, one leg up to support *The Monthly Review*, his nose well forward towards the page. It was his early afternoon ritual and, too late, I remembered his rage when he was disturbed. I walked softly into the room and was edging round the other side of his Sheraton writing table when he opened one eye and winked it at me like an amiable tortoise.

'Come here,' he said. 'I may as well see what the Academy's done for you.'

I went towards him and stood obediently in front of his chair while he looked me up and down.

'Where's Harry?'

'We'll talk about that, later,' he said. 'Not now. Well, they've taught you how to look like a young lady, if not to behave like one. Not bad, Lucy, not bad at all. But Gothic novels . . .'

I looked down at the floor. 'Are you very angry?'

'Damned silly to let them catch you,' said my uncle. 'That's all I'm going to say on the matter.'

I laughed and sat down by the fire. 'I saw the volunteer meeting in the village. Is it serious this time?'

'Never more so,' he said with relish. 'I've been waiting for it to happen. All that moonshine about peace and amity! You should have seen all the local ladies holding forth on the subject. Mrs Chaworth even painted a likeness of Boney from the report of a fellow who had once seen him! I told them they were fools.'

'Except for Lady Winter,' I said slyly. 'Or are you including her?'

My uncle flushed. 'Lady Winter is a woman of as much sense as . . .'

'A man?'

He chose not to hear. 'As if we hadn't had enough of French ways in Nottingham already! Damme last year if a Radical didn't win the election and go prancing through the streets with a bevy of local beauties dressed up in sheets and a trumpeter playing the Marseillaise! I heard one girl had nothing on at all, pretending to be a goddess, Reason or some such rubbish.' He sighed with faint regret. 'I missed seeing that.'

'I heard the riots were still going on,' I said. 'They talk of them even in London.'

'Oh, the town's not what it was,' said my uncle, shaking his head gloomily. 'Everybody shouting for liberty and their own terms, dressing up penny loaves in red paint on a pole and pretending it's Bastille Day. I always said that nothing good comes out of France.' He sucked at his pipe thoughtfully, not noticing it had gone out. 'Always a shoemaker at the bottom of it, too. I do hate a cobbler. In the old days, we would've thrown 'em in the Trent and had an end to it all.'

I leaned back, laughing. 'And Jackson's son, Tom? He's mixed up in it, I hear. I think you might be the first to end in the river, Uncle.'

His shout frightened me out of my seat. 'Don't let me hear his name! If I catch him again, if I ever see him near my land again . . .'

'What sort of a crime is that? He belongs to the village, after all.'

'What sort of a crime!' He put down his paper and glared at me. 'Why, he's after my best pheasants, the impudent young scoundrel. He and his scurvy town friends! You don't know what trouble they give me, Lucy, and you need not look so reproachful.'

'I only think that since they haven't got any land left of their own, they need to get food from somewhere,' I said. 'Does it matter so much to you to lose a few pheasants?'

'Of course I don't mind about the pheasants,' he said, so angrily that I knew he was feeling guilty. 'It's the principle that matters, not the damned birds.'

'I don't believe you for a minute,' I said, laughing, but he only grunted and put up the newspaper again. I wandered round the room, picking up half-remembered objects, seeing how shabby the curtains and carpets looked where the daylight caught them.

'What happened to all your plans for the house, Uncle?' I

asked, pushing forward a chair to hide a patch of threadbare canvas. 'When I was last here, you were talking of silk hangings and new pediments over the doors.'

He looked down suddenly at his old leather buckled shoes and then up at me, with a blankness in his eyes and a painful shake of his head. I went towards him and put my hands over his.

'It's Harry, isn't it? Something's happened to Harry.'

He nodded. 'Fetch me a glass of port from the side-table, will you, Lucy? Thank you.' He reached up to pat my cheek as I put the glass beside him. 'You're a good girl. You . . . you don't suffer from the vapours, do you?'

I smiled. 'Try me.' But my hands were trembling.

'I blame myself for it,' he said, looking away from me. 'The trouble started when I let him go to London. I should have made him stay here.'

'Trouble?' I repeated.

'Gambling,' said my uncle. 'He found a group of friends who went to the silver hells in St James's – and it took a hold on him. He was never here, only for a day or two to ask if I could pay his debts. Which I did. Well, I could hardly have let your brother be put in Newgate, could I? At all events, it got no better. The debts got bigger. Harry grew wilder. I sold some land and sent him the proceeds, hoping he would stop. He didn't, of course. He seemed to have lost all idea of money by last year and if I begged him to come home, he only sent another creditor to see me. By last January, I had no means left to pay and I told him so. He sent me a letter from Paris a month later, saying that he knew I could not pay his last debt, and he did not intend to return to England.'

I swallowed. 'Never?'

He sighed. 'The poor fellow wasn't left much choice, in the end. Boney rounded up all the English in Paris two weeks ago and I'm told they won't be allowed back for eight years or more. Perhaps it was as well for Harry.'

I stared at him dully, unable to believe that he was talking about my brother. 'And that last debt? Was it very much worse?'

'I'm rather afraid it was, my dear,' Mr Emerton said and he

walked over to the window with his back to me. 'Curiously, or, rather, unfortunately,' he said after a pause, 'it was to a new neighbour of ours, the tenant at Newstead.'

'Do you know the amount?'

'Lord Ruthven is driving here tonight to discuss what can be done,' he said. 'I suspect it is more than I could ever pay.'

I left him, as he seemed to wish me to do, and walked slowly up the great carved staircase, hardly knowing which way I went, past the cool, implacable smiles of the marble busts, the languid eyes in the family portraits meeting mine at every turn. The ladies looked down from fondling their pretty lap-dogs to watch me pass, tears rolling down my face for a brother I had never, after all, known.

* * *

I was sitting on my yellow silk bedspread, twisting the tassels in and out of my fingers, my head too heavy to think, when I saw a carriage draw up below the window. Cream and blue and drawn by two horses my uncle would have given his eyes for, it was the smartest, most dashing vehicle I had ever seen in the county. I pulled up the sash and leaned out for a better view.

A young man jumped out and sauntered over to the balustrade to survey the lake with as much authority as if he owned the house himself. It was early evening and the ducks were flying low over the water, skimming the ripples. The young man pulled a silver pistol from his side, raised it and fired. There was a splash, a squawk of fright as the birds rose in a cluster and fluttered away to the dark trees at the end of the water. I heard the man laugh, saw him slide his hand along the pistol as though it was a lover's arm before he turned to look up to the house. I stepped back, but not before he had seen me and swept a low, mocking bow in acknowledgement of my spying.

I had not intended to change my clothes but, passing my reflection in the mirror, I could not bear the thought that this elegant crack-shot who had come to rob us should write me off as a country dowd. I ran to the door and called for Rose, the village girl who had always acted as my maid at Alvedon.

She was plumper than when I had last seen her and very red in the face, as though she had been crying. I gave her my hand and asked after her family.

'Very well, thank you, Miss,' she said in a small voice and she began busying herself with turning down the bed. I frowned.

'Not now, Rose. Our guest has arrived. I think I'll wear my hair loose and, yes, the yellow silk with the low neck – Oh, do hurry!' I exclaimed, as she slowly turned down the sheet.

'Yes, Miss,' she said, but when she looked up, her face was twisted and her shoulders were heaving with suppressed sobs. I sighed and went towards her.

'What is it, Rose? Come, you know you can tell me. We've always been friends. I'm sorry if I shouted at you.'

'Oh, it's not that,' she said, shaking her head dolefully. 'I . . . I'm having a baby. Oh, Miss Lucy, what am I going to do? I'm at my wit's end with misery.' And she started to weep.

I looked at her sharply. Of course, that explained the plumpness. Silly girl . . . I patted her hair. 'And he won't marry you? One of the village boys, I suppose? Well, we'll soon arrange that. My uncle will make him see sense soon enough. I'm sure you'd be a very good mother,' I added, trying to find something comforting to say.

'Oh, Miss, you don't understand at all,' she said, clutching at my hand and looking up at me with her blue eyes round as two moons. 'It wasn't one of the village. It was Mr Harry.'

'Mr Harry!' I stared at her. She nodded and even began to smile a bit. She fumbled in her apron and pulled out a tattered sheet of paper.

'He left this by my door when . . . when he was last here. Oh, I can't help myself, but I'm sorry, Miss, truly I am! I know you think I'm a fool and I am, too!'

I was slowly reading the letter, sickened by its vulgar bravado. Had I been shown it without a word about the author, I would never have said Harry wrote it. But then, I reminded myself bitterly, I did not know Harry.

'Well, Rosy,' it began, '*Here's a fine to-do! The old man's clamping down on the money, there's bills to be paid and my heart broke in two to tell you that I'm off to Paris for a while till the air cools down, or to*

19

find myself a golden dolly to see me through. Here's something I bought for my little Rosy in London – keep it to remind you of – Harry E.'

'And what was the something?' I asked.

She looked away from me and I saw the flush rise up her throat to cover her face. 'A little silver locket, Miss – it was a very pretty gift.'

'With his name on the back and a lock of hair inside,' I said, and swallowed back my tears. 'Oh, I think I do remember it.' Remember it! I had sent it to him six months ago, when he turned twenty-one. I walked up and down the room two or three times, not daring to speak until I was in control. Rose waited by the door, clinging to the knob like a lifeline and 'Oh, Miss!'-ing me every time I looked towards her.

'He did not think to give the child a name, I suppose?' I was ashamed of the pride which rebelled against calling Rose my sister.

She looked down at her feet. 'There was what you might call a . . . ceremony. I went with him at night, together with two other young gentlemen. There's no use in asking me for proof of it, Miss. He put a scarf across my eyes and I only know it was a long journey. I couldn't say which direction. I've nothing to show for that night but this . . .' She burst into heavy, choking sobs. I felt quite desperate.

'No ring, no papers, nothing? What sort of wedding is that?'

'I know I put my name to something,' Rose said helplessly, 'but Mr Harry said he'd keep it with the ring lest I lose it. He was such a fine, honourable young gentleman . . . I thought he spoke from kindness.'

I was inclined to think she had invented this idiotic story to comfort herself. It sounded most unlikely. Better to forget it and think what to do about the child.

'Oh, of course you must keep it,' I said at last. 'You can't put an Emerton child in a foundling home. I'll help if you need money.'

'It's not money, but what my mam will say,' she wailed. 'Sunday school and in the choir and now this! She's reckoning on me to keep the family with a respectable marriage – she's told me so often enough.'

'Then go to Granny Smith's friend on Low Pavement,' I

said, turning away. 'You always say she lends a hand when needs be.' Silence. 'I'll come with you, if that's what you want?'

She clasped her hands. 'Oh, I shouldn't ask it, I know, but if you would, Miss Lucy! I've been so afraid.'

'Come here on Wednesday at ten o'clock,' I said. 'And keep it to yourself. My uncle would never forgive me for this.'

'As if I'd tell anybody! Oh, I do thank you for being so good to me!'

'I'm being nothing of the sort. Go on.' I managed a smile. 'Off you go and leave me to get ready.'

I dressed myself slowly and with care in a dress of golden silk, low-necked and high-waisted, brushed my hair into two heavy coils over my ears, the style which suited me best, unfashionable though it was. After a moment's hesitation in front of the mirror, I smiled at the reflection and added a silver rose to each braid, put a discreetly small black patch high on the left cheekbone to draw attention to the slant of my eyes and stood back to admire the effect before going downstairs. My heart felt like stone, but I was going to show nothing.

At first I thought the library was empty, but he was standing in a corner looking round the room with the proprietorial air which I had noticed before. By leaning back in the shadowed cubicle between the double doors, I was able to observe him, unobserved. Or so I thought. I had only time to notice that his face was thin and of the cultivated pallor of a hothouse lily, that his clothing was so carefully chosen as to show a high degree of vanity, before he turned and smiled at my hiding-place. After a moment, I was obliged to come out, feeling very much at a disadvantage.

'Perhaps I should be flattered by your interest, Miss Emerton,' the soft, slightly affected voice murmured and he leaned back against the bookcases and looked down at me through violet-lidded eyes. I dropped the smallest curtsey that politeness permits and moved further away from him. I was not inclined to break the silence which fell between us. He sighed.

'Silences are only tolerable between friends, Miss Emerton. I should be delighted to be shown the garden while we wait, if you have no prior engagements.'

21

Not to be outdone – 'The delight will be on my side, Lord Ruthven.' He took my arm. I shivered. He was all consideration.

'Your shawl, Miss Emerton? Allow me to fetch it for you.'

'No, no. It was only for a moment. Which path will you choose?'

'There!' He pointed to the lower lawn through the dark avenue of yew. 'My favourite trees,' he murmured as we came into their gloomy shadow. 'I love to shut away the light. May we stand here for a moment?'

'Would you not prefer to stand in a warmer spot?' I asked after five or more minutes had passed. He folded his arms and looked down at me with a thin half-smile.

'I see I must teach you, Miss Emerton. Please, allow yourself to relax and close your eyes – so.' His cold fingers touched my lids and a sudden giddiness made me take a step back. His voice came from a distance. 'You must not draw away from the chill. Absorb it, let it caress you and warm you as it flows into your blood . . .'

'I think we should go back,' I said, suddenly afraid, and without knowing why, I turned and ran towards the sun. He followed me, laughing.

'You are very like your brother, Miss Emerton.' I did not answer. 'He was a charming boy,' Lord Ruthven said after a pause. 'A little weak, but a very handsome fellow for all that.'

'And yet you took him for all he had, and more.' I turned to face him. 'Could you not see that he was still only a child?'

'Oh, come, my dear! No child would be spending all his nights in the silver hells, and your brother was a very . . . faithful customer.'

'And why did you go to them?' I asked, as he held a sweeping branch aside to let me pass. 'You speak as if they disgusted you, and yet you must have been a loyal client to know my brother as one?'

His thin lips smiled, but not his eyes, as he let the flowering branch fall to the ground, throwing white petals before us. 'Have you ever seen starvation, Miss Emerton? Despair? Passion? Yes, you know the words from books, but to see such things with your own eyes, the face of a man who has lost

22

everything, waiting without hope for the final throw, that is life! It is an extraordinary sensation. There is nothing to fascinate me in the ordinary and equable nature.'

I laughed, unwilling to take his declarations seriously. 'Then why did you choose Nottinghamshire for your home? There is nothing to excite your imagination here.'

'I am a creator, not a fantasist,' he said coldly. 'You mistake me for one of Mrs Radcliffe's admirers . . . Your uncle has fine shooting here, I see,' he said suddenly, looking at a fat pheasant strutting into the high grass beneath the elm trees.

'And you. You have excellent shooting at Newstead, I have heard,' I answered with relief. Never did I think to be so glad of such a dull subject!

'Ah, yes!' His eyes lit up. 'I have been teaching my young landlord to manage a gun and he proves an apt pupil.'

'What is he like, Lord Byron?' I asked curiously, as he guided me down onto the flagstones approaching the house. 'His great-uncle used to be the terror of the county, you know. I heard that he did terrible things. My uncle said he killed his coachman and threw him in the carriage where his wife was sitting, then drove them home together!'

Ruthven threw back his head and laughed.

'Indeed, sir, I do not see why . . .'

'Oh, but I remember the occasion,' he began, and then checked himself. I looked at him in astonishment.

'You *remember*! But the old lord died long before you came here.'

'I was thinking of another matter,' he said quickly and immediately began to chatter about Newstead, Byron and the local dignitaries with such malice and wit that I clutched my sides in laughter and wondered how I ever could have disliked him. Lord Ruthven always used charm when at a disadvantage.

My uncle was coming up the path towards us, his wig for once sitting straight on his head, white lace foaming forth under what remained of his chin and his buckled shoes scraped free of their usual coat of mud and grass. His affable smile was a little tight at the edges, and, knowing his anxiety, I looked for and found betrayal in the hand knotted like rope over the top of his cane. As he shaded his eyes to look at us against the sun, Ruthven glanced up and I saw my uncle falter and clutch at the stick. His face turned paler than his powdered wig. Horrified, I ran towards him to catch him before he fell.

'Come back, sir, you must sit. I'll call for some water.'

'No, no!' He pushed me back angrily. 'It was only for a moment, a passing similarity in Lord Ruthven to . . . Will you stop clinging to me, girl!'

'Perhaps it would be wiser to go inside,' Lord Ruthven said gently and I saw my uncle tremble, as I had, when our guest took his arm. We sat him down in the corner chair. Ricketts, the butler, brought some water and platitudes about going out in hot weather, both of which my uncle accepted with resignation. After a few minutes, he declared himself quite recovered.

'Well, sir, and what can we offer you, Madeira? Rum? A glass of wine?'

'No. Just a little Hock and Selzer,' Ruthven said hastily. A short silence fell as I listened to the pigeons beginning their broken half-chant in the trees. The warm summer light slid under the blinds into the room and a comforting feeling of eternity seemed to envelop the three of us until I remembered why our guest was here. After a glass or two, Mr Emerton was his usual hospitable self. He leaned forward in his chair to peer at Ruthven, who was sipping thoughtfully at his Hock and Selzer and smiling to himself.

'And how are you settling in at Newstead? I've heard Mrs Byron's been setting her cap at you.' His voice sank to the whisper he reserved for Radicals and French spies. 'You know she's a Whig, of course?'

Ruthven's mouth twitched as he offered my uncle a pinch of snuff and said with the utmost candour: 'To tell the truth, sir, if there is such a thing, it is the basis of our friendship.'

'Confound it!' My uncle snatched back his hand. (To be a Whig was as good as condemning yourself to eternal damnation in his eyes.) 'I'll have no foxy Whig in my house! I'll . . .'

'Uncle!' I said quickly. 'Not this time!'

He stopped short and glared at me, but I smiled demurely and called to Ricketts to fill Mr Emerton's glass again. He took it and subsided with an angry grunt. Ruthven shrugged and raised his drink to me in a silent toast.

Dinner was announced at six and we passed into the long, cool room where the best Sèvres plates and the heavy candlesticks of fluted silver had been put out. I was glad we were not going to cry poverty to our guest in the hope of grace.

The subject of the debt was not raised during the meal. Lord Ruthven amused himself and angered me by playing cat and mouse with my uncle. Some insight had told him that Mr Emerton liked to pretend to a much wider knowledge than he had, and could never bear to admit to ignorance. I knew for a fact that his reading did not extend beyond Fielding, Smollett and *The Monthly Review*, together with all the local articles which he studied with consuming interest. Ruthven dallied with his food and listened with a bland smile as Mr Emerton floundered out on a philosophical sea in the firm belief that he was discussing cattle breeders. I do remember him saying that he had not yet read Mr Locke's treatise on Jersey cows! Told of a Jacobin conspiracy in Nottingham to burn down the houses of the local squires, my uncle's face turned dark purple as he swore that he would stop them and made me list the servants to see if there were enough to hold the house. I could not tell him that he was a fool to believe such stories and so, with a look of indignation at our guest, I was obliged to go through with the farce; Lizzie and Susan to take the back door, Ricketts and Jackson by the gate, and so on. I could have died of shame for the poor old man, and yet he was clapping Ruthven on the shoulder and calling him an excellent fellow. He had long since lost the reason for the dinner in the port bottle.

The candles were lit, the curtains drawn. Ruthven looked at my uncle, whose head was nodding perilously near his plate. He drew his hands together, as if to pray, and softly said: 'And now?'

I rose, looking down at them, plucking nervously at the silk folds of my skirt. My lips were trembling and I bit down with my teeth. 'Shall I leave you, sir?'

Slowly my uncle raised his head. I looked at his face. 'I see we can provide you with the despair you call life, my lord,' I said scornfully and turned to go.

'Why, what's that?' My uncle cocked his head on one side. In the passage outside, a clamour of voices rushed towards us, then sank to a confused whispering at the door. As I hesitated, it flew open and Jenkins, the new footman, burst into the room. He was eighteen and had only been in service for a week, and I sympathised with his longing look back to safety as my uncle roared at him:

'And what is the reason for this, you young jackanapes? Damme, boy, I don't like it. Not pleased at all! No!'

I saw Ruthven smile as Jenkins cowered back into the corner. 'Come here, you,' he said in a soft, contemptuous voice. Shyly, the boy went towards him. 'Stand up. You're not in front of a gun butt. There's nothing to fear now, is there?' He rumpled the boy's hair lazily with one hand. Jenkins stood beside him, sheepish, all eyes and mouth.

'My dear fellow, charming though you look, we cannot sit in an agony of suspense all night,' Ruthven murmured. Like the boy, I was fascinated. I had never seen a man behave so with a servant.

Jenkins looked up at last with a quick, nervous smile and spoke to my uncle who was irritably drumming on the table with his fingers.

'Mr Emerton, sir, you said we was to tell you if there was poachers about. Susan was out in the Long Walk just now and says she heard some shots from the little copse up beyond Coney Field.' He stopped, head down, playing with the silver buttons of his jacket. 'That's all, sir.'

The veins in my uncle's forehead stood out like knotted tree trunks. 'Poachers!' He hit his temples with his palm, a habit he had managed to break except in moments of extreme fury. 'I've said I'll have no more poachers on my land! I'll have 'em hung at the next Assizes. I'll see 'em strung up in the market place and leave their bones to dry! They'll learn not to rob me of my pheasants, by God they will! Where are they? Let me at 'em!'

His face an alarming colour, he staggered to his feet and started shouting at the petrified Jenkins for his coat and gun to shoot the brigands down. I could have told the boy that my uncle, who hated physical violence, would never do more than swear and shout. My only worry was that he might murder his own health.

His face warmed by the candles, Lord Ruthven leant forward. His eyes were bright and I saw his knuckles whiten as he clasped the arm of his chair. My fear of the man rose again in my throat and I leaned back against the wall, suddenly breathless. The movement went unnoticed as Ruthven nodded to the boy to leave us. He almost ran past me and the door slammed, leaving a heavy silence. We waited for him to speak.

Slowly and deliberately, Ruthven turned to my uncle and said, 'Keep the matter in your own hands, sir. There is no need for judges in the matter.'

'Eh? What's that?' Mr Emerton scratched his head, perplexed.

'Listen . . .' He was smiling, but I saw my uncle shrink away from the soft, venomous voice. 'You are in my debt, to a tune you do not know. There were two wagers, you see.' He glanced round at me. My heart stopped. Surely Harry had not . . . I did not dare to think of it. 'I see that Miss Emerton understands the situation,' he said and turned back to my uncle. 'Money is, frankly, a less amusing wager to a man of imagination. Forgive my being direct. The condition of your charming house is evidence enough that you cannot pay it. Your nephew gambled beyond your own means as well as his. Oh, don't look so anxious, my dear sir. I am a generous man.'

'What do you want?' My uncle asked, staring at his empty glass.

'A hunt,' our guest said, leaning across the table. 'A manhunt – to the death. It's quite legitimate, on your own property. For me, it will be sufficient repayment. Well, what do you say? Come, you have no alternative. Your answer, sir?'

My uncle looked from his glass to Ruthven's smiling face, then turned towards me. 'No,' I said. 'We'll find another way of paying.'

'A hundred thousand pounds – I doubt it,' Ruthven remarked. 'Well, Mr Emerton?'

'Go and be damned to you,' my uncle whispered. 'You know I have no choice. Take your own guns. I'll have no murderer's hands on mine.'

27

'As you wish,' Lord Ruthven said. 'Miss Emerton, perhaps you would be kind enough to direct me?'

'I'll not come with you, but I can tell you the way from the door,' I said reluctantly, as my uncle nodded.

He followed me into the library, his step light and quick. All pretence of languor was gone as he stood beside me on the library steps, where the scent of flowers hung heavy as laudanum on the breathless air. I pointed to the clump of trees on the skyline, dropped my hand as a shot echoed back from the house.

'I pray to God your victim will escape,' I said fiercely as he drew from his sash the silver pistol and slid his hand down it. He turned and lifted my face towards his until I was forced to look into his eyes.

'Cease your prayers, my dear Miss Emerton,' he murmured, his lips almost touching mine. 'You would be wise to remember that I can always press the second debt, if I choose. You're a very charming girl.' I tried to turn but could not. His face melted into the dark and I saw only his eyes, grey, rock-hard and inescapable. My head was spinning. I could not breathe. From his black pupils, my face stared down at me and I heard his voice through a veil of terrible fatigue.

'You see, you cannot pray against me, my dear,' I heard against my mouth, and then he was gone like a ghost without sound into the darkness, leaving me to lean, exhausted, against the broad stone pillar outside the library door. I knew then that when Ruthven chose his prey, there would be no escape.

*　　*　　*

It was past eleven. There was nothing left to do but to watch the fat gold clock on the wall greedily counting the dead minutes. I looked up at a nightjar's vicious croak from the garden, then bent my head back over the embroidery. Sighing, I put it aside. My fingers trembled too much to hold the small needle straight. In the corner chair, my uncle sat motionless, his unlit pipe clenched in his fist. Every sound was distinct. At one moment, I could hear the faint music of a dance in the village, a girl's high-pitched laughter, the wailing strings of a fiddle.

'But it's within the law to shoot poachers on your own land, dammit!' my uncle shouted again, and again I nodded and reassured him.

'Nobody will blame you, sir.'

'Except myself.' He sank back in the chair, his eyes half shut. I never knew one night could age a man so much. I crossed the room to sit on the arm of his chair as I used to do when I was a child, looking down at the weary face under the rumpled bushy wig. He stared at me hopelessly. 'I'm certain the man has long ago escaped,' I began cheerfully when he started from his chair, clutching at my hand. The echo of the shot came back from the hill, gathering strength from each barrier it met, sounding its one, triumphant note over the prolonged scream, a thin, wailing cry of pain. The frightened chattering of a flock of birds rose from the back of the house, then the sound of running feet, the hysterical screaming of a girl. My uncle stood as still as if he had turned to rock, crushing my hand in his as he stared at the blind shutters.

'He's killed him,' I said. 'I never thought . . . Uncle, what are we going to *do*?'

He turned as I spoke, then sat down heavily in his chair, shaking his head. 'There's nothing we can do,' he said at last. 'It's done, and I'm to blame.'

A muffled sound of whispering and creaking doors broke the silence. 'I'll go,' I said. 'Somebody must tell them. Somebody must search the hill. . . .' My control suddenly broke and I began to laugh. 'You should be grateful to our guest: he may have saved twenty pheasants by tonight's work. Isn't that what you wanted?'

He stared straight ahead at the wall, not answering. I don't think he had even heard me. Slowly, I walked across the room and pushed open the door, blocking it so that they could not see the crumpled figure in the armchair. Their eyes were frightened: they huddled like a flock of sheep.

'You heard the shot,' I said. 'Somebody must go up to the little copse. If you find . . . anything, bring it back here.'

Silence. 'Well? Will nobody go? Must *I*?' After a long pause, two men raised their hands. 'Thank you,' I said. 'We will wait for you. Pray God, you'll find nothing.'

29

They nodded glumly and went back down the passage with dragging feet while I returned to the library, to wait.

There were ten minutes of awful and unbroken silence to be endured before one of the maids bobbed her head round the door, flushed with the excitement.

'They're coming down the Long Walk now, please, Mr Emerton.'

'Thank you, my dear.' My uncle's cracked smile was painful to watch. Silently, I fetched his heavy coat and wrapped my cloak round me. The blood was beating like a drum in my head as I followed him out into the back courtyard to join the circle of sharp, white faces under the light of the creaking lanterns. They turned to look at us. My uncle muttered a brusque greeting and pulled his coat closer to him, although the wind of the summer night was soft and warm. The heavy tramp of feet came nearer, the weight of their burden dragging down their steps. Their shoes sounded on the rough cobbles under the arch. The crowd drew back towards the house.

Pale as death, the faces of the two men as they laid the covered body on the stones and stood back. Beside me, my uncle trembled as he took the first step forward. I took one with him.

'Pull down the blanket,' he said. One of the men bent to draw it back, his face turned away as he held up his lantern. I looked down at the twisted face of Jackson's son, his throat torn open, his fists so tightly clenched that the nails had gone through the palm.

'Oh, God,' my uncle said quietly, and without another word he turned and walked back into the house, shutting the door behind him.

One by one, they crept up to look, their eyes wide in horror. Only Jackson stood apart in a corner of the yard, knowing by their glances whose body lay there. When all had looked but him, I saw him shake himself and cover his face with his hand for a moment. We watched as he walked up and looked down for a long minute at his son. We fell back as he laid the body across his shoulders and turned to face us. Tears ran down the wrinkles of his cheeks, but his eyes were dark with hatred as they met mine. I shrank away as he raised his hand, but he let it drop back against his side.

'Oh, I'll not hit you . . . Miss,' he said. 'I'll wait my time. Tell your uncle' – he spat the word like a curse – 'I'll not forget this night. You'll see me again. My son, too.'

He turned at the arch to give me one last look, then disappeared from sight.

I turned to the two footmen. 'Was there anyone else in the wood?'

'No, Miss Lucy,' one of them answered with a puzzled shake of his head. 'Nobody at all.'

'And the coach!' I cried, almost weeping as I stared up into his face. 'The coach? Is that gone, too? Lord Ruthven's coach, man, for heaven's sake!'

He looked as embarrassed as if I had taken leave of my senses. 'You should go and lie down, Miss Lucy,' he said gently. 'It must have been a terrible shock to you.'

The blackness was washing over me in waves. 'You must tell me,' I whispered.

'Why, Miss, you and Mr Emerton went out to watch him drive off after dinner. I never saw anyone kick up so much dust in the drive, the speed he was going at! Don't you remember now, Miss?'

'No,' I said as I sank back. 'I remember nothing.' And I fainted away.

2

Wednesday morning and the expedition I had to make with
Rose came almost as a relief from the oppression in the house
where my uncle and I circled endlessly on the rim of the one
subject in our minds.

I sat beside Rose in the light open carriage, our bonnets
nodding primly to the rhythm of the wheels. Behind the horses'
hooves, the dust blew up in a fine, sharp mist to make us choke
and spoil our dresses. I coughed and covered my eyes with my
hand. Through my fingers, I looked down on the charred
ruins of Jackson's home on the edge of the village. A chair,
its legs burnt down to squat stumps, lay upside down in the
ashes. Nothing else remained to show that anybody had lived
there.

Rose nodded. 'Mam saw him come back up the village
street, with poor young Tom over his arm and his face all dark
and strange. It gave her quite a turn. He went straight to the
house and set a match to it without a word to anybody!' She
stopped to smile at one of the village boys, loitering under the
lime trees, shouldering his pitchfork like a musket. One of the
regiment rejects.

'And then?' I prompted her.

'Well, Mam and all the rest came running out to stop him,
but it were too late by then. Poor Mr Jackson. Like a madman
he was, shouting at them to leave him alone, but they would
not, being afraid of what he'd do next, you see, Miss.'

I nodded.

'That's all,' said Rose, turning pale as we lurched into a
hole in the road.

'Go easy there, Ben,' I called up to the new coachman. 'You'll set no buck speeds in this old cart.'

'Sorry, Miss.' He grinned down at us, a half moon smile, and tightened up the reins.

'But where did he go to, Rose?'

She shrugged her plump, pretty shoulders.

'They watched him set off up Lantern Hill and that was the last anyone saw. But weren't it terrible the way he took it, Miss Lucy? We were all so shocked, really we were! As though Mr Emerton had anything to do with it! Why, everybody knows he wouldn't hurt a fly.'

I couldn't help but smile to think how angry my uncle would be to know that nobody believed in his bluster. 'How do you suppose it happened, then?' I asked, pretending to be busy looking through my silk purse. She stared at me, her blue eyes round as pebbles.

'Oh, we all knew at once what had happened to the poor young fellow,' she said and dropped into a confidential whisper. 'Mr Ricketts saw it straight away, and it was as plain as . . . well, plain as you like, the way he put it.'

'Put what?' My voice rose and she looked at me in surprise.

'Well, he must have run into one of those gangs of poachers from the town. They're rough fellows, I've heard, and we reckon they took him for the keeper. Although why they should have done it in such a nasty way . . . did you see his neck, Miss?'

'You're in no condition to be thinking of such things,' I said sharply. She bit her lip.

'You shouldn't have gone asking me about it, then,' she burst out after a moment, but I looked away from her face and watched the pale cornfields rolling past.

We came across the bridge over the Trent, past the silent row of anglers, heads nodding down in the long grass as their bait floated out, untouched, over the sun-splashed water. The town was a mile away yet, but our pace had slowed to a walk and the horses flicked their tails irritably back against the flies. For some unlucky reason, every soldier who had been recruited to fight Boney seemed to have chosen Nottingham for his practising ground. We were trapped in an unending file of

33

cavalry and foot and everywhere I looked I saw the uniform of the Yeomanry. Rose, who only had to look at a braided coat to fall in love, was enchanted. She leant out of the carriage, looking around and blushing and smiling, calling on me to give an opinion on this man, then that one: I believe she had quite forgotten the reason for our expedition. I sat well back, eyes shut, choked by the thick dust clouds, listening to the clink and tramp, the whistling and laughter.

'What's it about, Ben?' I called up, but Rose was quick to answer, her face shining.

'There's been another riot in the town. The women were out this morning, they say, breaking down the windows of all the butchers' shops because the prices were too high and they're burning all the doors and counters in the Market Place! Oh, Miss Lucy, what if we should meet with them?' Her voice yearned for such a drama.

'Listen,' I said, 'we are going to Cartright Street, which, thank heaven, is nowhere near the Market Place. We shall not stir from that part of Nottingham until we are collected by Ben to return home.'

She sat back in disappointed silence for a minute, but one of the soldiers tossed a bright hedge-flower into her lap as he marched beside the carriage and she began blushing and smiling all over again. A more feather-brained girl I never knew. I had expected to have her weeping and repenting in my arms for the whole journey and I was quite put out by her merriness. All the helpful tracts I had rehearsed the night before were quite wasted.

The high red roofs of Nottingham came in sight and I looked up, startled, rather shocked, at the disfigured board which had once welcomed visitors with the warning that all vagrants would immediately be put in gaol. The word 'vagrants' had been covered with a piece of black cloth on which somebody had scrawled in bold white letters 'tyrants!' I remembered Ruthven's story of Jacobin plots and wondered if it was I, not my uncle, who had been the fool.

The house on Cartright Street was a ramshackle, broken-down hovel. My spirits sank at the sight of it and Ben looked down at us doubtfully.

34

'You're sure this is the address you want, Miss Emerton?'
'Quite sure, thank you,' I said firmly. Rose shrank back
into the corner. 'I'm not sure if I want to do it, any more,' she
said in a faint voice. 'Then let's go home,' I began to say, a
smile of relief spreading over my face, but she shook her head.
'Anything's better than telling Mam,' she added mournfully
and climbed down the steps.

The woman was small and hatchet-faced, with red, washer-
woman's hands. I did not like her face, nor her manner. She
stared coldly at us from the low doorway, hands on hips.

'Mistress Smith said you'd help me out,' Rose muttered,
looking down at her feet as if she wished they were elsewhere.

'Maybe I will, maybe I won't. How many months?'

'Five,' said Rose, her head drooping lower still. A scrawny,
flea-bitten cat ran out of the shadows and I pulled my skirt
out of its way.

The woman nodded at me scornfully without moving her
hands. 'And what's she doing here? The less who know about
my little line of work, the better.' She folded her arms across
her chest and stared at me with small unblinking eyes.

'That's Miss Emerton. You mustn't speak so,' said poor
Rose, nearly crying.

'Well, let's hope Miss Emerton sees plenty of gewgaws to
waste her money on for the next three hours,' she said drily.

'But . . . I thought . . . can I not wait here?' I said, dismayed,
for the carriage had gone and it was not a part of the city I
knew. She laughed.

'No,' she mimicked my voice, 'you cannot wait here. You,
Miss, can come back when my work's over at four o'clock.
You're the one who's paying, I suppose?'

I handed over the money in silence. 'You needn't trouble
yourself,' I said coldly as she began to count it over, coin by
coin. She gave me a cool nod and continued. Rose gave me one
frantic look, her eyes as fearful as a hunted hare. I squeezed
her hand and walked slowly away down the narrow street.

Cartright Street was not a part of Nottingham to be seen
in, nor did I wish to ever see it again. I hurried past the low
houses which jostled each other's walls for a place on the hill.
Thin-faced and silent, the children ran past me, their faces

35

too old for their small bodies, their bruised legs thick with years of factory work. Only one, a tattered sprite with black slanting eyes and a gypsy's skin, stopped to look at me and swagger in my shadow. 'Leave me alone!' I said angrily as he pulled at my dress, rubbing the material in his grubby fingers. 'Oh, ain't we fine!' he said with immense contempt, but he kept a cautious five-yard distance for his persecution. He peered down an alley at the top of the hill and I heard a woman's voice over the splash of water being thrown out over the cobbles.

'Jimmy, yer little sod! Wilt come now, or shall I send Dad out to get yer with a beating?'

The sprite looked back at me with infinite regret. 'Coming, Mam,' he called back and scuttled away into the alley, spider-legged.

I looked down on the town. Below me, the Market Place. But it was not the hodge-podge of stalls and carts and country-women with baskets of fruit that I knew. It was a babbling, swarming mass of faces, an angry heaving of hats and bonnets and shawls, many as red as blood, and not for Mr Pitt's benefit. A bonfire had been lit, and its black smoke was pierced with flames, bright and fast as swordplay. Women, wild and witchlike, piled faggots on the blaze. Sparks shot out like red stars over the crowd. But, still on their horses, the soldiers sat, little plugs of red bottling up the entrance of each street and alley that fed the mass down into the square. Knowing nothing, I felt a fearful waiting, like the people packed below me. An explosion would be almost a satisfaction; one spark had to catch.

My day had dragged on already too hot and too long. I would not walk up and down Low Pavement or drink cups of lukewarm tea in the Assembly Rooms for the next three hours. I remembered how Ruthven had mocked me for only knowing emotions from books. I saw the scornful smile on his face. Below me, a single trumpet raised a forlorn Marseillaise over the crowd, and the red troops edged down a little nearer to the prey. I could not stand and watch any longer. Holding my dress up to my ankles out of the mud, I ran down the hill.

'Miss! Miss!' I looked up, frightened, at the soldier who had leaned down from his horse to grasp my shoulder as I crept by in the shadows. He shook his head at me.

'I'd take another road,' he said. 'You don't want to go down there.'

'Indeed I do not, sir, and you may take your hand away. I go in that direction.' I pointed away from the square. 'My uncle, Mr Emerton, has been waiting for me on Low Pavement this half hour. But I foolishly lost my way.' I smiled up at him, opening my eyes wide.

He lifted his hand. 'Squire Emerton's niece?' He was quite as red as his coat with embarrassment. 'Pardon me for interrupting you. If I'd known who you were . . . '

I nodded graciously and crossed the road through the scarlet ranks, looking back to make sure that I was well out of his sight before I changed route.

I was sucked into the vortex of the crowd as if it were angry water. A mill-race dragged me in, in, into the mass of them. God knows why I was not drowned or broken to bits. My pretty dress with its ribbons and bows made it clear enough that I had no place there, among the desperate faces, the hard corners of bodies. Now I was at the flames! The faces of the women were blistered and roasted like martyrs, yet their muscles swelled like prize fighters as they seized up their loot, heavy doors and wooden blocks, as light in their hands as new-born babies. They threw the weight on to their backs, tossing back their hair, then hurled it on to the blaze. One fury, her eyes mad above the mob, kept count like an incantation. The crowd caught the chant, stamping their feet to the rhythm of her cries . . . 'And a fifty! And a one! And a two!' More ominous than the singing, it swelled into a sullen requiem. Their hate was as real and solid as if I touched it. It terrified me, it was food to them. Behind me, the mass surged forward and back, and I swayed without will, to save my bones. 'And a six! And a seven!' The flames leapt over us, scorching and devouring. The very air was burning. By my side, a thin-faced boy staggered and fell. The crowd rushed in and his face was lost under the current. I heard the man who had stood with him cry out as he bent to search; he pulled away from the clasped hands to push towards one of the women as she staggered towards the

37

flames. I saw his mouth opened in a soundless scream as he pointed and wrung his hands. She stared at him as though she did not know his face, bracing her back against the weight, then hurled him back with a brutal blow that sent him reeling into the mob as she moved steadily on towards the fire. The women cheered her as she stopped to wipe the sweat off her face with her forearm, but she shook her head impatiently and fed the flames, which had sunk down, waiting for the next glutting. 'And a one! And a two!' I was dizzy with heat and weariness, my feet moved like lead and my hair clung damply against my neck, but there was no way back. I felt the fear rise in me, a choking blackness which I could not fight. I wanted to scream, to weep, to shout, but I could find no sound. I was drowning, my breath gone as I struggled for space and found none.

I hardly saw what happened. A woman passed like a black shadow in front of my dizzy eyes. Whether she was tripped or whether she fell, I did not know. I only heard the scream as she crashed forward into the pile, saw the flames shoot up to envelop her as she writhed and kicked on the ground, her body all fire.

The spark had been lit! With a great single roar of fury, the crowd came forward and I sank beneath it. They dragged me with them, sobbing, clutching, my feet bent back, my knees scraping along the stone. The sound rushed over my head like a torrent, the roar of the crowd and the clash of steel, the high whinnying of the horses and the frightened screams of the women. Before us, a red edge where the soldiers formed a line across the square. The crowd fell back, I lost my grasp, fell to the ground in front of two shining boots of black leather. At last, I looked up, not at a red jacket but a fitted grey coat.

Lord Ruthven bowed politely and offered me his hand.

'I am, as always, at your service, Miss Emerton.' He turned to survey the crowd as I struggled to my feet. 'The entertainment seems to be over,' he said as lightly as if we were returning from a play. 'Shall we go?'

I had no choice. Head bowed, I clung to his arm as he guided me through the square, languidly swinging his black cane from side to side to make a path. One man, the poor fellow who had lost his son beside me, pushed forward to bar our way, his fists raised. Ruthven paused, then said very gently:

'You wish to speak to me?'

The man folded his arms and looked at us. 'You'll not be leaving yet,' he said. Ruthven sighed. I gasped, blinded by the flash of steel in the light. The man stood back and cursed us as the sword slid back into the cane. We were not stopped again.

'Make your choice, madam,' he said, stopping abruptly on the edge of the square. 'Find your way alone, or bear with me. I have an appointment which I cannot break, even for the pleasure of your company.'

I was in no mood for mockery. 'I will come with you,' I said weakly. 'I dare not stay alone.'

His mouth tightened. 'That is quite impossible. Wait here.' He motioned me to a bench, bowed and strode away.

I fidgeted on the seat, too nervous to relax while the crowd still surged only a hundred yards away. I hesitated for a moment, tied my bonnet firmly under my chin, pulled it down to hide my face and ran after him. He was easy prey, standing at least four inches over the rest, but I was hard put to keep up his pace. He took a narrow street out of the square, looked round sharply. I slid into the shadows and held my breath as he stared suspiciously back. He shrugged and went on up the alleyway.

At last, he stopped below a dusty inn sign, a painting of a gamecock whose feathers had seen better days. I watched from a doorway three houses down as he rapped his cane twice on the cobbles, very precisely. A window over the sign opened, only a crack, and a dark-faced man peered out.

'Come down,' I heard Ruthven say in a low voice.

'Nobody followed you?'

'Don't be a fool. My time is short. Hurry!'

The window shut silently. A minute later, the man sidled out of the inn, his hat shadowing his face, his coat pulled up to his ears. He cried out as Ruthven caught his arm, tried to back away as it was bent back up to his shoulder-blade.

'Please, my lord!' He gave a sharp yelp of pain as he was lifted clean off his feet and flung back to lie against the door. I covered my mouth with my hand. Slowly, he got to his feet, brushing down his coat. He smiled ingratiatingly. 'One of your little jokes, my lord?'

I could see his face quite clearly as he peered up. Sunken eyes, sallow skin, thin hooked nose, with greasy black hair straggling down his collar: it was not a face I would easily forget.

Ruthven laughed shortly. 'If you like. Next time, perhaps, you'll remember not to sneak off to your lair to save your skin, eh, Richards?'

The other spread his hands deprecatingly. 'I'm more useful alive than dead, my lord.'

'I wonder,' Ruthven said coldly, and I shivered. 'Well, it went well. No doubt they'll make a good report of your work.'

The man rubbed his hands. 'You think so? Many taken?'

'Enough.' He smiled. 'But fear makes your masters in the government greedy, Mr Richards. For every ten victims today, they'll want a score next month. You'll have to work harder for your laurels. I'm afraid.'

Richards shrugged. 'It can be done.' I saw him give Ruthven a sly sidelong glance. 'Forgive my asking, my lord,' he said humbly, 'but what do *you* stand to gain by this?'

Ruthven's laugh was like a death rattle. 'Entertainment, my dear sir. Does that answer you well enough?'

Richards drew back. 'I don't follow your meaning, my lord,' he said in a faint voice. Ruthven gave him a scornful glance but did not reply. Their voices dropped and after a moment they went through the low door. I looked at my watch. Two hours still to wait. Slowly, I walked back down the street to the bench, going over the scene in my mind, reminding myself of the man's face. Caution told me that I would do well to forget it.

*　　*　　*

I was sitting smiling and composed on the seat when he came back, sauntering as idly as if he had only visited his tailor.

'I hope you were in time for your appointment?' I gazed up at him innocently. He took my arm as we walked slowly on in the direction of Low Pavement.

40

'Oh, it was not so urgent after all,' he said lightly. 'Some silk panels for the house which had not come, but the fellow had left with them this morning. A wasted visit.'

'Oh, but . . . How strange you must have thought it to find me in the square! I assure you it is not a habit of mine to join riots.'

'You amaze me,' he said with an ironic smile. 'I understand perfectly. You went, like me, from curiosity. I should not have said so much the other evening about seeing life, rather than reading about it.' He sighed. 'I always get carried away when the company is so charming. I must thank you for such a pleasant visit. What a delightful house it is! I was quite jaded by Newstead on my return and . . .'

'Lord Ruthven,' I said in a faltering voice which I could not quite control. 'I have a very foolish question to ask. When did you leave us? There has been some . . . misunderstanding on the matter.'

He looked straight at me. 'I remember precisely. The carriage was brought round at nine o'clock, and I was home by midnight. That reminds me . . . I heard a shot on the way up the street. Nobody hurt, I trust?'

'Yes, a man was killed,' I said slowly. 'The coachman's son.'

He bent his dark head. 'My sympathies. It must have been a terrible shock.'

'It was.'

'Well, we must take your mind from distress,' he said lightly. 'Would it amuse you to meet my young landlord? I have arranged to be at the Assembly Rooms at half past two.'

I held fast to his arm. 'But the debt? My brother's debt?'

He raised his thin eyebrows. 'It seems that I chose to forget one. Are you really so eager to discover the other, Miss Emerton?'

'I had rather know it than live in fear of what I do not know,' I said.

Ruthven laughed and patted my hand. 'But I adore suspense, you see. I suggest you learn to relish it. If reality could only live up to our fears . . .'

* * *

41

Low Pavement was predictably untouched by the riots six streets away. Its life was preserved in a state of remorseless stability; in my memory, nothing had changed but the hats. Outside the marble columns of the Assembly Rooms, carriages disgorged a steady train of visitors, stout matrons and pretty girls who came, not to meet lovers, but to talk clothes and scandal. Down jumped the feather-tailed lapdogs, taking their daily five-yard stroll before they were captured and clasped like animated muffs. The men were more to be pitied, bowing and smiling wearily, while their ladies called on them to admire expensive trinkets laid out behind the sparkling bow windows, glancing at their watches when they thought no one was looking.

Much though I feared my companion, he was a strikingly handsome man and many envious glances were directed at me as we strolled towards the Assembly Rooms. I was vain enough to be delighted: Lord Ruthven paid none of them the slightest attention. He paused outside the entrance to the Assembly Rooms and glanced at his watch. 'Late,' he said. 'As I expected.'

'We could go in . . .' I began, then broke off in surprise at the sudden change in his face. 'What . . . Oh, but it's Mary Chaworth! I didn't recognize her, she's grown so elegant.'

'He said he would come alone,' I heard Ruthven mutter as I ran from his side to greet her.

'Mary! Why, I would not have known you!' I stopped, suddenly conscious of my muddy dress and slippers as I looked at her, so smiling and assured, her curved lips redder than nature ever made them, her blue eyes slanting and full of practised mystery. I decided I had liked her better five years ago, when she was plump and much less pretty.

'But why did you not tell me you were home? I had no idea you were finished with your schooling,' she purred, taking in every detail of my appearance. I flushed as she raised her arched brows.

'You know how atrocious the road is from home. Even in the carriage, it's impossible not to be spattered with mud.'

'Mud! And the weather here has been so fine... How strange! Come,' and she drew me towards her. 'Tell me the truth, Lucy.'

'If Miss Emerton may be spared from inquisition for a moment,' Ruthven said dryly, 'I would like to introduce her to Lord Byron.'

I curtsied to Mary's companion, a slim, brown-haired boy dressed all in black, before looking up at the soft, arrogant face.

I was fascinated by it. I could not look away. Painted or scuplted, he would have passed as a sulky, good-looking youth. It was the mobility, the restlessness of his features which was so attractive. His mouth was full and discontented, turning down at the corners as if he had looked on the world and found it a dull place, but under the dark brows and long curling lashes, his slow, sleepy eyes studied me intently. I looked down, drawing my silk shawl over my neck and shoulders, wishing that the pavement would open and swallow up Ruthven and my dear friend, Mary Chaworth.

'I am enchanted, Miss Emerton,' he said in a soft accent which I took to be French. 'I regret that we have not met before. To live in ignorance of such refreshing beauty must always be lamented.'

I could think of nothing to say. All I could do was look and look at him, my face red as a poppy to betray me. Mary's laugh broke the spell.

'Poor Lucy's misfortune is in living so far away from us all. It must be at least six hours from Newstead – when the roads are usable. But you said they were intolerable, Lucy, even in fine weather.'

Byron turned to my companion with a smile. 'Ruthven? Didn't you tell me it took you three hours? You exaggerate sinfully, Mary!'

'It's a known feminine failing,' Ruthven said. Byron laughed.

'You will be at the ball, then?' he said to me. I looked blank.

'But of course,' Mary interrupted hastily. 'Had you not received the invitation? How could I have been so forgetful!'

'Remarkable,' Byron said with a grin. He turned as Ruthven, who had been out of temper ever since Mary's unexpected appearance, took his arm.

43

'Byron, I have a place reserved for us, but alas! It is only for two.' He bowed to us. 'Such dear friends will not find it hard to divert each other for an hour.'

'I don't think,' Byron began, looking towards Mary's stony face. 'That is, we had arranged . . .'

'Come!' Ruthven insisted and he bent to whisper, his mouth against the chestnut curls. Byron smiled, then burst out laughing and clapped Ruthven on the back. 'Irresistible! Mary, will you forgive me?'

'Oh, nothing could be more delightful than to walk up and down Low Pavement in the midday sun for an hour,' she said, her voice rising. I wondered how long she would keep Byron as he shrugged impatiently and turned on his heel to walk away, limping slightly on Ruthven's arm. 'God preserve us from hysterical women,' I heard him murmur, and smiled to myself.

'Poor Mary! He should not have deserted you!'

'Oh, it does not worry me! Usually, Byron is almost too attentive. He would do anything for me, anything I asked.'

'He's very charming.'

'I believe you're quite jealous,' she said, looking sharply at my face. I was caught off guard.

'I? Mary, how can you be so fanciful? I spoke five words to him. And what about Mr Musters,' I asked, changing ground before she could reply. 'My uncle wrote that you had an understanding with him.'

'I did,' she said airily, turning to admire a pearl-handled fan in the window. 'But then I met Byron and . . .'

'Poor Mr Musters,' I finished.

She turned to me, her face glowing. 'But, Lucy, confess! Did you ever see a more beautiful boy? You would have done the same. I know it! And the envy in everyone's eyes – oh, it's delicious! He's considered most disreputable, too, after the verses he wrote. You *have* heard of them?'

I was obliged to admit that I had not for fear of being caught by a lie. Mary giggled and whispered:

'They haven't been published yet, and I doubt if anybody will dare take them. We saw the manuscript, and Southwell was shocked to the core. You never saw such poems. Listen to this!

44

> *"Now by my soul, 'tis most delight*
> *To view each other, panting, dying*
> *In love's ecstatic posture lying*
> *Grateful to feeling as to sight!"*

Well, you can imagine what they thought of that!'

'And Lord Ruthven?' I asked with studied casualness. 'What is said of him?'

She stopped laughing abruptly. 'Little good,' she said after a long pause, and looked round as if she expected him to appear behind her. 'There are too many people here. Shall we find a table in the Assembly Rooms?'

We sat at a corner table, the sort usually taken by mothers who wish to keep an inconspicuous eye on their daughters. Nobody was near, but Mary leant forward and spoke in a hushed voice, her face pale and anxious.

'I'm afraid of him, Lucy. Does that seem very foolish? He pretends to be one of us, and yet he has an extraordinary power over people. I can't explain it very well, but when I talk to him, it is as if he had some way of entering my mind. I see the most horrible things, scenes which terrify me even to remember, and he looks at me as though he knew my thoughts. What can he want here, do you suppose?'

The scene in the alley came back to me. I was about to speak of it, but something held me back, and instead I told her of the evening Tom Jackson was shot. She clasped my hand, listening intently.

'How frightful, Lucy! But do you think it was him, or was it an extraordinary coincidence? I believe that he knew somehow what was going to happen and . . .'

'Don't!' I said, shivering at the memory. 'And yet . . . he can be so charming that it seems as if we were mad, not him.'

'I know,' Mary said, her hand falling back on the table. 'That is what I fear most. You see, he has a curious hold over Byron. I can say nothing to him against Ruthven, for he flies into a black rage at the slightest criticism. Ruthven snaps his fingers – and Byron follows. He wants to take him away from me, I think,' she added so slowly that I knew it was the first time she had spoken to anyone of her fear.

45

'He'll find that hard to break,' I said, playing my role dutifully. 'It's clear enough that Byron worships you.'

'I can't lose him,' she said fiercely. 'I won't marry Jack Musters and resign myself to a living death in the country like my mother. We must live while we're still young, Lucy. We have to escape, don't you see!' She sat back, head bent, while I thoughtfully sipped at the cold tea. 'Of course, it may only be that Ruthven dislikes feminine company,' she went on, half to herself. 'He certainly removed the women servants at Newstead very quickly . . . If only I knew.'

I wanted to question her further. If he hated women, I had less cause for fear.

A hat dropped between us on the table. 'A mystery?' Byron said gaily, his arm linked with Ruthven's.

'Oh, women's gossip, nothing more,' Mary answered lightly. 'And where did you spend your hour?'

'We went to the prize fight in the high field. It was excellent fun. Don't look so cross, Mary. You know you fainted the only time I took you.' He sprawled back in his chair, turning to outstare three young ladies who were peering at him like hopeful squirrels from the alcove opposite. Above him, Ruthven kept a silent guard.

'But you, Miss Emerton, I hear, are made of sterner stuff. Ruthven –' he looked up with a smile – 'tells me you went unaccompanied into the riot.'

'Lucy! You didn't!' cried Mary, horrified.

I looked down, scarlet with guilt.

'Please, Miss Emerton,' Byron said softly, leaning forward towards me. 'You misunderstand me. I admire your bravery. God knows there's nothing I hate more than a woman who preaches ideals and leaves others to practise them.'

'Yes, your mother is such a good example of acting on one's beliefs,' Mary said sweetly.

'If you refer to her Whig sympathies, yes,' he said angrily. 'Ruthven will tell you how much courage you need to declare your colour in a bigoted backwater like this.'

'Hush!' Mary said in alarm as heads began to turn and conversations around us faltered to a stop.

'I don't care a damn who hears,' Byron said, his face flushed

46

with excitement. 'We should always fight for what we believe. I, alone, saved Napoleon's statue from being destroyed at Harrow! Yes, I do admire him! But for me, the statue . . .' He picked up my cup and dropped it on the ground where it splintered noisily into a hundred pieces. Ruthven sighed.

'Better if it had been,' Mary said, fanning herself as she leaned back. 'He has a passion for shocking people, Lucy. Don't listen.'

'And what if I have?' he stormed. 'Must we never break the rules? Am I to sit and listen to the rattle of teacups until doomsday, and tell lies because they sound prettier? You know me better than that, Mary. Even the tamest lapdog must sometimes bite.'

An uncomfortable silence fell as Mary retreated, weeping, behind her fan. Nobody made scenes in the Assembly Rooms – it was the unspoken rule which preserved their dullness. A sober old gentleman, moustached and brown-coated, rose from the next table after a hurried consultation. His confidence seemed to ebb away through his shoes as he looked at Byron, and Ruthven behind him.

'Not here, my dear fellow,' he said nervously. 'You really should not . . .' His voice trailed away as Byron folded his arms and stared up at him silently. 'These are the Assembly Rooms, you see,' he added in a hushed voice. The magic of the words was wasted. Byron only laughed.

'Well, what shall we do?' he said, looking to Ruthven, not Mary.

'Miss Chaworth must advise you, not I.' He smiled. I saw the change in Byron's expression as Mary raised her tear-streaked face.

'Oh, my darling girl,' he said softly, taking her hand in his. 'You should not take me so seriously. I would not have hurt you so . . . I did not see. Come, we'll leave this wretched place and find a present for you. I saw a rose on a silver chain. We'll go and look for it.'

He left with only a brief nod to me, and not even a glance for Ruthven, who stood watching them, his brows drawn together.

'A pretty girl, Miss Chaworth,' he said in a low voice. 'Now she has a certain charm, but the freshness will fade in a year or so.' He shrugged. 'If the moth clings to the flame too long, its little wings must burn.'

'But he loves her.'

'It will pall,' he said, smiling.

'I must leave you, sir,' I said thankfully, looking at my watch.

'Where do you wish to go? I am happy to escort you.'

'I prefer to go alone, thank you,' I said, praying that he would not insist.

'As you wish,' he said listlessly and his eyes followed Byron and Mary through the marble doorway. For a brief moment, I pitied him.

3

Girls' slippers were never made for more than admiration on a *chaise longue*. My feet were bruised and sore when I reached the Cartright Street area. My ears jangled with the noise from the red-brick factory at the bottom of the street, the steady stamp and whirr of machines. I looked up, shuddering at the thought of working for fifteen hours a day behind the windows whose thick coat of black dust shut the sun away. I had seen those men once when my uncle took me to an evening play. We had passed a line of them, trudging home down the unlit streets, heads down, feet dragging as if they were chained. It was not easy to forget.

Impulsively, I took out my silk purse. Nothing soothes the conscience faster than charity.

The street itself was deserted, silent as if the plague had struck. Shutters, doors, all were barred against the soldiers who would come later, to question – and to take. I knocked at the low door and waited while the shuffle of footsteps came closer.

'I don't know anything. I haven't left the house all day. Try further down the street.' Her voice was high and frightened.

'Please don't be afraid. I've only come for Rose,' I said, full of pity.

The door opened a crack. 'Oh, it's you. Miss Emerton, wasn't it? Will you come in?'

Her whining voice irritated me. I pushed the purse which I had intended to offer her back in my sleeve. 'Is she all right?'

She gave me an uneasy smile. 'I just gave her a drop of gin. She'll be well, soon enough.'

I followed her down the sloping, gloomy passage, holding

my handkerchief to my face against the stench of cats and decomposing food. 'She's in there, lying down,' the woman said. 'I've done my best.'

She slid back into the dark and I opened the door. I blinked, trying to make shapes out of the shadows in the room. It was colder than a crypt, the only light a dusty shaft of grey from the high barred window at pavement level. She lay, white as marble, on a mattress in the corner. My first horrified thought was that she was dead, but she started and moaned as I walked towards her.

'Don't touch me again. I can't take the pain any more . . . Just leave me alone.'

'Rose! For God's sake, what has she done to you?' I whispered, terrified. Slowly, like an old woman, she turned herself towards me, and the faint shadow of a smile crossed her face. Tears trickled steadily down her pale cheeks, dropping on the straggling tendrils of hair. She tried to speak, shook her head and sank back, exhausted. I knelt down on the filthy floor, lifting her hair out of the dirt. She watched me mutely. Guilt-ridden, I blamed Ruthven for keeping me from her.

'How could she have done this?' I raged. 'I'll fetch her in and ask her what she means by it. God, and they call this mercy!'

'No,' Rose whispered, and her limp hand plucked at my arm as the door opened behind me. 'She had to. I'll be all right, by and by.'

'I've brought you a cup of tea, Miss Emerton. I'm sure it's not what you're used to, but it's the last I have.' She held out the cup and, as an afterthought, wiped the rim with her skirt.

'I won't deprive you of it. Can you give me an explanation of this?' I pointed to Rose with a shaking hand which I could not control.

'Oh, you mustn't frighten a lonely old woman,' she whined. 'I told you I did the best I could. But people are always so hard to please.'

'Pleased! Is that what you expect me to be when I come in and find her looking like a living corpse!'

She backed away, holding the cup in front of her like a

saint's relic. 'It'll be a lovely child. She won't be sorry, I promise you,' she said from the safety of the door.

'What!' I stared at her, dumbfounded. 'But you were paid to . . .'

'I did my best,' she said again. 'I earned that money. You'll not rob a poor woman of her living.' The door shut behind her.

I turned to Rose. 'Is it true?'

'Oh, she tried everything, Miss Lucy,' she said wearily. 'She said there was no more she could do . . . Dear Lord! This pain! Will it never go away?'

There was a rattle at the outer door. The woman returned, her fawning manner gone. 'You'd best leave,' she said quickly. 'The fellow that brought you's out standing in the street. He'll draw attention to my house.'

'I can't move,' Rose moaned. 'Just leave me to die here.'

The door rattled again. I looked at her ashen face in despair. 'Here!' I said, pushing my smelling salts under her nose. 'Breathe in, as hard as you can.'

She coughed and spluttered while I watched anxiously. 'I'll help you. Look, put your arm so . . . that's right, lean on me . . . now, slowly, one, two, one, two, that's good, Rose. You're doing very well.'

God knows what Ben must have thought as I dragged her out of the house, staggering under the weight, I did not dare to look at him as he took her other arm. Between us, we lifted her into the carriage.

'Don't worry, Miss Emerton,' he said as I climbed in, 'I won't say a word.'

In the carriage, there was a long silence which lasted almost to the edge of the village. I was deep in thought.

'Listen, Rose,' I said, making up my mind at last. 'You mustn't worry.'

She looked at me languidly through half-open eyes. I hurried on. 'You don't want to keep it, I know. I have a plan which may help. I must talk to my uncle first, but I have it in mind to bring up the child myself. We'll send you away – I have some cousins in Yorkshire, the Milbankes. They're very kind, Rosy, you would like it there. Then, when you've had the baby, you could come back and nobody would know.'

'Oh, Miss,' she said sadly, 'they ain't that stupid. If I go away so sudden and then there you are with a baby in the house, they'll know all right. It's no use.'

'Yes, it is,' I said impatiently. 'I know. We could say – if you don't mind, that is – that Harry fathered a child in France and sent it back for safety. It's almost true, after all. You'll just have to sign some papers, giving me the rights over the child. It's easily done.'

'And what when Mr Harry comes back?' she asked me doubtfully.

'Oh . . . We'll think about that later.'

She smiled for the first time. 'Well, if you're sure you won't change your mind, Miss Lucy. It would be better off with you, I know that, and I could see it just the same, couldn't I?'

I laughed. 'Better than that. He'll need a nurse. You can be his mother and nobody will ever know.'

We smiled at each other as the carriage rumbled home under the trees.

*   *   *

It was not hard to persuade Mr Emerton. Rose was sent away to Yorkshire and gave premature birth to a son, the week before the Annesley dance.

My uncle was delighted with him. He recognized that it was his only hope of keeping the house in the family, for I would marry and Harry, if he ever returned, would never settle down to becoming a country squire. The papers were signed before a lawyer: Orlando was ours. Lady Winter was summoned over to admire the young heir, for her approval set the seal on all Mr Emerton's decisions.

In my opinion, Lady Winter was an interfering old busybody with a weakness for titles with a lengthier lineage than her own. When my uncle remarked at dinner that night that Ruthven would make a good match for some pretty girl, I knew very well who had planted the idea in his mind.

Hesitantly, I told him of my fear that Harry had gambled me as his last stake to Ruthven. I felt sure it would bring an end to Mr Emerton's hints. It did not. He was shocked, but not unduly so. Under close questioning, I was obliged to admit that Ruthven had neither declared the nature of the debt, nor mentioned marriage.

'Well then!' Mr Emerton said triumphantly. 'You always did have a fanciful streak, Lucy. All those novels you read, I don't doubt. You could do worse than marry him, my dear. You know I'll not push you, but ten thousand a year . . .' He gave me a sudden sharp look under his bushy eyebrows. 'I don't care for the sound of the Byron boy. Lady Winter mistrusts him, and she's a perceptive woman. Making scenes in the Assembly Rooms . . . I've never heard of such a thing.' He paused. 'Lucy? You haven't fallen for him, have you?'

'Mary Chaworth would not thank you for saying so,' I said smiling.

He frowned and dug into the mound of cold salmon which lay between us on the table. 'He'll be at the Annesley dance, then? I wonder if you should go. That's why you put me off attending, I'll be bound.'

'Oh, Uncle, you mustn't believe everything Lady Winter says,' I said, blushing to the roots of my hair.

'And you haven't been eating enough. That's a bad sign.'

'Have you noticed, sir, Orlando's eyes are exactly like yours? Mr Ricketts was saying so just before dinner. It's really quite remarkable . . .'

'Don't try to fob me off, young lady,' he said sternly. 'I won't have it.'

'You won't stop me going,' I pleaded. 'I've seen nobody in three months, and you know how strange it would look if I refused at a week's notice.'

'No, I shan't stop you,' he sighed. I ran the length of the table to embrace him. 'Well, I shall hear from Lady Winter if you've been misbehaving,' he said, patting my hand. 'Yes, I thought your face would fall when you heard that. She very generously offered to take you in her carriage.'

*   *   *

The sky was black with the racing clouds of an approaching storm when we arrived at Annesley. The torches outside the

53

house leapt up against the walls, throwing shadows which towered like cliffs over the flames. The coachmen pulled their coats up over their heads as they hurried among the horses, soothing them with soft voices and knotting the reins tightly to the iron rings. In the house, the music and laughter drowned the wailing of the wind. Only the chandeliers creaked and swayed on their heavy chains. The oak-panelled hall had been cleared of its usual debris of hunting boots, shooting dogs and battered magazines. In the fireplace, flames crackled and spat as they ate their way into the logs, each big enough to fell a man. The stone floor echoed as the footmen ran to and fro, staggering under the weight of their silver trays.

I walked on at Lady Winter's side into the quiet drawing-room reserved for chaperons. On the stiff-backed chairs against the walls, the old ladies were nodding uncomfortably in a state of wakeful doze. The heavy tiaras, clumsy carriers of the best diamonds in the county, slipped sideways on their drooping heads and under the demure skirts of neutral-coloured silk, their feet crept out to spread wide apart. Sometimes one of them went through her small ritual, peering towards the clock, sighing and straightening her head-dress, before she staggered wearily away in search of an errant daughter. I left Lady Winter there, busy playing the eternal game of county scandal, the only exercise she ever took.

All country dances look the same at first glance. The situations never seem to change. I stood in the doorway watching the dancers take their places, their smiles promising what they could not say as they pointed their feet and looked expectantly at the orchestra. The music struck up, after a great wailing and sawing of fiddles. Mary was leading the set, partnered by a thick-calved, smirking boy who lagged behind her at every step, his face taking on a grin of fixed despair. Mary's sweet smile did not alter as he tripped on her floating skirt and fell with a resounding crash, nearly taking her down with him. By the walls the waiting girls wilted, only smiling and bursting into animated conversation when a man passed by and stopped to look them cruelly up and down before sauntering on. But men, too, could be made to suffer. I put up my hand to smother a laugh as I watched a foppish, weak-faced boy in a brocaded

54

coat being drawn along in the inexorable clasp of a large lady in green satin. They stopped before a girl I had once met, Jane Carlton, a long-nosed, pale-faced bundle of nerves with religious leanings. The mother smiled and kept her hold as she winkled Jane out of her chair, fuelled the languishing conversation into a flicker of life, and at last relented when Jane had written the young man's name down on her dance card.

Seeing no sign of Byron, I pushed aside the curtains of the nearest doorway and found myself in a dark, stone-flagged passage which ran the length of the house. The door at the far end was open into the garden and the wind whipped past me, drowning the music. I paused to wonder at myself, transformed in a looking glass where the old speckled silver gave back an illusion of beauty.

'You lie,' Byron's voice said very near me in the darkness. His voice sounded strained. 'Must you poison all my friendships with your loathsome insinuations? Even that pretty Emerton girl couldn't be allowed to speak to me before you were telling me that. . . .'

'My dear fellow, I merely said the blood was bad.' It was Ruthven speaking. 'With a mother in bedlam and a brother who was ready to gamble his sister's hand for a few thousand.' I froze. He laughed quietly. 'I still haven't decided whether to follow it up. She's pretty enough, but . . .'

I leaned against the wall, sick with fright. Better to be buried alive than married to a man who only knew how to inspire fear.

'Marriage isn't quite to your taste,' Byron broke in. There was a silence, a rustle of movement before he went on in a gentler voice. 'Oh, I know you mean to help me, but your friendship comes at a high price.'

'Byron, I crucify myself for you! Who was it who sat night after night with your mother, keeping her amused and listening to endless complaints and self-reproaches, so that you could visit Mary? Who told you the truth about your father, and saved you from a life of deception?'

'I wish to God you had not,' Byron said in a low voice. 'To think that I was brought up to worship a sponging braggart

55

who didn't stop at seducing his sister for money. I would rather never have heard the truth.'

'We should never keep secrets from those we love, it has been said. A charming sentiment,' Ruthven murmured.

Byron was walking to and fro restlessly. I knew his limping step and I pressed my back against the wall.

'And how can I know that you will keep it to yourself?' he asked suddenly, desperately.

'Your father's – what shall we say – crime?' Ruthven laughed. 'Your friendship is all I ask, Byron. You know that well enough.'

'A bought friendship? Is it worth having?'

'My dear Byron, if you feel so bitter, I will leave Newstead whenever you like. The choice is in your hands.'

Silence, then . . . 'Tell me that you lied about Mary,' he said pleadingly. 'She could not have spoken of me so cruelly. Ruthven, she loves me.'

'With what sort of love?' Ruthven replied. 'If you doubt my word, I can prove it to you easily enough. Come back to watch the dancing. Leave me alone with her when I make a sign, and stay in earshot.'

'Very well,' Byron said at last. 'And if you lie . . .'

'I forfeit your friendship. But of course.'

They walked away. I leaned back against the wall, pressing my hands to my head as I tried to think. I had come to try to steal Byron from Mary, and now that Ruthven was to do it for me, I only wanted to stop it from happening. I feared him enough to be sure he would succeed.

The dance was coming to an end as I walked towards them, my head held high. They were dressed in black and Byron's face was as pale as Ruthven's as they lounged side by side against the wall, flamboyant figures of doom in the mass of colours.

'Why, Miss Emerton, how delightful to see you!' Byron bent over my hand. 'Well, do you bring news of any more riots to amuse me? We must visit one together, I think.'

Slowly, I raised my head to look at him. Ruthven watched, his eyes glittering. 'May I speak to you, alone?' I asked.

'Alone?' He was startled. 'What strange secrets am I about

to hear, Ruthven? You claim to read minds. But it would be a pity to spoil your aura of mystery, Miss Emerton. It's too becoming.'

Ruthven smiled and turned his head. 'Perhaps the revelation can wait. The set is ending. Miss Emerton must desert us to join the next dance. Must she not?' His eyes met mine and I swayed under their command. The familiar wave of blackness was sweeping over me. I fought back this time.

'Please,' I said desperately to Byron, who stood caught between us, unconscious of the silent battle. But the music crashed to a stop, the dancers left the floor and Mary, careless of the scandalmongers, ran towards us. Turning her back on Ruthven, she leant against Byron, her hand eagerly seeking his. I had never seen her look more beautiful. Her hair tumbled in a rich mass down her white neck, her cheeks glowed and her slanting eyes shone with love. It would have been better if she had let them speak for her.

'Byron, you are cruel to desert me,' she said gaily. 'Must I dance with every clodhopping boy in the room before you will ask me? Oh, tonight I could dance until the stars fell out of the sky!'

Gently, he withdrew his hand.

'Well, won't you ask me?' Mary cried, her red lips drooping. 'How can I love a man who won't dance with me?'

The expression on Byron's face terrified me for a moment. Mary's eyes followed his down to his foot, her hand flew up to cover her face.

'Come, Miss Chaworth,' Ruthven said softly. 'This is cruel sport.'

'No,' whispered Mary, her colour draining away as Byron looked at her. 'I only forgot . . . I meant nothing. I'll dance no more.'

'But you look so pale,' Ruthven said, taking her arm. 'We must find you a chair to rest. The dancing has over-taxed you.'

She went with him through the door. The music began again and Byron and I stood isolated by the wall as the guests flocked to the floor.

'Forgive me. I must leave you,' he said.

'No!' I caught his arm.

He stared at me with heavy, drugged eyes.

'Oh, and I came with a hundred questions to ask! I scarcely know where to begin,' I babbled, my back against the door. 'I have been reading your poems since we last met and . . .' but even as I spoke I saw that it was useless.

'Another time,' he said and limped quickly past me through the door. I dropped my head in despair.

* * *

'Oh, my dear, I hope Lord Byron hasn't been shocking you. You look so pale. Have you seen Mary anywhere?'

I tried to smile and take the worried look from Mrs Chaworth's soft, round face. 'The heat, so foolish of me! Shall I go and look for her?'

'Oh, if you would, Lucy. Gracious, there's Lady Fielding and nobody talking to her! I must go. Bless you, my dear, I'm so glad you came.'

I went through the door. I saw Byron leaning by a half-drawn curtain, listening intently. I walked up to stand a few feet away, the heavy cloth hiding me from his sight. In the room behind us, I could hear Ruthven's soft voice. Mary answered him, not in her usual clear, high way of speaking, but strangely slow and heavy as if the words were spoken against her will.

'I?' she said. 'Why, do you imagine that I would ever marry that . . . lame . . . boy!'

I heard the door fly open, heard Byron's voice break as he shouted at her, 'You will never be asked, madam. For all I care you can go – you can go to hell!'

But the tears were running down his face as he left the room and hurried past me into the darkness. I stepped forward, and was caught by Ruthven's hand. I looked up at him in terror, tried to pull away, but he held me fast.

'And would you, too, try to get away from me? Your turn will come in time, my dear Miss Emerton,' he said softly. 'Keep to your spying instead – you seem to excel in it.'

'I could turn it to advantage against you.'

He let my hand drop, looked at me with a smile spreading across his face. 'Indeed!' he said, and pulled me towards him. My mouth was crushed, my head swam, my body trembled as if fever swept me. He pushed me back against the wall. 'Could you now, Lucy?' he said, and strode away up the passage after Byron.

Mary was lying face down on the floor, sobbing as if her heart would break. I knelt beside her.

'He made you say it, didn't he?'

She raised her head. 'I didn't want to. I tried not to, but I could hear the words over and over again in my mind. They were his words, Lucy, not mine! I only spoke them.'

'We must go back to the dance,' I said gently. 'You know what they're like, how they talk.'

She nodded wearily. 'He's gone, then?'

'Yes.'

'And – the other?'

'He followed.'

I had to support her as we went back to the noisy, brightly lit room. She was almost fainting.

'Mary, where have you been?' cried Mrs Chaworth, rushing up to us. 'Everybody's been waiting to say goodbye and I hardly knew what to say. You can imagine how bad it looked.'

'Yes, I must go, too,' I said seeing Lady Winter plucking the air with imperious snatches. 'Mary, come and visit me soon.'

She nodded and clasped my hand before slowly following her mother into the centre of the crowd, her red lips smiling brilliantly.

4

The months passed by, and my uncle's spirits rose as he foresaw the end of England. He positively revelled in his prophecies of doom. The outlook was bleak. The old king was openly said by everyone to be mad, and Mr Emerton raged at the extravagance of erecting the Martello Towers to protect a senile monarch when he took the sea air. It seemed that the French were never going to attack, although we were raring for a fight after the news that Boney had murdered the Prince d'Enghien. Beacons were put up all along the coast, but they only served to embarrass smugglers and bring help to a few shipwrecks.

The news from Newstead was equally frustrating.

Mrs Byron was still living in Southwell and Byron was never seen out of Ruthven's company at Newstead. The house and land, I heard, were going to ruin while they amused themselves by shooting everything which moved or flew. So much for Ruthven's influence. Mary, who had sunk back into the waiting arms of Mr Musters, kept me well informed. She welcomed a confidante too much to suspect my interest.

It was a warm day in early spring. My uncle had business to attend to in Nottingham, the servants were planning to go to the village fair as soon as he had left the house. I suddenly made up my mind. I took out my green riding habit, coiled my hair on top of my head and went down the back stairs, humming under my breath.

'Ben! Can you saddle up Luke for me?' I called across the cobbled yard. He looked up.

'Surely, Miss Lucy. He needs the exercise. I'll just call one of the boys to go with you.'

I paused. 'No. It's a shame when they all want to go to the fair. I'll ride alone, today.'

'What's Mr Emerton going to say?' he called back, grinning. 'I'm under strict instructions not to let you ride without a groom.'

'I'll take the blame. Quick! I want to go before the weather changes.'

It was a long journey, but I enjoyed it too much to care about time. I went by the fields and country lanes, trotting through the high, sweet-smelling grass past the thick hedges of thorn where flowers climbed in luxuriant chaos. The black-birds sang in the copses, and the soft new leaves brushed against my face as I rode through the tall trees, the sun flashing and splitting round me in gold splinters. One by one, the little villages of neat red houses and white railings rose from the fields to greet me, and I waved my plumed hat to the muddy faces of the children who scrambled and sprawled, shrieking and bawling, across the path. Over their yells rang the clang of iron on the blacksmith's anvil, and sometimes I caught sight of him, scarlet-faced, steady-handed, as he swung his arm down and down again.

I passed the little market town of Hucknall, its church tower rising above the trees, and took the lane to Newstead. My curiosity rose, urging me on, and we broke into a wild gallop up the last hill.

The abbey lay buried in the cold shadows below me. On one side, a ruin, on the other, Byron's home. Above the deserted roofless nave, a vast window rose to frame the piercing blue, spiking it with a sharp fretwork of stone daggers. The sky turned the lake in front of the house into a sapphire pool, unrippled. Above the far stretch of water, two forts for toy soldiers kept guard and on the nearest hill to me, another curious building hid behind the trees. Its empty windows and derelict air made me wonder if it was there that Byron's uncle had held his notorious orgies. A forlorn gloom hung over everything, from the stumps of the great oaks which had once formed an avenue to the house, to the black windows which caught none of the sun's reflection.

Luke, who had been cropping the grass, raised his head

suddenly, and I started. A bird twittered at me from the tree. I laughed at myself for being so nervous, slid out of the saddle and sank in the grass to look again at the house.

There *were* voices! I could hear them quite distinctly, floating up from the field below. Oh God, if I should be caught prying . . . I leapt up, turned to flee, then stopped. It sounded like a quarrel. I heard shouting and the angry squawk of a bird disturbed from its hiding place. I looked down the hill and saw Ruthven and Byron, boxing in the field. They were both stripped to the waist and their bodies shone with sweat. Byron was the steadier of the two, holding his ground and carefully placing his hard, deadly body blows. Ruthven, who had a good three inches advantage in height, moved like a cat, his attacks quick and provocative, throwing Byron on to the defensive. As I watched, Byron lunged, Ruthven danced to one side, and Byron fell flat in the grass. Ruthven's shadow swooped over him. I blinked. But I had seen. There was only one man. Then I heard his laugh, saw Byron struggling like a madman, pushing him up and twisting his body away in a quick, jack-knife movement. His face was deathly pale, as he stared at the other man. Ruthven moved effortlessly to trap him down, his arms spread to hold him fast. For a moment, the victor raised his face and I saw the expression on it as he bent forward. I screamed, and the sound echoed like a pistol shot down the valley. Ruthven looked up, startled, and Byron slipped his grasp.

'Quick!' I called. He looked up and began to run towards me Ruthven stood still, his eyes following him.

'Byron,' he called almost pleadingly. 'Don't be a fool. It was only a joke, a stupid trick. Come back!'

Halfway up the hill, Byron turned. 'To Newstead, but never, by God, to you,' he said. Ruthven stared up at him, his face ashen.

'I'm coming after you,' he called, starting towards the hill. Byron limped on towards me, his face pale with exhaustion.

'Your horse – can he carry two?'

'If he can carry my uncle, we should be light work.'

He held me in front of him on the saddle, his hands round my waist and we flew away down the hill, hooves thudding on the cropped turf as the wind rushed past us. We stopped short of the first village and flung ourselves down in the grass. I started to plait a chain of buttercups while Byron lay back, laughing uncontrollably.

'Well, thank God you came,' he said at last, raising himself on his elbows to look at me. I buried my face in the grass, hiding under my hat. He pulled it off and twirled it on his hand. 'I'm sorry that you witnessed such a vile scene.'

'What was he going to do? The look on his face, it was terrifying.'

'I'll tell you one day. God, to think I left Mary for that . . . Have you seen her?'

I tore the chain of flowers to shreds. 'She's gone back to Mr Musters. I think she plans to marry soon.'

'Do girls think of nothing else?' he said in disgust.

'Oh, I never want to get married,' I said. 'Well, you saw the boys at the Annesley dance. I can think of nothing duller.'

He laughed and tipped my face towards him. 'I like you, Miss . . . oh, you must have another name. I can't go on with this formality in the middle of a field.'

'Lucy.'

'Lucy,' he repeated softly, and his fingers traced the shape of my face. 'You aren't the sort of girl to plague a man, except with memories.'

'Do you get plagued often?' I asked, laughing. 'I never heard such a suffering voice!'

He smiled moodily, then rolled over on his back, pulled me across to lie beside him. 'Oh, Lucy, you don't know how the belles of Southwell take advantage of politeness. I only have to bow and say how d'ye do, before they begin swooning and making cow eyes at me.'

'You're very vain.'

'Possibly,' he said with a grin.

'And you must do more than that to make them fall in love with you. Do you write them poems?'

'Sometimes, when they're pretty enough.'

'Well, that's why,' I said. 'You mislead them. If you must write them poems, change their appearances, names, everything. It's true, I swear. All girls take poems to be a sign of love.'

'So if I write you one now?'

I smiled as he scribbled for a few minutes, blushed a deep crimson as I looked down at the piece of paper.

> *'Whene'er I view those lips of thine*
> *Their hue invokes my fervent kiss;*
> *Yet I forego that bliss divine,*
> *Alas! it were unhallow'd bliss.'*

'Not that that detracts from the pleasure. How strange! You look so like Augusta now, with your face in shadow,' he said as I shook my hair forward to hide my burning cheeks.

'Who is Augusta?' I asked, freezing at the softness with which he had said her name.

'My half-sister, the only honest girl I knew until I met you. Well, Lucy?' I leant towards him. It did not occur to me to resist. That was the power of Byron's attraction.

He kissed me hard and long, twisting his hands through my hair to hold me to him. I murmured weakly as he began to pull the green ribbons undone, slipped the dress down from my shoulders and pressed his lips to my breasts. My body burned and arched with the need for him, trembled at the sudden roughness against my skin. The muscles in his back swelled under my fingers. I clung, weeping, as his face stared down into mine, his eyes half-closed as he pressed me down and down. The last frenzy was on us, sweeping us up, straining towards each other, laughing with the joy of it as we came to the end together.

We lay flat on our backs, eyes shut against the sun. My hand lay loose in his, our faces close enough to warm each other with our breath.

'Was it better than . . .?'

'Quiet, Lucy. Don't spoil it with questions. It was what you knew it to be.'

'Perfection,' I said sleepily. 'I'm not even ashamed. But why, I mean, the first time . . .' I blushed.

Byron grinned. 'You ride horses astride, don't you? Mary

told me you were the only girl in Nottinghamshire who dared to ride like a man. There's a girl of spirit, I thought.'

I looked at him anxiously. 'Byron, does it show? Do I look, well, different?'

'Oh yes, your uncle will know at once,' he said and his smile broadened. 'Nobody could mistake that cream-fed look on your face for anything else.'

'I've been no better than a whore,' I said miserably, hiding my face in my hands. 'You can never respect me after that.'

Byron yawned. 'I never respected a woman in my life. Respectability's so damned dull. What can you do with it, for God's sake! Embalm yourself?'

I had begun to pull on the green dress, but he rolled over and snatched it off, threw it to land twenty yards away in the grass. 'Now let's remove the last of your precious respectability,' he said, and did so.

The sun was sitting on the green tree tops as I mounted Luke and bent for a last kiss. 'Be at the Assembly Rooms on Thursday,' he said. 'I'll show you a new side of the town.' He slapped the horse's rump and I cantered away down the hill, my hands as limp as putty on the reins.

*   *   *

I was there, trembling in case he would not come. As I looked round the room, I was caught by the arm. Eagerly, I turned.

'Well!' said Lady Winter. 'I've never seen you better turned out! You quite remind me of Lady Winchelsea in that blue – a little younger of course. Come and join us, my dear, all old friends. Mrs Carlton, Lady Bury, Miss Warwick.'

The sharp-eyed vigilants of the county dropped their voices and raised their smiles. I looked back at the door.

'Are you waiting for someone?' Lady Winter asked sweetly. 'I can see you find us dull company.'

'Oh, no!'

'Miss Emerton is the brave young lady who went all alone to a riot! Oh, you have no idea what excitement you caused, Lucy dear! But you must think us very old-fashioned.'

The ladies tittered and eyed me suspiciously over their tea-cups.

'Well, I'm thankful that dear Jane is not so . . . adventurous,' Mrs Carlton said with a thin smile. 'I know it's all the rage in London to flaunt respectability, but it doesn't fetch husbands.'

'I'm not looking for one,' I said stonily. Lady Winter fluttered her fan and exchanged a knowing glance with Mrs Carlton.

'Oh, Lucy, you can't . . .' Her mouth dropped open, and I turned to see Byron, shirt open, hair loose, sauntering towards me. 'Well!' she said, putting all she had into the one word. She drew back, throwing her pigeon chest out in defence, as Byron bowed, his eyes glinting maliciously.

'Ladies?'

Only Lady Bury, who could once have been beautiful, gave him a wistful smile. The others snapped their fans out in a united crack, and shut him out.

'Well, Luc . . . Miss Emerton?' he said. I curtsied, threw a parting smile at Lady Winter and left on his arm. 'Here, Bos'n!' He whistled a little black mastiff out from behind the doorman, patted his head as he looked thoughtfully back at the group of ladies. 'Next time, Bos'n. He's trained to sniff out an enemy leg.'

'I hope I'm there to see it.'

'Dear me! Such vindictiveness! Oh, don't look so anxious.' He put a hand lightly to my lips. 'Didn't we agree that you had lost your respectability? Now, you're free to speak the truth.'

He took me out to the flat fields on the edge of town. 'You can't wear that pretty dress, Lucy,' he said as we walked over the grass. 'Put on this.' He held out a bundle of blue velvet.

'What? Here?' And Rose had nearly killed herself to finish my beautiful blue dress in time.

He shrugged. 'There's no one to see, except me, and you won't mind that, will you? Here, I'll help you. We want to get a good place.'

I looked down at myself in the tight trousers and short, waisted jacket and began to laugh. 'I feel so strange.'

He kissed me. 'Halfway to paederasty. I never knew you'd make such a pretty boy. Now the hat, pull it down over your face. Very good, sweetheart. Can you try a man's walk?'

66

I swaggered towards him, my thumbs stuck in the waistband, my head on one side. 'Like this . . . my dear fellow?' I clapped him on the back and he shouted with laughter.

'Where did you learn that? Oh, I remember now. You have a brother.'

'Had.' I dropped my hand. 'He's in a French prison.'

He held me against his chest, fondling me gently. 'I know the story.'

'Ruthven's version.' I pulled away. 'He ruined Harry.'

'Don't be so quick to blame. Each man is responsible for his own ruin. Your brother chose his way of life.'

'He was led into it,' I said vehemently.

But Byron shook his head. 'Nobody has to be led. I'm afraid I have no respect for a man who could gamble his sister's hand. That damns your brother in my eyes.'

I leant forward, hiding my face. 'Please, Byron. Let's talk of something else. It's only with you I can forget about it. It haunts me day and night, the fear of it. . . .'

'And why did Ruthven take the wager? Have you thought of that?' Byron murmured. 'Love, marriage, all the natural ends of man, are of no interest to him. Perhaps he foresaw this, our love. . . .'

'Don't. . . .' I put out my hand, but he stared past me, talking in a soft, obsessive voice.

'You are the thread now, Lucy. He would have a purpose in marrying you. He could – and would – use you to hold me. *Is* that it – is that where our future lies?'

'Nothing could persuade me to marry him. You know that.'

Byron jabbed his stick at the wet tufted soil with little savage thrusts. 'I know Ruthven,' he said quietly. 'I know his powers of persuasion and his ability to arrange the future to suit his own purposes. You are right to fear, Lucy, but I doubt if you are strong enough to fight him. I know that I am not. That is why I must not see him again. It's the only way to save myself.'

His tone of quiet conviction terrified me. I had looked for reassurance or scepticism, not the confirmation of my fears. 'Is – is he still at Newstead?' My voice shook, blundering on the words.

'No, thank God.' Byron slashed viciously at the grass. 'Gone

67

on one of his London debauches, leaving my love-sick mother turning to me – me of all people – for consolation.'

I looked up at him curiously as we walked on. 'Why do you always talk of her so cruelly? She must have some good in her, to be your mother.'

'Bless you for that. Oh, I should tell you some pretty piece of lying sentiment, but how can I? I don't love her. She gave birth to me. Am I to thank her for that?'

I had an answer ready.

Five minutes' walk brought us to the scene of entertainment. A crowd of farmers and labourers pushed their way forward down the gently sloping hill to the ropes of the high platform. It rose over us like a forgotten watchpost, a makeshift wooden theatre. The smell of tobacco and sweat was overpowering, but Byron limped into the thick of it, and I was obliged to follow. The ground had already been trampled into a thick slush of mud, I was up to my ankles in it. Behind me, a bird squawked and a cloud of white feathers rose above us. Byron turned. 'There's no hurry. They aren't in the ring yet. Shall we have a look?' he said casually.

'Why not?' I said, swallowing. I could see the eagerness in his face.

'You're made of sterner stuff than Mary,' he said laughing and squeezing my arm. But I wondered how long I would last, as we edged our way into the circle of men. At either end of the square of rough turf, a man crouched over his bird, holding it down and coaxing it with gentle hands, crooning to it like a lover. 'Eh, my fine one, my beauty, easy now, easy!'

'Which is the favourite?' Byron asked a broad farmer.

He scratched his head thoughtfully.

'Well, Jack Bent's bird be the larger, but t'other's got the look of a good little fighter. Holds his head well, you see. It's going to be a close thing, but my money's on Jack's bird.'

'I'll take you ten to one against, then,' said Byron, digging a handful of coins out of his pocket. As he spoke, the men opened their hands, the watchers leaned forward. The cocks sidled out, jaunty-headed, scaly legs swaying as they circled, clawing at the grass. The crowd moved in, goading them on with shouts and whistles.

68

'Come on, then. Lost its courage, Jack?'

'Lose mine, first,' he said grinning and wiping his sleeve across his face. 'Never seen him back out, yet.'

With a sudden movement, they flew at each other, wings out and batting the air, eyes gleaming as their sharp beaks thrust forward. The bigger bird seemed to have it, driving the other back towards the circle.

'He's got him! Not a chance, now! Nah, you can see the little 'un's just waiting his moment.' Around me, their faces started to perspire. There was a sharp intake of breath as the little cock flew forward, went for the neck. The other struggled and fluttered, his claws pincering on the ground as he twisted his head to and fro. The little one held on; the head nodded forward, the sharp beak had found its way through to the gullet. I looked away, nauseated.

'First fight you've seen, lad?' said one of the farmers, grinning at my pale face. 'Well, they say the first's the worst. You'll think nowt to it next time. Here, get a drop of this in you.'

Gratefully, I tipped the flask back, choked and gasped as the fire burned down my throat. Byron watched me, his mouth twitching.

It did nothing to stay my sickness as the winner strutted its ground, tearing, ripping and crowing while the big bird beat his wings on the ground, his feathers sticky with blood and guts, his cut comb lolling in the dust. Now he lay still, claws up, but the blood lust was up in the brown cock. He pranced into the attack again, reared his little wings in rage as the owner pulled him off and tucked him under his arm. The crowd broke up, looking disappointed at such a quick victory.

'Enjoying yourself, Miss?'

I turned to see a dark, thick-set man in a shabby jacket, his hat pulled down over his eyes.

'I'm sorry, I don't . . .' He pushed up the cap and I fell back against Byron's side. Jackson nodded, a slow smile spreading across his face.

'What do you want?' I whispered, as he looked steadily at me.

'Nothing . . . yet, Miss. I'm glad to see you've not forgotten.'

'Strange friends you have,' said Byron as Jackson slouched

69

away through the crowd. 'One of your rioting acquaintances?'

Before I could answer, we were flung forward as the people pressed towards the ring. The first fighter swung up over the ropes, a slim boy, dark-skinned, his muscles gleaming as he looked down on us and held his arm high.

'Tait's looking in better form than I've ever seen him,' said a man beside me.

'He ain't got the strength, though,' said another scornfully. 'Wilks'll lay him out for dead, see if he don't.'

'Wilks!' He spat. 'Wilks is slowin' up, George. Thirty-five and he's lost his last two fights to young 'uns. He'll be slaughtered this time.'

Wilks, a heavy man, built like a miner with broad shoulders and muscular arms, came up into the ring, pushing his wife back with a gentle hand. A little brown-faced woman with sharp, bitter eyes, she clung on to the ropes, screaming at him to stop making a fool of himself.

'Let 'im go, missus. He's a big boy now,' called one of the men and the crowd shouted with laughter as Mrs Wilks fell back and shook her fist at us.

'His blood's on your heads, you bloody brutes!'

'You'd best go back home, Emily,' Wilks said gently. She looked up at him, threw up her hands hopelessly and walked back through the ranks of grinning men. The boxers took their corners. The referee came forward to shout us down. Wilks and Tait walked into the centre of the ring, shook hands affably as they sized each other up.

'All ready?' They nodded. 'Time!' roared the referee, scuttling back. Tait danced in, with a smile on his face to woo St Peter from the gates, lunged forward and gave Wilks a blow which sent him reeling to the ropes. He staggered for a moment, then walked slowly forward . . . and waited. Tait circled, looking for a gap, his feet quick and sure. He got in two blows at Wilks' head, no stunners though – then the crowd burst out in a great roar as Wilks' left arm shot up like a catapult and sent Tait down on his back.

I plucked at Byron's arm. 'He's good enough for the Fancy! He had it planned all the time and . . .'

'It wasn't a clean blow,' Byron murmured as Tait rose, his

hand clutching his throat. 'Yes, he'll punish Wilks for that if I'm not mistaken.'

The next round and the next – and the next, went to Tait, who gave Wilks one tremendous doubler in the ribs that drew a gasp from the crowd and knocked Wilks' breath out like smoke from a pipe.

Fifth round. Wilks' face looked like a ploughed field in the rain, but he wasn't finished. They fought at arm's-length, Tait going for the head before Wilks brought him down with a body blow. He packed huge power behind each hit: when Tait stood up, there was a spreading scarlet stain across his ribs. Byron shook his head gloomily at the sight of it.

'Of course, one can see that Wilks is the better fighter,' I said knowledgeably. 'More skilful.'

'Ah. You must give me the benefit of your wide experience of the art of boxing one day, Master Emerton.' Byron grinned and pulled my cap down over my eyes. And that was how I missed the blow that was said to have been the best in Wilks' career, the quickest, the hardest and the cleanest of them all. When I pulled off the cap, the crowd were pressing past us to the ring where Wilks stood holding up his hands and grinning. But Tait lay flat on the boards and what the Fancy term 'the claret' and I call blood, was streaming out of his mouth.

'Look behind you, Lucy,' Byron murmured. 'It's time for us to leave.'

On the horizon above us, I saw the line of advancing riders, and looked back at Byron afraid. He took my hand. 'Come! We'll have to run for it.'

I was breathless when we stopped. The velvet trousers were torn and spattered with mud, my body ached. 'Yes, I know, but see what you escaped.' Byron put his hand under my chin and turned it. 'Poor devils!' he said bitterly, as below us the horses plunged and reared among the frightened crowd, the great whips snaking through the air above them. 'Let's go. It's more to Ruthven's taste than mine.'

'Must we always talk of him?' It sounded more violent than I had intended, and he looked at me sharply.

'Does his name affect you so much?' he said, and spun me round to face him.

71

'Why, what is it? Byron, you're hurting my arm!'

'You were in love with him, weren't you? I was a fool not to believe him.'

'I? Are you mad?'

'Prove it, then. Show me you love me.' His eyes darkened as he pushed me back, I reached up towards him. Time passed. I swore I could never forget it, and I have – but I was happy.

'I don't want to go on with this,' he said afterwards, leaning over me and stroking my hair.

I rolled over. 'You're going to leave me?'

'Do you think I would, after that? No, I want to see more of you, not less, all of you, all of the time, pretty Lucy.' His hand slid down my body. 'Come and stay at Newstead.'

'Oh . . . But you know I can't! What would people say?'

'There speaks my bold girl,' he mocked me. 'Don't be such a little fool. I never said you should advertise the fact. Go and visit one of your girlfriends, a discreet one, make a plan to stay with her – ah, *now* you see!'

'I could.' With inward amusement, I saw the irony of making Mary be my alibi while keeping the truth from her. It would be a sweet revenge for her months with Byron. I touched his face, gazing at the curling lashes as they drooped down. 'I love you.'

'And I you, especially when you're plotting.'

I smiled, demurely. 'It's for your sake. Yes, I'll come to Newstead.'

* * *

I was never more calm and efficient than in protecting my love affair. Lady Winter's gossiping tongue was scotched when I laughed in her face and said that Byron had taken me from the Assembly Rooms to meet Mary, and to help choose a present for her. My tears were most effective and Mr Emerton was for the first time in memory moved to ask Lady Winter to have her carriage brought round. I watched her poker-backed departure through the window and smiled to myself.

The next step was to enlist Mary's help. I planned my story, invited her to stay and bought her a pretty, very expensive fan. I was sorry to see that she was still grieving over Byron. The black band round her bonnet seemed a rather extravagant gesture, but it turned out to be for a second cousin, or so she said. I softened her with a visit to Orlando. Always eager for anyone's love, he bounced, bubbled and beamed at her. Mary was wooed and won. I wondered if it was the dream of a Musters or a Byron brat which was clouding her eyes. It wasn't hard to guess.

'It's wonderful how he's taken to you, Miss Chaworth.' Rose said jealously, as she almost snatched the baby back. Mary smiled and looked wistful.

'Oh, Mary, how hard life is,' I sighed as we left the room.

'Why, I believe you're in love,' she said looking at me. 'Who is he?'

I bent my head. 'You're too quick, and I thought I had hidden it so well. I see I must tell you everything. Come, let's go into the garden.

'I need your help,' I said, dabbing at my eyes with a handkerchief, cologne damped. She took my hand and pressed it. 'He's an officer. They're sending him to fight. Oh, Mary, I have to see him before he goes, just once more for a few last days together, but my uncle has forbidden it.' I lowered my voice. 'He has no money, you see. His father cut him off without a penny.'

'Poor Lucy, but how romantic! What can I do?'

'You will help? Oh, my dear friend.' I put my arms round her. 'A little lie is all I need. Could you say that I had come to stay with you at Annesley, just for a week, or perhaps two? Would you do that for me, Mary? But it's asking too much of you. . . .'

'I'll do it gladly,' she said. 'I know what it is to be in love.' She looked down at her hands. 'I owe you something, too. Don't be angry with me, Lucy, but that first time we met, when I was with Byron, I thought . . . well, you looked at him so . . . forgive me.'

'You haven't seen him since the dance?' I said nervously.

She pulled up a handful of grass, shredded it in her white hands. 'He's still with – Ruthven, isn't he?' She stared ahead of her, her eyes shining. 'But when he sees how I was betrayed, he'll come back. I'm sure of it.'

'Do you still love him so much?'

She looked at me in surprise. 'Yes. They can make me marry John Musters, they can never stop me loving Byron. But you know what love is now, Lucy.'

'Yes. I do.' All the pleasure had gone out of my petty revenge, but it was too late to turn back, and I wanted Byron. I knew I loved him better than she ever could.

It was all too easy. My uncle never doubted the story. For two weeks, Byron was mine, in body and soul, if he could give that. All visitors were turned away, and I lived with him as his mistress. We let the days slip by, riding, talking, making love, and when night came and I had fallen asleep, naked and exhausted, lying across the bed, Byron sat on in the candlelight, writing until the dawn came up. In the mornings, he slept while I wandered through the house, wondering if he would soon talk of marriage. It was the only subject which lay between us, untouched. I did not dare do more than hint at it.

We went out once – I put on boy's clothes again – to see the young prodigy who had already taken London by storm, Master Berry. He was under-sized, with more determination than talent. The audience at the Nottingham theatre were not impressed. Byron yawned and I giggled as the unlucky actor retreated backstage, battling grimly against the shouts and cascades of rotten fruit. In the row opposite us, a man leaned forward and looked at us. My smile faded.

'Shall we go, Byron?' I nudged his arm.

'If you like. It's tedious stuff.'

He turned without seeing Ruthven and we left hurriedly. 'What upset you, Lucy? You're pale as a ghost,' he said as we came out into the cool street.

'It was too hot. Too many people.' I was nervous and on edge for the next few days, but he did not come. Perhaps he had accepted that I possessed Byron now.

The day came when I must leave. Byron lent me his horse to ride over to Annesley, where the coach would be waiting to take me home. I leaned down from the saddle, kissed him on the mouth.

'You should stay,' he said. 'I'll not let you go.'

'I must . . . My uncle.' He pulled me from the saddle.

'Come with me,' he insisted softly. 'I'll take you to London.

We'd be so happy together. You can stay with Augusta, if you're worried about the proprieties. She'd love you for my sake.'

It was not what I had hoped to hear. 'I doubt if I could love her as much as you do. You talk of her too much. No, I must go back. Shall I see you before you go to Cambridge?'

'Lord, yes! That's five weeks away, yet. I'll send word to you by next Saturday.' He lifted me on to the horse and looked up at me, smiling. 'I shall wait for you to change your mind.'

I looked down from the hill top, but he had gone inside. Heavy-hearted, I rode on to Annesley.

Mrs Chaworth gave me a nervous smile as she welcomed me. She was too friendly, too quick to accept my official story. I sensed that she wanted me gone. 'Where is Mary?' I asked.

'Mary? Oh, the poor girl's in bed with a chill. She's not well enough for visitors, I'm afraid.' She pressed my hand suddenly. 'My dear, I'm so very sorry,' she whispered and almost ran back into the house. As I looked after her in surprise, a curtain was pulled aside at one of the upper windows and I saw Mary. She drew back as I raised my hand against the sun. The curtain dropped.

*   *   *

Mr Emerton was standing in front of the library fire when I arrived. His face was grim.

'Why, Uncle, how well you look! Oh, how good it is to be back.' I edged towards the door. 'I must go and see Orlando – I never knew how much I'd miss him!'

'Come here,' he said quietly. I went up to him. He lifted his hand, slapped me hard across both cheeks. Tears smarted in my eyes. 'Now, why did you tell that pack of lies, Lucy? I want an explanation.'

'Lies, sir?' I faltered. How much did he know? 'These are hard words to come home to.'

'Mary Chaworth visited me yesterday,' he said. 'She was very distressed at having to tell me, but quite rightly, she felt it was for your good.'

'That was not her reason,' I said under my breath.

75

'I don't give a damn what her reasons were,' he roared. 'Do you think I enjoyed hearing what a fool you'd made of me? Oh, I'm sure you thought you'd been very clever, telling her one lie, me another, and then going off like a common whore, I mean it, Lucy, a common whore, with Byron.'

'I . . .'

'Do you suppose any decent man will be seen with you, let alone marry you, after this? And how do you suppose I look to the county? I can never hold my head up again. Oh, Lucy, how could you do it? How could you?' He sank back in his chair, his face buried in his hands.

'I do love him, Uncle,' I said. 'I'd do it again, if he asked me.'

'Little fool, that's all he will ask you. Well, did he talk of marriage? Of course he didn't. He'll marry somebody who sets a higher value on herself. You've ruined yourself, Lucy, and I'm damned if I can see a way out for either of us.'

The clock ticked loudly in the long silence. 'Go and change your clothes,' he said wearily. 'I'm not going to say any more. We still have to live in the same house, but I'll have no more shame brought on it by you or your brother.'

I turned at the door. 'Uncle, can I ask one question? Who told Mary?'

He made no answer.

'Was it Lord Ruthven?'

But he only lifted the poker and stabbed feebly at the fire with shaking hands. I sighed and left the room, too bent under my own woes to see what they had worked on my uncle.

It rained on the day of the funeral, but the bishop's address was given to a full church; he had been much loved.

I shivered as we stood in the wet grass round the open grave. The heavy clay sucked at the coffin: I threw down my handful of dust and turned away. Their eyes watched me coldly through the black veils. I knew what they were thinking. I was to blame. I had killed him with shame. That was what they thought, but they did not dare to say it. He had a stroke on the night of my arrival, and never opened his eyes again. But it was I, too, who sat up by his bed all night, listening to the loud breathing, cooling his forehead, smoothing the sheets. He never knew; he died, betrayed. I wept, but I was not repentant.

Two weeks later, I knew for certain that I had conceived. I wrote to Byron, asking to see him, saying nothing more. No answer. In my second letter, I told him everything. No answer. Panic gripped me. Rose urged me to go away, to stay with relations and rest, but I did not dare to leave the house until my answer came. God, how slowly those days dragged! A month had passed and I could stand it no longer. I took the hunter out and rode over to Newstead. It's a long journey for a heavy heart.

Nobody answered the door. I opened it and went through, my feet echoing in the stone hall. No answer came when I called. Slowly, I walked up the stairs into the gallery. The door of his room was open. He stood with his back to me, bent over some papers in a drawer. I sighed with relief.

'Byron,' I said softly. Lord Ruthven turned to face me.

'You're too late. He left a week ago,' he said, folding his arms and smiling at me. 'He's not coming back. Do you want these?'

I swayed as he held out my letters. 'What have you done? What did you tell him?'

He laughed. 'The truth. Do you need me to tell you?'

I shook my head wearily. 'No. I can imagine how neatly you twisted it to suit you. I suppose you said I was forcing him into a marriage. You put it onto a cheap, grasping level in the hope of winning him back. Poor Ruthven! What a victory! He left you too, didn't he? Should I weep for you?' I drew back as he moved towards me. 'Don't dare to touch me!'

'There's no one to hear,' he said, smiling. 'I have a debt to collect still. That's why I waited for you.'

I shuddered as his mouth brushed my neck, his teeth grazing the soft skin, but I could not draw away. 'Must you have everything which has been his?' I whispered as the cold lips touched my shoulder. My energy was draining away. With a violent effort, I pushed him back, drew up my bodice. 'You have the house to remind you.'

'We both do,' he said softly. 'You remember this room, don't you? Was it here . . . but I'm distressing you?'

'I gave him more than you ever could.'

'You're very hard,' he said, flushing.

'Since I met you.'

'Oh no, it's in your nature, Lucy. You're admirably . . . ruthless. That is why you will listen to what I have to say. Come down to the garden.'

'I'm going back.' I turned away towards the door.

'Back to what? There's no returning, not for you. Do you suppose they will take you back now? You have to marry, or be an outcast. And you were always mine, Lucy, You knew that when we first met. I did not need to tell you. Now, perhaps we should find a more appropriate setting for a proposal. Come.'

We walked through the wild, unkept garden to the enclosed stretch of black water behind the house. I stood beside him on the overgrown marble steps, remembering, remembering . . . Ruthven's stick was poised gently over a creeping beetle. It had reached the lowest step before he drove down the cane. Fastidiously, he flicked it into the water on the point of the stick. 'Well, what do you say, Lucy? I've been kind. You had more than a year to find another husband. Had you not chosen Byron, I might have released you from the debt.'

'But you knew I would choose him.' Ruthven smiled and said nothing. '*Why* do you ask me?' I stretched out my hands in despair. 'You don't love me. I have nothing to give you.'

'You have this. . . .' He stabbed a finger at my stomach. 'And we have so much to share. We both loved him.'

'That's not your reason.' I turned away from him. 'Why did you take the wager? Why me?'

Ruthven laughed. 'I'll tell you. I saw a drawing of you in your brother's rooms. The likeness intrigued me . . . I half guessed the future from that pretty sketch.'

'Likeness?'

'My dear Lucy, surely you know it! Neither you nor he suffer from modesty. Did you never stand with . . . your lover, in front of a glass?' I shuddered as he caressed my features with bloodless fingers. 'Here, you see, and here. The same full lips, the vain white hands, the high brow. Even the colour of the hair. And you came from Nottinghamshire. Vanity will always

78

find a mirror for its love: I knew then I had found my answer.'

'But why did you not take me then for your wife?' I faltered. 'How could you have been so cruel, to wait until I loved him . . .'

'Cruel?' Ruthven raised his eyebrows. 'Byron has deserted you, not I. I merely offer myself as a substitute. And a necessary one, my dear Lucy. You will not refuse.' He paused. 'But you are correct in thinking I have other motives. I need an heir.'

'So you'll take his.'

'You put it so delicately. Well, what is your answer?'

I looked across the water. To live here, but as Lady Ruthven . . . I laughed harshly as the sob ached in my throat. 'As you say, I have no choice.'

He smiled. 'We'll make all the arrangements. Alvedon must be sold of course, your servants dismissed. I want none of your past.'

'But the baby and his nurse?' He turned quickly. 'I owe it to Harry,' I added in a low voice.

'A child? Tell me.'

I explained Orlando, as well as I could. He followed the story attentively. 'You have the papers giving you control over him?' he asked.

I hesitated. 'Yes . . . and they will remain in my possession.'

Ruthven shrugged. 'We'll talk of possession another time. The story interests me. Ah, one more point, Lucy.' He held my head up towards him, forcing it back until I nearly choked. 'I want no interference with my life. Do you understand? No questions, no gossip. I am a private man, and I expect loyalty.'

'You shall have it,' I said between my teeth. 'And no more.'

*   *   *

Alvedon was sold to a rich factory owner from Nottingham, the type of man my uncle had most hated. He paid a low price, but I took it. The servants were dismissed, the wedding preparations made. The neighbours called in their carriages to congratulate me and I sat, hands folded, in my uncle's chair while they told me how fortunate I was to have made such a good match, killing me with their kindness as they remembered Byron and shook their heads. Only Rose knew the true story and bridled as she said that Miss Chaworth had come to pay her respects.

'I won't see her.'

'You'll have to, Miss Lucy. I told her you were here. She's waiting in the hall.'

I went to the corner table and poured out a large glass of brandy, drained it in one swallow. Rose grinned. 'That's the way to do it, Miss. You show her. I'll bring her in.'

She was all smiles, preening herself like a sleek cat. 'How good of you to come!' I kissed her rouged cheek. 'So, we'll be near neighbours, Mary. And what could be more delightful?'

'Dear Lucy, but you look so pale and tired. I looked to find you blooming like a rose. It's supposed to be so good for the skin.'

'I don't know what you're talking about,' I snapped, forgetting to smile.

'You mean there's another reason for your marriage? Do forgive me, but I had no idea.'

'I wasn't aware that you were marrying for love,' I said in as sweet a voice as I could manage.

Her lips drew back over her white teeth. 'Were you not?' She fingered a little locket round her neck, turning it so that the dark stone flashed in the light. 'Isn't it charming? Byron sent it to me. "To the Rose of Annesley." I think he has regrets.'

I tugged viciously at the bell handle by the fireplace. 'Forgive me, I must ask you to leave. Rose, fetch Miss Chaworth's cloak.'

'My dear, I wouldn't stay a moment longer than was necessary,' she said, flushing a deep red, and swept out of the room. As the front door slammed, I collapsed in a chair and buried my face in my hands.

* * *

I moved through the crowd of guests on Ruthven's arm, nodding and smiling, trembling as I saw how they shrank away from him. All the illusion was there: candles glittered in the heavy wall-sconces, the orchestra tuned up their instruments, the girls' bright dresses fluttered up and down the staircase, but it was all a pretence. There was no joy at my wedding.

'Well, will nobody dance?' Ruthven said, abruptly. 'Mrs Musters? I remember how *you* love to dance.' Mary winced.

Lady Winter came towards me as he dropped my arm. 'My dear, I hope you know what you're doing.' She lowered her voice. 'You must try to look a little more gay. People are talking.'

'Let them talk. I married him, didn't I? Wasn't that what you wanted me to do, Lady Winter.'

But she only shook her head. 'Quiet, Lucy. You've caused enough scandal already.'

The outer door crashed open and a gust of dead leaves blew in, scattering the guests. One of the servants went out. They looked round curiously as he hurried back to me. 'It's a gentleman to see you, my lady,' he said. I looked at him, ashen-faced.

'I forbid you to go,' Ruthven said softly, taking my arm. 'Your place now is here, at my side.'

I looked up at him and laughed. 'But what do you have to fear, my lord? I married you. You have me for life, so may I not see him for five minutes? Or are you too jealous to allow it?' I spoke clearly and several of the guests turned to listen, as I had intended that they should. Ruthven was white with anger, but he forced a smile and released my arm. My head high, I walked to the door and let it swing shut behind me.

'Byron?' I leant out over the balcony. 'My love?' I could not keep my voice steady, nor reproach him.

He looked up from the shadows at the foot of the steps. 'Lucy . . . I heard of it this morning. *Why* did you do it, in God's name! I would have married you, if I'd known that was what you wanted, but to take him!'

I drew back. 'Surely you knew? My letter – you had my letter, Byron. It was cruel not to answer, cruel to believe him.'

'Come here,' he said quietly. Mutely, I let him take me in his arms. He looked down at me. 'You wrote to tell me this? It's my child, isn't it? Forgive me, but . . .'

I nodded. 'It is yours, and I wrote. Ruthven said he advised you against me.'

Byron laughed bitterly. 'He did far worse than that. He never told me at all. I never saw your letter. I knew nothing.'

'But why did he want to marry me? Because I belonged to you, still do, my dear, my sweet love?' I clung to him, sobbing. He stroked my hair and kissed me again and again, but the sourness of their finality made them bitter in my mouth. I broke away from him and leant against the wall. 'Byron, why? He doesn't love me.'

'He married you because he's incapable of fathering the heir he longs for,' Byron said slowly. 'All the devilry in the world can't give him that, but you can.' He clenched his fists. 'And it's mine, damn him!' His eyes glanced past me at the door. He felt in his pocket. 'Listen, my sweet love. Keep this, to remember me by and if you can, use it to buy your way to me. I won't forget you. I'll wait, I swear.' He laid a weight in my hand.

I turned the ring over in my hand, a flawless square-cut emerald surrounded by diamonds and set in gold. I dropped it in my bodice, caught his hand as he turned away. 'A ring cannot love me. Don't leave me now, Byron. Please . . . don't go.'

'Darling girl, I must. I want no part in your wedding dances.' He looked up at the walls, his face dark with fury. 'And I pray the day will soon come when I can afford to dismiss him as my tenant, when I can come back to my own home.' I put my hand against my mouth to stifle any sound as he swung himself up into the saddle. I must not cry, must not . . .

I watched him ride away down the drive, turned as Ruthven came through the door.

'The guests are waiting, Lucy. Come.' He held out his arm and his hand closed over mine as he bent over me. 'What did he say to you? Tell me! Did you tell him of the child?'

I drew back, terrified by his expression. His eyes shone and flickered like alien spirits in his white face. 'He – he's gone, Ruthven. The child will be yours. You have nothing to fear.'

He shook his head. 'You'll run away to him to have my son. He gave you money, didn't he?'

'No. No! I swear it.'

He stared at me, smiling-lipped. 'Come, Lucy. What did you plan? Tell me, or . . .'

I stepped back again and saw my fate in his face a second too late. There were fifteen stone steps. As the doctors said, I was lucky not to break my back.

But he said that I'd done it to spite him, and from that moment on, our marriage was dead.

5

Six years had passed, and not one day had gone by without my regretting my marriage. I had known that it would be loveless: I had not known the isolation I was to suffer as Ruthven's wife. The fear he had once inspired had turned to a silent hate, and it was shared by everybody who crossed his path. I did not need to hear the stories, although Rose was always ready to tell them. I only had to walk through the villages to see how the men turned away, how quickly the women pulled their children back into the doorways. No family wanted their sons pressed into Ruthven's service – too many had gone down that path already.

Yet, he could be kind. He brought back presents from his journeys, a length of silk or a pair of painted velvet slippers for me, a stick and hoop or a wooden sailing boat for Orlando. He gave me dolls dressed in the latest fashions from France, taught me what colours to wear to complement my hair. My appearance could always make him kind. I knew he saw his lost love in my face. My crime lay in being a woman.

But I had come to dread the evenings when he came home. Solitude was the only grace I looked for, now. I used to make an effort in the first years, talk of the books I had read, of Orlando's nursery feats. But my words were always twisted to turn against him; I was reminding him of the son he could not have. I was almost glad to have miscarried Byron's child. It would only have served to torture me more.

The first year of my marriage had taught me to sit stone-faced at the end of the long oak dining-table, while Ruthven called in his siblings and sat them beside him, telling me to listen to them if I wanted to learn how to amuse him. I had learned that

I must watch in silence as he ruffled their hair, poured the wine down their throats until they were too drunk to stand. I had learned when I was permitted to go up the stairs alone, while he lay back in his chair and stared down at the bodies sprawled at his feet, his face slipping back into the pallid mask of boredom.

I could endure even that better than the nights when he persecuted me for having loved Byron. It was like a chain, choking me to death, the bond of passion that bound us to the same man. His jealousy bordered on madness. In every smile, every journey outside my prison gates, he saw danger, pulled the chain a little tighter . . . I shuddered and put my hands across the looking glass to hide my face as the words rose from the blackness of my mind . . . 'You'd better forget him, Lucy. He forgot you long ago . . . You hadn't heard? A choirboy, a pretty, fair-haired boy . . . Tastes change, my dear . . . His sister, no, don't run away . . . but you should be flattered. She has a look of you, or was it you who always reminded him . . .'

He had planted the seeds of doubt well, and they had taken root. I could not forget them. The memories were fading, and the suggestions remained. Only once did I dare to tell him the truth. I turned as I went wearily up the stairs, looked down at him as he sat, laughing softly to himself.

'Do you realise how I pity you sometimes?' I said slowly. 'It's your obsession which has to be fed, not mine. Six years have passed and yet you still have to follow every rumour because you can never have the reality. Do you suppose I haven't noticed that every one of your – protégés – has his hair, the same soft eyes, full lips? Think of this next time you mock me: he left *you* by his own choice. Good night, my lord.'

It was worth the pain I suffered later.

But life had changed during the last few months and, thank God, he had little time for me. There was talk of a new rising among the people. The county, as usual, shut their eyes to it. They had managed to survive the war without letting it disturb their way of life: how should a riot succeed where the French had failed? But I, I was forced to be aware of it. They came to the house late at night, the soft-voiced men in shabby coats, and Mr Richards was among them. I had not forgotten his face. I had listened at the door, and I knew now what Ruthven's work was, that took him away for months on end. It was dangerous knowledge. He was helping the government agents in their search for spies. It was a job which he could enjoy; hunting a fox was dull work to him when there were men to be chased. But I knew my rôle. I saw nothing, and I asked no questions. It was easier that way.

I sighed and turned away from the glass. Rose looked up from her sewing. 'Is the Master coming home tonight?'

'I doubt it. Oh, don't look sad, Rose. You know my feelings well enough.'

'It's a shame the way he treats you, though. I don't know how you stand for it.'

'You know what happens if I fight against him. It's not advisable. Oh God, how I wish . . .'

'Yes, my lady?'

'Nothing.' I went past her down the stairs. 'I'm going out. Will you bring Orlando down later?'

I walked slowly along the side of the lake, beating my hands against each other in frustration. The wind whipped up the ripples into a small storm, the trees bent down, groaning. Through them, I saw a carriage. I knew the two black horses well. I hurried back to meet it.

Mary had changed more than me. Her prettiness had faded and four children had altered her slim figure, but we were friends again. We had both suffered too much to bear grudges. I kissed her warmly.

'How glad I am to see you! My first visitor since Christmas! I need company, today.'

'That you do. I came to tell you . . . may I come in for a moment? We'll freeze to death out here.'

We sat in front of the great fire in the hall, warming our hands. 'You must come away from here, tonight,' she said at last. 'You know there's been talk of a new outbreak of riots? I've heard that they plan to come this way.' She looked down at the floor. 'We know that Ruthven is not . . . loved around here. I think you'll be in danger if you stay.'

I poured out the tea and noticed that my hands were shaking. Nerves: I shrugged and took a firmer grasp on the painted handle. 'They can hardly burn down the abbey. The job's half done already. Anyway, Ruthven's away, as usual. There's nothing to fear.'

She sighed. 'You always were stubborn, Lucy. You won't consider coming to stay with us?'

'And face him when I come back?'

She set down her cup. 'Oh, it's too ridiculous! You can't let him keep you a prisoner here like this. The man's a fiend!'

I looked at her and smiled. 'You don't have to live with him. Thank you, but I'll stay. It's probably a false alarm. How's John?'

'Well . . . He's found a new admirer. I hear she's quite pretty.'

'Anyone I'd know?'

'Naturally not.' She stood up suddenly and turned away from me to feign interest in a crayon sketch of Orlando which stood on my writing table. 'How many times have we had this conversation, Lucy?'

'Five times. Six? I can't remember. Does it still hurt?'

'A little less each time. It's better once one knows. I'd mind so much less if I didn't have to be warned by some well-meaning outsider like Lady Winter, who manages to convey the fact that everyone knows but me. Why do men ever think it's kinder not to tell us, Lucy?'

I laughed. 'All men are cowards about that. They only say it to their wives when they think the girl will stay, but they can never be sure.'

She nodded eagerly. 'And the hateful way they have of always being more sensitive than us, just when it suits them. That's John's usual way. When I tell him that I know, he turns on me for having driven him to it, because I can't understand his sensitive nature. Him! Sensitive! Oh, Lucy, it's such a relief to talk to somebody.'

'Have some more tea.'

'No, I must go back. He likes me to be there when he arrives home. Part of the room as he expects to see it.' She laughed as I shook my head, then gave a small sob of despair. 'What would Byron say if he could see his 'Rose of Annesley' now, I wonder?'

'You haven't changed.'

87

She tossed back her hair and smiled. 'No, I've kept my looks well, haven't I?'

'Not a day older,' I lied. 'Bless you for coming, Mary. I'll let you know if a siege takes place.'

She clasped my hand. 'I'm perfectly serious about it. Are you sure you won't change your mind?'

I watched the carriage roll away, then drew across the heavy bolts on the door.

*　　*　　*

The branches rattled against the window. I turned over again in the bed, pulling up the sheet, trembled as I heard a scream. I pulled a silk shawl round me and ran out into the dark passage. 'Is anyone there?'

Silence, then a small wail from Orlando's room. I laughed with relief, pushed open the door. He was sitting upright in bed, his eyes wide and frightened.

'What is it, darling? Did the wind wake you?'

'He came in here. I looked up and he was bending over me.'

'Who, Orlando?'

'Him,' he said stubbornly, shaking the mass of fair curls forward over his pointed little face. He would never say Ruthven's name. 'His face was . . .'

'Yes, was what?'

'I don't know. Different. Don't laugh at me.'

'I won't,' I promised, 'but you must be tired, darling. He isn't here tonight and Rose has gone out. We're all alone.' I hesitated as he clutched his fingers round mine. 'Do you want to sleep in my room, just this once? I get frightened sometimes, too, when there's a storm.'

He fell asleep almost at once in my arms, but I lay awake, listening to the wind. They wouldn't come here. They were frame-breakers, not murderers. They had no reason . . . I started at the heavy crash below. It came from the hall. I waited for the next, trembling. It came, and with it, the splintering of wood. Slowly, I lifted myself on my elbows and looked round the room. I saw what I needed.

'Where are you going?' asked Orlando, waking as I slid past him.

I put my finger to my lips. 'Stay here, Promise me you won't leave the room.'

'Don't leave me, please don't,' he whispered. 'I'm afraid.'

I sighed. 'Stay behind me then, and do exactly what I tell you.' I took him by the hand, grasped the pistol with the other and hurried down the stairs, pulling him along behind me.

The door was still holding them back, but a thin crack in the wood split it between the top and bottom bolt. As I looked at it, the blunt nose of a ram splintered through. I knelt down by the little boy as he shivered in his thin nightgown, hiding my fear as well as I could.

'We're going to play a game, darling. There's nothing to be afraid of, you see. There are some men outside the door and what we must do is to try and keep them out.'

He looked up at me suspiciously. 'If it's a game, why did they start first, and why is your face all white?'

I shook him. 'Never mind that. You stay here and watch the windows. Tell me if you see anything.'

I dragged the heavy refectory table towards the door, every muscle strained to breaking point with the effort. The dull thud of the ram came again; the crack opened wider. Frantically, I piled chairs, carpets, everything in sight onto the barricade. Then I turned in fright as Orlando shouted: 'The window! The window!'

I waited with a grim smile as the man put his hand over the sill. The face, coated in black, rose up, bodiless, terrifying: it bent forward between his straining shoulders as he heaved himself up. I lifted a stick and brought it down with a vicious crack on the nape of his neck, splitting the skin. He slumped over the sill, arms dangling, flaccid, by the wall. I managed to push his body back, heard it crack on the flagstones outside.

But now the ram was through the door, pushing the chairs back as fast as I piled them up. The wood fell away from the iron bolts; the door swung forward in two pieces. I fled back to the stairs, held Orlando tightly to my side as he began to whimper. I put my finger against the trigger.

'If you want my husband, you'll have to look elsewhere. The first man through the door gets a bullet through his head.'

'We don't want your husband, yet,' said Jackson as he

pushed the halves of the door apart. 'I've come to keep my promise.'

I held the pistol steady and looked down at him, my heart thudding like a hammer. The black paint glistened on his broad cheeks and forehead: his eyes were narrowed under brows like thorn thickets. I would not have known him.

'I've waited a long time for this,' he said, leaning against the foot of the stairs and looking down at his gun.

'I had no part in it,' I whispered, dry-mouthed.

'You married the man who killed my Tom. You didn't stop him then. Reckon that's enough for me,' he said slowly, and lifted the gun. 'Don't you think you owe me something?'

'This,' I said and squeezed the trigger. It clicked back, dead. I dropped it, watching it clatter down the stairs to his feet.

He laughed. 'It would have done you no good. I've got ten men out there. Any one of them would do the job for me, if I asked him. Put the child in front of you. Quick, now!' He trained the gun on me and I pulled Orlando forward.

'Nice-looking boy,' said Jackson, as Orlando hid his face against me, sobbing with fright. 'You must have grown fond of him, like he was your own son.'

I clutched him to me. 'You wouldn't kill the child? Listen, Jackson, I'll get money for you. I'll see that you get a good job, anything you want. Nobody ever need know that you came here tonight.'

He spat at me and I felt the warm saliva trickle down my arm. 'That's what I think of your offer,' he said, his face darkening. 'My work lies out there, with Ludd's men.'

'Ludd?'

'Aye. You'll not live to hear more of him, but others will. They'll live to wish they'd never heard his name before we're through.'

'Tom!' A low voice called from outside. 'Finish what you have to do. We've fifteen miles to go tonight.'

He smiled at me as he raised the gun towards Orlando. 'One son for another, lady.'

A shot rang out. The gun dropped from his hand as he fell to his knees with a scream of pain. There was a scuffle of feet outside the door as his comrades fled away into the night. I looked up to see Ruthven coming down the stairs. He brushed past me and bent over the body. Jackson groaned and turned over, his face grey with pain.

'Yes, you'll live to face your trial,' Ruthven said softly. 'I think you may come to regret that I did not kill you.'

'You saved me from him,' I whispered as I came unsteadily down the stairs. 'How can I thank you?'

He laughed abruptly. 'You flatter yourself, Lucy. I have my heir to protect.'

I flinched as if he had struck me. 'And if his gun had been trained on me,' Ruthven said slowly, 'would you have fired your pistol so quickly? I wonder. Get me a piece of rope. We'll tie the brute up to the table for the night and give him time to cool down.'

I looked at Jackson's sagging body, the useless arm which flapped loose from the shoulder. 'We can't leave him like that.'

'He's a killer. It's more than he deserves.' Ruthven kicked him savagely, smiled as he twisted on the floor, his face contorted.

'Where are your friends bound next? Come, tell me?' His leather boot drove savagely down. Orlando trembled beside me, his face white and frozen.

'For God's sake, the child!' I sobbed. 'Orlando, come with me, darling. I'll put you back to bed.'

'No, let him stay. Come here, boy. Take a look at the man who tried to kill you. Here, take my stick.' He stooped to clench Orlando's hand round the cane, looked into his face. I saw the dazed blank look on the little boy's face as he closed his fingers, stared up into Ruthven's eyes.

'You devil!' I whispered. 'Would you corrupt a child?' I pulled him back and dragged him, weeping, up the stairs.

*   *   *

'King Ludd' was on everybody's lips that year, but there was no sympathy for the weavers whose bare cupboards and empty bellies had driven them to revolt. It seemed to me that they had a good cause, but it would not have been wise to say so. The countryside was in the grip of terror; men talked again of Jacobins and spies. In the town, the riots broke out once more: the military were brought in to crush them. Hay-ricks blazed like warning beacons in the midnight skies, a hundred or more of the master hosiers had woken to find that their frames had been smashed in the midnight raids – and a letter from the mysterious King Ludd was always pinned to the wreckage. No one knew who Ludd was then, but the stories were wild. Some said he was a convict, some said he was a weaver. Many said that he issued his orders from near us, in Sherwood Forest. But nobody knew, and the unknown leader was greatly feared.

Ruthven's own dedication to hounding down the rebels had reached fever pitch; the sweating flanks of the horses told me how furiously they had been driven every night. The county applauded his efforts: I was sickened by them. I took great pleasure in showing him a report in *The Times* of Byron's maiden speech, supporting the Luddites and saying it would take twelve butchers and a Judge Jeffreys to condemn one of them. It deterred Ruthven – but only for a moment.

The only thing which gave me cause to hope was a near miracle. His coldness to me would never change – that I knew – but he seemed to have repented of his treatment of the little boy. Every morning, he set aside an hour for a walk with Orlando. With him, his face became gentle, his words were soft, and I smiled as I saw them walking under the trees, hand in hand. They came back with their faces flushed, laughing quietly as if they shared a secret. I let myself dream of impossibilities, not of love, but of quiet nights and peaceful days. Bitterness is hard to live with for a lifetime. Its demands are too high.

When Ruthven suggested that I should sign the papers making Orlando his heir, I barely hesitated. I had nothing to give the child for a settlement and there was no news of Harry. Ruthven had an easy task in persuading me that Rose's story of a marriage was beyond credulity. I had never really believed in it. I had not wanted to believe in it. Her distress when she heard what I had done gave me a moment of anxiety, but the new tenderness in Ruthven's nature allayed my fears. I began to hope that Orlando, the future, would obliterate Byron, the past.

Rose came into my room one morning, some weeks after Jackson's visit, her round, sweet face unusually solemn. I put aside my embroidery.

'It's about Orlando,' she said hesitantly. 'I'm worried about him, my lady.' She brushed her eyes with the back of her hand, tried to smile. 'It's hard not to feel a mother's fears.'

'Come and sit down beside me,' I said gently.

'He mustn't stay here any longer,' she said with a sudden fierceness which took me back. 'It's against nature to bring up a child in this house.'

'But he seems happy enough when I see him on his walks.'

'Does he?' She lowered her voice. 'Come and look at him, my lady. It'll bring tears to your eyes to see the poor mite.'

I followed her up the stairs. Softly, she opened the nursery door and I looked in. His wooden painted toys lay, untouched, in a pile by the wall. On the window-seat, the little boy was kneeling, his face against the window. I could see the mist of breath veiling the glass.

'Every day,' Rose whispered. 'All he does is sit there and stare out. It's not natural in a child.'

'Orlando?' I said.

'Leave me alone,' he said, without turning round. Rose looked at me warily. I walked across the room, made my voice light and gay.

'It's only me, my darling. I came to take you for a walk. You'll get ill if you sit inside all day.'

He turned and stared at me coldly. My buried fears flooded back as I forced a smile onto my lips and held out my hand to him.

'Come, here's your coat. Now, your hat. Shall we take your new boat out on the lake? Rose tells me you're quite an expert at sailing it.'

I gave her a look of triumph as he followed me slowly out of the room.

The wind bit into my flesh as I knelt beside the water and pushed the little boat out. When I looked up, his eyes had turned away. I felt that he was watching something I could not see, and I trembled as I bent over him.

'What are you looking at, darling? Is it the trees you like so much, when they bend over the water? They're vain, you see. They want to admire themselves.'

But he only looked at me with the blank, unchildish eyes and said nothing.

'It's that night, isn't it?' I prompted gently, brushing back the soft fringe of his hair. 'You were so brave, too.' I could not keep the harshness from my voice. 'It was Ruthven who . . .'

I started as he stared up at me, his eyes blazing. 'You're not to say his name, I won't let you, I won't!'

I tried to smile, but I was paralysed by the look on his face. Was it the same expression . . . no, I was being imaginative. The wind sobbed ever the dark water, tugging the little boat away. I knelt down to grasp at the string.

'Well, we'll go back, since you don't want to play. Come!'

'Look!' said Orlando, and held out his hand. In it lay a dead fledgeling. He brushed the feathers down carefully. It was the first human gesture I had seen him make and I almost wept with relief.

'Poor little creature. We'll make it a grave by the water, shall we, where the ground is soft?'

I took it gently from him. 'Why, it's still warm. It must have died only a few moments ago. . . .' I stopped, appalled. He smiled and looked up into my eyes. I was the one who turned away.

* * *

I put on my old green riding habit and rode over to Annesley that same afternoon. There was a tumbling, shouting group at the door to welcome me; Mary pushed the dogs down and called the children to stop plaguing me. She gave me a distracted smile.

'Forgive them, Lucy. They're impossible when they see a visitor. Annie, will you let go of Lady Ruthven's skirt! She doesn't want your muddy little fingers all over her.'

'I like you,' Annie announced, pulling at my sleeve. 'Your dress smells nice.'

I laughed and patted her silky yellow hair as I followed Mary into the house.

'My dear, I was so worried about you. I heard what happened,' she said breathlessly as she pushed the last hopeful head out of sight round the drawing-room door. 'You must have been frightened almost to death. I hear Ruthven's been doing splendid work in hounding them down.'

'Yes, it's a job he does well. Mary,' I leaned forward in my chair. 'You know children better than me. I want your advice.'

She listened attentively, her face glowing in the light of the flames which leapt and snapped on the hearth.

'Well, tell me what you think,' I said. 'Am I being imaginative, or is he exerting some horrible influence over the child?'

She sat back. 'You don't think the poor boy is still overwrought from his experience?'

'I should like to think that is all it is.' I sighed. 'You don't know how much I had hoped that life was changing for the better. He seems so fond of the child.'

'He always has to possess something, someone, doesn't he?' Mary said slowly. 'He lost Byron, he lost you . . .'

'He never . . .' No, it was not true. There had been times. Times when desire drove out despair, when revulsion became a fever, when his lightest touch made me tremble, when I wanted to be of one skin with him, to let him reach into my soul. Power must always fascinate the weak. 'He could never keep me,' I said.

'Then why do you stay? For me, it's different. I have the children. But you, Lucy. You were always the scandal-maker, the rule-breaker.'

'Believe me, when I say I would,' I said slowly. 'But he's made it impossible for me to leave. The lawyers have seen to that. I have no access to any money, except through him. And now, he has Orlando. How can I go?' She lay back, watching me as I wandered round the room. 'Oh, I've thought of it. I could have gone to Byron once, but *Childe Harold*'s made a celebrity of him, now. With all London at his feet, what place could there be for me? I'd be an embarrassment to him.'

'Because of that Devonshire House girl, you mean? What's the silly creature's name?'

'Caroline. You know it as well as I do, Mary. Don't pretend.'

'All flash and not much else, from what I've heard,' said

Mary, poking vigorously at the fire. 'He's just a feather in her cap. Well, feathers fly away soon enough.'

I laughed. 'So much for her. But the fact of the matter is, I can't leave Newstead, and Byron does not choose to return to it while Ruthven's still his tenant. So, what am I to do about the child?'

'Why don't you say it?' she said with a smile. 'Of course you can bring him here. I only hope he's strong enough to stand up to my little tyrants!'

'I'd have to ask Ruthven.'

She shook her head. 'Just bring him. You're a fool if you think he'll let the child go.'

'The problem is, will Orlando come?' I said.

*   *   *

'No! You shan't take me away.' He stood with his back to the corner, his little face flushed with rage.

Ruthven glanced at me and raised his eyebrows. I compressed my lips and said nothing. He laughed and walked across to the small and furious figure.

'But if I tell you, you must – you understand?'

Orlando's cold eyes fastened on me. 'She wants me to go. She wants to take me away from you.'

'That's right,' said Ruthven with a curious smile. 'But not for long, eh? We'll be together for a lifetime yet.'

I turned and walked away down the stairs.

He was driven over to Annesley the next morning. The last thing I saw was his face, pressed against the window of the coach. Three days later I looked up, startled, to see the Musters' barouche at the door. Orlando came down the steps, very composed, his hair neatly parted. I saw him look up at the house with a slight smile on his face.

'Why darling, I expected you to be gone for three weeks,' I said, puzzled, as he held up his cold cheek for a kiss. He drew a letter out of his pocket and handed it to me.

'Mrs Musters told me to give you this.' I saw that the seal had been broken, but I let that pass. I peered at Mary's thick, ink-spattered characters.

'My dear Lucy,

'Forgive me. I know you will try to understand. I had to send him back to you. It is not possible to keep him in this house for a day longer.

'He arrived in good spirits and was put to bed. The next morning, we were disturbed at breakfast by the most appalling screams. I rushed up to the nursery, terrified, as you can imagine, and found my children in tears, huddled in a corner, while Orlando was carefully disembodying the last of their dolls behind a barricade of chairs and rugs. As he completed each job, he flung them over the top to join the pile in front of the children. Lucy, I cannot tell you what horrible things he had done to them. It looked like a scene at the foot of a guillotine — and worse. There were heads with the eyes pulled out and paper stuffed in their mouths, there were sockets filled with the hair torn from their wigs — it looked like the work of a demon.

'We made him apologize to poor Annie and Lizzie, who were in a terrible state. He showed no flicker of conscience about it. Not a sign. I could have stood that, but his next performance was so much worse that I simply did not dare to keep him here.

'I was walking with John round the garden, planning where to put down the new trees, when we heard the most dreadful laugh. It was low with a soft chuckling sound in it, not the little boy, evidently. We turned and looked up to see Annie's white dress fluttering on the top balcony. John ran like a madman back to the house and up to her bedroom. Lucy — it was too awful, I can hardly write it — Orlando had a stick in his hand and he was leaning out of the window, pushing it at her. Thank heaven, John reached her in time and snatched her off the edge. He said the boy's face was like the mask of a devil when he pushed the stick out of his hand. I'm sorry, my dear friend. I had to send him away. God knows how a child of that age could have even thought of such a thing. . . .'

I folded the letter up and looked at him. 'Orlando, come and sit beside me on the window-seat. I want to talk to you.'

He perched beside me, his feet three inches off the ground. I looked down at my hands, wondering how to begin. 'Is it true? You did that to a little girl of three years old? Perhaps you didn't know how dangerous it was?'

'I wanted to come home,' he said. 'I knew they wouldn't keep me there after that. You shouldn't have sent me away.

97

You knew I didn't want to go.' He swung his legs to and fro, drumming them against the wood. 'You're afraid, aren't you? That's why you sent me there.'

My hands dug into his shoulders as I forced him to look up at me. 'He told you to do it, didn't he? Orlando, listen to me.' I pressed the small, cold hands in mine, tried to keep my voice calm. 'You must not think he loves you. He doesn't even know what love is. I've known him long enough to see that he corrupts everything he touches. . . .' His body stiffened against me. I sighed. 'Perhaps you should go to bed. It's asking too much that you should understand.'

'Why don't *you* go away?' he said softly. 'We don't need you here, now.' He nodded towards the servants' door. 'He goes there every night, you know. He likes them better than you.'

My fingers met round his throat; he choked and tried to pull them away. 'Never say that again, do you hear me, never!' I whispered. He screamed, but only after Ruthven had come through the door. He broke away from me to run to him.

'I came back,' he said simply.

Ruthven smiled, pulled him in front of him to face me. 'You see how hard it will be to separate us,' he said softly. 'We have an understanding, don't we, Orlando? *"Thou art mine. . . ."* '

'*. . . and I am thine,*' the high unchildish voice went on, '*"Till the sinking of the world,*

> *I am thine and thou are mine,*
> *'Till in ruin death is hurled –* '

'Except in birth,' I added viciously, to break the intimate smile which excluded and terrified me. 'Go to bed, Orlando dear. Rose will be surprised to have you back so soon.'

*   *   *

'You look tired, my love,' said Ruthven, as I took a seat opposite him by the fire. 'I thought we might spend a pleasant evening planning some of the new furniture for the house.'

'I'm sure Byron will find furniture of his own when he takes back Newstead.'

'I've brought back a copy of Smith's *Household Furniture*,' he said, ignoring me. 'I rather liked the look of the lyre-backed

98

chairs for the dining-room, or do you think Hepplewhite camel-backs would look better?'

I sat back, half-listening as he weighed the merits of one design against another. It was only a form that he should ask my opinion; I had no say in the matter. The shutters were drawn: overhead, the floors creaked gently as our rooms were prepared for the night. Ruthven sat forward, the book laid open on his beige-breeched thighs, his dark hair falling forward as he studied the drawings through half-closed eyes. I had moved to sit at the little satinwood writing table, a pile of politely refused invitations growing into a small mountain by my side. I tried to remember the last time I had been permitted to write an acceptance, and laughed suddenly. 'What a vision of domestic happiness we would present to anyone who saw us, now. Your sense of drama must be fading with age.' I saw him wince, but only because I had leant back in the elbow chair: he was afraid for its tapered legs. I pushed it back violently. 'Orlando suggested that I should leave,' I said, watching him. He shrugged without raising his head.

'I heard. You only have to walk through the door. I wonder if one hung a little inlaid cabinet between the windows – perhaps it would look more interesting if the room was slightly asymmetrical.'

'To whom? Nobody ever sees the house but us.'

He looked up at last, his eyes black slits in his pale face. 'You're in a very difficult mood, Lucy. As I said, if you want to go . . .' He twisted the glass of wine in his hand and raised it towards me. 'Try it.'

'The wine?'

'A departure. To your health, my dear.'

He lay back smiling, as I walked towards him, looked down at his face in disbelief. 'You won't prevent me?' He shook his head. 'And leave the child to you?' I said slowly. 'Why, that's exactly what you want. You don't care what happens to me, now that you have him.'

'I did once,' he said, and pulled me down to him. I closed my eyes as his mouth met mine. Byron's face rose in front of me and I moaned from the sickness of my longing. His hands were ice against my breasts: I cried out as he thrust me back

99

until my hair lay spread on the floor. His lips were soft on my naked skin, I felt the heat of the fire on my body before he let me fall and turned away. I looked up. He stood, with his back to me, his head buried in his hands on the mantelpiece.

'I don't understand . . . what did I do?' I whispered, stretching up my arms. He turned to me, his face dark with anger.

'So many years, Lucy, and you still have to close your eyes to forget who's bedding you; it's a martyrdom I don't greatly enjoy inflicting on myself.' He looked towards the servants' door. 'Do you wonder that I prefer their company?'

'You pay for it well enough.'

'There speaks Byron's trollop,' he said with a cold smile. 'Go. Get your clothes and go.'

I bent my head. 'And the child?'

'He stays, of course,' he said in even tones. 'You signed the papers; he's my heir.'

'Unless Harry comes back.'

'The father of a bastard has no claims, my love. It's time you accepted the fact that Harry's probably in a French graveyard by now. The world won't lament his passing,' he said brutally. 'To all intents and purposes, Orlando is my heir.'

'Heir to what? The house is Byron's, the land is Byron's – and as to the money, it'll be gone soon enough on your little stable-court.'

'A spiritual heir, you could say,' he said, and laughed.

It was a trick. I knew it, even as I laid my dresses in the morocco case, but I would suffer more by not appearing to be deceived. I came down the stairs slowly, playing my part, knowing that he was watching me go through the charade for his amusement. It was not the first time. He stood by the door, sipping the wine and humming under his breath. He drew back the bolts and the night wind rushed in to sweep the papers up from the long table. 'Well,' he said, 'all you have to do is to walk out.'

I smiled and put down the case. 'The game ends here, doesn't it? Now, you can ask me what my feelings were and settle back to enjoy your second-hand sensations again. I wonder you don't get bored.'

'No, no,' he said anxiously. 'You don't understand. I want to see you walk through this door. Come!'

I drew back, looking at him suspiciously. 'It's a trap. I know the look on your face too well. I'm not going.'

He led me to the threshold. The wind caught my hair. 'Now, just three steps more and you're free.'

I shrugged and walked out, determined to deny him the pleasure of any reaction. To my surprise, he did not follow me, but closed the door. One by one, I saw the lights go out. I caught my breath, not daring to believe that he had meant it. It was no night to leave in, a cruel night, alive with the unseen. Through the great ruined window of the abbey, the moon glittered down, and the straggling clouds tore gently apart on the high chimneys. Beside me, the black mirror of water moved, trembling, under the trees. I put the case down, looked around nervously, afraid of the silence. If I could sell the ring. It had been given to me for a night like this. I pulled aside the clothes, pressed the little spring that released the secret drawer. It glowed up at me, splintering as it caught the stars into its emerald depths. I turned it over in my hand and slowly replaced it.

My heart in my mouth, I walked over the wet grass towards the stables, stopped dead at the sound, a soft, heavy snuffle. I froze in my steps, staring down into the yellow, basilisk eyes. The wet jaws opened with a snarl, the teeth gleamed as the tongue curled back. I flung my hand across my face as he sprang. A whip cracked. The dog cringed back, padded away into the night.

'You must admit, that is a superb example of training,' Ruthven said with a pleased smile. 'To stop at the very moment of attack . . .' He turned me towards him in the moonlight. 'I'm afraid I used you to try him out. It's no use if the victim knows. The smell of fear is a vital part of the experiment.'

I shuddered and tried to draw away from him. He laughed. 'Poor Lucy, did you think I'd let you escape so easily? I'll never let you go to him. You know that. Why should I? I loved him, too.'

I stared up into the white, cruel face. 'Let me go, Ruthven, for God's sake. I swear I won't go near him. I'll go abroad – I'll work as a governess.'

'Most convincing,' he said dryly. 'And how will you go without money?'

I breathed a sigh of relief that he had not seen me take out the ring. He would steal it from me, I knew. 'No, you will stay,' he said softly. 'You know too much.'

'Why, what's that?' I exclaimed, as a long, deep baying sounded across the lawn. His face lit up. 'They must have heard a prowler. I've been looking for a chance to exercise them and those damned magistrates won't let me use them on the frame-breakers. You're too valuable a prey, but . . .' he squeezed my arm. 'Come! We'll call them out.'

I was half-caught by his excitement. 'But if it's one of the servants?'

'No, no. They're all warned.'

'And yet you never thought to tell me. . . .'

'Hush!' he said impatiently. 'Damn! I can't find the lock on the gate. He'll be gone at this rate. There, out you come, my beauties!'

The black shapes streaked past me, scarlet tongued, dragon teethed. 'I'm going in,' I said, without moving. 'You can feast your eyes on the delights alone.'

'No, you must come,' he said eagerly. 'You want to. I can feel it. I'll teach you the only truth, the aesthetic of terror,' he said, dragging me behind him across the lawn. 'It's the one moment of real beauty, of true understanding, when we rise out of ourselves towards the supreme quest. Now, now! Watch, Lucy! See how they spring for the throat . . . Down, you brutes!' He stopped dead and drew back. I ran forward to the man lying still in the long grass. The moment was gone. I only felt a sick horror as I looked up at Ruthven. 'He's still alive, thank heaven.'

'But hardly heaven-sent,' Ruthven murmured with a curious expression on his face as he stared down at the body.

'What?'

'I wonder *you* don't know him,' Ruthven said. 'It's Harry.'

6

'I wouldn't refuse another glass of cognac,' Harry said, leaning back in his chair. Four hours had gone by since the incident, long enough for me to understand that the Harry I had known was as dead as if the dogs had torn his throat out, instead of being called off as he fell in a dead faint.

'Your recovery seems complete,' Ruthven said dryly, as he refilled the glass. 'I don't want to hurry your departure but . . .'

'I thought I'd stay, as a matter of fact,' said Harry, swinging his legs up on the fragile sofa and sprawling back. He blinked as he tried to focus on Ruthven, and his words were slurred. 'I could be very happy here. Food, drink, a comfortable bed – what more can a man want? I only need little Rosy to unharden her heart and she'll do that soon enough. She always was easy with her favours.'

'Don't you have anywhere else to go?' I asked coldly.

'You sold the house, remember, my dear sister. The house that would have been mine. Not a thought for poor Harry, languishing in his prison.'

'Prison?' said Ruthven, raising his eyebrows. 'I may be mistaken, but I thought that Bonaparte merely restricted your exit from Paris.'

'The house felt like an accursed prison, damme,' said Harry, his sallow skin flushing red.

Ruthven smiled. 'Ah, yes. I misunderstood you. But I'm afraid you can't stay here. It's quite impossible.'

'I don't think so,' said Harry slowly and a cunning look came into his eyes. I remembered an out-of-work quack I had seen one year at the Goose Fair; thin-mouthed, hard-eyed, weak-chinned. Thank God that Mr Emerton had died before

Harry's return. He walked over to Ruthven and tapped him on the shoulder. At a distance, his clothes had smacked of fashion and money; next to Ruthven's, they looked tawdry. The gold buttons were, after all, only common metal. 'I've a prop . . . proposition to put to you, old fellow,' he said carefully.

'Well?' said Ruthven, moving away. His face was deathly pale, but his voice was emotionless.

'I went back to the old place before I came here,' Harry said, looking at me as he spilled a fifth glass of cognac from the decanter. 'I found the new owner there – a very helpful chap. Not quite to our uncle's taste, but good enough for me. He told me where I'd find you, Lucy, and that you'd married – him. Kept the debt in the end: I never thought he would, you know. Mustn't hold it against me, sister.'

'Go on,' said Ruthven.

'Oh, I will, I will.' Harry drained the glass and looked reproachful. 'Can't you afford anything better? It burns the throat, this stuff. So, I went down to the village. Saw old Jackson's house was burnt down, by the way. Sorry about that. I thought I'd look in on little Rosy and see how she was, to while away a dull afternoon.' He paused, then turned to face Ruthven. 'I needn't go any further, need I? I've come to collect my son.' He raised his hand as Ruthven moved towards him. 'Now, don't be so quick. I haven't finished. I'm not a rich man, old fellow – you saw to that. Not that I bear grudges. No, that's not my way.' He smiled and swayed on his feet as he looked down at the swirling pattern of the rug. 'I'm not demanding. Ten thousand a year would keep me in breeches.

'Well, what do you say?' he said loudly as the silence lengthened. 'You've grown quite close to the little boy from what I've heard and if he goes, well, it begins to look bad after seven years of marriage, doesn't it? Old Harry can father a son with no trouble at all, but . . .'

'For God's sake, Harry,' I whispered, shrinking away from them.

A couplet I had heard the other day suddenly crossed my mind. 'It will have blood they say; blood will have blood.' Hate and fear struggled in Ruthven's ashen face; the serpentine smile twisted as he tried to control himself. 'Your sister signed the papers,' he said slowly. 'He's mine.'

'Not without my agreement, old fellow,' said Harry. 'Do you take me for a fool? I know the law as well as you.' He thrust his hands into the pockets of his blue cloth coat and unearthed a grubby sheet of paper. 'Here.' He pressed it into Ruthven's unwilling hand. 'That should satisfy you that my claim's in order. What a rum way the world works! I only went through with it for a bet – the clergyman was drunk as a pieball and little Rosy never knew what she was signing.' He laughed loudly, enjoying the spectacle of our dismay. 'Damme if I ever thought I'd use the certificate again. Lucky I kept it, wasn't it?'

I did not dare to look at Ruthven.

Harry leant forward, speaking softly. 'It's quite simple. Keep me here, living in the manner of a gentleman, and I'll behave like one and make no trouble. If you won't, then I'll take the boy. Fetch him down, will you? I want to see if he takes after me.'

'Give him the money and let him go,' I said, walking over to stand by Ruthven. 'I don't want Orlando to see him.'

'You're a hard girl, Lucy,' said Harry. 'But it won't do. I want a home. You sold mine. I'm staying here, on a reasonable income and we'll be one big, happy family. The idea doesn't seem to appeal to you?'

'For your sake, I hope you're more efficient as a blackmailer than as a cardsharper,' said Ruthven coldly. 'We'll discuss it tomorrow. Lucy, have a room prepared for your brother.'

I was half asleep when Ruthven came into my room. I lay back on the pillows as he sat wearily down on the edge of the bed.

'Well, did he stay?'

He gave a short laugh. 'Of course. Not in a bedroom. He keeled over when he finished the second decanter. Damn him! He shall not have the boy!'

'But he doesn't want him. He's only using him as a pawn for the money. He said as much.'

'Oh yes, he believes that now. When he sees his son, it'll be another matter. I've no illusions on that score. He's done

105

nothing else in his life, so, like any other fool, he'll take pride in having fathered a son. They all do.' His mouth twisted and he hid his face against the bed post.

'It would be natural for him to go with his father, I suppose,' I said.

'I am his father,' Ruthven said flatly. 'Can you tell me that a man who cared so little that he left the country while the child was still in the womb has more right to him than I have? He is mine, Lucy, body . . . and soul.'

If Harry had been anything other than himself, I would have moved heaven and hell to get him away with the boy at that moment. I turned away and shut Ruthven from my sight in the soft pillows.

*   *   *

Sunlight filled the room when I woke. Rose was laying out my clothes, her neat coil of hair moving like a sleek spaniel's head across my line of vision from the bed.

'It's a fine day for your ride, my lady,' she said brightly, throwing open the window. 'Look, I picked these for you up in the woods. I took Orlando up there after his glass of milk. He was so good, the little lamb, quite himself again.'

'I'm glad,' I said slowly, separating the heads of the delicate blue flowers. 'I know you were worried about him.'

She looked at me with an uncertain smile and seemed about to speak, then hurried towards the door. I caught her arm. 'Rose, what is it? Have you seen our . . . our guest?'

'No, my lady. I was only going to say . . . no, you'll laugh at me for being superstitious. I know what you think of old wives' tales.'

I drew on the cream silk dress and turned to let her button it. The reflection in the long glass showed me how becoming it was, high-necked and close-fitting over the breast with a deep ruche of soft pink at the hem. 'Well?' I said, fanning out the skirts.

'I hung a cross over his bed when he came in last night,' Rose said slowly. 'He didn't like it, but I tied it out of his reach. It's something my mother told me to do if I wanted to frighten away the spirits.'

'Spirits? What do you mean, my dear? There are no ghosts here, unless the wicked lord has risen from his grave.'

'I'll go on doing it, if you don't mind,' Rose said quietly. 'We all have our own fears and they're best conquered by our own means.'

I shrugged. 'Well said. No, I shall not stop you.'

There was a clatter of feet on the passage floor. 'Rose!' Orlando called eagerly. 'Where are you?' I ran to the door, terrified lest he should go downstairs, unwarned. He looked away as I came out, his face sullen. 'Where's Rose? I didn't call you.'

'She's in my room, darling. Would you like to come in? You used to like being brought in to sit on my bed.'

'No. I don't want to go in your room.'

I sighed. 'Very well. I'll bring her out.'

'You mustn't speak like that, Orlando,' Rose said as she came through the door, her pretty face flushed. 'I don't know what gets into you to make you so rude. I'm sorry, my lady. I'll take him back to his room.'

He tossed back his fair curls. 'Don't you want to hear the news? I shan't tell you, now. Well, perhaps I will,' he said anxiously as we turned away. 'A messenger came with a letter from Yorkshire, and he said that Bonaparte's abdicated and gone to Elba. Where's Elba, Rose? Is it near England?'

'Your messenger is behind the times,' I said, closing the door. 'I have some news, too. I think you'd both better hear it.'

Rose took it hard. I had been afraid she would. She always was too soft for her own good. Her eyes misted over and I knew she saw it as a romantic gesture, the keeping of a bond which would never have occurred to Harry. Well, she would find out soon enough. I lacked the courage to dispel her illusions.

Orlando's reaction threw me into a further dilemma. I had hardly known what to expect, but not joy. He seemed overcome. When Rose had left the room, he sat on in the window-seat, asking me so many questions that my head began to spin. I could not bring myself to tell him that money had brought Harry to Newstead, not his son.

'Is he taking me away today? Shall I go and live in France with him? What's France like?'

'I don't know. I've never been there. I thought you never wanted to leave,' I said gently.

'I didn't know I would have a father to leave with,' he said. 'You always told me he was dead. But then you never told me that Rose was my mother. You should have guessed that she would tell me in the end.'

'No woman is safe with her own secrets,' I said with a rueful smile. 'You're right – I should have known better.'

'Do I look like him?' asked Orlando, eyeing himself in the long glass.

'No!' I said vehemently, and pulled myself up, too late. 'There is a likeness, of course, but . . . come, we must make you look elegant for such an occasion. Your father dresses . . . very well.'

With my heart like lead, I put on his white nankeen trousers and a blue jacket and sash. He fidgeted restlessly, his eyes on the door, his lips framing the next question.

'Stay here,' I said, pushing him back, and on impulse drew him to me again. 'He will love you, darling,' I whispered. 'He must.'

Blithely, he smiled at me. 'I know he will. You shouldn't worry so much, my dear.' His considerate little nod as he patted my arm brought me to the verge of tears.

Harry was sitting alone at the breakfast table when I came down, the *Nottingham Journal* spread in front of him, his legs straddling the chair.

'What happened to your clothes?' I asked, startled by his immaculate appearance.

'Oh, Ruthven went out early, so I took the opportunity to relieve him of a coat and a pair of breeches.' He laughed uneasily. 'They might have been made for me. No objections, I trust? You don't want the boy to see his father looking like a tramp.'

'No, no. Everything we have is yours, Harry,' I said with a sweet smile. 'All you have to do is ask.'

'Very prettily said.' Harry aimed at the cup with the silver coffee pot, his hand trembling violently. 'I'll do it,' I said hastily. He caught my sleeve as I leaned over him. 'Lucy, we used to be so close, you and me. What's happened?'

'You know very well. If you had any decency at all, you wouldn't ask.'

He shrugged and let me go. 'Ah, well, if you feel like that . . . I met an old acquaintance of yours at Angelo's fencing rooms, by the way. He talked of you . . . most affectionately.'

I stood very still. 'Who?'

'Your landlord,' Harry said with a grin. 'It took a bit of time to persuade him who I was. Still, it's fair enough to be cautious when you're a celebrity, I suppose.'

'You thought you'd touch him for some money, did you? I hope he gave you none.'

'He's generous spirited, unlike some I know. Capital fellow. I liked him.' He paused before adding in an offhand voice: 'He fences tolerably . . . for a cripple.'

'He is not a cripple!'

'Well, well,' said Harry as I bit my lip, furious at having been tricked into betraying myself so easily. 'You're very defensive. Still love him, do you?'

'Yes, I still love him,' I said slowly.

'That's a pity,' he said. 'He's getting married, you know.'

My heart stopped. 'Are you sure? Harry, please don't joke about it. When memory is all one has, it can't change. It must *not* change.'

'I'm sorry, believe me,' he said with unexpected gentleness. 'I didn't mean to spring it on you. I thought you must have heard. Don't cry, Lucy. You'll laugh when you hear who it is.'

'Laugh! I'm afraid my sense of humour doesn't stretch that far.'

'He's marrying Annabella Milbanke,' he said, offering me a cambric square with Ruthven's initial embroidered on the corner. 'Our sweet cousin, the ice princess! I tell you, Lucy, it won't last. On my word, it won't. How can it when everyone in London knows he's besotted with his half-sister – did anyone ever tell you how like Augusta you are?'

'Tact never was your strong point, was it, Harry?' I said savagely. 'Thank you for nothing.'

He shrugged. 'It's better than reading of it in the paper. Why worry? You're happy enough here.'

'Happy! With him! Don't be such a fool.' I was shaking with anger. The cup clattered and rolled over as I put it down. 'Seeing nobody, being kept a prisoner, having my friendships vetted, knowing how I'm hated just for being his wife, oh, I'm very happy, Harry. I must thank you, I suppose . . .'

He held up his hand defensively. 'For God's sake, I'm sorry I spoke. How was I to know? He is rich, though,' he added anxiously. 'That makes up for a deal of sins.'

I laughed harshly. 'Oh, you need not worry yourself on that score. He can pay you, if he chooses.'

Silence. 'I'm going out . . . ' I began.

'No, don't go,' Harry said, looking up. 'I've been thinking. There's no reason I can't escort you for a few outings, if that's what you want. We could take the boy if you like.'

'I had rather you took him away. You *are* his father, Harry.'

'Can't do it,' he said. 'I need the money and to be frank, he'd be a millstone round my neck. Where is he, by the way? I want to see him.'

I looked at him anxiously. 'You will be kind to him, won't you? Please. He's expecting so much . . . '

'And getting so little? You put it very succinctly, my dear. Quite a gift with words. Where's the decanter gone? I know it was in here last night.'

'You finished it. You can survive on coffee for another hour,' I said. 'I'm not letting Orlando see you for the first time when you're drunk.'

'What have you turned into, a Wilberforce convert or a Wesleyite?' said Harry angrily. 'Our father always started the day off with a glass of port.'

'Yes, and he was dead at forty. Don't be a fool. I'll get the boy.'

Ruthven had been right. I saw Harry's face soften as Orlando walked up to him and held out his hand. 'No need for that,' he said gruffly and pulled his son to him.

'When are we going?' Orlando said eagerly.

Harry coughed. 'Well, not yet awhile. Here, let's have a look at you. Don't hang your head down. Yes, you've got an

Emerton face, hasn't he, Lucy? Now we'll see if you've inherited some of their pluck. Have you ever tried sliding down that spiral rail, Orlando? That's what I used to like doing at your age. Do you remember, Lucy?'

I smiled, seeing a sudden look of the old Harry in his sharp face. 'Yes, I remember.' I sat down at the writing table and dipped the quill in the silver inkpot. 'My dear Annabella . . .' I stared down at her name and swallowed back my tears. Byron and Annabella: her, lying in his arms, sharing his bed? Orlando's eager voice interrupted my thoughts:

'And what did the Prince say then?'

'Why, he put his arm round me and said, "Emerton, old fellow, I can't thank you enough. Treat Carlton House as your own home." '

'I wish I'd known you then,' said Orlando wistfully. 'Were there parties every night?'

'Aye, and all day too.' Harry sighed. 'Now the one when he became Regent, that was an evening to remember.'

'But you were in France,' I heard Orlando say suspiciously.

'To and fro, to and fro,' Harry lied glibly. 'What a night that was! A river running down the table, full of little gold and silver fishes and flowers, and as much iced champagne as any man could ask for.' I choked back my laughter. Harry had read his papers as thoroughly as I had myself.

'And what about Boney? Did you meet him, too?' I looked round. Harry had his arm round him and the little boy was staring up into his face with eyes like saucers.

'Didn't I ever tell you, Orlando?' I said with a faint smile. 'He fought Harry in a duel for the hand of the Empress. Napoleon won, but it was only a matter of policy, wasn't it?'

The door slammed and I turned round hastily. 'Well, Orlando,' said Ruthven, flicking the dust off his top boots. 'Are you ready for your walk?'

Harry stood up, holding the boy against him. 'I thought he might come with me,' he said coolly. 'I'll teach you how to make a sailing boat, if you like.'

Orlando looked from one to the other, lifted his hand and placed it in Harry's. 'I'll come with you.'

'Have you told him why you're here, Harry?' Ruthven asked, leaning against the door.

I put out my hand. 'No!'

The cruel smile slanted his eyes. 'He's come for money, not you, I'm afraid, Orlando.'

'It's not true, is it?' said the boy, and a better man than Harry would have lied when he heard the catch in his voice.

'No, it's not,' Harry said slowly, watching Ruthven. 'It's not.'

'Orlando, look at me,' said Ruthven. 'Would I ever lie to you?'

His eyes brimming with tears, Orlando slowly shook his head. With a little sigh, he took his hand out of his father's and walked over the stone floor to Ruthven. The door shut softly behind them.

'Damn!' Harry said furiously and kicked over the nearest chair. I bent over the table, driving the pen across the paper so hard that it sputtered across the hail of lies.

'Now, that's as pretty a piece of hypocrisy as anybody could ask for,' I murmured, signing my name with a flourish at the bottom. I folded it neatly into an envelope and ground the amethyst seal deep into the hot wax.

'What did you expect me to say?' Harry muttered, staring out of the window at the figures moving away under the tall elms. I put the letter down on the table and picked up the *Household Furniture*, studying it with feigned interest. Harry pulled it out of my hands. 'Well?' he said angrily. 'You called me a hypocrite. What would you have done?'

'I was speaking of the letter,' I said coldly. 'I have no idea what I would have done. He's your child.'

He stared at me. 'But you said . . . '

'Listen,' I said, leaning back in my chair and half-closing my eyes – one of Ruthven's postures. 'If I had not seen what a drunken trickster you've become, I would help you. But I don't believe in you any more, Harry. I'm sorry.'

'I meant it,' he said slowly. 'I admit I hadn't thought of the boy when I came here except as a way to get some money, but now I've seen him and, well, I can't help liking the little fellow. He took to me, didn't you think?'

I shrugged. 'Then prove your words. Let him see that you spoke the truth.'

'How? I haven't got a penny to my name, Lucy. You don't suppose Ruthven's going to subsidize me if I carry off his only heir?'

'If you play fair with Orlando, I'll do what I can,' I said slowly.

'You? Why should you care, Lucy? You don't give a damn for me. I can see that.'

'Hush!' I said, listening. 'They're coming back.'

'Answer me! Why?'

I pushed away his hand. 'Not for your sake, brother. For mine. When you leave, I'm going with you. There's nothing to keep me here but the boy.'

Harry whistled softly. 'I see. Well, you may have a lifetime of waiting. I can be a better father to him here, in comfort. Where's Rose, by the way? I'd better go and make my peace, since I'm going to live under the same roof.'

Silently, I led him up the staircase to her room, turned back down the gallery with a half-smile to hear how he meant to talk himself into her forgiveness. 'Rose,' I heard him call softly. 'Rosy, it's Harry, come to find his little rosebud.'

'Ugh!' I said, as he rattled the doorknob. I heard him go in, paused as he called my name.

'Here, Lucy, what sort of trick is this, showing me into an empty room? Are you trying to make a fool of me?'

'What?' I went towards him, astonished. 'But she's always here.'

He stood back. 'Look for yourself.'

I walked into the centre of the room. The windows were shut, the bed neatly made. Every vestige of Rose had vanished; only the faint smell of musty lavender sprigs remained. I pulled open the empty drawers, threw back the cupboard doors. Nothing. But not to leave so much as a note . . . she must have been driven into flight. But why?

'Well?' Harry said in a bewildered voice. 'As jokes go, I've seen better.'

'But she was here this morning! Three hours ago. Look,

this is the table where she keeps all her boxes and bottles. They've all gone!'

We looked at each other in silence as voices echoed up the stairs. 'Rose!' I heard Orlando call. 'Rose, where are you?' He raced down the passage towards us, looked up with panic in his eyes as he saw the empty room. I patted his head.

'Ruthven will tell you. I'm sure he knows the explanation.'

Harry glanced at me. 'I'm curious to hear it. Come down, old fellow.'

But Orlando snatched his hand away; we followed him down the stairs, watched as he went across the hall to Ruthven. 'Where's my mother?'

Ruthven looked up, startled and angry. 'Who told you that? Is it your doing, Lucy?'

'No,' I said, coolly. 'She told him herself. Well, why don't you answer the boy? Where is she?'

'Go to your room, Orlando,' he said slowly.

Orlando put his hands behind his back. 'Not until you tell me.'

'Very well. She's gone. She left you, just as your father did,' Ruthven said savagely. 'Does that satisfy you?'

Orlando backed away towards us. I held my breath. 'You've sent her away,' he sobbed. 'She would *never* have left me!' He turned to Harry, his face defiant. 'Well, I have my father now. He'll stay with me.'

'Well said, Orlando. Now, that sailing boat I promised you . . . ' He pushed the boy ahead of him up the stairs.

'Children don't like broken promises, Harry,' I said softly and went towards Ruthven. His face was grey. 'You made a mistake, I said, smiling. 'Orlando will never forgive you for that. Really, for one who says he knows character so well . . . '

'She was too close to him,' he said abruptly. 'I found she'd been frightening him with peasant superstitions. He'll forget.'

'You did it because you were afraid,' I said, rearranging the bowl of flowers and leaves on the long table. 'I know that – and so does he.'

I watched him fighting for control, playing for time as he took out a pinch of snuff, dropped it on his wrist. 'You want

114

Harry to have him, don't you?' he said in a low voice. 'You're siding against me.'

As he came across to me, I moved away, sweeping my dress in a wide arc. 'Lucy, we must stand together in this,' he said pleadingly. 'It's for the boy's good. What could Harry offer him that I could not? Life in a London lodging house, shut up in the care of some slattern while his father went gambling in the silver hells until there was no money left. Is that what you want for Orlando?'

'Give a man a chance, and there's a chance he'll make something of it,' I said softly. 'You could give Harry an allowance.'

'If he stays here. If he leaves and takes the boy – nothing. It must not happen.' He looked down at me with a thin smile. 'It's as well that we tied you up in trust, my dear. I don't think I have much faith in your judgement.' He looked over my shoulder at the letter on the table. 'Who's this Miss Milbanke? You know I expect to be shown your letters.'

'A cousin. She's marrying Byron. Perhaps he'll bring her here one day,' I said sweetly. 'You wouldn't let your distress show too much, would you, my dear? It could be a little . . . embarrassing to explain your feelings under the circumstances.'

'Married? Byron?' he said in a stunned voice.

I laughed viciously. 'So there *was* something you could not offer him. I think perhaps I'll go and change for dinner. I'll leave you to send our congratulations to Byron.'

* * *

The strain mounted as the weeks crept past. Harry was given money to buy clothes, cognac and a black mare which must have cost the best part of two hundred guineas. Ruthven's patience was wearing thin, but he did not dare to gainsay Harry's demands for fear of losing the boy. And Orlando knew it. He hid his preferences, if he had any, and played one against the other as skilfully as a girl with two lovers. It was hard to think of him as a child, now; he had forgotten how to behave like one.

It was strange, too, to see Harry acting the part of a doting father. For three weeks, he threw himself into it, but Ruthven was always there – and Orlando's smiles remained opaque. I was fearful that it would all end in nothing. Ruthven waited . . . and Harry was getting restless.

I came back late one evening from a peaceful day at Colwick with the Musters family to find lights blazing from every window. My brother came unsteadily out onto the steps and peered down into the darkness.

'Is that you, Compton, old fellow?'

'It's Lucy,' I said. 'And who, pray, is Compton?'

There was a long pause. I heard him swear under his breath. 'I thought you were coming back tomorrow,' he said accusingly. 'It's damned inconvenient of you to arrive just now.'

'I'm sorry to disappoint you. Who have you got in the house, Harry? Did anybody say you could give parties here?'

He looked at me uneasily. 'You aren't going to be difficult, Lucy? I just asked a few friends. Ruthven's gone to London for two days and it's damned gloomy being alone.'

'I've stayed here by myself more times than I can count,' I said coldly, walking past him into the hall. The noise and light blinded me for a moment. I looked round, bewildered. 'Is this what you meant when you said you wanted to be kept like a gentleman?'

The weak, raddled faces gathered round the table turned towards me. One, a heavily built man in tight green satin breeches and waistcoat, rose unsteadily to his feet. 'Your servant, ma'am.'

'Where did you find such a pretty face on a night like this, Emerton?' drawled another, raising his eye-glass to examine me. 'Come and sit by me, my dear. I need some luck. Skeffington here's been sweeping the board since six o'clock. Can I offer you a glass of wine?'

'Don't kick up a row now, Lucy, for Lord's sake,' Harry whispered. 'Gentlemen, may I present my sister. Lord Skeffington, Lord Alvanley, Mr. Blewitt, Lord Flyte.'

Lord Alvanley, the man in green, stared at me and laughed. 'So she's the one you gambled Ruthven for! Do you remember, Skeffington? It was the talk of the clubs.'

Harry pushed me towards the spinet. 'Give us some music, Lucy. Gentlemen, to the game. You to play, Flyte.'

My cheeks burning, I sat down and began to play a new piece open on the stand. I put down the pedal and quickened the pace as I heard footsteps. 'Let me turn the page for you,' Lord Alvanley said, bending over me. I tried to move away from the fetid smell of his hot breath. 'You play charmingly,' he murmured as I reluctantly came to the end, and his hand brushed my cheek. 'Don't look down, I want to see your pretty eyes.' He tilted my face up. 'Well, well . . . My dear, you're wasted on Ruthven. We all know women aren't to his taste. What a sad fate for such beauty. It should be rectified. It could be – very easily.'

'Please remember you are in his house, drinking his wine before you say any more,' I said, standing up. He laughed and before I could stop him, he had pressed his mouth to mine. The soft, wet tongue moved against my teeth. I gasped and slapped him with all my strength across the cheek. He caught my hand and held it. 'I like a girl of spirit,' he said softly. 'We must get to know each other better.'

I smiled coldly. 'I can see no pleasure in furthering our acquaintance, my lord. It's gone too far already. Harry!'

He was laughing at some story of Flyte's. 'Tried to take the footman to Almacks! I'll wager Lady Jersey didn't stand for that, although her own taste . . . Lucy, can't you see we're occupied?'

'If you don't send your – friends away, I shall bring down Orlando and let him see exactly what sort of a father you are,' I said slowly. 'I'm giving you five minutes.'

Harry stared at me, his mouth open. 'You wouldn't! Why, you little . . . '

'*I* keep my promises, Harry,' I said. 'Excuse my leaving you, gentlemen.'

I waited in the darkness at the stair top with held breath, sighed with relief as I heard the chairs scrape back across the stone, the raucous voices die into a mutter as they went out onto the steps. Slowly, I came down the stairs as Harry slammed the door.

'Don't you dare to say a word,' I said savagely as he opened his mouth. 'I promised to help you over the boy, but if you ever do that again, I swear I'll tell him everything bad about you – and more. I'll make him wish he had never set eyes on you, you understand?'

'Now,' I said gently, as he sank back in a chair. 'You listen to me, Harry. Tomorrow, you and I are going to take him on an excursion – it's the only chance while Ruthven's away. You are going to behave decently and perhaps – we have to keep trying. That is, if you still care about the boy. I begin to wonder after tonight.'

'Oh, this?' Harry flicked the cards and sent them fluttering into the air. 'I still want the boy, don't worry about that. But I need this, too, Lucy. It's no use thinking I'm going to reform. Nine years is a long time.'

'I can't think why you ever started,' I said, gathering up the cards. I put them neatly back in the drawer of the Pembroke table and – a useless precaution – locked it.

Harry laughed. 'Do you want a long story? At least, it'll show you why I loathe Ruthven.'

'I'll listen, if it's a true one,' I said, taking a chair opposite him.

He half closed his eyes. 'It was long ago, when you were still with the Quentin woman in Hans Place and I had come to London for the first time. I was drinking with some friends in a St James's club – White's, I think – and Ruthven came across and joined us. He was an elegant-looking fellow, a bit of a dandy in those days, and we were very green and easy to impress. He seemed to have an entrée everywhere, his friends were the sort you don't meet without the right introduction.' He laughed harshly. 'You could say he put a spell on us. At any rate, he had us sitting in his hand like tame parakeets. He told three of us to come along to his house that evening. We turned up, dressed to kill, scared out of our wits. The place looked like the Pantheon and Carlton House rolled into one – double arches, black pillars, chandeliers of Venetian glass, the lot. He softened us up with a few drinks and stories, the tables were laid out and . . . he let us win.'

He poured out a glass of cognac and looked at me with a grin, half-ashamed, half-mocking. 'It seemed so easy. I couldn't understand what had happened when it all went wrong. I always won at first, then the big stakes came and my luck went.

I was caught by then. Couldn't stop. Everything went, money, clothes . . . '

'And me.'

He looked down at the glass. 'I never meant it to happen, Lucy. It began as a joke. They were all laughing and making mad bets, and then Ruthven said he'd play me for my sister. He'd seen your sketch, the one I used to have. Well, I couldn't back out.' He covered his face with his hands, muffling his voice. 'He never took his eyes off me. I had a good hand, good enough to win on, but I couldn't play it right. He just stared at me with those cold ghoul's eyes and I went to pieces. I left for Paris the next week. I couldn't face coming back.'

The blood drained from my face. 'But the other debt, Harry? My uncle said there was another, too high for him to pay. Ruthven came to collect it and . . . ' I told him the story of that night.

Harry shook his head. 'Whose word did our uncle have? Only Ruthven's. It was the same debt. So he was paid twice over, with a murder and a wife.' He whistled softly. 'What a bastard, if you'll forgive the term. Oh, if I could . . . '

I blew out the candles. 'You'll win this time, Harry, and we know it's the loss he'll suffer most. Come, it's three o'clock.'

7

It was early in the morning when we set off in the barouche for
Nottingham, a soft golden morning, very still. The ducks rose
in a great cloud from the lake as we passed: to our right, in the
park, the cattle looked up at us broodingly, their heavy heads
monstrous in the long silvered grass. The air was very cold and
thin: I wanted to swallow it like an essence as it brushed my
mouth. I smiled as Harry took Orlando up on his lap. The little
boy leant back against his father's blue velvet coat, playing
with the embossed buttons and swinging his legs on either side
of Harry's knee. Under the broad brim of his nut-brown cap,
the childish face was composed, reflective. I longed to know
what was in his mind. Ruthven? I shrugged it off. The carriage
rattled steadily along and the hills opened out into the soft
slope leading down to the village of Papplewick. Behind the
discreet mask of trees which overhung the village, the new Hall
by the Adam brothers shone out like a fresh sepulchre.

'Doesn't Ruthven ever take you for an outing?' Harry looked
down curiously at his son. Orlando shook his head.

'He takes me to Southwell sometimes, though.'

'That's a dull place. Full of old ladies and their dogs from
what I remember. What do you find to do there, eh?'

Orlando smiled and looked at me. 'Oh, nothing much.
Where are we going to first?'

I sat back with a sigh of relief. Harry would hear of those
visits, but from me, not the child. I wanted no shadow to be
cast over our expedition.

It was an unqualified success. Harry insisted on taking the
boy to drink with him in The Black Moor's Head, an idea which
appealed to Orlando. They emerged an hour later, flushed and

wonderfully loquacious, and the rest of the day was in Orlando's hands. Fairs and food were the chief entertainments, as far as I can remember, and Harry did not stint with Ruthven's money. The boy only had to glance at something to be given it, and his affection for his father increased with every gift. We ended the day with a visit to the playhouse to see *School for Scandal*, and Harry took the best box in the house. I hardly noticed the acting: I was watching Orlando as he whispered with Harry before turning to repeat with ardent accuracy the slightest witticism his father had made. I was delighted.

The play over, we returned home in a mood of drowsy contentment. Dusk made a snug haven of our carriage and the soft wind blew all the bittersweet scents of summer evenings in our faces. Orlando had forgotten his resentment of Harry: he lay curled up against him like a little dog, humming under his breath. But Ruthven was waiting for us in the hall, and his face was bleak.

'Listen, sir!' Orlando cried, running ahead of us, hat in hand, tousled curls flying. He stood in front of the cold, unsmiling face, legs apart, hands behind his back and started to sing in a high piping chant:

> '*If he'll take t'other boat out, we'll let Tallard out*
> *And much he's improved, let me tell 'ee*
> *With Nottingham ale at every meal*
> *And good pudding and beef in his belly.*'

'I don't admire tap-room ditties as much as your father,' Ruthven said, then forced a smile on his unwilling mouth. He knew as well as Harry how easily Orlando's affections might swing. 'The next expedition is promised to me, remember? Our little excitement.' He looked mockingly at Harry over the boy's shoulder. 'We know things your father never dreamed of, don't we, Orlando?'

Harry stared after them, his face perplexed. 'What the devil's he talking about? Where do they go that attracts the boy so much?'

It was time to play my last card. I led him out onto the stone balustrade. The sun had sunk, leaving the sky cold, tinged with the faint pink of early winter dusk. We leaned on the parapet, watching the ducks skim down over the lake, wings spread as their claws broke the surface. 'Have you ever been into Ruthven's study?' I asked. 'He has a painting by Fuseli hanging over his desk – a man leaning over a child in a dark room. The window is open and they look through it with terror – but their eyes are full of blinding light.'

'Well, what of it?' Harry moved restlessly.

I gripped his hand. 'You don't understand. Ruthven doesn't *play* with the aesthetic of terror like the others. They write about it, paint it, frighten themselves by invoking it. Children's games. He lives it, Harry, night and day, and he needs Orlando because, like all mad men, he must have his disciple. The boy is drugged with terror, fed it daily until it becomes a natural way of life, the only way, and Ruthven possesses him – body and soul. He failed with Byron, but this time . . . '

He stared at me and gave an uncertain laugh as he drew back. 'Lucy, do you expect me to believe that? You're alone too much. You mustn't frighten yourself with these ideas.'

'Listen,' I said fiercely. 'He once tried to convert me to his beliefs. I went with him once. I never forgot. It was the most appalling experience.' I lowered my voice. 'There's an old house in the centre of Southwell. They call it the House of Correction. The first floor has the appearance of a normal dwelling, clean, white, looking through high iron gates onto Burgage Green. Nobody who goes through those gates as a prisoner sees the light of day again – until they carry out his corpse. There's a small trap-door in the floor of the back room, leading down to a hole, high enough to stand in, wide enough for a man to lie, but not to walk. In the corner are two iron bedsteads; on the floor, chained down, are the prisoners. Some are mad, some sane; when the door opens, you wouldn't know the difference. The guard has a whip in his hand to keep them back; otherwise, they'd tear you to bits. Ruthven took the whip, I remember. The guard seemed to expect it. That's where they go, Harry.'

'And you have allowed Ruthven to do it! My God, Lucy . . . '

'It's too late to be self-righteous, Harry,' I said impatiently.

'You know quite well Ruthven forced me to sign the papers, handing over the boy. I was powerless.'

'But Orlando – he could have refused to go. How could he bear it?'

'Children don't have morals,' I said. 'They know what they're taught, that's all. Why do you suppose Ruthven is so terrified of letting him go? He's spent a long time indoctrinating Orlando with his beliefs. Left alone, there's no reason he shouldn't enjoy every success. You've waited long enough. Now for heaven's sake, act!'

Drama loses its effect if it is prolonged. I went inside and closed the door.

* * *

Jackson was being tried the next day and Ruthven had insisted on my going with him to the court. I woke with a heavy heart. The fine weather had been blown away and when I had scraped the frozen surface off one of the window panes, my eyes were burned by the hard whiteness of the frost. I shivered in my chemise as I rolled up a piece of cloth and pressed it down into the crack above the sill. Many changes had been made at Newstead since my early married days, when starlings and pigeons had built their nests above the stairs and the heavy furniture had been shrouded in dust sheets, but even Ruthven could not conquer the cold. It crept like a malign spirit through the house from October to April, blowing the winter wind into every corner and cranny, laying the chill of death on everything, everywhere. If they were right that this would be the winter of the great frost – I sighed and knelt down by the timid, insubstantial fire, prodded the flames into an attack on the damp logs. There was a knock at the door.

'Come in!' I pulled the wool blanket from the bed and folded it round me. Harry came in, his teeth chattering. He crouched beside me, his hands spread towards the grate.

'The wind blew mine out. God, look at my fingers; they won't even move.'

'I dare say you'll recover. Harry, I must get dressed.'

'I'll sit in your dressing-room, then. Damned if I don't envy old Boney. I'll wager Elba's hotter than this. Lucy . . .'

'I wish you'd stop walking about. You make me nervous,' I murmured, rubbing my finger round the rouge pot.

'I'm going to do it. I've thought it over and, well, I can't let it happen. I'm going down to tell Ruthven now.'

'Oh, Harry!' I looked at his pale face in the glass. 'Promise you'll be careful. You know how strange he is.'

'Typical of a woman,' Harry said, without concern. 'I never knew one who didn't wait until I was on the field for a duel before conscience struck her. You're all the same!'

'If you say so.' I went to the morocco case and pressed back the little catch. 'Look, Harry, this will buy you enough to leave on.'

He whistled. 'Enough to live on, you mean. Do you know how much it's worth, Lucy?'

I shook my head as he held the ring up to the light. He put it in my hand. 'Keep it. I'll manage. I'll sponge off Ruthven, but not off you.'

He sauntered out of the room, swaggering slightly. I hesitated, then ran after him. 'Wait! I'm coming too.'

Ruthven was carving himself a slice of beef at the sideboard when we came down for breakfast. 'You're late,' he said, without turning, then looked at me coldly. 'I cannot believe your appearance kept you so long.'

I poured out some coffee without answering him. 'Toast, Harry?'

'No, thank you.' He paced up and down the room, head down until Ruthven had taken a chair. 'I've decided to take the boy with me,' he said and spun round on his heels as if he expected an attack.

'Really?' Ruthven continued neatly cutting the meat into small squares.

Harry leant on the table and stared at him. 'You raise no objections?'

'I? My dear fellow, it's quite reasonable. I'm surprised you took so long to decide. When would suit you? Tomorrow?'

'I suppose so,' said poor Harry, looking as though he had been knocked down by a feather bolster. 'Well, that's all I wanted to say.'

'Good,' Ruthven drawled, rising to his feet. 'Then it's all settled. Lucy, we must leave.'

I followed him down the steps, hurried into the carriage as a dull boom of thunder rolled through the sky. 'I'll take the reins,' Ruthven said to the coachman with a soft smile. 'And – tell Jenkins to have the south and north gates barred, except to me.'

He cracked the whip viciously over the horses and they sprang forward. I lay back, sick with fear as I heard him urge them on. He looked to me like the devil himself, standing on the box, his black coat flapping in the wind, the hair blowing back from his drained, lily face. The horses could miss their footing at any moment on the icy track; I dug my nails into my palms as the carriage swung round the corners, the offside wheels spinning in the air. We came down Papplewick Hill, the verge fell away and I stared down the drop. The horses fled before the whip like hounds into hell; behind them, the rumbling carriage swayed and lurched. A flash of light opened a wound in the shadowed fields below, as if they had been split by a sword. The horses reared up on their haunches, straining back, their white manes whipped by the wind, their eyes rolling. With a cry of terror, I flung myself onto the floor as the fields came up to meet me, the wheels slid away. . . . Slowly, I opened my eyes and sank back on the hard seat. Ruthven glanced round, his eyes clear and calm again. 'You look a trifle distraught, my dear. Did you think I'd lose control?'

'I wish you could,' I said savagely. 'It would be a relief to see you capable of failure.'

'But I lost to your brother this morning.'

'Did you? Who are you trying to deceive? I know you better than that, Ruthven.'

He laughed and turned round, his hands tight on the reins, although his arms moved with easy languor. I sighed. Always the pretence, the false situation. I longed for an end to it all.

* * *

The courtroom was crowded. The Luddite movement was dead, but the fate of the last of the rioters attracted the curious. The benches creaked with anticipation as the Judge's gavel fell. Jackson was brought out with six others. I stared at him, horrified, as they pushed him into the dock. He staggered and clutched the side, his eyes blinking in the soft, vellum-yellow light. What could prison do to age a man so much, to turn him from a sturdy, black-haired fellow in the prime of life into a trembling, grey-faced beggar! They took the chains off and he rubbed the ugly sores on his wrist, wincing with pain.

The names were called by the clerk in a sonorous, rolling voice cultivated for just such a purpose: 'William James Roberts, Arthur Prittie, Thomas Jackson . . . '

I looked over the shoulder of the boy beside me as he sketched in light crayon, his eyes half-shut as he looked towards the dock. Jackson's face emerged from the paper; intrigued, I turned to the young sketcher.

'What's your name, boy?'

He looked up for a moment. 'Bonington, ma'am. What a face that man has to draw!'

'I know him,' I whispered. 'His face is prison-made, it's not real.'

'Oh, I know that.' His face brightened and he laid down his crayon. 'Would you like the drawing to remember him by? Family friends often buy one from me. It's a good likeness.'

I shook my head. 'It's too good. I'm sorry, I don't want it.'

'As a gift, then?' he asked, thinking he understood.

I smiled at his bright, quick little face. 'Not even as a gift, Mr Bonington.' I turned as I heard Jackson's name. It seemed he wanted to defend himself. The Judge, a thin, frowning man, dissatisfaction in his drooping mouth and restless hands, decided to let it pass. He called on the prosecutor to open the case.

I did not like the prosecutor's face. His features were very small and neat, polished for display in a round bullet head. His eyes were bright black beads: they glistened as they swivelled to the man in the dock. 'Well, Thomas Jackson,' the prosecutor said, leaning forward. His smile opened a black trap to catch the unwary. 'And in what profession did you serve your country?'

'As a carter, lately,' Jackson said quietly.

'A carter. A noble trade,' the prosecutor mocked him, and waited for laughter. 'And how, pray, did you come to feel the call of his most regal majesty, King Ludd?'

'I carried the cloth and I used my eyes,' Jackson said in a

calm, steady voice. 'There's no shame in men wanting to produce good work. We all know the new machines were being used to turn out shoddy stuff which brought discredit on them. It's hard, sir, when Nottingham workmanship's been famous for over two hundred years, for good craftsmen to be turned on to making gloves that fall to pieces the first time a lady slides them on her hand. I went with them because they're hard-working men trying to do their job. There's no crime in that.'

'There's nothing to complain of now,' the prosecutor snapped, sensing the crowd's sympathy veering away from him. 'The wages have been raised by two shillings a week.' He picked up a sheet of paper. ' "Long last the reign of Ludd, the only King over us all." ' He tossed it down contemptuously. 'Tell us how you came to be handling seditious material in the Feathers Inn on the night of March 24th. Treason is a serious matter, Jackson.'

Jackson turned round, his eyes searching the room for some-one. I shrank back. His gaze rested on a man in a brown hat, standing in the thick of the mob below me. 'Ask him.'

The prosecutor shook his head. 'But Mr Oliver has already given us all the information we need.'

'Mr Oliver, is it?' Jackson said bitterly. 'Mr Richards when he came to us with his plots and pamphlets. Yet he goes free while I stand here.'

I stared at the man I had known as Richards. His face twitched; he pulled the hat down, moved back.

'He gave us that bit of paper. He was the one who told us where to go, listed the names, was never there when the soldiers came. Damn you, Oliver!' he shouted suddenly. 'Damn you for your lying treachery, aye, and damn you for coming here to see us hanged!' He covered his face with his hands.

'Silence in the court!' The Judge brought down his gavel as the crowd rustled and murmured. 'Now laying aside the question of your political activities . . . '

'They were not political, sir,' Jackson said, with a painful jerk of his head. 'I toast our poor king as heartily as any man, and I pray for his recovery to set our country on the right road again.'

'Very laudable,' the Judge said coldly. 'I do not come to this court to be preached at from the dock. You will confine yourself to brief answers please – Mr Jackson. Mr James?' He nodded to the prosecutor who continued smoothly:

'Now, on the fourth of April, you broke into Newstead and attempted to brutally murder the wife and child of Lord Ruthven. Perhaps you have another moving defence to offer us.'

Jackson looked up at us. 'Ask Lord Ruthven. He knows why.'

'Would you care to enlighten us, my lord?' The prosecutor looked up at us. 'Naturally, if you prefer to remain silent, there is no compulsion. None at all.'

'I am delighted to be able to assist,' Ruthven said with a gentle smile, and rose to his feet. 'I rather think the poor fellow is referring to the death of his son.'

'Well?'

'I caught the boy poaching.'

'On your land, of course?' The prosecutor looked anxious.

Ruthven hesitated. 'No. My wife's uncle, Mr Emerton of Alvedon gave me permission to deal with the affair. My wife will confirm this, if you wish.' His thin fingers closed over mine, crushing the bones. I wondered at his complex nature, inviting danger when by silence he could have eluded it so easily. He had no need to confess. It was the drama which appealed to him. And he was safe. If I spoke the truth, I would be laughed out of court. He would go free, as always.

The Judge's intervention spared me the dilemma. 'I hardly think we need a witness for a man who has done so much to quell the recent riots. Your actions speak for your reputation, Lord Ruthven.' He lay back in his high-backed chair, his restless hands pressed together in a controlled lock. 'So . . . you decided to take revenge into your own hands, Jackson. You deliberately utilized the followers of King Ludd for your own ends. You prepared to kill a mother and child who had done you no harm . . . '

'My Tom was eighteen when he died, my lord,' Jackson said flatly. 'He was all I had, my boy.'

'He would have hung by the Poaching Act,' the Judge said. 'By law, I should hang you now.' Ruthven leant forward, his lips parting in a smile as he glanced at Oliver. 'But I am not a harsh man,' the judge went on. 'I shall be lenient. You will be given a chance to see the error of your ways under a sentence of transportation – for life.'

Jackson turned deadly pale. His mouth opened but not a word came out. Ruthven stood up, his hands grasping the rail in front of us.

'My Lord, I question your decision. This man is dangerous. I owe it to my child and to my dear wife to request that he should be hanged as he deserves. Your leniency can serve no purpose here . . . '

'I do not expect the decision of the court to be questioned,' the Judge said coldly. 'Please return to your seat, Lord Ruthven. I accept that you speak from deep personal feelings, that love of your family has temporarily overruled your head . . . '

I stood up, trembling with rage. 'Sir!'

'Please,' the Judge said wearily. 'This is a Court of Law, not a university debate. The sentence is pronounced.' He brought down his gavel and two men came forward. Jackson was led out between them, his head bent, his feet dragging on the floor. I turned so as not to meet his eyes.

'He promised me, damn him,' Ruthven hissed through his teeth as he beckoned to Oliver. I never saw a more uneasy face than that of the spy as he edged towards us.

'Well . . . A most surprising verdict, my lord.' He rubbed his dry palms together and his lips twitched as he saw Ruthven's glacial expression.

'You promised me a hanging, Oliver. You swore it.'

'I did my best, my lord.'

'If that's your best, you should find another profession, my friend,' Ruthven said. 'I could make . . . things difficult for you, remember.'

Oliver drooped, limp as a doll. I saw Ruthven smile. 'Go back to the carriage, Lucy,' he said. 'I have a private matter to discuss.'

His expression bred mistrust. I nodded and made as if to go towards the door. As two ladies came together to discuss the possibility of staying for the afternoon session, I stood behind them, listening intently.

'You're most kind, most, I really . . . ' I heard Oliver murmur.

'It's a plant – a very easy job. I'll give you the situation, you provide the evidence.' Ruthven laughed gently. 'And the more incriminating it is, the better. It's a matter of some urgency.'

'Where?'

'Home territory. I suggest that you come to Newstead tomorrow. Now, the man on whom you will plant the documents is . . . ' Their voices dropped. All I could hear was Oliver's high laugh taking its cues. I hurried back to the carriage and was sitting watching the passers-by when Ruthven came through the pillared doorway.

I was silent on the journey home, pleating and crushing the folds of my dress with nervous hands. It was no longer safe for us to stay, now that he had decided to act against Harry. We must leave as soon as possible, but how? I had seen his trained hounds at work, knew that they could outstrip a running man. He was capable of anything in his present mood. I smiled as he turned towards me and I put my hand on his.

'Ruthven – I was wondering if we might give a small party tonight for Harry and Orlando's farewell. We could call on a few neighbours on the way home, the Middletons, the Musters. They always ask us, although we never go. It would be kind, and it would stop the talk if we offered a return of hospitality, don't you think?'

He smiled with the ease of a man who has set his mind at rest. 'Why not, my dear? Something for Harry to remember.'

The acceptances were embarrassingly ready. Hardly surprising with so many years of anticipation. Countless ratafias and slices of rich fruit cake later, we had twenty guests for the party and had left a flutter of excitement behind us. Ruthven, soothed by the pleasant prospect of Harry's imminent transportation to some distant quarter of the world, was at his most charming, and the three plain daughters of Lord and Lady Middleton did their best to forget my existence as they gathered round him, putting each other down with the most ruthlessly barbed compliments as they strove for attention; their mother sighed and smiled at me, thinking, no doubt, that my expression came from jealousy.

When we arrived at Newstead, the house had a deserted air; the door was open, creaking gently on the hinge. Ruthven looked at me. 'Orlando! Emerton!' he called, his voice harsh. No answer. He clenched his whip, and an evil smile crossed his face. 'So,' he said softly. 'Your brother chose to ignore me. How very foolish.'

I leaned against the doorway, my heart thudding as he brought round the hounds, straining forward against their chain leashes. He looked up at me, laughing as they pawed the balustrade, thrusting their muzzles towards me. 'I grieve that you never saw your brother to say farewell,' he said gently. 'Poor Harry! But I credited him with a little more wisdom.'

'The boy, Ruthven,' I said to him. 'Think of that. You'd lose him, too. Is it worth that price?'

He grinned at me and held up a piece of cloth. 'I think they know this smell by now. That's the scent they'll seek. We'll be alone again, Orlando, I – and you. I'm sorry it seems to give you so little pleasure. However . . . ' He stooped to unfasten the leashes. A shadow brushed past me. I saw Ruthven's face change as he looked up. 'You?' he said in a strange, cracked voice.

'What are you doing?' Orlando said, staring at him in horror.

Ruthven avoided his gaze. 'Oh, they need exercising now and again.'

'He was going to set them on your father and you,' I said.

The boy spun round. 'What?'

'She's lying,' Ruthven said. 'Would I have arranged a party tonight, if that was my intention?' He led the dogs away across the grass as Harry sauntered up from the path by the lake, whistling to himself. I beckoned him. 'Harry – here, before he comes back. We have to plan quickly. Stay here, Orlando. This concerns you . . . ' I told them what I had heard.

'Leave tonight!' the boy said. 'But why, when Lord Ruthven . . . '

'Damn Ruthven. If he has his way, Harry will be transported, sent a long, long way away, Orlando, for the rest of his life. You would never see him again. Well, do you want that to happen?'

He shook his head, tears spilling down his cheeks.

'Stop it!' I shook him. 'We've too little time, as it is.' I turned to Harry. 'Ruthven keeps laudanum in the drawer of the desk

131

in his study. Use it to deal with the hounds. Not now, you fool, while he's with them. Later. We must all be very calm. Nothing must show, nothing.'

*   *   *

It was seven o'clock. The first carriages were due to arrive at any moment. I clenched my hands in my lap as Rose's replacement painstakingly twisted the dark curls into place. I sat forward, went through the motions of examining her work in the glass. 'Yes . . . it'll do well enough. Now, fetch me the blue dress, the embroidered one. Good girl. Quick, now . . . ' I was still able to be amused by the thought of leaving Newstead in my ball dress. Byron would have appreciated the situation, but God only knew what the Londoners were going to make of it when I arrived. The material was as fragile and as subtly indecent as only a Frenchwoman could make it, showing the outline of my breasts as clearly as if I walked naked, clinging to my thighs as I walked back from the glass. The girl stared at it, her mouth open. 'Don't you need to wear anything underneath it, my lady?'

I fastened Ruthven's diamond necklace round my throat. To rob him of it seemed no great crime to me. 'That, my dear, is the point of the dress. You can go now.'

As the door closed, I fell on my knees and pulled out the brown morocco case, thrust the necklace in beside the diamond ring and flung my dresses on the top. I turned as the door rattled, pushed it out of sight. Harry came in, pulling his white cravat into folds worthy of Mr Brummell. 'Nobody could say we aren't leaving in style,' he said, taking in my dress with an admiring nod. 'Well, we're all ready. The dogs are dead to the world and I've laid the horses to a temporary rest with the last of my brandy. Orlando knows what to do, and the back door is on the lock. So, sister . . . '

I clasped his hands in mine. 'I'm so frightened, Harry. What if it goes wrong?'

'Don't think of it. Come, we must go down or he'll begin to wonder.'

I paused on the turn of the staircase, looking down on them. Ruthven was too patronizing to be a good host, too conscious of their covetous glances as they took in the yellow silk hangings, the delicate Sheraton and Hepplewhite furniture – he heard the faint sighs as the ladies drew their comparisons and found them to be not entirely satisfactory. The dresses were high-necked, low-waisted, ten years out of date. I looked down at mine and drew a deep breath. Well, let them think what they would . . . It was the last time. I walked down to join them.

'Miss Willoughby, Mr Charles, I believe supper is laid out in the dining-room if you would care to – why thank you, sir, I rejoice that it meets with your approval.'

'I have a nightgown which is very similar,' said the eldest Miss Willoughby, and tittered. 'Perhaps I should have worn it.'

I looked at her plump arms and her squeezed-in waist until she blushed. Her brother was cruder. 'You're too fat, Jane,' he said brutally. Mary came towards us, making a wide arc to avoid Ruthven. She had lost her looks so quickly in the last year; I looked at her thin, flushed face, and, by sudden intuition knew why. I took her arm. 'Mary, my dear, how glad I am to see you! Come and look at the new Stubbs painting Ruthven bought the other day.'

She looked at me in surprise. 'Lucy, dear, don't you think it's enough that I have to look at ours all day? You know that John's only criteria of a painting is that it must contain a horse.'

'Come,' I said. 'I insist.'

We looked up at the glossy bay and his currant-eyed groom. 'Mary,' I whispered. 'I'm taking you over to Ruthven. I want you to talk to him for at least half an hour. Don't let him out of your sight.'

She winced. 'You're asking the impossible. You know what I feel about him. Does it matter a great deal to you?'

I nodded. 'I'm leaving. It's not safe to stay here any more. But if he knew . . . I'll write to you when I reach London.'

'But where will you stay? If you need money, Lucy . . . '

'I have means. Don't fret about me – and Mary, don't torture yourself by thinking I'll go to Byron – he's married.'

Mary laughed and turned away as the racking cough shook her. 'And I thought not to tell you!' she gasped. 'We keep secrets well for women, don't you think?'

I looked away as she glanced down at her handkerchief and crumpled it quickly in her hand. 'You should not have kept this one from me, Mary. How long have you known?'

She smiled drearily. 'Four months. The doctors say I should go away, but how can I leave my little darlings? They're so young. . . . There! It's gone. Now I'm ready to try, at least, to fascinate Ruthven.'

I led the way to where he stood, politely stifling a yawn as the Reverend Becher – heaven knows what had made me ask him! – pressed him on his religious beliefs. He hastily averted his eyes, as I approached. I put my arm through his. 'Come, my dear sir, you must not think that a dress can proclaim one's virtues – or vices. Is Ruthven converting you to his atheist views – he can be most persuasive.'

The Reverend Becher's smile was agonised in its carp-stretch of politeness. He was thinking of funds for the church roof. 'The ladies will have their little jokes. Lord Ruthven has promised that you will both honour us with your company one Sunday at the Minster. And your brother, too, perhaps?'

'Yes, where is Harry?' Ruthven asked, looking round.

'He said he felt a little unwell, but he'd join us during the dancing. Ruthven, Mrs Musters has a hundred questions to ask. She plans to refurbish some of the rooms at Colwick and there is no one who knows more about such things than you.'

On cue, Orlando's wail rose over the noise of the party. Ruthven turned.

'No, no, my dear. I want you to help Mrs Musters. I'll go. We have no nurse since Rose left, you see, Mary, so I am learning a new profession.'

Calmly, I walked up the stairs, collected my case, threw on a heavy travelling cloak – and ran for my life. They were waiting by the door, looking so nervous and white that I felt heroically calm. 'Quick! the laudanum will be wearing off,' Harry whispered. I gave him a cool smile and a shrug before stepping out into the night.

Nothing followed us but the soft glare of light from the windows and the confused murmur of conversation dying away into the distance, as we struggled through the damp, clinging grass up to the drive. We were left with the nightjars to cry our farewells as we stood at the high, wrought-iron gates and then, we were free!

The black shapes of the carriages were barely visible outside the inn across the road. The lights were extinguished. I bent over my case and drew out the diamond necklace.

'Ruthven's paying for our journey – I'm sure he'd be the first to appreciate the irony. Harry, you go – they don't know you. The necklace is for any man who will get us to London tonight.'

'He's sure to have discovered by now,' Orlando said in a terror as Harry vanished into the darkness.

'Hush, child!' I held him against me.

A patch of light appeared. I saw Harry push his way through the door, hold up his hand. I waited anxiously. It was a long ten minutes before he came back with a startled, sleepy, red-faced fellow, his nightcap still clutched in his hand. Harry laughed excitedly. 'He'll do it for us. We'll be in Piccadilly by the morning.' He pulled Orlando towards him as we hurried towards the coach.

'It is legal, I suppose?' the man said, barring the way as he gazed at the glittering pile in his hand. 'No, I'll not ask. That way, I don't know nothing about it. In you get, lady.'

The horses were harnessed, the whip cracked and I fell back in my seat, half fainting with exhaustion as we pulled away on the London Road.

Part Two

LONDON

8

Three days later I sat in Hyde Park, cold, disillusioned and alone, almost ready to admit defeat and return to Newstead. London had seemed the most delightful of cities when I was not in it: now that I was here, I felt as alien as an atheist in a packed church. Society has no time for runaway wives who lack the money or the courage to force their way into it, a truth which I was coming to understand now that Harry and Orlando were gone.

I never thought that Harry would leave me, but we had not been in London for two days before he announced that he was going to make his way to Brussels with the child. He wanted to join Wellington's troops and he was adamant that I should remain behind. After all, he said, I had a ring worth a couple of thousand pounds. I wouldn't starve.

The Dover coach left early the next morning and my spirits were never so low as when I stood alone in the grey shadowed street, watching it roll away down the cobbles with Orlando perched on the top at his father's side, wrapped in Harry's greatcoat. Neither of them looked back.

Indeed, I had the ring, but it was a useless security when I had no idea of how or where to sell it, nor even of the value. I would have given ten such jewels for a safe roof over my head . . . but where? Byron had told me to use it to come to him, but I could not bear to go to Devonshire House as Annabella's homeless cousin. Pride and commonsense forbade it. I wanted his love, not his pity. Suppliant women have never appealed to poets – they only write of them.

I sat on a bench by the Serpentine and stared at the pages of my morocco address book with blurred eyes. No comfort for me, there. Ruthven's friends, country acquaintances, girls from the Academy who had long since married and settled into provincial life. Mrs Quentin: I looked at her name, wondering. After the disgrace of my expulsion? No room for forgiveness in that corseted heart. But who else?

I put the book back in my purse and watched the world hurrying past, too bent on pleasure to give me more than a glance. A group of young officers swaggered along the path, their shoulders like red chairbacks, their moustaches curling to perfection. Beyond them, the little boys crouched by the water, pushing out their wooden boats, backs turned to the pretty girls who leant from barouches to admire the children while glancing at the officers. . . . I watched them all with an increasing sense of exclusion which eventually drove me to my feet. For better or for worse – and I could not help think the latter was more likely – I would ask Mrs Quentin's assistance.

Hans Place was just the same, an ugly curving street of four-storey houses in red brick, wearing its tired air of genteel respectability like the faded pots of flowers behind the windows. I knocked on the door of Number Forty-one. A bland-faced woman in a brown dress came out, wiping her hands on her skirt. She looked blank at my request.

'Mrs Quentin? There's no one of that name here.'

'But . . . Is the Academy closed, then?'

She nodded. 'It does seem like it, doesn't it – Miss? I've been here for four years and it belonged to a Colonel Fairweather before then. Your friend may have sold it to him. It's apartments now: that's how I keep myself in pocket.' She sighed. 'It's a hard life for a widow when you're reduced to taking poets for lodgers – and their ladies.'

I took her sudden friendliness to mean that she was sizing me up as a prospective lodger. She leant forward, confidentially. 'Mr Shelley and his wife – well, that's what he *says* she is – they live up on the top floor. The sooner they leave the better, I say. Four of them up there, and I've eyes in my head to see what's going on. But the first floor, that's very nice and quiet. It might suit you very well, if you're looking for lodgings. Three pounds a week and no gentleman visitors: that's the terms.' She leant back against the door, her arms folded.

'It sounds very reasonable,' I said, 'but I don't have any money at present – only this?' I held out the ring with an uncertain smile. The woman's face froze.

'I keep a respectable house,' she said. 'I'm not asking where the likes of you would find that ring. I don't want to know. You'll not find *me* handling stolen goods. Academy indeed! A fine tale to spin!' And she slammed the door shut in my face.

The railings blurred in front of my eyes as the sobs thickened in my throat. When I heard footsteps coming down the steps, I tried to turn aside to hide my tears. A soft hand touched my cheek.

'Is there anything I can do?'

I looked up and saw a sharp-faced girl in a green velvet cloak, her brown hair blowing out like a soft cloud. I shook my head and turned away, but she held my arm. 'Come, we can't let you go like this, Miss . . . ?'

'Ruthven, Lucy Ruthven,' I said.

She caught her breath. 'You aren't related to *Lord* Ruthven, are you?'

'I was his wife,' I said. 'I ran away, and now . . . and now . . .'

'I think you'd better come in,' she said. 'I know enough about your husband to understand. You'll be safe with us. But we should introduce ourselves. I am Mary Godwin Shelley and this is a very dear friend of mine, Mr Hogg.'

Mr Hogg, a sturdy, rather solemn-faced man, shook his head. 'Mary, there's no room.'

'Yes there is. She can sleep in Claire's bed – my step-sister,' she added for my benefit.

'But she and Shelley come back tomorrow.'

'What of it?' Mary asked. 'Claire can go to my father's house. I wish to heaven she'd stay in it. Come, Lucy. . . . May I call you that? We will give you lodging and in return you are to tell us all about Ruthven. Shelley will be beside himself with joy to meet someone who knows him so well. He's been the inspiration of all our Gothic tales and imaginings, hasn't he, Hogg?'

'Less of an inspiration to his wife, I'd imagine,' said Mr Hogg in a dry voice.

* * *

141

I turned restlessly to and fro on the hard, unsprung bed, trying to remember all that I had learnt of my new home from Mary and Hogg. The walls were thin. I could hear the soft murmur of their voices in the next room and outside, the echoing rattle of the last hackneys going home.

It had taken me a little time to realize that Mary's Shelley was the man of whom I had heard so much from Ruthven, the author of the Gothic novel, *Zastrozzi*. Inadvertently, I had entered a circle for whom Ruthven was a charmed name, as the man who had inspired the personification of evil around whom the romantic novelists wove their plots. *Zastrozzi*, which I remembered seeing on the shelves at Newstead, had an anti-hero whom Shelley had based on all that he had heard of Ruthven.

Mary was an insatiable inquisitor. She wanted to know everything about him.

'You're plotting your own novel again, I see,' Hogg said, stroking her hair.

Mary sighed. 'Plotting . . . the plot is what I lack. All I have is a title, *Frankenstein*. One day, I shall find the story to follow it. Perhaps Lucy will provide me with the theme. Come, tell me about him, tell me everything. What good fortune it was that we met!' She leant forward with an eager smile, her pointed chin resting on her hand. I told them all I could – an experience which I found very painful – and then they told me of their one meeting with him, when he had conducted a galvanic experiment before a selected audience.

I could not have produced a more successful passport to their friendship and one that I was less willing to display.

They were very patient with their own explanations of a history which bewildered me in its complexities. Mary's Shelley, it seemed, had been born the eldest son of a respectable Sussex family whose life had been turned into a maelstrom of disappointments and misunderstandings by the wilful brilliance of their heir. Hogg had become his closest friend at university and they had been sent down together for publishing an atheist pamphlet. Shelley had then proceeded to cut himself off from his family and renounce his inheritance.

Mary sat in compressed silence while Hogg spoke of Shelley's

142

first marriage. Evidently, it had not been a happy one. That was all I could gather and Mary's expression denied my curiosity. Her face only resumed its natural sweetness when she spoke of her own first acquaintanceship with Shelley.

Mary was the daughter of William Godwin, the philosopher and author, by Mary Wollstonecraft, whose *The Rights of Woman* I had to admit I had not yet read. Godwin had since married a woman they all disliked whose daughter, Claire, lived with Shelley and Mary in Hans Place. It had been Shelley's admiration of Godwin's work which first drew him into their circle. Later, he had fallen in love with Mary. I smiled in anticipation of the romantic ending, but Mary forestalled me with a mournful look.

'Shelley is still married to Harriet, you see. It was distressing to a man of my father's principles.'

And so they had eloped. Mary was not yet married to him, but was carrying his child.

'And Mr Godwin is reconciled?' I asked.

She sighed. 'He is a man of very high principles,' she said in a tired voice. 'But yesterday he came here for the first time . . . '

'Yes. To ask about the will,' Hogg said angrily. 'I think it's abominable. He refuses to forgive either of you, yet he takes money from Shelley without a qualm.'

'I have a great respect for my father,' she said quietly. 'He needs the money in order to write. It is not for us to judge him.'

'But Shelley has no money left to give!'

She gave him a thoughtful look and he subsided in his chair with an angry shrug.

I began to think that my own ideas were very *vieux jeu* and provincial as they tried to explain their household in simple terms. On an idealistic plane, it might have sounded better.

Shelley was trying to realize his dream of the ideal life in which he and Claire, Mary and Hogg would live together in perfect harmony. The more they tried to convince me, the more apparent it became that the scheme was not enjoying much success. Hogg loved Mary. That I could see with my own eyes. She liked him and was feigning love to please Shelley. The drawback in it lay here. Hogg spoke of it as a *ménage à quatre*, Mary as a *ménage à trois*. In her version, there was no part for

Claire. All she would say was that Claire's jealousy made life difficult for Shelley and that it was a pity she could not get herself a husband.

'But you can make your own judgement of Claire tomorrow,' she said, seeing that I was falling asleep. 'She insisted on going with Shelley to hear the will read, heaven knows why! They'll be back in the morning.'

'With good news, I hope?'

She shook her head. 'I doubt it. Shelley's drawn too far away from his family to be forgiven now.'

We had finished eating breakfast and I was listening politely to a long dissertation by Mr Hogg – I forget what about, it seemed very dull to me – when the door burst open and through it came a . . . being. I couldn't describe Shelley as a man: there was nothing so solid about him. His face was more strange and beautiful than any that I had ever seen, a Peri with golden hair, a skin so pale and translucent that the great glowing eyes seemed to belong to another body. Mary dropped her cup with a little cry and ran towards him as her sister, Claire, pushed past. She was pretty, but in a heavier, more sensual style than Mary, with sly, heavy-lidded eyes, dark hair and a creamy oval face that was just beginning to show signs of a double chin. She stared at me resentfully. 'I hope you haven't damaged my shawl. It's a new one.'

'Our possessions are to be shared, Claire. Remember what Shelley told us,' Mary said, without turning round. 'The lady wearing your shawl is Lucy Ruthven. I have given her your room.'

'I am not going back to Skinner Street!' Claire said furiously. 'You're trying to get rid of me again. Shelley, tell her to stop it!'

Shelley looked at Mary reproachfully. 'Claire's very sensitive, Maie,' he said. 'You must remember that. And we cannot have another presence in the commune. Any alien force would destroy it – surely you understand?'

'Ah!' Mary said triumphantly, 'but she is married to *our* Ruthven. Poor Lucy, we've exhausted her with questions but later . . . ' She smiled. 'She understands your terror aesthetic better than any of us – even Claire.'

144

'Really? How extraordinary!' Shelley glided towards me, his great eyes fixed on my face. I moved back hastily as he bent and whispered: 'Can *you* see . . . look, on my skin . . . ' His fingers traced circles on his face as if he was outlining the ravages of some horrible disease.

'Oh, Shelley!' Mary said, pulling at his hand. 'You don't still believe in that? Your skin is quite untouched, my love. Not a mark, not a mole. Tell him, Lucy.'

'I can see nothing, Mr Shelley,' I said, anxious to reassure the beautiful creature. He sighed and laid his hand against his cheek. 'I felt it on the stairs, a sudden, horrible fear. Claire nearly fainted with fright.'

'Oh, Claire would faint if she saw a dead sparrow,' Mary said impatiently. 'She encourages you. But tell us what happened.'

'Wait!' Claire said, raising her hand dramatically. 'Do you realize what day it is, what a risk we took in travelling? A day of bad omens.' She looked towards me. I laughed, refusing to be drawn.

'Friday the thirteenth,' I said lightly. 'You should meet Byron: he's as superstitious as you.'

'Byron?' said Claire, her face changing. 'You know him?'

'Intimately,' I said coolly. 'I feel I must apologize for having taken your bed, Miss . . . '

'Clairmont.' She rolled it out impressively, then gave me a dazzling smile which I did not return. 'I was joking, of course. Why should I mind? Any friend of Lord Byron's is welcome here, isn't he, Shelley?'

He gave me a smile of peculiar sweetness. 'Why, yes, but her name has made her already welcome. How strange that fate should lead you here.' He sat down opposite me and leaned forward. 'I've just sent some poems off to Byron's publisher. Do you think that perhaps you might . . . ?'

'Later, Shelley,' Mary said firmly. 'I want to know what happened.'

He sat back in his chair, his legs curled up, his face as wicked and gleeful as Puck. 'Oh, we made ourselves felt, and you too, Maie. The funeral was over, so we went straight to Field Place. The first person we saw was my father, standing on the steps. He gave me his hand with a very affable smile, nodded to Claire, and then said that he was sure we would understand that there was no question of our entering the house.'

'Which broke your heart, naturally,' Hogg said, looking up from his writing for the first time.

'Oh, we were desolate!' Shelley cried, rocking his chair wildly to and fro. 'To be banished into exile! Unthinkable! So, we sat ourselves down on the front door-step where we were sure of being seen by every one of the arrivals, and Claire had the inspiration of holding up your copy of Milton's *Comus*, Maie, with it open at the flyleaf where your name is written. We fairly flourished it in their faces, and not one of them didn't look down and then hurry past as if he'd seen the devil. Of course they tried to get rid of us, but short of whips, we weren't to be budged.'

'But the will,' Mary said quietly. 'What of the will, my love?'

'A hundred thousand pounds!' Claire burst out. 'Enough for us all to be free!'

'What!' Mary stared at Shelley in disbelief. He shook his head fondly at Claire. 'What a declaration! You know it's not as simple as that. A hundred thousand pounds, but on my father's death, and then only if I entail the estate.'

'But now!' Mary said desperately. 'We must have something to live on, Shelley! The bailiffs were round again yesterday and there's nothing left to sell!'

'And I had made your father a definite promise,' Shelley said in a low voice. 'I know he was counting on it. By next year, we can hope for something, but now . . . ' He shrugged. 'We'll manage: we can always borrow against the expectation of the will.'

'We never do anything else,' Mary said. 'Oh, I forgot. This came for you yesterday from Chapel Street. Harriet, I suppose.' She took a letter from the dresser and handed it to him. He read it rapidly, his face darkening, crumpled it into a small ball and threw it savagely at the window.

'She must have seen the announcement in the paper. She's pressing for a settlement.'

'You'll have to do something about her soon,' Hogg said, putting on his spectacles and looking earnestly at Shelley. 'You know what a depressed state she's been in. She's talking of taking her life again.'

'Oh, really, Alexy, you know Shelley gave her every chance to join us and make something of herself,' Claire said angrily. 'If she chooses to be so wilfully misunderstanding about Mary and me, I don't see that she's entitled to anything.'

'Hush, Claire,' Shelley said mildly. 'Perhaps it was my fault for thinking that she had a finer spirit than she had.'

'She's a foolish, selfish creature – that's my opinion,' Claire retorted, tossing her head. 'Unable to think of anything but the mundane and the trivial.'

Hogg looked at her and turned back to his desk. There was silence for a moment, but for the scratching of his pen. Claire went across the room to Shelley and laid her hand on his. 'Well,' she said softly, 'are we going to see the new gas experiment in Highgate? You did promise.'

'Perhaps I'll come too,' Mary said, looking at her with narrowed eyes. Shelley shook his head.

'No, Maie, you stay here with Hogg. Peacock may be coming round, so I won't be late.'

She sighed. 'If that's what you want. . . . Oh, I nearly forgot. You're so quiet, Lucy. You should have reminded me. Have you got the ring? She wants to sell it, Shelley. Well, can you do it for her?'

I gave it to him and watched anxiously as he tossed it from one hand to the other, fascinated as a child by the spinning prism of colours. 'If you could . . . I'd be so grateful,' I said as he put it on his white hand and stared at it raptly.

'The moon's image in a summer sea – are you a witch sent to tempt me?' He laughed. 'Will you give it to me?'

'Don't be silly,' Mary said, but she smiled affectionately. 'She doesn't want it wasted.'

'What would you do with it?' I asked.

He looked down at the ring thoughtfully. 'It would settle Mr Godwin's financial problems. I don't want to disappoint him.'

'It would – but I need it more,' I said.

'Do you? Well, I'll make you an exchange,' he said, leaning across the table. 'I will sell it for you, but you must arrange for us to see the raising of the dead which your husband promised us when we attended his experiment.'

'Oh, yes!' Mary said eagerly. 'If you could do that . . . '

I offered him my hand across the table. 'If I ever have the misfortune to see him again, I will ask. That's all I can promise.'

He laughed gleefully. 'I shall make it my business to bring you together again, then.'

'Shall you?' I looked at him nervously. He looked so confident, so strange that I found it quite credible, but Mary smiled at me reassuringly.

'Shelley's the gentlest soul in the world. Come, tell her you're making fun of her. She's as white as a corpse.'

Ignoring her, he laid his hands flat on the table and pressed them down, watching me as he spoke in a slow, vibrant voice. 'Ruthven . . . Ruthven . . . I summon you . . . '

'Stop it! You're much too convincing,' I said, half-laughing, and pushed back my chair.

He frowned at me. 'You've broken it.' He looked up at Claire as she leant over him. 'We'd better go now and visit Phillips with the ring on the way. He'll buy it. Maie, promise you won't go out. I want you to continue with the Greek translation . . . you haven't touched it for a week.'

She sighed and put her hands on his shoulders. 'No, I don't feel like it. Perhaps I'll go to bed and read *The Italian*.'

'Well, remember to leave it down here before you go to sleep,' Claire said. 'Shelley and I are reading it to each other.'

'Yes . . . I've heard you,' Mary said flatly. She looked down at Shelley with a sad little smile and touched his golden hair, but he was tracing lines and circles on the table with his finger, his head bent forward.

Hogg turned round when they had gone, laying down his pen with a sigh.

'Is it not going well?' Mary lifted back one of the heavy red curtains from the bay window to watch them going down the street. She saw me watching her face and turned round with a quick smile. 'Poor Alexy! Still, you've finished one book, which is more than I've done.'

'I'm beginning to think one's enough,' he said, putting on his

148

coat. 'Perhaps I'll leave it and go and watch the cricket at Islington.'

'Oh, you and sport!' Mary said wryly. 'I can't think why you waste your time at it. Why don't you stay and help me – I'm making a new fire balloon, a golden one, as a surprise for Shelley.'

'It will be a better present for being made by your hands,' Hogg said hastily, opening the door. I jumped up.

'I'd like to come, if you'll take me with you,' I said, forestalling Mary's next suggestion – that I should help her. I can't abide sewing.

'Oh . . . very well,' he said, looking taken aback. 'Get your cloak and hurry, then. With luck, there'll be a hackney on the Sloane Street rank.'

*   *   *

'Well, how do you find the ideal life?' he said mockingly as the carriage rattled along past the Hyde Park promenaders.

I frowned. 'I haven't seen enough to know. . . . Mr Shelley's so extraordinary. Have you always been friends?'

He stretched out, propping his feet up. 'Do we seem such an odd couple? No, don't tell me. I think I know him better than anyone.' He laughed suddenly. 'God, I'll always remember when we met again last year. I was just settling comfortably back to a hard-working, thoroughly boring, respectable life. I was sitting in my rooms one night, just like every other for the previous two months, reading through law cases, when the door opened and in he burst like a bolt of lightning, wild and unearthly as ever – and just as irresistible. Shelley's so much more, I don't know, alive than other people – just to be with him is like breathing ether. A somewhat rarefied air, if you're not accustomed to it.' He paused, looking at me quizzically. 'It's most curious to think of you as Ruthven's wife,' he said suddenly. 'I can imagine Byron wanting to marry you, but it's not a state which I would have expected to attract Lord Ruthven. Why?'

'Why did he marry me? Because I was the person who most threatened him, then,' I said. 'I would have taken Byron from him.'

149

'Interesting,' Hogg said. 'I hadn't realised he was so . . . obsessed with Byron. A fanatic's obsession, by the sound of it. And why did you do it?'

'Circumstances,' I said, looking out of the window. 'Please – can we talk of something else? I came to London to escape, not to remember.'

'You'll never be allowed to forget while you remain at Hans Place,' Hogg said. 'It's one reason why you should seek another home.' He leant forward. 'Turn right when we come to Portman Square, cabbie. We want to look at a house.'

As we came into the elegant square, Hogg pulled down the window. 'There – that's the home for you. A good area, well-placed, respectable – it's just what you want. It was refurnished only last year. Very elegantly, I gather.' His voice was dry. 'One way to waste a fortune.'

'You sound like an agent,' I said, looking up at the long sash windows and newly faced walls. 'Anyway, I can't afford it.'

He smiled. 'You think not? It happens to belong to the friend of my best client. I know for certain that you could rent it for five hundred a year. The famous ring will stretch to that, won't it?'

'But I'm very happy at Hans Place,' I said. 'Why are you showing me this? I thought we were going to watch cricket?'

'So we are,' he said. 'Later. I'm trying to tell you something, Lucy. Mary's taken you in on account of your name. They're all infatuated with anything Gothic at the moment.' He paused. 'Nothing wrong with Gothic fancies – until they take on flesh and blood. You see, I know another side of Lord Ruthven. He's been working with the *agents provocateurs* for Sidmouth, hasn't he? A very efficient administrator, I've heard, if a little . . . bloodthirsty.'

I nodded. 'But what . . . ?'

'What has that got to do with Shelley?' He glanced at the cabbie and lowered his voice. 'He's been under surveillance for the last three years. He was nearly caught in Lynmouth, when they found the sort of pamphlets he'd been sending out. I've heard that Ruthven has been showing a remarkable interest in the case.' He patted my hand. 'Too close to home, my dear. You're better advised to take Portman Square.'

'I'll risk it,' I said. 'I'll stay.'

'But you risk them, too,' he said. 'You're still his wife.'

*   *   *

It was late when we came back to Hans Place, past twelve and
no link-boys to guide us through the pools of mud and flotsam
with their lanterns. There was one light still burning in the
Shelley's home, and it slid across the narrow passage floor in
front of me. I paused outside the closed door, listening. Of
course! The raising of the midnight ghosts. An opportune
moment to present myself. I turned to share the joke with Hogg,
but he was still on the stairs.

I held back my laughter as Claire's throaty, slightly ex-
aggerated accent sank to a dramatic whisper: 'The hooded
figure came towards him, remorseless as death, and as he looked
into that awful face he beheld the flames which played within
the sunken sockets of its eyes . . .' I pulled my hood forward and
opened the door just before Hogg reached me.

'No!' Claire, ashen-faced, dropped the book and cowered
back against the wall with a shriek of terror, while Shelley
broke into a piercing, almost fiendish laugh, staring up at me
with his long fingers creeping on his face as if he meant to tear it
open. I was paralysed into immobility.

'Fool!' Hogg said savagely as he pushed me out of the way.
'Go and wake Mary. She'll soothe them. Shelley, Shelley?
Come, old fellow, you were dreaming. There's nothing there.'

'But the eyes!' Shelley screamed at him, shrinking back in
his chair until I could only see the golden halo of hair. 'Her
eyes! I saw them. They were scarlet, Hogg, and they . . . they
wouldn't close.'

Hogg shook his head. 'It was only the light. Look – if I turn
the lamp so, it throws strange shadows. That was all you saw.'

'No, I saw it too,' Claire sobbed. 'It was there, just as I read
it. We raised the spirit. Oh, what shall I do! Shelley! Shelley!'

Hogg motioned me to hurry. I ran down the passage to
Mary's room, shook her frantically as she stirred in her sleep.
She opened her eyes in a troubled stare. 'What is it . . . ? There
were voices. . . . Oh, it's you, Lucy.'

'It's terrible,' I said, half-crying. 'I only opened the door and they . . . they went into a sort of fit. I didn't do anything, I promise, I didn't. I didn't mean to do any harm. . . .'

'No, no, it's my fault,' she said quickly. 'I should have warned you. They will do this wretched witch-raising, and it always ends like this. Shelley? Percy, I'm coming, my love.'

I watched from the doorway, helpless and excluded as she rocked his head against her breast, whispering to him as he moaned and clutched at her hair. 'You'd better get the laudanum,' she said hurriedly to Hogg. 'Claire, you can sleep with me tonight. You must stop doing this, do you understand? I thought you promised me in Nelson Square that it was all over.'

'It was!' Claire wailed. 'Oh, Mary, it was so vile – we mustn't stay here any longer!'

'Go to bed,' Mary said in a strained voice. 'Alexy, give me the bottle and help me put him on the sofa. There's a cover in the chest. Oh, my dear love, look at me! You're quite safe now. Now, drink this. You'll sleep until the morning and all the spirits will have gone.'

'They're never gone,' I heard him murmur. 'Claire's right. We mustn't stay here, must move, the eyes keep coming back, you see.' His voice slurred and his head dropped back until he lay as pale and quiet as a ghost-ridden child in the darkness.

'Thank God,' Hogg murmured as he and Mary looked at each other across the sofa. She let him lead her out of the room, brushing past me as if my existence had been forgotten.

I was woken in the morning by Mary, already neatly dressed in a dark brown gown with a white embroidered collar. Her hair was drawn tightly back and the harsh morning light showed no mercy to her pale, drawn face as she looked down at the bed. I smiled nervously, alarmed by her detached expression.

'You were dreaming,' she said softly. 'I heard you calling out; it sounded like oleander?'

'What? Oh.' I sat up and started to drag back my hair with the heavy wooden comb. 'No, I remember now. I was dreaming of the child, I forgot he'd gone.'

'Do you miss him? You sounded so lost.'

'I suppose I do,' I said slowly. 'Not having a child of my own, I'd grown so used to thinking . . . no, of course it's right that he

152

should be with his father. Dreams always confuse the truth, don't they?'

'No, they tell you what you don't want to think. You should have a child of your own,' she said thoughtfully. 'Still, it's your affair.'

'That's not a very good joke,' I said sadly. 'What could I do if I had Byron's child? He wouldn't want it.'

'But you do,' she said, watching me. 'It shows in your face. Well, you'd better hurry your plans before Claire overtakes you. She's very determined, and with Shelley's brain behind her, and her looks . . . '

I looked up at her, understanding. 'You want me to go now, don't you?'

She gave an embarrassed smile and started to fold up the bed cover. 'Lucy, I don't like saying this. I know what you must think. But after last night, it's really better that Shelley shouldn't see you – for the time being, at least. When he has these fancies, hallucinations, call them what you like, it's important that nothing should upset his recovery and, as he saw you as part of it . . . '

'But it was all Claire's doing. She persuaded him,' I said desperately. 'Surely if he saw me in daylight, he'd know. Please, Mary, I'll be no trouble, I promise, but I've nowhere else to go.'

'Hush!' she said sternly. I dried my eyes, seeing there was no hope of moving her with tears. I wondered that I could ever have thought that she was sweet and gentle. There was nothing docile about her now. 'Well, when do you want me to go?'

'Oh, come, it's no tragedy,' she said briskly. 'Claire has the money and you certainly won't starve.'

'How much?'

'Two thousand pounds.' She paused. 'Minus forty shillings. They bought Shelley a new microscope as he had to pawn the last one, but you won't mind that. Hogg is going to make all the arrangements for you. There's a house in Portman Square . . . '

'Yes,' I said. 'He showed me.'

'Oh, do stop looking so martyred,' she said in an irritated voice. 'We've never lived anywhere so grand, and goodness knows where *we* shall find to live. Shelley's decided we must move after last night. Don't worry about that, it would have happened soon, anyway. You don't know what real misery is, Lucy, that's the trouble. You've never been on the run from the creditors, cut off by your family, had to beg like a pauper when and where you can. Well, have you!'

'It's not my fault that I wasn't born to be an idealist,' I said indignantly. 'I suppose eight years of hell count for nothing?'

'A very luxurious hell compared to some. Oh, I'm sorry,' she said, putting her arms round me. 'I don't want us to be enemies. Listen, when you're a beautiful queen of society with nothing to do but talk and lie in bed until four in the afternoon, we'll come and visit you.'

Her conception of my own ambitions was particularly mortifying because it was, in part, true. I carefully buttoned up my blue silk dress, while Mary planned my future.

'And you're to tell me all about Byron. What will you do, Lucy? Shall you go and visit him at Devonshire House? That would be very brave, to run the gauntlet of his wife and sister!'

'Oh no, that's not at all my intention,' I said, beginning to feel happier at the prospect. 'First I shall go and leave an invitation to both of them. He'll remember my hand. . . .'

9

I walked up the shallow steps of the graceful staircase of
Melbourne House behind the footman, the courage ebbing a
little faster out of my new kid slippers on every tread. Lady
Melbourne might be one of London's most famous hostesses,
but she had never shown the slightest interest in our side of the
family, the connection being by marriage, not blood. This, I am
bound to admit, had never prevented my parents from following
her career with an unflagging and, in company, a possessive
interest. My own curiosity had been aroused in later years. Her
name had been closely linked with Byron's at the time when he
was trying to disentangle himself from the toils of her daughter-
in-law, Caro Lamb, and I had heard that Lady Melbourne's
role had been active – and far from disinterested. And yet she
was said to have encouraged his marriage to her niece,
Annabella. I was intrigued, but it was not that which had
brought me to her.

My name was announced and I was shown into a long,
elegant drawing-room, hung with Chinese wallpaper. My first
impression was of simplicity, then of the skilful disarrangement
which prevented the room from appearing contrived: the
leather music books casually heaped by the stand on the painted
harpsichord, a magazine lying open on a silk-covered stool, and
on the sofa near the Adam fireplace, the silky brown hair of a
sleeping dog. I corrected myself with a smile as a slipper came
into sight on the sofa, and Lady Melbourne's head turned to
look at me. I hurried forward, my hand outstretched.

'Lady Ruthven?' she said quickly, before I could embarrass
her with the more familiar address permitted to a relation,
however distant. Her voice was brisk and business-like, her

eyes discomfitingly penetrating. I could understand Byron's liking for her; old enough to deter the gossips, she had both the directness of a man and the deviousness of a woman. 'I believe I saw you in Hyde Park last week,' she said, 'not that I knew who you were, but it's not usual to see a lady driving her own phaeton, unaccompanied. Take my advice and don't do it again – it gives rise to talk. I asked your name, and Lord Alvanley was good enough to tell me.' She looked at me sharply. 'He praised you in very fulsome terms.'

'Indeed!' I laughed uneasily, aware that I must have made a very bad impression. 'I hardly know him, I assure you. His praises must be won easily.'

'Won't you sit down?' she said in a kinder tone. 'I'm afraid I'm not well enough to stand for long. These English winters – they grow longer every year.' She sighed. 'It's most tedious – had my health been better, I would have gone abroad by now. Really, I'm in no state to receive visitors.'

I rose to my feet with an expression of gentle understanding. Damn her if she sent me away now! 'But, of course – you must be exhausted. Let me fetch a cushion for your head and I'll leave.'

She sat up quickly. 'No, no! I'm delighted you came to see me.' She paused and I had the uncomfortable feeling of being assessed before she gave a little laugh and said lightly: 'To be frank, it suited me very well. Tell me, my dear, are you on friendly terms with your cousin, Annabella?'

Wondering what was coming next, I hesitated, then shook my head. 'We have very little in common.'

'One thing, surely?' Lady Melbourne said with a sudden spark of malice. 'Byron is a very open confidant, you see. Well, are you still in love with him? He was devoted to you . . . quite boringly so. De-voted,' she repeated, watching me. 'Well?'

I blushed and looked at my feet, 'Perhaps, but . . . '

'But nothing,' she said sharply. 'He always told me you reminded him of his sister and you must have heard those rumours?'

I nodded without raising my eyes. 'I couldn't believe that he would do anything so ruinous to his reputation.'

She shrugged. 'Poor B. That's gone long ago. Listen, my dear. If you have – and I imagine that you came to see me in order to see how the land lay – designs on reviving your love affair, I have two pieces of advice for you. One, use discretion. He's had enough of public love-making. Two, swallow your pride and use your resemblance to Augusta. It's there that your attraction to him lies. Tell him I'm ready to help.' She gave a little laugh, and added, 'You timed your London visit very well.'

'Oh?'

'Annabella's with her parents in Seaham,' she said. 'Nursing a wounded heart. Understandable. Byron's been the soul of indiscretion about his feelings for Augusta. But I hold no brief for Annabella. She's a cold, stubborn girl – no wife for Byron.'

'But you encouraged his marriage,' I said. 'I don't understand.'

'Then you have as little intuition as your cousin Bella,' she said crushingly. 'I'm very fond of the silly boy. He was like a favourite nephew to me before he became one.' She sighed and rearranged the folds of her grey silk dress. 'When you reach my age, you'll learn that the penalty of arranging matches is that you bear the blame if it fails.'

'And I am to be your sacrifice to the god to make him smile on you again?' I wished the stupid words back in my mouth too late, as she frowned.

'A willing one, I don't doubt,' she said dryly. 'Don't be foolish, my dear. You look as if you have a cool head. Keep it.' She lay back against the cushions. 'There! I've told you enough. Now, run away and remember to keep me informed – and to tell Byron that it was I who sent you.'

I twisted my hands nervously as I stood up, uncertain how to frame my question. 'Lady Melbourne, I know that it is imposing on you to ask, but – I know so few people in London. My connections were all from school.'

'That comes of running into marriage instead of doing your London Season, my dear.' But she gave me a smile of great sweetness and went to her writing table. 'I'll write to Lady Jersey – that gives you an entrée to Almacks, and after that, you'll be sure to be asked everywhere. But Ruthven is known,' she added, poising her pen over the page. 'There's no need for this.'

'I – I am no longer with Lord Ruthven,' I said in an unsteady voice. Lady Melbourne put down her pen and turned round in her chair. I quailed under her stare. 'I have left him,' I hurried on. 'I have taken a house in Portman Square and . . . ' My voice trailed away into a dismal silence as Lady Melbourne's frown deepened. 'Yes,' she said. 'Well, I imagine your carriage is waiting for you. I trust after this betrayal of friendship you will have the goodness to forget what I have said to you. Had I known . . . !'

'But how can you judge me without knowing the circumstances!' I exclaimed as she put her hand on the bell-handle. She rang it. 'Well?' I demanded.

'I have no wish to hear of them,' she said coldly, 'Even my poor wretched Caro would never behave so abominably. To take a lover is always forgivable, but to take a house on your own in London with not even a pretence of respectability and then to expect society to call – surely you can understand that there is only one class of person who does that, and of that class you will be assumed to belong. I'll give you one piece of advice. Send for Ruthven, or your reputation will make Harriette Wilson look like a Mother Superior. Next time, I shall look forward to seeing you *both*.'

I curtsied. 'At that price, I prefer to forgo society, Lady Melbourne. Thank you for your frankness.' I paused. 'And for your advice. It will be followed, I promise you.'

She looked past me to the footman in the doorway. 'You will conduct this young lady to her carriage,' she said. 'See to it that she is not admitted again, on any occasion.'

I never met Lady Melbourne again.

I knew it was the moment to visit Byron, with Annabella safely out of the way at Seaham, yet for four days I did nothing. Now that it was possible, I felt only fear. It had been so many years. Perhaps I had changed, he would not find me beautiful, would not even remember me. Had I been more confident, I would have given Lady Melbourne's suggestion no further thought. But I was afraid of being rejected as an embarrassing reminder of a past Byron might have no wish to remember, of being turned away at the door.

I knew Augusta well from Byron's descriptions. I knew, too, that there was a likeness between us. He had often remarked on it. In a hooded cloak, I might briefly pass as her, long enough to gain entrance to his house, long enough to feel his arms around me before I showed my face. A coward's trick, but I was too uncertain of myself to be courageous.

The sky had slung a sparkling cobweb over the slate roofs of Piccadilly when I arrived: the gas lamps flared brightly up at long sash windows where silhouettes paused, then crossed as in a magic lantern. In the street, groups of young men were sauntering home from the theatre, their laughter raucous in the quiet night: the cabbies on the hackney rank jolted awake, then pulled down their hats with a sigh as the prospective clients turned away down St James's.

At last, I raised my hand, knocked at the black door, pulling my hood further over my face as I waited for an answer. The footman's face registered surprise, then pleasure.

'Why, Mrs Leigh! We didn't know you were coming . . . I'll tell the housekeeper to see your room's warmed and ready for you.'

'No, please don't trouble her,' I whispered, 'I shall only be here a short time. I'm afraid I've lost my voice.' I could not mimic hers was the truth of it. He nodded understandingly. 'I'll tell his lordship you're here.'

'I'll announce myself,' I said. And I went past him into the marble hall, to be confronted by the reproachful stare of Lord and Lady Milbanke, with dog, from above the fireplace. 'You'll find him in the drawing-room,' the footman said. 'Shall I say that there'll be two for dinner, Mrs Leigh?'

I nodded and started up the curving staircase.

The light shone dimly under the mahogany door of the drawing-room: for a moment, I wanted to turn and run away. Having achieved this much, what if . . . what if . . . 'Oh God,' I said, gripping the stair rail. 'I can't do it. I can't!'

Weeping silently, I retreated towards the steps, took the first one down, the second, paused as the door opened, trapping me in a sudden flood of light.

'Who in hell's name is it creeping around out here?' I heard him say angrily. Slowly, I turned. 'Gus?' he whispered incredulously, as I shook the hood forward. He limped quickly across the landing, bent over me and pulled it back from my face. I looked up at him, unable to speak.

'Come here!' he said furiously, pulling me back into the room after him. He slammed the door and turned towards me. 'Now, what the devil do you mean by coming here dressed as her? Did you think I'd want to take you as my sister, you fool! Get out of those clothes and pull your hair down, or I swear I'll have you thrown on the street – naked.'

I looked at his blazing eyes and did as I was told. Not until I stood in my underskirt and blue camisole with my hair hanging loose to my waist did the fury die out of his face. He lay back on the black japanned sofa and looked at me silently. 'Well, have I changed enough, my lord?' I asked. Slowly, he shook his head. I looked down at my breasts, more than half visible above the blue cotton. 'I should be embarrassed . . . '

He laughed. 'You didn't come for tea and sympathy, my love. Come here.'

I quivered as he reached out his hand, caressing my body as if to remind himself of it, staring at my face with heavy eyes.

'Do you think that . . .?'

'Later,' he said softly, pulling me down to him. 'We'll renew acquaintance first, shall we?'

I had been half afraid, so easily does one man's love-making obliterate another's, whatever the comparisons, so treacherously does memory blur one body in another to make a confused and imperfect whole. But not his. It was as if we had never been parted. Each fantasy was understood and played; the fight, the rape, the submittal that clings and clenches, the pulsing, rising fury, the spent lassitude as the sweet musk smell of it enveloped us.

'Oh God, how I do love you!' I whispered, burying my face in his soft brown hair.

'Lucy,' he murmured. 'But you should not have done that to me. To come as her . . . '

'I thought you would not want me as myself,' I said in a low voice. 'I could not know, I only had intuition, not knowledge. . . . I'm sorry. The last thing I wanted was to anger you.'

He shook his head as he looked down at me, studying my face. 'Why did you take so long to come? When I gave you the ring, I thought you'd use it to follow me.'

I shrugged. 'It wasn't possible. Ruthven guarded me like a prisoner of state and you – well, you were very quick to console yourself, Byron. I heard that even Madame du Stäel joined the throng.'

He lay back on the carpet, roaring with laughter. 'Well?' I said, reaching for my clothes. Byron leant forward and tossed them up on to a screen, a collage of pugilists. 'You don't need those,' he said. 'My dear Lucy, if you'd seen her as I did, when the amiable lady lost her corset at dinner and had to have it fished out of her dress by a footman . . . I do assure you that any thoughts of love were killed stone-dead! No, for God's sake don't ask for a résumé of my affairs. None of them have lasted – that's all you need to know.' His hand slid down my body. 'You never had a child,' he said slowly.

'By him!' I shuddered.

'And mine?'

'I wanted to write and tell you, but I never got beyond writing your name. I couldn't find the words. They looked so much bleaker on paper. I'm sorry.'

Byron turned away from me and lay face down. 'If I had a child now,' I said hesitantly, looking at his bitter face.

He shook his head. 'It's too late. I must get away, Lucy. I'm sick to death of England. I can't write, I can't think, I'm getting soft in domesticity . . . and the damned creditors don't give me a day's peace.'

'Well, I suppose if they see you here . . . '

'I'm selling Newstead,' he said abruptly. 'The money has to be raised and I'll burn in hell before I beg off the Milbankes.'

I stared at him, dismayed. 'But Ruthven – he's certain to come to London if Newstead goes. Was there nothing else you could do?'

'Do you suppose Newstead would keep him away if he thought that you were with me? We'll talk about it over dinner – I've had nothing to eat today.'

I ate my way with zest through turtle soup, cold salmon and

a roast partridge while Byron toyed with three biscuits and a glass of watered wine and talked.

'Perhaps you should come abroad with me,' he said suddenly. 'We'll dress you as a boy – do you remember when we went to the fight?'

'I often thought you loved me better then than as a girl,' I said and stopped, frightened by his expression.

'Why do you say that?' he said furiously. 'Do you think I'm like Ruthven?'

'I was only joking – I meant nothing. I promise you.'

He pushed a bowl of strawberries towards me and sat back with a sigh. 'I know. Scandal sets one's nerves on edge. I used to enjoy it, but now, well, it's not pleasant to find yourself cut by every little nobody when you walk down the street. It's another reason to leave.'

'I can't see any point in it. You'd have to come back again.'

'Not this time. I tell you, Lucy, I'd rather join Ali Pasha's skipetars than live in the Regent's pocket like Southey.'

'Ali Pasha? He'd make short shrift of you,' I said, sipping at the golden Sauternes.

'He fell in love with me, as a matter of fact,' Byron said. 'I'll give you one of his presents to prove it – there's a chest full of 'em in the corner.'

He came back to the table with a necklace of plaited silver and laid it by my plate, then destroyed all my pleasure by adding, 'I was going to give it to Gus, but if you like it . . . '

'Not if you meant it for her,' I said, looking away. He kissed my forehead. 'It's yours.'

I smiled and lifted up the necklace, looking at the jewel-studded clasp. 'I never imagined Albanian ladies wearing such beautiful things. Don't they have to go about in veils and black robes?'

He laughed. 'Only widows and the poor. You're just like Gus. All she wanted to know was what the ladies wore.'

'You're very kind.'

'It's as cultivated a beauty as the European,' he said, not noticing my change of tone. 'They dye their hair mahogany at the age of ten and whiten their faces with a witch's brew of cowrie shells and lily roots. Their eyebrows are grown very thick, sometimes joining in the middle, which, curiously, isn't unattractive – what is it, Lucy?'

'Oh, nothing.'

'It was hearing me mention Gus, wasn't it?' he said abruptly. 'You came here posing as her, and yet you can't bear me to mention her name.' He laughed. 'And I was fool enough to think that *you* understood.'

'I'm trying to.' I leant forward. 'Byron, dear love, you can't let it go on. The whole of London talks of it. *Childe Harold* is dead, don't you understand? It's the only crime . . .'

'That's why I must go,' he said slowly. 'What is there to stay for?' He buried his face in his hands.

'Oh, to hell with Gus!' I said softly and ran round the table to kneel by him. 'Byron, I'll come with you wherever you choose to go. I don't ask for anything else, just to be with you. Let me. Please!'

'Sweet Lucy.' He stroked my hair. 'If I had married you . . .'

'No! It would never have worked. I'm as jealous as any other woman. Better to be like this, with what might have been than to have lost it. But I could follow you.'

'Limping in my footsteps?' he said with sudden savageness. 'What a touching pair we'd make.'

'You're too conscious of it,' I said, looking away from the raised leather boot.

'Do you blame me, when if I give a beggarwoman a coin, she ups and mimics me behind my back, and at every waltzing party, it's "Oh Lord Byron, why don't you dance?" '

'You can't blame every young lady with aspirations for wanting to be in your arms,' I said, trying to relieve his mood.

He grinned with sudden malice. 'You should hear their dinner conversations, telling me about the exquisite autumnal tints of the Scottish hills, in die-away voices.'

'To which I suppose you gallantly reply that you prefer the tint of Scottish whisky?'

'Not a bad guess.'

'Do I understand you as well as Gus?' I said, stroking his hair. He frowned.

'Come here before I forget what you look like with your clothes off.'

163

'What, here? But if somebody . . . ' My hands met behind his neck as he pulled me down on to his knees.

'When do we see each other again, my love?' he said softly.

'Any . . . ' No, no charm in availability. 'No, not tomorrow, or Wednesday, perhaps late on Thursday?'

'You sound very occupied. Who are you seeing?'

I smiled. 'Oh, I really can't remember.'

'Who is he?' Byron demanded, his face darkening.

'Why should it interest you? Where shall we meet?'

'You won't tell me?' He pushed me back. 'Then you can go. I don't like sharing my mistresses.'

'You don't mean it,' I said, dismayed, as he walked away across the room.

'I most certainly do,' he said coldly. 'A pity. I would have taken you to see Mrs Siddons at Drury Lane. You know I'm on the committee now.'

'Byron,' I said after a long pause. 'I . . . I'm not seeing anybody. As a matter of truth, they won't see me. I'm more ostracized than you. Lady Melbourne says I'm socially unacceptable without my husband.'

He kissed me. 'I'll fill the role if you've nerve enough to take the gossip. Your reputation or me: take your choice.'

'And what if he doesn't come back?'

'A clever woman doesn't force a man's hand,' Byron said slowly. 'I won't be pushed, Lucy. . . .'

* * *

A week passed and I was never so happy, so careless of what people thought. I dropped the precaution of wearing a mask in public and sat openly at his side in the theatre and when we drove in the Park. Together, we went to the opening of the annual exhibition at the Academy and drew more attention than even Lawrence's portrait of the Regent. The Prince himself was there, fatter and redder than his favourite's brushstrokes chose to show, but splendidly dressed and very graceful in his manner. Byron frowned at my admiration, and pointedly turned away to inspect one of the two Turners. 'No doubt you applaud his behaviour towards Princess Caroline, too,' he said dryly.

'I'd say she deserved it – she's made an absolute fool of herself abroad, by all accounts. Imagine what they must have thought at Genoa when she appeared with that dreadful Bergamini, with her skirt halfway up her legs. I don't know how she dares.'

'Driven to it,' he murmured, bowing very low as the Regent gave him an affable nod. I began to see that what Byron said and what Byron did seldom accorded.

I guarded my happiness with jealous determination. Nothing was going to take my lover from me. My promised introduction for the Shelleys was pushed to the back of my mind, for I knew they would bring Claire with them. But it was not Claire, nor Annabella, nor even Augusta who threatened me.

Every night, it was the same. However hard I tried to distract him, there came a moment when his smile grew remote, his eyes dulled, and I knew that he was thinking of the past. Of Ruthven. I had no weapons to fight what I could not understand. Byron was vehement in his hatred of the man, yet he spoke of him so often and in such a strange, despairing voice that I began to comprehend, terrified, an obsession deeper and more dangerous than love.

He did not notice that I sat in silence, oppressed by the feeling that Ruthven was now, would always be, with us. He was absorbed, caught up in the web of his rambling monologue. One night when he began to tell me of the disgust and loathing he felt for Ruthven, I was driven beyond caution and burst out: 'I don't believe in your hate. You used to worship him. You still do. It's as if he possessed you . . .'

'Don't say that,' Byron said. 'Never say it again, or I'll throw you out of my house.'

I looked up in astonishment. He had his back towards me. When he turned round, I saw that his face was as white as chalk, his eyes huge and staring like those of a haunted man. He sat down on the sofa opposite me and leant back. 'What did you mean when you said that?' he asked. 'Tell me. I'm really most curious.' He was trying to make his voice sound light and amused, but it was not convincing.

'It's only a feeling I have,' I said, looking away from his face. 'A feeling that he's trying to, I don't know, take you over in some way. I know that he is fascinated by you, that he is totally possessive, that he feels a kind of kinship with you. He follows your career as if it was his own, keeps every cutting and review, knows who are your friends, which parties you attend, where your coats are made, everything. He even visits your mother's grave every week, as if he were her son.'

'It's as well someone does,' Byron said.

'Is that all you can say? Byron, you must tell me! I *have* to understand.'

He leant against the marble lintel shelf, looking down at me, his face in shadow. 'Every man has two sides, dark and light,' he said slowly. 'His nature is composed of opposites, as clearly marked as if he had two souls in a single body. Ruthven claims to be my darker half. Yes, you can laugh if you like, Lucy. You don't know what it is to be the object of that sort of fixation. He lives my life, you see, to a certain point. Newstead, and you, were mine. Usually, he prefers to link himself by opposites, to score each sin of mine as his victory.'

'But how did he form such an idea?'

'Oh, don't call it an idea,' he said. 'I half believe in it myself. How? I'll have to go back to when we first came to Southwell, and Ruthven rented Newstead. He was very good to me – and I was so damned lonely. You know the sort of charm he can exercise when he wants, and he used it to the full. I never felt in the way or that I was boring him, although he was two years older than me. He always had time for me, and I suppose I was flattered. Two years is a deal of difference at that age. It never occurred to me that it was the other way round, that I was the prey.'

'I could have told you that,' I sighed. 'It was very obvious.'

'Then in God's name, why didn't you!' he shouted. 'I can't abide wisdom after the event.'

'I don't think you would have listened,' I said.

He shrugged, his anger evaporated as quickly as it had exploded. 'Perhaps not. I admit that I was very much under his spell when I first met you. No, it was after then that his possessiveness started to get on my nerves, and I found the friendship becoming more of a strain than a pleasure. I felt that I was beginning to lose my own identity in him. I couldn't get away from him. When I was writing, he would come in and look over my shoulder, frightened that I was sending love letters, I suppose. If I went out, he put me through an inquisition afterwards – he behaved, in fact, like a jealous lover. The only power he still had over me was his knowledge of evil: the stories he told me were quite extraordinary, more so because of the man's identification with them. The difference between us, the one he never understood, was that I am amused by horror. He believes it.'

'He lives it,' I said quietly. 'It's his weapon against the world. He's always used it to get what he wants.'

'But what fascinates me is where the myth stops and the truth begins,' Byron said, staring down into the fire. 'Who is the real Ruthven, man or monster? See what you think, Lucy; I'd like to know. One night he told me the story I'm going to tell you, and said he was telling me more about himself that he would ever say again. I remember it very clearly.

'Darrell, a young buck, came to London, where he became fascinated by Lord Digby, the most notorious social figure of that time. Digby's generosity was as famous as it was dangerous. Everyone who benefited from it met with disaster. Gamblers were ruined overnight, innocent girls became depraved harpies.

'Time passed and Darrell's beloved died in inexplicable circumstances. Heartbroken, he agreed to go with Digby on a tour through Europe to try and forget his sorrows. On the journey, his companion sickened and became daily more feeble, but he insisted that they must reach a certain cemetery in Turkey before he died. They found it at last and the dying Digby confessed to Darrell that he was a vampire and this was the resting place to which he must always return, that he made Darrell his, by letting him share in his secret.

'Knowing now that Digby had caused his beloved's death, Darrell still carried out the vampire's last request, namely that he should cast his ring into a certain lake in Turkey.

'When, some years later, he returned to England, a dying man, his younger sister told him that she was about to be married to a certain Lord Marsden, then opened her locket to show him the portrait of Digby . . . or should I say, Ruthven?'

'No, it's absurd,' I said slowly, as his eyes met mine. 'Completely implausible.'

'You should have heard him tell it,' Byron said, leaning back and staring at the shadows of flames on the ceiling. 'He convinced me enough to make up my mind that our relationship must end. I told him so out in the field that day you saw us and that was when he told me the last and the strangest story of all, that he was my other self . . . he had searched me out and was bound to one aim, to house his soul in my body. . . .'

I suddenly remembered watching them fight and how, for a moment, the two shadows merged into one. The moment of Ruthven's victory.

'Hush,' I said softly, drawing his head down on my breast. 'What can Ruthven do to harm you here? We won't talk of him any more. I only want to think of you.'

Yet even in our love-making, the fear did not leave me. He was there, as real as if he lay between us in the bed. But I did not dare to say it, and Byron did not choose to question me.

'Stay here tonight – to hell with writing!' he said, putting his arms round my waist as I raised my arms to fasten my dress.

'I can't. The milliner's coming round at nine o'clock tomorrow morning.'

'But you've at least fifty hats already,' he protested.

'Oh, those!' I smiled down at him. 'They're old. She's very clever, used to make Lady Bessborough's hats.'

Byron sighed. 'That's a bad omen – there'll be so many feathers on your head that I shan't be able to kiss you for sneezing. Well, come here at eleven, hat and all; we might drive out to Richmond in the evening for dinner.'

He bent to press his lips to my forehead. 'To hell with Ruthven,' he said softly. 'We'll never talk of him again, only of you . . . and your precious hats, my sweet love.'

I looked up at him, my eyes blurred, and suddenly buried my face in the soft ruffles of his shirt. He stroked my hair gently, knowing what was in my mind. 'We've another week before she comes back,' he whispered. 'We mustn't darken it by thinking of the next.' He kissed my mouth and pushed me towards the door.

* * *

I found a letter from France waiting for me at Portman Square. Guiltily, I took it to my room to read. I had barely given a thought to Orlando in these past few weeks.

Harry's writing sprawled up and down six pages like grasshoppers' legs, telling me first how France had welcomed back Napoleon, who could still fire the imagination of the people more than their prosaic Bourbon king ever had. On their journey from Deauville, they had seen troops on the road everywhere, marching to join the Little Corporal on his triumphal progress towards the capital. Paris had fallen without a murmur, Harry said. The king had fled and Napoleon's carriage clattered up the Tuileries, unchecked. His sins were forgotten; everyone remembered the glory of the Empire – and that the Bourbons had stayed abroad, dissociating themselves from it. Orlando, apparently, had been wild with excitement and had morever been their passport to safety, declaring to anyone who would listen that they only had to give him a gun and he would join the army at once! His blond hair and misleadingly candid expression had stood them in good stead; food and lodging had been forthcoming and payment indignantly refused at every village along the way. '*In fact,*' he went on, '*I begin to see profit in being a father, and am happily preparing to live off my son's charm into a luxurious old age! You should have come, Lucy. It's been devilish good fun. Now we're off to the Netherlands where the allies are gathering: I'm hoping to get taken on by Wellington, and from all accounts, it shouldn't be too difficult. Any able-bodied man who can handle a gun stands a good chance, I'm told. Don't worry yourself about the boy – I'll find a family to take him in, if anything should happen to me. At present, he's trying out my sword on the table-cloth: he'll make a fine Major one day.*'

Under his father's flourish of a signature, Orlando had added two lines:

'*I wish you were with us. I have thought of you nearly everyday. I miss you very much now. Your loving O.*'

I folded the letter up and sat motionless for a long time, reproaching myself for not having kept him with me. Poor child, wandering through France like a vagrant, begging for food . . . I knew my brother well enough to see when he was putting a coat of varnish on a sorry picture. And London was no place for me to be when Annabella returned next week. I put down the letter, then looked at the sad little message again. Yes, I would go. I must.

It was still dark when I heard the carriage draw up in the square. Half-awake, I turned over in the bed and buried my head in the pillows. In the hall, the outer door shut with a click . . . I sat up as the footsteps came up the stairs, looked at my watch. Four o'clock. I smiled and lay back, closing my eyes. I would not stay with him, so he had come to me. Perhaps I should be a little angry at such a peremptory awakening, but not for long. I turned towards the door as his shadow crossed the passage wall.

'Byron, you should not have come. What am I to say when your carriage is seen here in the morning? Would you tear my reputation to shreds?'

He laughed softly and I felt his breath on my face in the darkness. 'Come to bed,' I said, stretching up my arms. He pulled the bedclothes back, and flung himself on me. Too late, I knew my error. My mouth opened in a soundless scream as my head was forced into the pillow. I gasped, choking in the treacherous softness as he forced his way into my rigid body.

'Is this how he takes you, whore?' he hissed as I sobbed with the pain. I bit on the back of my hand to keep myself from making any sound, turned my face away as he stood up.

'Look at me,' Ruthven said softly, and he twisted my head towards him. As I looked into his eyes, I believed everything that Byron had told me about him and it was all I could do to keep my fear from showing.

'Well, have you come back to seek Orlando or to hear about Byron?' I asked scornfully. 'I'm delighted to oblige you on the second score.'

'Cover yourself, my dear,' he said. 'A naked woman with a vicious tongue is like a thorn in the flesh.' He walked over to the dressing-table and picked up Harry's letter. It was not in his nature to show sorrow. His face had the calm detachment of a doctor studying his patient as he turned to look at me. 'Very shrewd of your brother to leave,' he said, taking a small bottle out of his pocket and unscrewing the top. 'We must make sure that your . . . maternal spirit does not lead to your making a second flight.'

'What is it?' I whispered.

'A sleeping draught,' he said, coming towards the bed. 'Drink.'

I tried to turn my head away, but he twisted my hair round his hand, forcing my head back until he could thrust the cold lip of the bottle into my mouth. Languor crept up, slow and inevitable as black silk over a corpse, shrouding me coldly, dragging me down into dark sleep.

IO

I did not know how long I lay alone in my dreaming, half-lit world, nor the moment at which I realized I was with child. It was as if I were trapped in a small, dark room which shapes and faces could enter at will, but I could never find the way out. The dreams and the reality were inseparable. Fear made all things real. Once, I thought I was back at Newstead in front of the house. Ruthven stood by the door, holding a black stallion by the bridle. He smiled and called to me to come and admire it, but as I came up to him, he melted away. I reached out to touch the animal . . . and it changed. The hoofs reared up at me and they were bronze and vast; sparks flew up as they touched the ground and the crescent horseshoes glowed white hot. The mane was of twisted iron snakes, the eyes were red like fire. I ran back, screaming, but it trapped me against the wall – and behind the window, Ruthven watched, laughing. The horse's head fell back: it was Ruthven, it was Byron, and as I hid my face in my hands, the voices began to whisper and laugh, round and round, louder and louder, in my mind, no, in the room, no, stop, only stop, I can't, I can't . . .

It was a month before I was free of that closed world of ghosts. I woke to the scene I last remembered. Ruthven stood beside me, staring down at my face with a small black bottle in his hand. He was so pale and still that I thought he was the spectre of my dreams, but then he leant forward and I felt his cold breath on my face.

'What . . . was it?' The syllables slurred together: I pressed my hands to my forehead, trying to push the confused thoughts into place. 'You drugged me.'

'Laudanum,' he said. 'Very effective. I've given out the news that you're suffering from a bout of fever – unspecified.' He paused. 'I thought Byron might find time to visit you, but his love seems to have waned with my return. We'll find another way to bring him here.'

'Not through me,' I said. 'I'll go to him. I'll never bring him to you.'

He laughed and looked down at the bottle. 'One escape is enterprising, my love. Two might prove . . . regrettable.'

I dragged myself up against the pillows and whispered the truth to shatter that pallid mask. 'But why should I wish to escape when I'm bearing your child?' I held my breath, waiting for his reaction.

'A child?' He put down the bottle. 'My child?' I nodded, almost sorry for him that it was not. I never saw a man look so appalled as he did at that moment. The horror slowly spread from the eyes to the furrowed brow to the parted lips before he finally stammered: 'The laudanum! God, had I but *known* . . . I may have . . . '

'You'd better fetch a doctor,' I said. 'There'll be time enough for guilt.'

He left the room in hurried silence and I lay back, content, secure in the belief that it lived and that it was Byron's child. And Ruthven would never know. He would not choose to raise the doubt.

It was because there was only certainty in my mind that I raised the question of the date of conception with so little concern. It was a matter of curiosity, no more. The doctor put away his instruments and began to calculate on pink, uncreased fingers at a speed remarkable to watch. It was only an instant before his final deductions that I had my first qualm of doubt. It was like being stabbed twice with a broken sword to hear his bland voice confirming my fears.

He looked up at me with a pleased smile. 'I'll run through it again, but that seems to be the day. Six weeks ago, March the twenty-fourth. . . . What is it, Lady Ruthven? What can I have said to distress you?'

I grasped his arm and clung to it, staring up at his face. 'Are you sure that was the day? You can't be certain. . . . There must be a mistake. Oh, there must be!'

'No,' he said. 'The twenty-fourth. I'd swear to it.'

'Oh, da-damn your certainty,' I stammered. 'Leave me alone. Leave me, I said!'

When he had gone, I lay back, staring at the yellow canopy over the bed, still as a corpse. The twenty-fourth. The day of Ruthven's return. The last time I had lain with Byron. 'Whose? If you could tell me that,' I wept, pressing my hands to my body. 'If I could only *know*.'

But nothing could tell me. I could only wait in an agony of ignorance.

Slowly, drearily, the months passed by. Ruthven was always with me, watchful, coldly polite, making the excuse of my pregnancy to make a prisoner of me in my own house. No one saw anything strange in my confinement being made actual, only the evidence of Ruthven's love. I had no means of protesting. Alone in my rooms, I brooded on the fluttering creature inside me – Byron's child, Ruthven's heir? Time played tricks on my secret longings: it seemed as if this was that first, miscarried child of love.

On the twenty-second of June, Lord Wellington's despatch was printed in the *London Gazette*: that week, Waterloo was the only subject in the city. They cried it in the streets, reworked the battle in the clubs and coffee houses, discussed every detail in the political saloons. The war was over! England had triumphed! Every bell in London from St Martin-in-the-Fields to St Paul's at Deptford rang to shake the marble spires: the garlanded coaches clattered into every village in England with one word: 'Victory!'

A week later, Ruthven walked into my bedroom and dropped a copy of *The Times* on my lap. 'Read it,' he said. 'I've marked the place.'

I looked down at the death list and turned white. 'I don't need to look. Harry?'

'A better death than he deserved, in my opinion,' Ruthven said.

'And Orlando,' I whispered. 'What of the child? Well? Tell me.'

'Nothing,' Ruthven said, staring out of the window. 'I've asked. He's vanished. He was last seen with Harry a week

174

ago, just before the battle. Since then, nothing. Not a word.'

'Oh God,' I said. 'And I let him go.'

He turned round and walked towards me, his mouth set in a thin line, his hands laced as if he meant to murder me. I shrank back on the bed. 'He's better dead than in your hands. I'd do it again. I would!'

'Not with this child, Lucy,' he said softly. 'You'll never have the opportunity. I've made all the arrangements.'

I stared at him. 'What arrangements?'

'Don't look so dismayed,' he said. 'They should suit you very well. I've bought this house for you. I shall make you a generous allowance and, in due course, return to my old home in Albemarle Street. The appearance of our marriage will remain. Nothing more. The child will, of course, live with me.' He smiled. 'It should be most interesting to tutor it from birth.'

'To become like you,' I said. 'I suppose you plan to do to him what you would have done to Byron?'

'*Would* have done?' Ruthven said. 'When will you learn that nothing ends, only progresses?' He leant over me, staring down into my eyes. 'You know what I want of you, don't you, Lucy? I've waited long enough.'

'I won't do it,' I said. 'I'd rather lose Byron myself than persuade him to see you.'

'You don't understand,' he said in a different voice. 'There is a reason why I must see him. I wanted to conceal it from you, but . . . ' He sighed. 'Tomorrow is time enough. I act for your own sake, as well as my own. You must help me, Lucy. I'll never ask you again, I promise you.'

I stared after him, bewildered, as he walked out of the room, his head bent. The distress in his voice had sounded real enough.

When I came down to breakfast the next morning, a small book bound in white vellum lay beside my plate. I glanced across at Ruthven who stood by the fireplace, smiling at some article in the newspaper. 'Is this a present for me?'

'In a sense.' He frowned. 'Well, open it.'

I opened it at the frontispiece, a crayon portrait of a boy. He was shown leaning over a table, making an anagram with the scattered letters of Ruthven's name. I turned the page and caught my breath. They were love letters, and they were written by my husband. I read two of them and closed the book. 'Have these been published?'

'Not yet,' he said, laying aside the paper. 'I'm sure it would interest you to know that Byron sent them to me. The boy whose face forms the frontispiece sent him this little effort and asked Byron to see that it was put in the hands of a publisher. I begged Byron to burn them, but his answer was to send me this copy.' He bent over me, his cold fingers fondling my neck and shoulders. 'I admit defeat. He won't see me, but this must not be published. It would ruin you, as well as me. He must be prevented. Ask him here, tell him I'm away. If once I can see him, I'll persuade him.'

'No,' I said abruptly. 'I'll go to Devonshire House. He'd never forgive me if I led you to him. You want to create a rift between us.'

'Please, you must bring him here,' he said pleadingly. 'Only I can explain this to him. Listen. I'll even compromise. I'll leave you to dine with him alone first.'

'Well,' I said doubtfully, 'if you make it clear that I have nothing to do with your plans.'

'I promise,' he said eagerly. 'And I won't interfere.'

At last, I nodded. It was against my instinct, but I had not seen Byron for so long. To lie in his arms again, if only for a little while. . . .

* * *

He came, rather late, very suspicious. 'I hear you're with child,' he said as he sat down facing me. 'I didn't want to see you: the thought of it, of you and him, was abhorrent. Loathsome, do you understand? You degraded what was between us. I don't know if I can trust you now. You may be in league with him.'

I flushed. 'It's very easy for you to condemn, Byron. I always admired your ability to stop relating to life when it suited you. Do you suppose I welcomed his return? I couldn't prevent it.' I looked towards the door fearfully, then went towards him, my hands outstretched. 'It's your child, my love. I'm certain of it.'

'Is that why you brought me here, to tell me of your fantasies?'

My eyes filled with tears as I shook my head. 'I . . . I didn't know you could be so cruel.'

'Ask my wife,' he said with a savage laugh. 'My Pippin will blacken me to the world before she's finished, and I'm hanged if I won't live up to it. Oh God, how weary I am of it all!'

He buried his head in his hands and as I looked down on the thick chestnut curls, I noticed the first threads of grey. 'What an odd sham marriage is,' I said softly. 'You and Bella, Ruthven and I, all that sadness tidied away behind the façade, and all for the sake of a society which doesn't even care.'

'They don't care, but they talk, my dear,' Byron said bitterly, 'and a scandal cannot be permitted, only a supposition.' He looked up at me. 'Lucy, if the child is mine . . . '

'Yes?' I knelt beside him.

He sighed as he lifted my hair aside to kiss my neck. 'I pity it. Why so sad, my darling? We're together again – that should make you happy.'

I looked down at the floor. 'I don't suppose you heard. My brother died at Waterloo and the boy, Orlando, vanished. He may be dead too, by now, for all I know.'

'I lost a good friend, too,' he said quietly, 'and poor Hobhouse's brother, Ben, died at Quatre-Bras. I must be getting old, for I'm weary to death of politics and slaughter. Men die and nothing changes.' He shrugged. 'But we'll keep sad stories of the deaths of kings for another time and talk of love instead. Why do you move away?'

I smiled, awkward with embarrassment. He caught my hands in his, laughing at me. 'Oh come, Lucy, should *that* stop us? You look more ravishing than ever. I never saw eyes so pretty and wicked as yours when you want something. And I want you . . . ' He pushed down the ruffles of my dress until I lay half naked in his arms. Laughing softly in the sure knowledge of pleasure, we slid down in the soft cushions of the sofa, so closely wrapped that we were like one body.

Behind me, the door clicked.

'Well, well,' Ruthven said calmly. 'Don't let me disturb you. I always wondered how you managed with that leg of yours, Byron. Most intriguing.'

He walked away to the window, out of sight behind the

screen, and I looked up, terrified by Byron's expression. 'Please, it's not what you think,' I whispered as he pulled on his shirt. 'He was going to come later, about the letters.'

'What letters?' Byron said in a stifled voice.

'A small deceit, I'm afraid,' Ruthven said without turning round. 'Byron returned them to me and left publication to my discretion.' He came towards us, smiling. 'I *had* to see you, you understand.'

But Byron looked at me. 'How could you do it, Lucy?' he said and his voice was cold with disgust. 'Is that how you repay my love?'

'I didn't know. Believe me, I thought it was true,' I wept, clinging to him. 'Don't look at me like that. I – I can't bear it, not from you.'

He pushed away my hand and walked towards the door. 'Let me pass,' he said coolly as Ruthven put his hand on his shoulder. 'I don't wish to appear rude, but I have nothing to say to either of you.'

Ruthven looked at him with his wide, strange eyes, and I saw Byron falter. 'But you will stay for a just a little while,' he said softly and his fingers touched Byron's cheek. 'You know that you cannot separate yourself from me for much longer. You felt the fusing, you feel it now, in the darkness of your soul, drawing you . . .'

I ran across the room as I saw Byron sway before that hypnotic stare, seized a jug of lemon water from the side table and flung it in Ruthven's face. For a moment, he was off guard, and in that moment Byron had gone through the door. I fled after him. 'Byron, wait! Wait!'

'You'll never have him now, Lucy. He's mine, I tell you, mine!' Ruthven's hand held me back, a manacle, until the door in the downstairs hall had slammed, and I leaned against the stair rail, my throat aching with tears as he laughed and went back into the room.

*   *   *

Shortly after this episode Ruthven returned to his house in Albemarle Street. I had served my purpose. He knew now that his power over Byron could be re-established. I heard that he was often to be seen at Devonshire House, and that Annabella liked him well enough to be influenced by him. I was very uneasy, but there was nothing I could do. Byron showed no wish to see me and I was too afraid of meeting Ruthven to go to him.

August came, and with it a scorching heat, rising off the pavements in a quiver of mist, turning the parks into sepia deserts: when the wind blew, the yellow leaves crackled like parchment on the tired brown trees in Portman Square.

Society followed the Regent to Brighton to take the air, and London slept, exhausted. The gardens at Ranelagh and Vauxhall were taken over by London tradesmen: merchants' sons could safely ape the gentry in late summer when there was no competition to hand. The Academy was closed, the great houses shut up and the voices of the newspaper boys echoed plaintively down the deserted streets.

I was lying on the green silk day bed by the drawing-room window with the curtains drawn against the glare of the sun when I heard wheels rattling to a halt outside the house. Hastily pinning up my loose hair in front of the glass, I wondered who it could be. Byron had retired behind the Devonshire House shutters for more than a month, and Ruthven, if not a frequent visitor, was both punctilious and pre-announced. That victory, at least, I had won after he had come in to find me in Byron's arms. Neither of us would have wished to repeat the occasion.

'No, please,' I heard a girl's soft voice murmur outside the door. 'I'd prefer to announce myself.'

'Mary!' Delighted, I flung open the door. 'Come in! Oh, but you should have brought Shelley and Claire. I thought you had all forgotten me.'

She looked pale, but otherwise unchanged. The cobweb of golden-brown hair still floated around her pointed face; her sharp eyes looked past me to take in the grandeur of the room. 'Well, how elegant you've grown, Lucy,' she said, disapproval in her tone, envy in her eyes.

I laughed and put my arm through hers. 'No, I won't let you lecture me. You can talk about anything you like so long as you don't try to reform me. I'm not in the mood for it.'

She smiled and sat down beside me on the day bed in the window. 'No, I came for quite a different purpose,' she said in a quiet voice. 'You may not have heard. My little girl . . . died. She was only ten days old, Lucy. She died in my bed, beside me, while I slept.'

I took her hands in mine. 'Poor Mary. I didn't know. You should have written to me.'

'I almost did,' she said. 'I kept having dreams, you see, that the little girl was calling to me, begging to speak to me . . . I thought perhaps Ruthven would help.' I turned away my head. 'I know,' Mary said. 'I knew you would not like it. But now . . . ' She stared at me with huge, fever-bright eyes. 'Lucy, Claire has met a man who claims to be able to raise the dead to life, to call back spirits. I *must* find out. You will come?'

I looked down at the swell of my stomach. 'What else does he claim to be able to do?' I asked in a low voice.

'Oh, extraordinary things, miracles,' Mary said eagerly. 'He can see into the dark parts of our minds, he knows things that ordinary men do not. . . . What is it, Lucy? You look so strange.'

'Nothing,' I said. Oh, but if I could know that Byron was the father of my child, be put out of the misery of ignorance. . . . 'But are you sure it was not Ruthven that Claire met?' I asked, and as I spoke I was certain that it was so. But Mary shook her head.

'No. I forget the name, but I would have known if it had been his. It was very strange. He came up to her in the street, as if he knew her, told her things about us which nobody could know, and gave her an address at which he could be found when we wished to see him prove his claims.'

'What sort of things did he tell her?'

Mary looked round, then spoke in a low voice. 'About our political activities, a time when Shelley spoke in Ireland, of pamphlets he had printed . . . '

'Oh, it must be Ruthven!' I exclaimed. 'He works with Sidmouth and his spies. Hogg will bear me out on that – he knows.'

'I think you're mistaken. And if it is him, what of it? Let him prove his powers.'

'Well, how much do we pay to see his tricks?'

'We! So you will come!' She smiled. 'I'm glad of it. He asked for nothing: that is what convinces me that he must be genuine.'

As she spoke, the weather had changed swiftly and ominously. The sky was dark: a rushing wind tossed the trees as violently as if they were dry sticks in a breeze. 'It's too much of a coincidence,' I said, half to myself. 'I don't like it. No, you shall tell me about it later. I'll have nothing to do with it.'

Mary looked at me scornfully. 'Listen,' she said. 'I know your feelings about the aesthetic of terror, but it *is* fear which causes true inspiration. What strength does anybody gain from a quiet, untroubled life? If Shelley was not pursued by his fiends and visions, he could not write as he does. You can always choose to run away, to live a second-hand life, but what satisfaction is there in that? Better to be like Byron, or Ruthven for that matter, and seek notoriety, than achieve respectability through non-participation. Is the unthinking church-goer better than the questioning atheist, the man who accepts his role without trying to change it more worthwhile than one who fails in his reforms? I don't mean to lecture you, but you have no right to live vicariously. No one has.'

'Vicariously? Like Claire?' She had already stung me out of apathy.

'No. Claire is bolder,' Mary said cruelly. 'You have had the chance to make something remarkable of yourself, but you prefer to let experience pass through you without gaining from it. Had *I* been you, I would have learnt at your husband's feet, instead of shutting your eyes to his beliefs. When you were with us, you were never a part of us, you never wanted to be more than an observer. To my mind, there is not much difference between observers and spies.'

The windows creaked uneasily in the wind. I stared down into the grey square where rain spattered angrily across the pavements.

'Well,' she said in a gentler voice. 'I'm not sorry if you are angry. I would not have said it if I did not like you.'

I laughed painfully. 'Cruelty and kindness make bitter bed-mates. No, I'm not angry. There is a little truth in what you say. But Byron . . . '

'Your love hasn't been tested yet,' she said passionately. 'When you give up all this to follow him, let your name be splashed with mud, go through such misery that you feel your heart is being twisted out, then you can talk of love.'

'You judge me by your own experience,' I said.

'What else do I have?' Her skirts rustled as she came across the room and put her hands over mine. 'Come, Lucy, I'm giving you the chance to experience something extraordinary, which you may never see again. You'll regret it as soon as I have gone, and wish that you had been bolder.'

I kissed her gently on the lips. 'If you want me to come, I will. But no more lectures.'

*　　*　　*

The storm had driven the people off the streets. The carriage wheels echoed noisily as we passed through the deserted city. I was silent. The brief moment of bravado had faded away and I wished now that Mary had left me alone in the comfort of the drawing-room. She glanced at me once or twice, but seeing that I was not disposed to talk, she turned to stare out of the window. As we drew up outside a dripping portico of marble, I saw two figures huddled beside one of the pillars.

'Oh, she should not have brought him!' Mary murmured.

'If I am to face fear, why should he not do so?' I said savagely.

She stepped out of the carriage, ignoring me and so, I observed, leaving me to pay the driver, while she ran towards them. They moved forward and I saw Shelley's strange, pale face under the flickering lamplight as she took his arm. 'Percy, there was no need for you to come,' I heard her say in a strained voice, 'You are not well yet. Come, take the carriage.'

'No, you shan't coax me out of it,' he said stubbornly, then shrank back towards Claire. 'Who is it who stands behind you, shrouded in black? Show your face!' I pulled back the dark velvet hood with an uneasy memory of our last meeting. He looked, if anything, a little disappointed, but he held out his hand with a sweet smile. 'Now, of course, I remember – you were to introduce us to Byron. But why did you forget?'

I began to apologize, but he waved it aside. 'No matter: I had rather meet him as an equal when I have completed *Alastor*. I don't want the patronage of his success.'

'Never mind that,' Claire said impatiently, pushing him forward. 'We should go in. I'm tired of standing here in the rain.'

Conversation ceased as we followed the footman into the black marble hall. Slim columns rose to a high vaulted ceiling, from which hung two circles of grim spikes, each one staking a heavy altar candle: as the door closed behind us, they swayed, throwing a ghostly, uneven light into the shadowed depths. Beyond the rows of pillars, a broad passage extended into the distance. The footman turned and beckoned us to follow him down it. Tall censers were the only ornaments, exuding an aromatic and subtle vapour over our heads. Their fretted metal bowls threw distorted beams of light across the walls, but the effect was sinister rather than comforting. Claire's nervous laughter jarred on my nerves.

At the far end, we came to an ebony door, about nine foot high, composed of six polished panels which were richly edged in gold. Torches flared up on either side, carried in the arms of sturdy wooden blackamoors. We passed them and entered a low, windowless room, very dark, very quiet. I looked back as the door swung shut to trap us. In silence, we took our places on the small, gold-painted chairs facing the dais. Nobody spoke, but the seductive heavy odour of incense began to have its effect. A subtle easing of the senses, a gradual loss of any physical being, were all that I can remember. Behind us, I heard a soft creaking and whispering of late arrivals, but in the darkness I saw no faces. I longed for escape, but there was none. Shelley suddenly started from his seat and tried to drag Mary from hers. 'We must go!' I heard him whisper. 'Come!'

She shook her head. 'Not now. I've waited too long. Claire will go back with you.'

'Not I!' Claire laughed boldly, then looked startled at the sound. A soft murmur and rustle rose from behind us, as the crimson curtain drew back on the dais. It was empty, but for a high cloth-covered block and a metal connecting wheel.

He came on from the left, a tall, thin man in a black frock coat, grey trousers and a short hooded cloak, shadowing his face. 'Mr Shelley, if you would care to return to your seat,' he said in a gentle, melodious voice. Shelley started at hearing his name, but he resumed his place. A slight bow acknowledged the rest of his silent audience before he leant forward on the block to address us.

'Now, many of you are no doubt asking yourselves why you came here tonight,' he said softly. 'You have all seen the galvanic tricks by which a frog or rabbit may be made to jerk along a board in a brief imitation of life. My business, ladies and gentlemen, is with the grave. I have made my studies in many countries and in places that I dare to say few of you would dare to tread: in charnel houses where the bones are painted to look as if they still lived, in crypts where the undead are said to lie, in cemeteries where the wind moans as if the dead were begging to return. I have studied alongside professors in Paris, in Ingolstadt, and in Geneva, and I have conquered the secret that all men yearn to discover, the answer to life itself. I can look into your minds, my friends, and I can see things which you do not dare to look upon. Not yet,' he smiled, as the chairs creaked in anticipation. 'First, I will show you a little of my art. There are some among you who do not yet believe.' I stirred uneasily as the light caught the glittering eyes beneath the shadowing cowl. And yet the voice was not his. . . .

He walked across the stage to the wheel and gestured us to silence. I watched, fascinated, as he began to turn it. Faster and faster it revolved; now I saw the sparks flying out in the darkness. Beside me, Mary leant forward, her eyes on the cloth-covered block. No sound, but the whirr of the wheel. Now I could see what had been imperceptible, the wires linking the wheel to the obscured shape, as they turned from dull red to an electric white. The man breathed stertorously, rapidly, as if in a trance. . . . Did I dream or did I see the cloth move? My eyes stung as I concentrated on it. Beneath it, something was stirring. I could see the outline of a leg, an arm. I shuddered as the sound of someone sighing broke the silence. A sigh that was neither human nor animal, a grating, tearing sound, like dry stones rubbing against each other. Shelley's face was pale as a mask of death, his breath sobbing in dry gasps as the thing

184

turned over, showing us its form clearly under the thin material. I covered my face as the man spun the wheel for the last time and held his hand over the cloth.

'Well, my friends, will you look on it or not? The choice is yours.'

'No!' I murmured trembling, clammy as if fever gripped me.

'Show us!' they sighed, and the sound was like the wind dying. He laughed and plucked it back . . . and then I saw that the thing had a face, the face of a demon child with crazy eyes and I knew what it had once been. Far away, I heard my voice screaming, as it sat up on the block, nodding and chattering, stretching its skinny hands towards us.

The man's glittering eyes held me, all of us as he pushed the creature back and came forward down the dais. Mary grasped my hand. 'It *is* him!'

'Now look into yourselves,' he said, holding up his hands. 'The truth is there, if you choose to see it.' A rushing sound filled the room: I started. I could have sworn I had heard a child crying. Beside me, Mary stretched her arms out, smiling, then shuddered and drew back – as if she had touched death. She hid her face on Shelley's shoulder, but he seemed unconscious of her. His face was tranquil and his lips moved. 'Such a gentle sea,' he murmured, smiling, and Mary raised her head to stare at him, her face white with fear. I watched them covertly. I did not dare to look up. Claire's lips parted, soft and wet. 'When?' she said eagerly, and as she glanced furtively at me, I wondered what she had seen. Her face was ugly in its wanting; her breath came quickly, her eyes narrowed. 'All dead, all dead,' Mary murmured, and her hands fluttered like broken bones in her lap. Through a veil, I stared up at Ruthven's face, and in it was Byron's, as it had been in my dreams. They were his features, and yet they were not: the expression of evil, supreme, the evil of Milton's Lucifer, altered them so completely that I could have looked for a year and never seen the truth. Now, I knew it and I could not look away.

Behind me, a chair crashed over. I turned and Ruthven's laughter rang in my ears as I saw Byron, slumped sideways, his face buried in his arms. Half fainting, I pushed my way past Mary and Shelley, seized his arm and dragged him to his feet.

185

'Hurry, for God's sake!' I cried as he stared at me with dull eyes. 'Byron, come – before it's too late! Come!' He followed me slowly out of the room, but I saw him turn again towards the dais, as if to confirm the horror. Ruthven made no attempt to stop us. He had done all that he wished to do – for the present.

In the cool, rainwashed street we clung to each other, and I felt the violent tremors passing through his body. 'You saw it,' I whispered. 'You saw his face.'

Byron threw back his head and pulled his cloak tightly to him as he stared sombrely at the dim stars. 'We saw what he wanted us to see,' he said harshly. 'Stop trembling, girl. Don't you understand that our fear is his victory: it makes him what he thinks he is . . . God, what a man!' he exclaimed. 'One can't but admire such obsession. It's extraordinary. To go to such lengths, and for what?'

'He wants to destroy you,' I said slowly. 'That's what he means by possession.'

Byron smiled grimly. 'He's doing well. At the moment, I'm half inclined to destroy myself, if the world doesn't do it for me. Oh, if I could be rid of him . . . '

'Is it impossible?' I asked.

'You know him,' Byron said. 'And we saw his powers tonight. Ask yourself whether one can fight such a man.'

I held his hand to my cheek. 'You must fight him. You *must*. Shut him out of your house, don't let him see Annabella. Send back his letters. He'll have to give up in the end.'

Byron smiled. 'Do you think so? When will the child be born?'

'December,' I answered dully, seeing my words had had no effect. He took a ring off his little finger, a seal of a mermaid set in gold.

'There. If it's a boy, and it has my face, send me this. I'll let no son of mine stay in his hands.'

'And I – what of me?' I cried. He kissed me, stopping up my mouth.

II

The wind blew cold that autumn. Heavy with child, I offered no resistance to the doctor's urgings that I should avoid society and employ myself quietly at home. I knew that Ruthven was seeing Byron, but for the moment I was helpless to fight. When the child was born, Byron's son, would be time enough. For the present, I swallowed my pride and accepted what scraps of information Ruthven chose to drop before me. I was waiting for him now, sitting by the fire, my tapestry idle in my lap. Downstairs, the door slammed. I pressed my hands together, automatically patted my hair into place. He came in, soft-footed as a panther, his thin lips smiling, his pale cheeks flushed with colour by the bitter wind. He looked exultant.

'You look tired, my dear,' he said, touching my face with his long fingers.

I flinched away.

'How is he?'

He sat down opposite me and I fixed my eyes on his black leather boots rather than look at his face. 'I heard a very interesting remark today,' he said after a pause. 'Somebody described Byron as having become a split character.'

'How very astute of them.' I picked up my tapestry.

'How is he?' He sighed, mocking my voice. 'Rather yellow in complexion.'

'You know my meaning,' I said quietly. 'The violence, your side of his nature, if you choose to call it that.'

He nodded. 'It increases daily. He writes nothing, talks to himself, smashes furniture for no reason. He broke a china clock to pieces with a poker the other day.'

'I suppose that woman kept the fragments to show you.' I laughed scornfully. 'Don't you find it a little demeaning, gathering information at the housekeeper's door?'

'Yes, the signs of madness are there,' he said softly, as if he had not heard me. 'The other day, he had a forged letter delivered to Annabella, saying her mother was dying. Untrue, of course. But it increased her doubts.'

'He probably thought it would keep her out of his sight for a time – if *he* wrote it,' I said, looking at him sharply.

'You're very loyal,' Ruthven sneered. 'How unfortunate for Byron that he does not have you to reassure him. Poor fellow, you'd quite pity him if you saw how tortured he is by his own nature. He hasn't learnt to accept my power yet. Still, I can wait.'

'Do you suppose that your pretences deceive anyone?' I said, mildly. 'I've watched how you manipulate people. There's no sorcery in it.'

'Did I ever pretend to be a sorcerer?'

'You don't object if you are thought to have unnatural powers, do you? That's how you control them, through fear. That night when you played the scientist, magician, or whatever name you wish, it was by tricks that you made us see what we did. You created an atmosphere of expectancy, and our own fear did the rest.'

'Very facile,' Ruthven said gently, 'but how do you know that fear did not show you the truth? I suggest that it did. With insight and knowledge of men's secret demons, anything is possible.'

I stood up, pulling my silk shawl over the discreet, full-skirted dress. 'You know that when I have had the child, I shall fight to destroy any harm you have done. I'll never let you have him, never!'

Ruthven laughed. 'Quite the little Gothic heroine. Child-bearing may leave you a little weary, my dear. I doubt if you'll cause me much trouble.'

* * *

The child was born that winter, a month before the doctor's calculations.

The pains started late at night, and for two hours, nobody came. Ruthven was out, the servants did not answer and I lay alone in the carved black bed, tearing at the silk sheets as the pain gripped me. I tried to reach the door, but there was no strength left in me, and I lay, comfortless and exhausted on the floor until the doctors came. I was barely conscious when they lifted me up on to the bed. I remember sobbing and clinging to their arms, but they put down my hands and went away into the corner, murmuring together.

Dawn came, bringing no change. With every fresh bout of pain, I thought I'd die of agony: Ruthven came and stared down at me as I begged for laudanum to deaden it. A slight smile curled his lips, and he called the doctors to help me by laying on the leeches. They vigorously dissented, but he pressed them, and I shuddered as the clammy underbellies of the slugs fastened on to my arms and chest.

Dimly, far away in a grey, half-dead world, I heard the baby cry, a cry that rose to a piercing wail as they took it away to wash it and cross it. Weakly, I tried to raise my head. God, the weariness of making that one little movement!

'Let me see it,' I whispered. 'Please. I *have* to know.'

They brought it to me, wrapped in a shawl and I stared down at the tiny crumpled face, no bigger than a man's hand. Byron's nose, his mouth? His coloured hair, certainly. Wonderingly, I touched the soft little cheeks, the tiny curls of his ears. So beautiful. The lashless lids opened suddenly and two flat-blue eyes, old and dead as sea-rock, glittered up in an unfocused stare. His eyes. I drew up the shawl to cover them.

'What is it, my lady?' The doctors hurried towards me.

'Its eyes,' I muttered. 'Have you seen the eyes?'

They looked at each other across the bed, came to a silent understanding and smiled at me. 'Would you like your husband to come in now?' one asked, patting my shoulder paternally. 'There now, if we prop you against the pillows, perhaps you'd like to hold your little son.' I sat, unresisting, as they arranged their little spectacle, as they laid the baby in my arms and combed my hair over my shoulders. All that pain for this, for his child, I thought. It seemed so cruel, so unjust.

Ruthven came in slowly, dark rings under his eyes, his stock loosely knotted. 'Well?' he said in a low voice, without looking towards the bed.

The doctors bowed, jocularity passing into respect. 'A son, my lord.'

'A son!' he repeated. I turned my face away as he came towards me, his eyes fixed on the creature who lay at my breast.

* * *

Thank God, I was too weak to suckle the child. It was put out to nurse for three months. The doctors said that I must rest and see nobody: every day they came with their leeches and laudanum, to drain away my blood and dull the pain. I was sure Ruthven was behind it, that it was part of his plan to keep me in isolation, but I was too tired to fight. My depression was absolute: I had lost all pleasure in existence. My pretty dresses hung in the cupboards while I lay on the gold day bed in a pink and coffee lace morning gown, either staring at the wall or aimlessly turning the pages of a book, seeing no more than blurred lines of print. Newspapers and periodicals were prohibited, in case they disturbed me: visitors were turned away at the door. The outside world was dead, dead as the leaves that lay in decaying heaps behind the iron railings of the square.

The child was at Guildford, and Ruthven drove down every Thursday to visit it. Coincidence brought a carriage to 15 Portman Square one Thursday in January and Dickon, the new footman, knew no better than to send the visitor up.

It was Annabella.

Had she not been announced, I would not have known her. My memories were of an apple-cheeked little girl, neat and precise as a miniature governess, always ready with good advice when it was least required. Of that child, not even a vestige remained in the sunken-eyed woman who came through the door. She looked ten years older than Byron. I dropped my outstretched hands and stood staring, as she peered short-sightedly about the room, then, unwillingly, turned to me. 'Where's Lord Ruthven?'

I raised my eyebrows. 'You're very cool on greetings, cousin.'

'Where is he?' she repeated, as though she had not heard me. 'I came expressly to see him. He *must* be here.'

'You've chosen the wrong day to come. He's visiting the child in the country.'

'Will he be back soon, then?'

'I doubt it. Bella, I find this intrusion extraordinary. I want, no, I demand, an explanation.'

Surprise parted her lips. 'You don't know?'

'No,' I said. 'So perhaps you'd be good enough to enlighten me.'

'I had to do it,' she said desperately. 'It's for his own good. There was no choice, but I need Ruthven's advice on what to do next.'

'What did you have to do, Bella?' I asked, leaning back in the sofa.

'Leave Byron.' She shook her head at my expression. 'Oh, my dear, if you had seen him as we have, you would understand. Heaven knows how I would have stood these past three months without Ruthven and my dear Mrs Clermont to support me.' (I gave an involuntary smile at the unlikely thought of a friendship between Claire and Bella before realizing my mistake. Bella's Mrs Clermont was the housekeeper at Devonshire House.) I listened with mounting fury as she continued: 'Lucy, if you could see how Byron returns Ruthven's friendship, you would not doubt his state of mind. But your husband has endless patience, and he's been so clever in observing the symptoms.' She sat down opposite me, gazing earnestly into my face. 'I'll prove to you how perceptive he is. It had never occurred to me before, but the way B. looks up under his eyelids is just like the poor King since his mind went. Your husband remarked on it at once.'

'Oh, for God's sake, Bella!' I exclaimed. Of course I knew that look. Byron was famous for it. It was half of his attraction, and nothing to do with madness. How like a little harpy she looked, crouching forward in her chair, bright-eyed, fork-tongued! 'Yes, of course you were the one Ruthven chose to work through,' I said savagely. 'Your longing to crucify someone else for your own martyrdom is just what he'd need. The perfect tool. Now listen to me for a change. I want an answer, yours, not Ruthven's, mind. When did the violence start – in September?'

'It increased,' she said stiffly, 'but I really don't see . . . '

'And when did my husband find his way into Devonshire House? September. Put that together, my dear. I know how charming Ruthven can be when he wishes, but I promise you that no good will come to you from his friendship. Go home, Bella, and next time my husband comes calling, shut the door in his face.'

She stood up with a cold little smile. 'I'm afraid you don't understand. Ruthven and I act in Byron's best interest.'

'The worst act you ever did was to marry him. What have you ever done for him, except to slander his name? He was right to prefer Augusta to you: she did him no harm.'

'How can you say that when she allowed herself to be seduced into the most horrible relationship known to man?' She hissed at me. 'Do you suppose God will forgive them that? Would you have me tie myself to a damned soul?' She cast a pious look at the ceiling. 'Thanks be, Augusta has seen her errors and, it is to be devoutly hoped, will publicly renounce him.'

'Publicly!' I stared at her, horrified. 'What, will you destroy him completely!'

'He's destroying himself,' Bella said flatly. I could find no answer. She seemed to take heart from my silence, and went so far as to pat my hand with her cold little claw. 'Come, Lucy, Ruthven and I have his good at heart. I shall write to him cheerfully and persuade him to follow me to the country where he can be put under medical supervision. Ruthven knows of an excellent doctor.'

'And I thought you loved him!' I pressed my hands to my forehead, bewildered. 'I cannot understand your listening to Ruthven. If you knew the man as I do . . . '

She looked up at me sharply. 'You wrong your husband. Oh, I know his reputation. It's worse than Byron's, but the world has terribly misjudged him. He is a good man, truly good. Listen to me!' she cried as I turned away. 'If you knew how he has been hurt by your lack of understanding. How often he has

192

told me of it, how you deliberately blacken his name, how you refuse to see the child.'

'I see he's done his work well. There's nothing more I can say to you.' I cut across her. 'Perhaps you should leave.'

'No!' she said passionately. 'Not until you understand.'

'I do. Please go.' I put my hand on the bell.

'What would you have done?' Bella demanded. 'He made me listen while he told me of his affairs, he told me to leave without him, said he hated me, everything to do with marriage. . . . How could I stay – and let myself be damned with him?'

'You have damned him today,' I said. 'There will be no peace for him now, and it will be your doing, yours and Ruthven's. You should be glad to have done one effective act in your life.'

Her face froze. 'You never liked me, did you?' she said softly. 'I know why. Did you think I hadn't heard about your little provincial affair with him? You couldn't bear it when he married me instead.' She put her face very close to mine. 'Ruthven told me he married you after B. threw you over, to give your child a father. He told me, too, what Byron used to say about you, when he was sick to death of your empty-headed rubbish. Don't you want to know, cousin? He said you . . .'

'Spare me Ruthven's lies. I've heard enough of them,' I said wearily. 'If you'll forgive me, I'll go up to my room. You can wait here for him if you wish, but I think you'll find that his use for you has ended.'

She left without another word and I hurried upstairs to put on my prettiest clothes in which to visit Byron.

I had forgotten how to dress for a man, it was so long since I had made the effort. It was at least an hour before I was satisfied with the reflection in the cheval glass. In a dress of ruched organza, with a rose velvet sash tied round my waist, a pair of pink kid slippers on my feet, all that I lacked was the hat. Byron had always loved me in hats. I pinned on an extravagant nonsense of ostrich feathers and velvet and went down the staircase to order the carriage in as calm a voice as I could contrive.

The house was as dead as the grave when I arrived. The shutters were closed, and the hall echoed in its emptiness as I walked towards the stairs. In the side passage, a door opened quietly. A sharp face looked out. I recognized it with a sinking heart from the days when Mrs Clermont had been in the Milbankes' employment. For a moment, I wondered what to do. I had thought she would leave with her mistress. She was in Ruthven's pocket. If he should hear of my visit . . . It was too late now for flight. Taking a deep breath, I glided towards her with a charming smile. She looked up at me stonily as I offered her the tips of my rose-silk gloves. 'Mrs Clermont, surely you remember me?'

'Your voice is familiar,' she admitted reluctantly. 'I don't seem able to place the face.'

But wouldn't you like to! I thought as her darting eyes came up to meet mine. I laughed gently. 'Mrs Wraxall, from Kew. I came in a large dinner party some months ago. Lord Byron very kindly said that I might come one day to look at an Albanian costume he has. I wanted to borrow it for a masquing party. No, no, don't trouble to show me up. I know where it is. I may be a little time as I need to look very closely at the stitching.' I offered her another smile as she looked dubiously at me. 'Mrs Leigh is here, I suppose?'

'No, she's out in the Park with young Mr George. I'll tell her you called.'

'Please do. Adieu, dear Mrs Clermont. I mustn't keep you from the path of duty, must I?' My arch innocence seemed to convince her. She gave me a last hostile glance and then went back down the dark passage.

I rehearsed what I must say as I walked up the stairs, for I could afford no mistakes this time. It might be my last chance and I would have to tread very carefully. He might not know that Bella had gone for good, and there was the problem of Augusta. I found myself hoping that Bella would persuade her away and stopped, appalled at my own callousness. I was no better than Ruthven. I, too, was waiting for Byron's destruction before I tried to possess him wholly. 'No, he could never be happy with her: the world would not allow it,' I said aloud. 'I am his only chance.' But the thought soured in my mind. A second-hand life, Mary had said. 'You let experience pass through you.' I shook my head. Not this time.

I opened the drawing-room door. It was empty. The white shutters closed out the day, the fire lay ready but unlit, and a damp, deserted smell clouded the air. The silence was deafening as I walked over the Aubusson carpet, picking my way among the sheaves of scattered papers which looked as if they had been flung down in a sudden mood of despair. On impulse, I stooped to look at them. All bills, pressing behind their obsequious veneer. I knew how little those pleas to honoured lords from their obedient servants meant. It was Byron who was the slave, by the looks of things. I sighed. It had always been his trouble, the feeling that he must play the peer's role with all the accompanying show, and yet the only person of any merit who gave tuppence for the pretence was himself. Sometimes, I had secretly reproached him for being quite so conscious of his title. Even to me, he had often shown a hint, the slightest of shadows, of patronage, although I'd back the Emertons against the Byrons any day. My eyes slitted as I noticed an envelope, half hidden under a cushion. It was addressed to Byron in Ruthven's hand. I turned it over and pulled out the single sheet of paper. It bore two lines:

'*To Lord Byron, the sum of ten thousand pounds,*
    Guaranteed by Lord Ruthven.'

I pushed it back with a shaking hand. Here was the solution: Its simplicity staggered me. It had made no sense that he would weakly allow Bella to bring Ruthven into his house. I had been unable to understand it. This was the true explanation, and one, I reflected, which made my position extremely difficult. How on earth could I persuade him to leave with me when he was so indebted to Ruthven? But why had I not thought of it before? It was what he had always done, with Harry and the rest of them. There was a stirring in my mind, the rising of a distant memory, sitting in this very room, listening to Byron's version of Ruthven's story. '*Digby's generosity was as famous as it was notorious. All who benefited from it met with disaster.*' Destruction, disaster, always the same morbid thoughts, all coming to the one conclusion.

There were voices on the stairs, murmuring together. Panic-stricken, I looked around for somewhere to conceal myself. If Augusta and Byron's cousin found me here, prying in his papers, what possible explanation could I give?

Trembling, I pulled the red curtains shut in front of me and leaned back against the shutters, holding my breath. The door opened.

'She's in here,' Mrs Clermont said. 'I knew she was up to no good when I saw her face. Mrs Wraxall, indeed! It was lucky you came when you did.'

'Yes, indeed.'

I pressed my hands together in an agony of fear. What evil stroke of fate had brought him here! I heard the deadening of his feet as he walked forward on to the carpet. I knew that he was examining every corner of the room. The horror was to stand in the shadows, unseeing, not knowing whether I was unseen. I heard his soft laughter, very close to me.

'You can go now, Mrs Clermont. Thank you for your assistance.'

I looked down and saw that the curtain had moved, just a fraction, revealing the point of my left slipper. I held my breath, waiting for him to move away before I drew it out of sight. I could hear nothing now, except the drumming of my heart.

'Come, my dear,' he said silkily. 'I'm offering you the chance to leave in a quiet and dignified manner. The alternative will be unpleasant for us both, I assure you.'

I did not move an inch.

'Very well, I'll give you one minute to consider it.' He counted out the seconds in a slow, deliberate voice. ' . . . fifty-nine . . . sixty.' A long pause. 'You leave me no choice.'

I felt as if I had been stripped naked as he tore the curtain back to discover me, cowering back against the shutter. He looked at me dispassionately. 'I warned you not to interfere,' he said. 'It was extremely ill-advised of you to come here. I shall have to be more forceful in future.'

I touched my lips with my dry tongue.

'Nothing physical,' he said coldly. 'I'm not quite so boorish

196

as to assert my power through your bed. No, my method is more permanent in its effect.'

I stared at him, terrified, not understanding.

'Come!' he said, and grasped my arm. I twisted away and ran across the room, slamming the door behind me.

'Byron! Byron!' Tears poured down my face as I fled from door to door – and found every room empty. Ruthven's feet echoed on the stairs behind me.

'There's nowhere to run to, Lucy,' he said softly as I reached the last flight of the staircase. 'You've lost.'

At the end of the dark passage facing me, a door opened, throwing a sharp light across the faded carpet. Byron came through it, but he stood still, making no move towards me. His face was that of a man haunted by his own dreams: it stopped me dead in my tracks.

'Go home, Lucy,' he said harshly. 'This is no place for you.' He turned back, shutting the door behind him. I started down the passage, but Ruthven pulled me back.

'You heard him. Now come, before I get impatient.'

His iron hand forced my unwilling feet down the stairs, each step taking me further away from Byron. We crossed the empty marble hall, but as we reached the door, it opened from the outside. I caught a glimpse of a soft, pretty face, an untidy bundle of hair, then Ruthven pulled me viciously towards the street. It was the first time I had seen Augusta Leigh.

*　　*　　*

I sat at my desk, keeping a watchful eye on the door. He had told me to come down to the drawing-room at eleven. I glanced at the clock. Ten to the hour, and I had not finished it yet. I picked up the pen and started to write again.

I was sending a letter to Annabella, a full account of everything that I knew of Lord Ruthven. She *must* be made to see the danger. If the Milbankes could pay Byron's debt to Ruthven, he would be free. Whether she would believe it or not, I did not know. Seeing it in writing, I was conscious of the absurdity of my accusations. I read it through anxiously, unable myself to believe that he was capable of so many crimes. Murdering for blood-lust, corrupting boys, possessing spirits, assisting spies: I tore it up in despair. It would do no good. He'd deny it with a smile, as he always did when it suited him to play the victim, and she'd believe him. Eleven o'clock. . . . I slowly crossed the room to the door.

Ruthven was standing in the drawing-room with a small, sallow-faced man, dark haired, probably younger than he looked. I gave him a nod and a careless smile. I thought I was past fear now.

'This is Doctor Millingen,' Ruthven said. 'He has my orders to care for you here, and he answers only to me. Do you understand?'

I nodded, unimpressed. Doctors were always easy to manage. You only had to flutter your eyelashes, promise a little more than you gave. Millingen looked perfectly corruptible.

'His orders,' Ruthven said in a calm, distant voice, 'are to drain you of precisely the amount of blood each day which will ensure that your movement is – restrained.'

I smiled. 'I have a strong will, Doctor, I warn you.'

He made me a little bow, very precise, very correct. 'The will is subordinate to the body in the last resort, my lady, but I shall watch your progress with the greatest interest.'

'Thank you,' I said dryly. 'Lacking the concern of my husband, I must be satisfied with that of my doctor, I suppose. Is that all?'

Millingen turned to Ruthven with a puzzled smile. 'But your wife seems in excellent health, my lord. Are you sure that this is necessary?'

'Your fee will answer your questions, my dear sir,' Ruthven mocked him. He glanced at his watch, then turned to me. 'I have an appointment with our mutual friend. I'll remember to send him your regards, my dear.'

'How long am I to be kept under this treatment?'

He smiled. 'As long as I wish. Doctor Millingen will reassure you if you fear for your health, and I shall visit you daily.'

'Now my cup of happiness is overflowing. How could I have rested happy without the comfort of your presence!' I said viciously.

Ruthven patted the doctor's shoulder. 'Isn't she delightful? I'm sure you'll enjoy your work.'

'Oh yes, certainly, certainly!' the doctor said with a bewildered smile. I almost laughed at his perplexity.

'Excellent!' Ruthven drawled. He gave me the honour of a languid bow, threw his coat over his shoulder and sauntered out of the room.

Turning to the doctor, I caught him with a look of wistful admiration on his face, but I was in no doubt as to who had put it there.

'Sit down, my dear sir,' I said softly, sinking back gracefully on the sofa and allowing my skirt to rise just above my ankles. 'I see no reason why we should not dispense with formality now.'

'As you wish, my lady.' He took the stiff, high-backed chair in the corner by the curtains, and looked down at his knees. I fanned myself gently, watching him.

'How solemn you look, Doctor Milligan.'

'Millingen,' he corrected me unsmilingly.

'Millingen. Of course! How could I forget! Well, my dear sir, I am sure we can come to some arrangement.'

'I'm afraid I don't follow you,' he said stonily. 'The arrangements have already been made.'

'So they have, but surely they can be amended.' I raised my skirt an inch higher.

'I don't think you quite understand,' he said. 'I am here on Lord Ruthven's instructions, and I shall obey them. Implicitly.'

'I see. He must be paying you well?'

'Lord Ruthven is known for his generosity. I don't wish to betray his trust in me.'

'How very honourable of you.' I was more afraid than I cared to show. There was a cold bloodlessness about the man which reminded me of his master. 'Do you enjoy your work, Doctor Millingen?' I asked suddenly.

He glanced at his watch. 'It's very specialized. Now, Lady Ruthven, if you would be kind enough to lead me to your room, I can make my examination.'

'Rather an unnecessary formality,' I said dryly. 'As you were kind enough to observe, I am in excellent health.'

'Please don't make my job difficult,' he said, and there was a note of menace in his voice. 'The sooner I can begin, the easier it will be for all of us.'

'I'll soon be too weak to fight. Is that what you mean?'

Without giving me an answer, he opened the door and stood aside to let me pass. I went up the stairs in chilly silence, and into my room. He closed the door behind him, hesitated, and then locked it, putting the key in his pocket.

'Perhaps you'd like to examine my bag to see if I've concealed a pistol in it,' I said sweetly. He took it from my hands and peered inside, then shook the contents out on to the floor. A few coins, a comb and a rouge pot rolled out.

'If you would lie down, my lady, and unbutton your cuffs. Thank you.'

I lay still, watching as he first listened to my wrist pulse, then bent my arm and stared at it reflectively. 'Good sized veins, Doctor, or are you afraid the leeches will go hungry?' I asked with a last effort at bravado.

'Oh, we won't be using leeches,' he said, his back towards me. 'This is my little weapon.' He laughed as I looked away from the thick, blunt-ended needle. 'He's a hungry little fellow, but you'll soon grow quite fond of him. He can give back as much as he takes, this little one.'

'What do you mean?' I said slowly as he came towards me.

'That's the progressive element in my work,' he said, staring down at me. 'The part that makes it all worthwhile. Feeding in a combination of drugs to substitute for the blood. It's difficult, of course. One never knows what the measure of success will be, but the results are always fascinating.'

I felt the drops of sweat forming on my forehead. 'And if I die?'

'Oh, you won't *die*,' he said. 'Shall I bandage your eyes, my lady? You may find the sight a little disturbing the first time.'

'How thoughtful of you to consider my feelings. No. I can close them myself if I wish.'

I shut them involuntarily as he plunged the needle down.

When Millingen came again, he brought Ruthven with him. I lay still, inert, as he looked down at me. His face confused me as I tried to concentrate on it, then it swam away into the blackness where my mind wandered aimlessly. I could not hold on to my thoughts. They passed through the darkness, drifting elusive across my consciousness, gone before I could catch them. I was not unhappy nor was I in pain. Sensations remained, or illusions of them. I saw, but not as I had seen. Shapes were intense, alive. My hand would shrink into nothing, then suddenly expand to become a giant's paw as I moved it on the coverlet, while the curved pilasters at the end of the bed undulated gently towards me.

'What did you give her?' Ruthven asked curiously.

'Laudanum and a little of the Turkish essence. Yes, it seems a good combination. If you would stand to one side, my lord.'

Ruthven held up his hand. 'I'll give her my news first.'

'I doubt if she'll understand,' Millingen answered in a low voice.

He laughed gently. 'Then you must lessen your doses.'

I tried to ask him to tell me about Byron, but my mouth would not make words. I lay still, staring at Ruthven as the needle sank into my flesh. It pained me no longer: there was something near to sensual pleasure in the feeling. I looked down drowsily. So much blood. It flowed out steadily into the cup which Millingen held above the sheet, a thick, red stream.

'You see how docile she is now,' the doctor said cheerfully. 'They grow to enjoy it after a time.'

'I know,' Ruthven murmured. 'No, don't take it away. I brought a bottle with me for the purpose.'

I looked vaguely at him as he carefully emptied the cup with steady hands.

'What use will you make of it, my lord?' the doctor asked timidly.

Ruthven laughed. 'Oh, experiments of one sort or another. I play with science on an amateur's scale. When do you come again, by the way? I'll make a note to be at home that day.'

I closed my eyes as they walked away, arm in arm.

No, my chief pain came not from the needle but from Ruthven. He came smiling, venom-tongued, to drop his poison in my ears, and helpless, I could only listen. I heard it all, how Bella, in the hands of her advisers and her family, was being forced to keep her word, how Augusta's rambling bulletins from Devonshire House were being stored by the Milbankes for use against him, how Mrs Clermont was accelerating the process with her lies and misrepresentations. He told me that Byron's name was openly linked with sodomy and incest, that it was the talk of London, that he was cut dead in the House, loathed in the streets for daring to praise the Tricolour after Waterloo, and that he even passed as the devil in some circles.

Last and most painful of all was the news he brought me late in March, that Byron was finding solace in the arms of Claire Clairmont. Naturally, he did not tell me all the story. He wanted to cause me pain.

Later, I learned the truth, that Byron had flatly rejected Claire's first overtures. Only by extreme persistence and by nagging Shelley into writing a highly complimentary analysis of her character to show to Byron, had she managed to arouse his fleeting interest.

But then, I only knew that Byron had betrayed me. That he had rejected me at our last meeting I could understand, but to find consolation in her arms. I brooded on it: Claire and Byron. *Claire* and Byron . . .

'I'm sorry it distresses you so much,' Ruthven said, selecting one of the grapes from the silver basket by my bed. 'Of course, it could be an innocent friendship. I know Byron wanted to give six hundred pounds to old Godwin. Perhaps he's sending it through her. You don't think so?' He laughed. 'Then it would seem he's forgotten you, my poor Lucy. Out of sight . . .' His hands played with the tassels of the bed canopy. 'Don't you sometimes wonder if he continued his affair with you in order to provoke me into returning to my . . . pursuit? Think on it. Who's that?' He turned quickly, but it was only a nervous maid bringing the morning papers. He took them from her and leafed rapidly through the pages, smiling to himself. 'Well, well, a wholesale attack. I wonder if he's seen them? I think I'll take the carriage round to Piccadilly.' He looked down at me. 'You do understand how near he is to destruction, don't you? The options are closing and soon, very soon . . .'

'For what purpose?' I asked. 'Why is it that you want to destroy him?'

'To save myself, Lucy,' he said. I shook my head, bewildered. 'I don't understand.'

'I hope you never will,' he said. My perplexity must have amused him, for I heard him laughing as he went down the stairs. To save himself . . . I turned the words over and over in my mind. From what? From death? From death! Was that the answer?

Dr Millingen's drugs were a welcome relief from the ability to think.

*   *   *

A week passed.

I lay patiently waiting for the doctor's usual morning visit to return me to sleep. It was past the hour, and he was always punctual to the minute. Ruthven entered the room alone.

'How do you feel?' he inquired, drawing back the curtains to let the April sun slip in.

'Tired,' I murmured. 'Always tired.'

'Too tired to go to Lady Jersey's tomorrow?'

'After being bled today?' I laughed weakly. 'You must be insane.'

'Millingen's leaving you alone, today. I want you to be present at the party, in fact, I insist upon it. If you think it would be too exhausting, I'm sure our little doctor can supply a restorative.'

'No. I don't want one.'

'You don't seem to appreciate his efforts,' Ruthven said lightly. 'Well, no matter. Look – I have a new dress for you. I'll hang it here where you can look at it. Perhaps it'll tempt you out of bed faster.'

I looked at him in astonishment. His voice was sweeter than treacle – and the dress was ravishing, a concoction of ruffled lace that frothed in his hands like whipped cream.

'We might lunch together, downstairs,' he said. 'Then, when the wine's put some colour in your face, I'll have the carriage brought round and we'll take a spin in the Park. No arguments,

Lucy. I want you there tomorrow.' He pinched my cheek affectionately and went out down the stairs, whistling under his breath.

'Well, I'll be damned!' I said, staring after him. 'He means it.'

*   *   *

We arrived early at Lady Jersey's, but a surprisingly large number of carriages had already drawn up. The curtains and shutters were closed, but through the open door I saw the guests moving slowly up the curved staircase in a flood of yellow light. Fanning out the folds of my dress, I went up the stone steps. Ruthven was conspicuous at my side in a coat of black brocade ornamented with knots of roped gold. He had had it copied from the costume worn by Cesare Borgia at his murdered brother's funeral. Later, I realized what lay behind Ruthven's choice.

Lady Jersey was in the hall, fluttering from one group to another like a little painted bird, the gold of her clinging, high-waisted dress rivalling the cluster of carefully-arranged curls at the nape of her neck. Her helpless appearance was all artifice: she was extremely ambitious, a demanding friend and a relentless enemy. She turned from a bleating flock of youths as we came in and laid her hand on Ruthven's arm.

'So you brought your wife out of Purdah at last. Don't take her away again.' She smiled kindly at me. 'She's too enchanting to hide away. A credit to your taste, my dear.'

Ruthven bowed. 'You command me, Madam. What can I do but rejoice in obeying?'

She laughed and tapped his arm. She must have been irresistible in the days when she had ruled the Regent's heart. 'And you promise to behave this evening? I've implored everyone, and I know you would not wish to wound me.'

'I shall be myself,' Ruthven smiled.

'That's all the promise you'll give me?' She sighed prettily, and turned to me. 'See that he keeps it, my dear. I want this party to show Byron that he has some true friends left. It's the least I can do.'

204

We were pushed forward by a wave of new arrivals and I found myself mounting the stairs beside Ruthven. 'You should have told me,' I muttered. 'Why did you come? Why make me your witness?'

'You jump to conclusions too quickly,' he said. 'Are we not his friends? *I* came to show myself as one.'

Scorning to answer, I passed ahead of him into the long, brilliantly lit room. They were all there, waiting, their chatter breaking off as they turned to the door at every new entry. We joined the central cluster under the huge chandelier, dragging down on its heavy chain like an overblown crystal wedding cake. The noise made me dizzy: I had grown used to the silence of my room. I took a glass from a passing tray and drained it rapidly.

'Nervous?' asked Ruthven, solicitous.

'Not at all,' I smiled. 'I'm flattered by your attention, but shouldn't we talk to someone else? Social conversation is impossible within a marriage: it lacks the spice of novelty.'

'In a marriage of love, yes,' Ruthven said cuttingly.

I found myself turning to look at the door as anxiously as the rest of them. Vainly, I hoped he would not come, and cursed the sense of melodrama which would bring him. At least, Caro Lamb was not here to see. Rejected, she was the most remorseless of them all in hounding him down, spreading the rumours as fast as she denied them with faint words.

'I'm going,' I said suddenly. 'I won't be a party to this.'

'Too late,' Ruthven murmured as silence fell. 'To leave now would be more insulting than to stay.'

I looked up as Lady Jersey moved forward. Byron stood in the door, Augusta by his side, a tremulous smile on her face. She was far gone in pregnancy and she leant heavily on his arm as they came down the steps. The crowd moved back, a silent unit of complicity.

'My dears, I speak for us all when I say how delighted I am that you came,' Lady Jersey said in a clear, ringing voice. 'You are among friends here.'

Byron looked over her shoulder with a cynical smile at the circle of faces. I saw Augusta's expression suddenly change to a look of frozen terror as she saw Ruthven, knew that Byron was conscious of her fear by the set of his mouth. They came towards us.

'Well, my *good* friends,' he said mockingly. 'Here are the devil and his wife come to join you. Isn't that what you call us now?'

'Oh, my dear!' Lady Jersey hurried to his side. 'You must not heed what they say in the streets. Come.' She took his arm, but he withdrew it gently and walked to one side of the room where he stood surveying us, his arms folded. I moved forward to join him.

'Not yet,' Ruthven said, stepping in front of me. 'We will observe.'

Augusta left. Not one person had addressed a word to her, except her hostess. She had approached one or two women she knew well, greeted them with a timid smile. They turned their backs, brutal in their virtue. I did not hate her now, as I had once. I would have spoken to her, had Ruthven let me. Weak and silly she might be, but who else had dared to stand beside him through all the scandal? If they had – I forced myself to think of it – lain together, was it such a crime? As a child, I had been Harry's follower and slave. Curious innocence had been explored and satisfied, then laid to rest at the back of our minds by an unspoken understanding. If only Byron had been more circumspect. Useless to lament it: secrecy was as alien to him as solitude.

Helpless, I watched. Their cruelty was masterly in its refinement, the skirts twitched aside, the raised fans, the excluding backs and the conspiracy of silence. I remembered how they had fawned and crawled for *Childe Harold*, and wondered at the nature of envy, the mediocrity which will feed on success, drag it down and humiliate it before it can be tolerated.

As they gathered at the far end of the room, Byron's mask of indifference slipped, unobserved. Pain made his face old. Now at last Ruthven moved forward, walking with slow, deliberate steps across the room until they faced each other. I was conscious of the guests as the conversations drifted into a murmur, then silence. They were watching, every one of them, waiting.

'Look at me,' Ruthven said quietly as Byron took a step towards the door. He stopped, turned.

'We both knew it would come to this in the end,' Ruthven

murmured. 'You won't fight me now. There is nowhere else to go.' He laughed softly. 'You should have listened. It is easier to accept when you understand.'

'I understand,' Byron said, his voice very low.

'Yes, now. You know. Come, we shall go together, you and I. Give me your hand.'

Byron's eyes never left Ruthven's face. Slowly, he unfolded his arms, placed his left hand over his right with a gentle, sliding motion. Ruthven smiled and held out his arm, the first movement he had made. It broke the spell which held us all. With a sudden, violent movement Byron threw up his hand and flung it forward. A diamond ring rolled across the floor and lay in front of me. Ruthven raised his hand and touched his cheek. The ring had bitten deep into the flesh, leaving a long thin line of red from the cheekbone to the left nostril. The blood trickled down the cut and ran past his mouth. His tongue curled out to draw it in with a languid, repetitive movement, and his lips smiled. Byron saw me stoop to pick up the ring, then he turned on his heel and walked out of the room.

Nobody laughed. Nobody moved. Nobody spoke. And in the middle of the room under the swaying chandelier, Ruthven stood alone, his tongue red with blood as he licked his pale skin.

*   *   *

Byron left England two weeks later. He sent me a letter from abroad, explaining that he had been forced to keep his departure an absolute secret, although he had been planning it since March. I understood. It was the only alternative. There was no safety for him in England while Ruthven lived.

Slowly, dry-eyed, I folded the pages over, wondering that he had not heard of the strange event which filled the papers the day after he had gone. It was curious that he made no mention of it.

Ruthven, and the child, had vanished, silently and as inexplicably as ghosts. Nothing had been taken, everything was in order. In his study, all his papers, accounts, letters, bills, lay neatly arranged and indexed. In his bedroom, his evening clothes were laid out in preparation. All the evidence pointed to a prepared departure.

Then a body was found, drowned, in the Thames. Sick with dread, I went to the mortuary to identify it. The hands had been gnawed to the bones by fish, but the rings remained, and they were his. Yet the face, horribly changed though it had been by water, bore no resemblance to Ruthven's. I hesitated for a long time before putting my signature to the certificate which would free me of him.

12

London is an agreeable city in which to be widowed, and rich.
I emerged from the initial shock and the family lawyers' offices
in Lincoln's Inn, as a woman of property and an object of covert
interest in society. Ruthven and Byron grew in disrepute as in
retrospect: those who had known them were much in demand.
Caroline Lamb provoked a new flood of speculation by saying
the hero of her wretched *Glenarvon* was Ruthven, while giving
him the character of Byron. The unsubtle intimation did not
hold back the sales of her book. For myself, I had no wish to
write of it, although I knew the story far better than she. But
in conversation, I was ready to take up the cudgels on Byron's
behalf. It pleased me to think that I was thwarting Bella's
efforts to blacken his name. I tried to enlist Augusta's help, but
it was too late. Bella had already ensnared her, and convinced
her of her guilt.

At first, I had intended to follow Byron to Geneva, but then
I heard that Claire was going there with the Shelleys and
revised my plans. It was bitter to know that Claire was bearing
him the child that I had longed to have: all Byron's letters of
assurance that he found her a damned bore and longed to be
rid of her could not convince me. He had not asked me to join
him.

I took lovers, naturally. Women will always use them, in
order to forget love by acting it. There was no pleasure in those
affairs, only comparisons and regrets. They understood my
reasons, and why it was that I sometimes turned away from
them in the bed and lay facing the pencil drawing I had made
of him, which stood on the bedside table. For them, it was a sop
to their virility that they could be said to have replaced Byron,

something to be boasted about in the clubs and coffee houses. I don't know quite what made me decide to visit Newstead again before it was sold. A sudden mood of nostalgia, a wish to escape from the *ennui* which is a way of life in London, a desire to evoke the past. . . . It's hard to say which motivated me.

It was late in the afternoon when I arrived, and bitterly cold. I stood for a moment looking up at the silent house. With the shutters closed and no sun to warm the grey walls, it had the forlorn appearance of a magnificent and forgotten tomb, such as one comes across occasionally in a little country churchyard, erected in love, decaying in indifference. I knocked on the door, but nobody answered. Behind me, the wind rattled in the dead leaves. Shivering, I turned away and walked down to the lake, watching the black ripples as they lapped through the damp yellow rushes. The sky was very dark, the silence heavy. I had wanted to remember Byron, I was aware of Ruthven. I turned round with fearful eyes.

As I stared across the water, I saw a figure on the opposite bank, dressed in black, looking directly at me. There was something sinister in its stillness, almost unreal. Afraid, I hurried back towards the carriage, stumbling on the rough grass. Across the lake, the figure kept pace with me. It crossed the bridge as I reached the entry to the drive. There were barely fifty yards between us. My breath came faster. I bent my head in order not to see it, and half ran towards the house, meaning to come to the carriage from the opposite side without crossing its path. A rustling of skirts on the gravel stopped me in my tracks. I scarcely know what I had expected, but not that. Slowly, I looked round and saw Augusta Leigh. She extended her hand without speaking or smiling. I hesitated a fraction too long before taking it. Knowing she had as good a cause as I to come back, I resented her presence as an intrusion.

'What brings you here?' I asked. 'Memories?'

'Yes,' she said. 'I . . . I was very happy here.'

'You carved your name with his on the tree. I often used to pass it and think of you.'

'I am laying ghosts, not recalling them,' Augusta said slowly. She looked troubled and unhappy, very pale in her black dress.

'Does Annabella know you came here?'

She looked up under her eyelashes, Byron's manner. 'You wouldn't tell her? I don't think she would understand.'

'I'm sure she wouldn't,' I said dryly. 'She's not an understanding woman.'

'She's very good,' Augusta said.

'In conventional terms.'

'In all terms.'

I shrugged. 'Have you heard from him since he went to Venice?'

She nodded. 'He wanted me to go to him. . . . I didn't answer. Bella says that silence will be more effective.'

'In doing what? Making him more unhappy, making him more vulnerable to Ruthven . . .'

'Stop it! Ruthven is dead,' Augusta said in a low voice. 'That danger is over, thank God.'

'How can you be so sure? Whose word do you have?'

She looked at me. 'Why, yours! You saw the body. You identified it.'

'I identified *a* body,' I said. 'As he knew I would.'

And again I felt the eerie sensation of a third presence. I turned at the same moment as Augusta, staring fearfully towards the lake. 'It's only the wind,' I said.

Augusta clasped her hands in her agitation. 'But why did you not speak of it at the time? You should have disclaimed it. How could you do it, Lucy, knowing his nature, his obsession . . . ?'

I shook my head. 'You would have done the same. The money, the London house, everything, passed to me on his death, you see. If I denied the body, I was left with nothing.'

Augusta's eyes filled with tears. 'And I didn't understand, I didn't answer him. I thought he spoke of her.'

'Tell me,' I said urgently. 'What did he say?'

'The poem he was writing in Geneva,' she faltered. '*Manfred*. He sent me a single stanza in an uncovered letter. It must have been the reason.'

'Can you remember it?'

'I wish I could not.' She looked away from me as she spoke the lines in a flat voice which was more frightening to me than all the expression an actor could have given them:

Though thou seest me not pass by,
Thou shalt feel me with thine eye
As a thing that, though unseen,
Must be near thee, and hath been;
And when in that secret dread
Thou hast turn'd around thy head,
Thou shalt marvel I am not
As thy shadow on the spot,
And the power which thou dost feel
Shall be what thou must conceal.

And in the silence which followed, I thought I heard someone laughing softly.

* * *

If I had wanted further confirmation of my fears, I was given it in 1818, when Mary Shelley's *Frankenstein* took London by storm. Everybody had a different theory to offer. Some thought Shelley was Frankenstein, others were convinced it was a portrait of Byron. For me, there was only one conclusion – the one I had struggled not to draw from my meeting with Augusta at Newstead.

It was dark when I laid down the book. My hands were like ice. The fire hissed and spat like a basket of snakes, the shadows of the flames crept up the walls, threatening spectres. I drew the curtains, lit the candles, closed the doors, but the fear was in my mind, not the room. I could not drive it out. I was alone, and never had I longed so much for company. Each sound made me start. Each spasm of silence was intolerable. The verse that Byron had sent to his sister jingled, persistent, deadly, in my mind. '*And when in that secret dread, Thou hast turn'd around thy head* . . .' I stared into the darkness, trembling.

If I could but find another explanation, but there was none. Mary had seen at Geneva the truth which I had always known, never dared to admit, that the pursuer and the pursued can never escape from each other, not in this world. But only she could tell me whether Ruthven lived, if he preyed on Byron still, or if some twist of circumstance at Lake Geneva had evoked the ghosts of the past . . . I could not know. I did not dare to think.

I sought company during the following month with an almost frenzied determination. No invitation, however dubious, was rejected. When Lord Alvanley asked me to the opera with him, I put aside my dislike of the man and wrote a cool note of acceptance. Any company was better than my own terror-haunted thoughts.

Time and port had not improved Lord Alvanley since our first meeting at Newstead. Watching him as he leant against the marble fireplace in my drawing-room, I saw in his face a resemblance to the portraits of the corrupt princes of Renaissance times. His eyes were small and cruel, his pursed lips buried in a mass of heavy, porous skin which age and ease had pulled down into loose pouches. He carried, however, an arrogant conviction of his own charm, which rendered him impervious to insults. After his allusions to our first meeting had been met with silence and a frozen smile, he entertained me with a string of anecdotes in which he featured as a man of remarkable wit and as a veritable Sampson of sexual prowess. Happily, I lacked the opportunity to test the truth of either claim. In fact, by the time we reached the opera-house, I was heartily sick of Lord Alvanley and ready to seek the first convenient excuse to leave.

The curtain had gone up when we arrived, but only just, for the audience were still murmuring and leaning back from talking to their neighbours. I glanced up at the boxes to see who to avoid and who to visit, and there, looking earnestly towards the stage with her white arms resting on the balustrade, was Mary Shelley. I was astonished. They were so retiring by nature, yet there she sat in the very best box, in a low cut dress of crimson velvet with her soft hair bound up in two curling shells over her ears, and her face flushed with the consciousness that she was being pointed out as Mrs Shelley, the authoress. Shelley stood behind her chair, a lambent spectre in the gloom, a most elegant spectre in a dark blue coat with round gold buttons marching down the front in double file, cream trousers of excellent cut and a neat white stock held in place by a diamond pin. I could only conclude that Byron had given him some lessons in dressing at Geneva, or a new valet.

I turned back towards the stage.

'Charming, isn't it,' Alvanley remarked as the curtain fell on the first act. 'And what a pretty voice! Angelic! If only all operas were by Mozart, I'd go every night.'

'It would be like eating sugar bonbons for breakfast every day, a surfeit of sweetness,' I said, smiling. 'Will you come with me to see the Shelleys in their box?'

'The Shelleys!' Alvanley's voice made our neighbours turn round nervously. 'Good God, no! Damned Radical!'

'He is a poet, too, in case you'd forgotten,' I said.

'That's worse,' Alvanley said indignantly. 'I'd tolerate the *Examiner* bunch better, if they weren't so damned vulgar. Hunt and Cobbett! Who are they to have views, I ask you?'

'Hush. I'll go alone,' I said, seeing the apoplectic purple mounting in his cheeks. He leant across the seat, barring my way.

'Please don't stop me,' I said quietly.

He leant back. 'You haven't thought how embarrassing it will be for me if my name's linked with them. I shall have to explain it in the House, and it'll be damned difficult. Had that occurred to you?'

'You'll manage,' I said, edging past him into the aisle.

I hurried through the crowd of people at the back of the theatre and down the warm dark passage leading to the boxes. I opened the door.

'Mary? Shelley?'

Their fair heads were close together, intimate, excluding, and Shelley's eyes were politely blank as he turned. Mary pushed back her chair with a shrill little laugh and ran towards me.

'Oh, I saw you, I saw your face! I knew exactly what you were thinking – "Why, what are *they* doing here?" Am I right?' She laughed coquettishly and patted my hand. 'Well, come and sit. Yes, we're having a month of frivolity and it's utterly delightful! Operas and ballets and museums – I'm drowning in culture! Oh, but it's been so long since we saw you. When was it?'

'At Ruthven's spirit raising,' I said deliberately, and watched her face change.

'So it was,' she said in a completely different voice, and her

214

false manner dropped away. Shelley was leaning out of the box, staring down at the chattering audience, lost in some vague dream. I turned to Mary and said in a low voice: '*Frankenstein*. You must tell me. Was *he* there? Was that why . . .'

'Not now,' she said, turning very pale. 'Please, let's talk of something else.'

'But I *have* to know!'

'No! It's better that – I wish you had not read it. I was afraid that you would, and that you would think . . .'

'Would think what, Mary?' I said softly.

'The curtain's going up,' she said with a sigh of relief. I looked at her pleadingly. 'Yes, I will tell you, I will, but now is not the time. I must think. Can we meet tomorrow perhaps? I'll come to Portman Square.'

*   *   *

She came. She talked. How she talked! She told me everything and nothing. On any other occasion, I would have been interested by lengthy descriptions of Alpine scenery, her meeting with Monk Lewis, the young Gothic novelist, and how she had persuaded him to release the slaves from his Jamaican plantations. But when she went into a second volley of raptures about Mont Blanc, with Shelley's impressions of it playing first violin, I decided I had had enough. I leant forward and touched her arm. 'Mary, will you please tell me what *happened* at Lake Geneva?'

'What happened?' She laughed uneasily. 'Why, I've told you everything that I can remember. As to why I wrote the book, it's easily explained, and a little mundane, I'm afraid. We were all going to write ghost stories, and while the others quickly tired of the scheme, I determined to carry it through. I had a dream which gave me an idea for the subject. That's all there is to it.'

'And why are your hands shaking,' I said softly, 'and why do you not look at me?'

She put her hands inside her muff and looked down at the floor. I waited nervously.

'Very well,' she said at last, and raised her eyes with a curious look of defiance. 'I felt, from the moment we arrived, the presence of evil, that one of us was wanted, was being taken over by . . . I don't know what.'

'Which?'

'You know,' she said emphatically.

The clock ticked steadily through the silence. Mary looked coldly at me. 'Say it,' she said, 'you asked for the truth.'

'Was he there, then?' I whispered.

Mary shook her head. 'Something was, that is all I can say, something which was not of the place. At first, I thought it was Byron's mood which was affecting me. He behaved so strangely at times, quite unlike himself, as if he were fighting with something which we could not see, only sense. Naturally, we assumed that he was still suffering from the scandal, from the failure of his marriage, but it was more than that. He hated to be alone, was too pressing with his invitations. When he suddenly agreed to let Claire come to his rooms at night, I think it was only for the same reason that he had brought poor Doctor Polidori from England. Any company, however objectionable, was better than none.'

'But that's only natural,' I said.

'That was the least of it,' Mary said. 'There were times when he – it was as if the devil possessed him.

'Once it came when we were on the lake. He'd been in a black, silent humour all day and while the rest of us were talking and laughing, he sat in the prow by himself, arms folded, staring down into the water. Claire, poor silly Claire, was prattling endlessly, why did he look so glum, why would he not smile and talk to her? He threw back his head suddenly with a choked, savage laugh and said he would not talk, but he was in the mood to sing. And he howled, like a beast. It echoed so strangely as the mountains threw it back. There was nothing human in it. I felt that we were outsiders, that he was defying something, something that only he could see.'

'Go on,' I said eagerly as she paused. 'What else?'

She shook her head wearily. 'Oh, all the time. We used to go up to the Villa Diodati every night, at his invitation. It was very ordered, the evening ritual. At midnight, the candles would be extinguished and we would gather round the fire to talk of ghosts. They felt it, too, I know it. It was as if another person sat with us, but nobody dared to mention it. Then, one night, Byron, without saying anything, drew up a sixth chair. Trembling, I asked him why and he fixed me with the most dreadful look and said: "You know, don't you?" I couldn't answer.

'The only time he spoke of it was when Shelley raised the subject of whether man is an instrument or not. He quoted Rousseau for his own beliefs, and I saw Byron's face turning dark with rage. He suddenly pushed back his chair with a violent movement and said: "And what if one is the instrument of evil, and the evil is yourself, yet you were not born with it, what does M. Rousseau suggest then?" Shelley laughed, thinking it was some sort of a riddle, but Byron rushed across the room and flung open the window on to the balcony. It was a terrible night of summer storm. Lightning played over the sky, brilliant, dazzling, turning the lake into a blazing inferno, then plunging it into darkness. I saw Byron turn and stare up into the stormy mountains as if he expected to see someone, something. Claire rushed after him, but he threw her back with such fury that none of us dared to move.'

'Oh God, and how cruel he was!' She suddenly buried her head in her hands.

'To you, my poor Mary?'

'No, no. He was always kind to me, courteous, understanding . . .' She smiled wistfully, not at me.

'Why, I do believe you lo . . .' I broke off hastily. I was voicing my thoughts aloud.

'No,' she said, not noticing. 'It was to Shelley. It was so strange. Everything indicated that Byron liked him immensely. They talked together all the time, went on a tour together to Chamonix and Chillon, were wonderfully close. Byron knew how easily Shelley is upset, how his imagination can be manipulated, and he was very considerate, protective almost about him.'

'He had been in a strange mood all day.' She paused, reflecting. 'Yes, how curious. It was always with the weather, his mood. We were inclined to postpone our evening visit, but he was so pressing that we should come as usual that, somewhat reluctantly, we agreed. He talked very violently at first. In a less abstemious man, I would have said he was drunk, and he harped endlessly on the aesthetic of terror.'

'You used to be its disciple,' I reminded her with a wry look.

'Yes, when it is of one's own making. This was not. It happened through Byron's action, but it was not from *his* mind. Midnight came. Byron talked on, gently now. Shelley was leaning forward on the table, listening to him, mesmerized. You know how Circean that soft languorous voice can be.'

'Yes,' I said flatly. Sweet Jesus, must she remind me, knowing what torture those memories must bring! I must have shown it in my face.

'You were the one who forced me to talk of this, remember,' she said.

'I know, I know. Finish it quickly,' I muttered.

'Fear was like a living being in the room, yet none of us could admit what made us turn with a shudder every time the wind rustled the leaves, or the outer door creaked on its hinges. Some fears are too strong to be spoken. I felt that something horrible was about to happen, that it must be stopped. I stood up to go. "Not yet," Byron said and he lay back in his chair, staring at Shelley through half-shut eyes. It was very quiet. In a soft, flat voice he began to recite that terrible verse from Coleridge's *Christabel* – you know it, of course?'

'*Behold! Her bosom and half her side – Hideous, deformed and pale of hue,*' I murmured. 'Terrible indeed, but surely . . .'

'Listen!' Mary said fiercely. 'You wanted to hear. Shelley suddenly gave the most dreadful scream. His eyes were fixed on me. I looked down . . . and I saw what he had seen. It was not my body. I sat. I couldn't move. Shelley fled past me out of the room, shrieking like a fiend and when I forced myself to look again, I saw only the brown bodice of my dress. We were alone, Byron and I. Claire and Polidori had rushed to Shelley's assistance. He stared at the window, I never saw a man look so. I turned my head, and I saw . . .' She swallowed.

'You saw?' I said thickly.

She shook her head. 'Nothing. The calm lake and the starry sky. There was nothing more. In the next room, I could hear Shelley sobbing, Claire murmuring to him. When I turned to

Byron, he was dreadfully pale, his hands clasped in front of him, staring at the table. "Shall I ask the doctor to come in?" I asked hesitantly. "No," he said, quite violently. "No. It's my battle. Nobody can fight it for me. You do understand," he went on, looking at me very earnestly, "that *I* could not do that to Shelley of my own free will." I had seen them together so often. I know he spoke the truth. It was out of Byron's love for Shelley that that night came. Lucy, that creature half possesses him, that thing which was your husband. What are you going to do?'

'I? What can *I* do?' I lay back among the sofa cushions with a sigh.

'Nothing,' Mary said and she took my hand. 'That's the horror of it. There's nothing any of us can do. Oh, I should not have told you. . . .'

I shook my head. 'You don't know the relief of seeing that my fear is real. I was terrified that. . . . My mother lost her mind. . . . I thought perhaps. . . . Yet, I could never find a rational explanation.'

'There is none,' she said flatly. 'Not for such an obsession. No, it's not in you that the madness lies, my poor friend, but I'm afraid for Byron. He's so sensitive, so much a victim of himself, so vulnerable. . . .' She looked up with a smile. 'But you know all this. He told me you understood him better than any other woman.'

'Annabella would disagree with you,' I said. 'Did he really say that?'

'Come, you don't need me to tell you how he loves you,' Mary said. 'And now that Augusta is lost. . . . You're very like her, Lucy.'

'I have been told so.' I stared down into the fire, the tears pricking my eyelids. 'If you knew how much I miss him. . . .'

She stood with her back to me, her silhouette sharp against the flames. 'You could come with us if you wanted,' she said slowly. We're leaving for Venice tomorrow with Claire and the child. He needs you. There's nothing I can do for him. . . .' Her voice trailed away. I leant forward.

'Do you love him too, Mary?'

'I?' She turned, her cheeks glowing. 'Why should you think

that? I share Shelley's esteem and affection for him, and for his work. That is all.'

I looked at her intently. 'All?' She looked down at her hands. 'No,' I said abruptly. 'Go without me. Looking after Claire will be a full-time occupation. Tell Byron . . . tell Byron . . .'

'Yes?' she said questioningly. I shrugged. There was nothing to say that he did not already know. I'd trust no woman as my messenger. 'It doesn't matter. Send me news of him, but none to pain me.'

'You should come,' Mary said. 'You're wasting your life here.'

'I know,' I said, my back turned towards her. 'It's quite painless, I assure you.'

'You won't be persuaded?'

'No.'

I heard her sigh, then the rustle of skirts as she went towards the door. 'For his sake, I wish you would come,' she said softly. 'I think he needs you.'

'I . . .' I spun round, but she was gone.

You must not think that I had ceased to love Byron because I did not go to him. Yet how should others not think I had forgotten when the years passed by and lovers with them, and still I stayed in England?

It was pride that kept me from him. Pride and fear. Not the pride I felt in having been the mistress of the man whom exile had made society's idol, the author of *Don Juan* and *Beppo*, but the pride which feared rejection, disillusionment. Mary wrote to me that he had grown stout and languid in Venice, that he was living in a mixture of grandeur and squalid chaos with a black-haired baker's wife whose ranting seemed to amuse him. I tried to laugh – and found myself in tears. If he would but write. . . . But the years were passing, and all news of him was second-hand.

Had I wished to forget, it would not have been possible. Polidori's *The Vampyre* saw to that. Everyone knew that the doctor had the story from Byron himself, and the fact that the vampire hero was named Ruthven was enough to make me the darling of the drawing-rooms for a month. Memories were forced out of me by demanding hostesses: everyone wanted a scandal to commit to their diaries. It was a story to rival the Regent's divorce – but I wanted none of it. I was no Caroline Lamb to live on the stories of past affairs. I loved Byron to well for that.

Curiously, my only defendant against the drawing-room jackals was a woman I hardly knew, although I often saw her at the Castlereagh parties. On more than one occasion when I was being pressed to tell all I knew, or suspected about Ruthven's relationship with Lord Byron and about the actual circumstances of my husband's death, Princess Lieven came to my rescue with an adroit remark and slid the subject into another channel with the graceful charm for which she was famous. I did not know her reasons. She shrugged aside my gratitude.

Four slow years passed before I heard from Byron. My hands trembled so violently when I saw his writing on the envelope that it slipped from my fingers. It was another hour before I could summon the courage to read the contents.

It was short, imperative, more than I had hoped for, worse than I had dreamt. No love letter, but the cry of a lost soul:

'*He is here, Lucy. Wherever I go, he follows. I've fought it for four years – God knows how much longer before I go mad. I've tried to drive it off, with the easy whores of Venice – no rivals for you here! – with writing into the dawn, but it's the cold hours of morning when women lie sleeping and I've no words left . . . I can't stand it, Lucy, not alone, not any more. Come, I beg you, come. . . . You, only you, can understand what hell it is I'm living in, the despair of knowing I can't escape. I love you, but more than love, I need you. Take what terms you like, marriage if that's what you want, but come tomorrow. . . .*'

Ruthven haunted my dreams that night. I saw him again, a spread-eagled shadow over Byron in the field, a thin figure in black walking towards my bed with the laudanum bottle in his hand, strolling with Orlando in the garden at Newstead, licking the blood from his pale cheeks at Lady Jersey's ball. . . . I woke in a cold sweat, my nightgown clinging to my skin, seeing his face in the shadows of the gas lamps that stalked the bedroom walls. In the morning, the room reeked of my own fear. . . .

I made the arrangements that week to sell the house in Portman Square. The servants were dismissed with a month's wages, my farewells made with as much discretion as is possible in a society whose food is scandal. An unchaperoned journey to Italy was ruin to my reputation – and I knew it. I positively enjoyed the thought of defying the social rules which had defined my life for so long. I had lost the taste for caution.

Two days before my departure, I was surprised to receive a letter from the Princess Lieven, asking me to visit her the following morning. Surprised, flattered, and a little intrigued, I went.

I arrived at eleven o'clock and was shown into the drawing-room. The princess did not rise from her desk but gave me a charming smile and asked my forgiveness for a few moments while she finished her letters. The minutes passed slowly. I stared at the marble fireplace, the titles of the books spread over the table beside the sofa, then back at the clock. . . . A quarter to twelve, and the princess's pen scratched on against the quiet. After the initial courtesies, she had shown no more interest in me than a butterfly collector would think due to a cabbage white. I rustled my skirts and offered a timid cough as a reminder.

The princess laid down her pen with a small sigh which reproached my lack of patience, then rose and glided towards me with a smile that would have disarmed even an avenging angel.

'You are angr-ry with me for keeping you so long? I am afraid I may make you a little angrier now. Please, si down.'

I placed myself among the blue silk cushions on the sofa while she moved about the room, talking in her quick, pretty way a she twisted a flower to another angle, altered the position of porcelain figure. 'You will have vondered why I sent for you I will tell you. I hear you are going to Venice to seek your love That is char-rming. But you must not do it.'

My smile faded. 'Not go, Princess Lieven? Why do you say that?'

'Because I know a little more than you, child,' she said, no unkindly. 'Ach, I know what you think. There is nothing lef

n England. It is better to be enslaved than to have slaves. It is
pleasant to have lap-dogs, but one cannot love them. You are
afraid of growing old, of forgetting the pain – the – what shall
I call it – masochistic sweetness of real love. Oh yes, I understand your feelings very well. They are natural, they are good.
So why, you say to yourself, does this tiresome voman tell me
to stay?'

'Your interest is an undeserved honour,' I said awkwardly.
She looked at me sharply.

'Well, enough of pretty words.' She sat down gracefully in the
chair opposite me, her hands drooping over the arms, and gave
me a long, penetrating look. I smiled uneasily, wondering what
was coming.

'You know something of Italy's political situation?' she asked
abruptly.

'That Austria has the power, yes.'

'And Lord Byron has no doubt expressed his feelings on this
subject to you?'

I hesitated. It was rumoured through unofficial channels
that the Princess had been Metternich's confidante since the
Congress of Vienna in 1815. I was afraid of making trouble for
Byron by being incautious.

'Come, come,' she said gaily. 'I am not so cr-rass as to ask
you to betray your lover to me. It's vell known that poets are
always for democracy, and it would be strange indeed if Lord
Byron supported the Austrian system. It would be to betr-ray
his principles.'

'I'm no political manipulator, if that is the cause of your
anxiety,' I said. 'There are no quixotic ideals in my going to
him. For myself, I am so apolitical as not to care whether Italy
rules herself or not. It is not my country. I am going because I
love him. I know now that the memory of an affair is not
enough. There is no more to it.'

'I'm afraid there is,' she said quietly. 'Lord Byron is an
eloquent speaker, and his verses have made him something of
a hero among young revolutionaries. Consequently, he has to
be watched, reported on, accounted for in his every movement.'

'Spied on.'

'If you wish to name it, yes. Now, you know the saying that

every man has his price? Some can be bought for money, others have a private motive.'

I nodded, puzzled. Byron would never inform for money, I thought to myself.

'You know, naturally,' she said in a mild voice, 'that your husband is not dead?'

For a moment, I thought I was going to faint. 'What do you know of it?' I whispered.

'I played a – minor part in the arrangements,' she said coolly. 'I expect that you remember as well as I do a curious little scene which took place some years ago at Lady Jersey's house: it caused a great scandal. Shortly after that, approaches were made through certain channels by your husband. He had an interesting proposition. There was already concern in some quarters at Byron's departure, the possibility of a revolution abroad being ignited by his presence – and his financial assistance. Your husband, Lord Ruthven, is an intelligent man. He comprehended the awkwardness of the dilemma, and placed himself at the disposal of – certain parties to assist. Evidently, there was no altruism in it. He had his own reason for wishing to follow your friend incognito, although he gave none.' She smiled at me. 'I imagine jealousy had a part in it.'

'Oh no!' I said vehemently, and stopped myself with an effort. 'No, I doubt if that was the reason.'

She shrugged indifferently. 'I do not interest myself in motives. He is an efficient man.'

'And that is why you would have me stay!' I stood up. 'I am sorry to have wasted your valuable time.'

She laughed with genuine amusement. 'So impetuous! You must learn the art of patience, my dear, not rush at life in such a headlong way. It will do you no harm to stay in England and wait for your Byron to return.'

'He will never come back. He left in too much bitterness. If I don't go now, I shall lose him for ever, I know it!'

'Listen,' she said sharply. 'I am not inter-rested in your emotions, but your safety. Ruthven's name is not popular in Venice. There have been – scandals. He cannot be protected for much longer from the Italian government. I have heard that he may have to leave the country. He has an estate, a castle, I

224

believe, in that part of the vorld – Albania? I don't remember. If you arrive bearing his name on your passport, you may find yourself in a very awkward situation. You follow me?'

'Scandals,' I whispered. 'Of what nature?'

'Does it matter?' she said. 'Myself, I don't know what he has done, only that he has caused considerable embarrassment. So, I assume they are not love affairs. Venice is not known for her – puritanism.'

She gave me a long glance which did not allow her meaning to be mistaken. I flushed darkly. 'If Lord Byron is already involved, I will return, but I am not going to alter my plans for departure. If there are any difficulties, he will protect me. But I thank you for your kindness in offering your advice.

'And you will not take it. Well –' She offered me her soft, powdered cheek to kiss. It smelt of roses, the Bohemian attar. 'You are a brave girl, but a silly one. I wish you good fortune, and you may give Byron my compliments. Tell him I remember him with affection.'

believe it, and given the world a discovery? I don't remember.
If you come here now, I'll move up the message. You may and
you call in a few awkward resignation. I am following—"

"Scandal," I observed. "Of what nature?"

"Does it matter?" she cried, Mr. Holmes. I know whether his
done, or that pronounced some terrible embarrassment. S...
I assume they are not free affairs. Venice is not much the better
particular."

She have men long enough. I did not allow her mounting
to see clearer. I finished, darkly, "and force is already in—
volved. I will reward her but I am not going to Alice my plans for
departure. If there are any difficulties, he will protect me—but
I thank you for your kindness in mentioning yourself."

"And you will not refuse." Wait— She offered me her soft
powdered glove: realise: "It surely cries if the Bohemian scent.
You are a dangerous man, Mr. Holmes, I wish you good fortune,
my greatest esteem and my compliments." And I remember
him with elation.

Part Three

THE JOURNEY

13

My inclination for adventure and independence was brief as the life of Solomon Grundy in the nursery rhyme. The journey through France and Northern Italy was plagued with all the trivial disasters which become insurmountable catastrophes when you are tired and alone. Robbed by my *voituriers* at Calais and Besançon, stranded for a fortnight by an avalanche at an Alpine inn, jolting down at last to Italy in a carriage with no springs and a loquacious driver whom any tortoise would have beaten to a standstill: only the thought of seeing Byron kept me from turning back.

I had hoped to make the journey in a month. Ten weeks had passed before, exhausted, nervous and suddenly afraid, I looked out of the carriage window and saw the domes and towers of Venice, rising in the violet dusk from a still lake, unearthly, dreamlike, more delicate than the palest watercolour. I glanced down at Byron's letter, open on my lap. The Palazzo Mocenigo, Venezia. . . . I pressed it to my lips and leant back, laughing and crying together, so wildly that the driver turned to stare at me.

'You wish to stop, signora? You are ill?'

I shook my head. 'Ill! Why, I'm happier than I've ever been in my life. Oh, hurry, please hurry – I must see him tonight! I'll . . . I'll give you two guineas if we reach Venice by nightfall.'

He grinned. 'The horses are old, senora, and the road is long.'

'Four guineas,' I said. I lay back, smiling, as the horses broke into a rapid trot.

There is no new word, no phrase, no feeling that has not already been used to describe the spell that Venice weaves around her visitors, the calm voluptuousness of sliding through the lapping night water beneath the pointed windows of the grey stone palaces, watching the swaying silhouettes of the gondoliers, hearing the murmur of conversation echoing back through the arched bridges down the narrow canals, seeing the stars of light spreading away from the dip of the oar, feeling, the sense above all, of having come home.

We slipped quietly under the last arch and out into the broad sweep of the Grand Canal by the Rialto, trembling in its own reflection. The quiet palaces slid by. 'Here! Stop here!'

He turned round. 'The Palazzo Mocenigo, signora?'

'Yes, isn't that it, over there?'

'Yes, signora,' he said, 'but it is closed.'

'Closed,' I repeated dully. 'Closed? Are – are you sure?'

He lifted his dripping oar to point. 'Look for yourself, signora, if you do not believe me. The windows, the doors, they are all barred. Lord Byron left two weeks ago.'

He leaned on the oar, his body gracefully tilted, looking down at me.

Slowly, I turned my head away from the dark palace. 'Do you know where he has gone, when he returns?'

'I?' He laughed. 'I am a gondolier, signora, not a spy. I can only give you the gossip of the canals about Lord Byron. The British Consul, Signor 'Oppner, he would know, perhaps. But it is late. He will be sleeping.'

'Then I'll ask for him to be woken. Yes, take me there.'

The gondola slipped forward through the water and I leaned back against the velvet cushions, fighting desperately to control my tears. To have come so far, only to find him gone. It was hard to bear. All that had kept my spirits high through the last, murderous leg of the journey was the thought of the reunion, of seeing his face, of hearing his sweet, languid voice caressing my name, and now, in a moment, there was nothing, nothing but the desolation of knowing I had come too late.

I sat by the dead fire in the Consul's neat, brown study, my eyes fixed on the dull gold paperweight on his desk. Mr Hoppner, a drab, grey-faced man with a thin mouth and a sharp chin, pulled his dressing-gown sash around his waist with a vicious tweak of his fingers.

'My dear Lady Ruthven, I have told you all I know. Lord

230

Byron is with the Countess Guccioli, his – mistress, at her husband's house in Ravenna. The child, poor little Allegra, whom my wife had cared for like her own daughter, is being placed in a convent, and the whole affair is a social disaster. Lord Byron's mode of behaviour in Venice was regrettable: his association with a family of liberal sympathies and, er, revolutionary tendencies, is deplorable. All I can suggest is that you return home to England as soon as possible.'

I shook my head. 'Nothing on earth would persuade me to go back to England, Mr Hoppner. I am not helpless. I have other friends here, the Shelleys. . . .'

'I also have the *honour* of knowing the Shelleys,' Mr Hoppner said with unpleasant emphasis. 'I am sorry to hear you term them friends.'

'Indeed?'

His mouth thinned, avid in its spite. 'Their ménage is a scandal, a league of incest. The begetting of children by sisters is a sin that I, at least, cannot condone.'

'Nor, I, if I was witless enough to believe it,' I said shortly. 'It's a vile rumour, and a man of your position should be above repeating it so readily.'

'And how, if I may presume to ask, do you intend to set about finding your "friends", Lady Ruthven?' he asked silkily, turning the gold paperweight over in his hand. 'I ask only from interest. Do you know their whereabouts?'

My head drooped. 'No.'

He smiled triumphantly. 'And even such an – intrepid traveller as yourself will not consider wandering through all Italy alone in search of *them*?'

Dislike is a healthy antidote to despair. I felt my strength seeping back as I stood up. 'Thank you for giving me your time, Mr Hoppner.' I smiled. 'You have provided me with a solution, if only by negation. I shall stay here in Venice.'

'No, no, you can't possibly do that,' he said quickly. 'It's out of the question. You should never have come.'

'Really?' I raised my eyebrows.

'Surely you know the embarrassment of your being here? Your name is enough to discredit you. I cannot afford to protect you against what will happen.' He glanced nervously at the door. 'It was bad enough that the servants should have heard it.'

'What in God's name has Ruthven done to put the fear of God in the British Consul,' I said mockingly. 'Corrupted the gondolieri – I thought Venice was well-versed in that?'

'Please,' he said, covering a nervous cough with prim fingers. 'This is no matter for laughter. It really is most unfortunate that you should arrive now. Had I only known, you would have been stopped on the route. But you had to come this very week, just when the whole affair came to a head. . . . Did nobody warn you? It really is too bad!'

'Please, Mr Hoppner,' I said as his voice rose. 'How can I understand if you do not tell me? I was under the impression that my husband was, for certain reasons, under the protection of the Austrian police.'

'He was, until last week. But naturally, they would not associate with him when he had betrayed them.'

'I see. To whom?'

'To Lord Byron,' he said wearily. 'Don't ask me to tell you why. I have no idea.'

'I think you'd better start at the beginning,' I said. 'I may as well tell you that I've no intention of leaving until I know the full story.'

'Oh, very well. Yes, I suppose you are entitled to know,' he said, pressing his fingers against his forehead. 'Forgive me, but it has been a most exhausting week. Let me see. . . . Lord Ruthven arrived here at about the same time as Lord Byron, accompanied by his children . . .'

'Children?' I interrupted eagerly. 'But it's obviously a case of mistaken identity. There is only one, a boy of five.'

'Was,' said Mr Hoppner. 'Diphtheria – I gather the best doctors were brought in, but . . .' He shrugged. 'A merciful release, in my opinion. Lord Ruthven is not a fit father for a child.'

I tried to look grief-stricken, and felt only relief. It had always been Ruthven's spawn, never my child. Its arms had never reached up to me. It had never lain at my breast. How should I weep for the loss of something I had loved so little? 'You said children?' I repeated.

The Consul stared at me over his desk as if I had lost my senses. 'But, naturally. One never saw Ruthven without his son. They were inseparable.' He shook his head. 'Oh, we were all enchanted by Orlando. Such a beautiful boy, quite angelic. . . .'

'*Orlando!* But how . . .?' I sank back in my chair, not knowing whether to laugh or cry. To know that he lived was more than I had ever dared to hope. To know that he was with Ruthven plunged me into despair.

'Do you wish me to continue?' the Consul asked.

I started. 'Forgive me. Yes, please go on.'

'Yes, we all thought Orlando a model son,' he said, looking down at his hands. 'Quite devoted to his father. The affection they had for each other was often remarked on, more so when the scandals began.

'The first was last year, about the same time that Lord Byron became enamoured of Teresa Guccioli. A boy was found, drowned, in one of the side canals. Not such an uncommon occurrence here, I'm afraid. There was an autopsy, but no satisfactory explanation. Then the mother came forward with a statement which put a very different complexion on the case. The boy, it appeared, had been the constant companion of Orlando Ruthven and was a frequent visitor to their house. On the night of his death, he had talked of dining there. Accusations were made – and denied. It was very unpleasant.

'Just two weeks later, an identical case came up. There was, of course, talk. People wondered. There was no proof, but Lord Ruthven was warned. I believe a payment was made, all rather sordid.

'In less than a month, another body was found, but this case was far more serious. The boy was the only child of a Venetian nobleman, the heir to a large estate. There was now no doubt as to what was happening. The boy had been a close friend of Ruthven's son, was with him every day. Evidently, Orlando was acting as his father's decoy, and indeed, at the autopsy, marks were found on the neck of the drowned boy.'

'Marks?' I repeated, startled by the change in his voice.

'I don't know the precise details. The Italians are a very superstitious race. There was a rumour put around – ridiculous,

233

of course – they were the marks of a vampire, but that, of course, was the reaction of hysteria. It was obvious that the poor boy had been strangled and then thrown into the canal. During their inquiry, the police discovered that Ruthven was working for Austria, as nothing more than a spy on Byron. This meant that he was, to some degree, under protection. The Venetian police were furious, the boy's father was more so, but while Ruthven was with Austria, they simply did not dare to do more than threaten him.

'And then, the most extraordinary thing happened.' Hoppner leaned over the chair, looking at me as if he hoped that I would be able to provide an explanation. 'Somehow, Ruthven got wind of the fact that Byron was not treating his new affair like the others. It appeared that he was genuinely in love with the little countess and was following her to Ravenna. There was a meeting between Byron and Ruthven, and it seems that Ruthven lost his head. I saw Byron afterwards and he told me that Ruthven had begged him not to go, and when he refused, had disclosed the whole Austrian network in Venice. It was an act of absolute insanity. He gave him the names, details of reports, everything, and then, if you can credit it, reported his own betrayal to his employers. It was almost as if he had decided to risk his life in the effort to win Byron's trust.'

He paused. 'But, of course, Byron went. It made no difference to him. The last part of the story has taken place in the last two weeks. The Austrians put out an official denunciation of Ruthven. They threw him to the wolves, or rather, the Venetian police.

'The evidence was assembled, and he and the boy would have hanged for less. There was no question at all that they were both guilty. Even if I had wanted to assist, I could have done nothing for them. Two days ago, the police went to his house at dawn, and found him and the boy gone. God knows where. The search is still going on. Now, perhaps, you understand why you simply must not stay here.'

'And if I told you where he has gone?' I asked. 'Could you hang him? He has a castle, I believe, in Albania.'

'It's outside our jurisdiction,' the Consul said.

I took a deep breath before breaking the silence which

followed. 'But I had nothing to do with it. I share nothing with the man but his name!'

'In the present climate, that's more than enough,' he said dryly. 'They want a scapegoat. Legally, they can't touch you, but there are – other ways. I can't give you protection. I have to live and work here. All I can tell you is that you stand as much risk as the heir to the usurper of a throne. It's what you represent, not what you are, that is the danger. You *must* go.'

'But Mr Hoppner, I . . . I.' The tears rushed up to my throat and, too tired to care what he thought, I leant forward on my hands and wept. 'Oh God, what am I to *do*!'

'You have my sympathy,' he said awkwardly. 'You've had a long journey. It must be very embittering.'

'And he's gone. . . . Tell me, is she very beautiful? Does she make him happy?'

'Who? Oh, the Guccioli girl!' He frowned. 'You shouldn't waste your tears on Byron. His life's a moral disgrace.' He paused, drumming his fingers on the leather top of his writing desk. 'Really, I cannot understand what women see in him. A pretty girl like you, what can he give you but a lost reputation?'

'You don't know women very well, if you weigh love against a reputation,' I said sadly. 'But if he loves her. . . .'

The Consul's face softened slightly as I looked up at him. 'I see. No, my impression is that he is resigned to being loved by her. What is she like? Pretty, voluble, and not very perceptive. Yes, it's a pity you came so late. Perhaps he would have made his choice another way, in other days. Well . . .' He brought his hands together. 'I'm afraid there is no more I can do, except to suggest that you make arrangements to leave Venice tonight.'

But I did not follow the Consul's advice. There are three ways of taking an unendurable situation: to write it out, to work it out, or to walk it out. I chose the latter without being aware that I was seeking a cure. For two hours, I wandered alone through the dark, whispering alleys, crossing the same bridges and empty piazzas over again without noticing that I had done so. Then, when my feet would go no further, I leaned on a stone parapet and gazed down into the still, black water. It is the only moment of my life in which I clearly remember being tempted

235

to end it. Then, I heard voices, the tramp of feet, and I drew back into the shadows, pulling my veil over my face.

A group of Austrian officers came up the shallow steps, their arms linked, their voices battling against each other for attention. They stopped as they caught sight of me, their long shadows swaying down the bridge. I smiled nervously and tried to make my way past them. But one caught my arm and held me against the wall. 'Buona sera, signorina,' he said softly. 'Dove va?'

'Buona sera, signore,' I muttered, without raising my eyes. He laughed and turned to speak to his comrades, without letting go of my arm.

'Français?' he demanded. 'Ingleesh?'

'English,' I said. He grinned.

'You talk to Franz. He understandt.'

One of his companions lounged forward, his spurs clicking on the stone. He put his hand under my chin and lifted up my face. 'Please. Let me go!' I said angrily as he winked at the others.

'Soon,' he smiled. 'We have a little time on our hands. I am sure your hurry is not so great. What is your name?'

I turned away. 'Oh, a lady of mystery,' he laughed. 'Well, we shall soon solve that. As an officer of the Austrian guard, I demand to see your passport. Come, or we shall be suspicious of your pretty show of secrecy.'

I shook my head, terrified. They were not smiling now. I could see the others whispering together behind his back. All I could remember was that they must not know my name. 'I'm going to Lord Byron at Ravenna,' I said at last.

Franz glanced at his friends and spoke to them rapidly in Austrian. They nodded and, before I had understood what was happening, he had reached down and snatched the purse from my hands. I trembled as he flicked over the page of the passport. 'So . . . o,' he said with an indrawn breath. 'This is very intriguing. I think you should, perhaps, come with us, Lady Ruthven.'

'Ruthven?' I heard one of them murmur, then they all started to talk at once, and I caught the names of Byron and Ruthven several times. My heart sank when I saw how they looked at me. 'Please,' I said imploringly. 'I haven't seen my husband for four years. I came only to see Byron.'

'Yes,' Franz said. 'That is what will interest our commander. Why did you come to see him *now*?'

'I – I don't know what you mean.'

'I think the commander will help you to follow the meaning,' he said quietly. 'If you are wise, you will tell him the truth.'

* * *

Wearily, I leant forward in the chair, my eyelids drooping with fatigue. Opposite me, across the heavy table, the grey-faced Austrian commander stifled a yawn as he let the papers drop back from his hand in an ordered pile. Franz, my captor, sprawled in a chair by the fire, his boots propped against the red flock wallpaper, his fingers playing with the silky ears of a brown and white spaniel. He hummed to himself under his breath, tapping time with his spurs against the wall. His superior gave him an irritated look.

'For God's sake shut up, Franz, and put your feet where they belong. You're not in a bordello.'

'More's the pity,' he murmured, but the humming ceased abruptly.

'Now!' The commander turned to me with a smile which hardly moved his mouth. 'Shall I repeat the questions again or are you ready to answer?'

'I told you. I don't understand what you want from me. I have nothing to do with my husband's murders.'

'Did I suggest that you had? Please, do not try to confuse the issue.' He leaned across the desk. 'All we want to know is what messages you were taking to Lord Byron?'

'Messages?' I looked at him in bewilderment. He sighed.

'Must I explain it to you in words of one syllable? We have been watching Lord Byron since he came to Venice. We know that in Ravenna he is heavily involved with the Italian revolutionaries, a branch of the Carbonari. The Countess Guccioli's family, the Gambas, are also of liberal sympathies. It all makes a composite picture, you see.' He looked down at the papers on the desk. 'Lady Ruthven, we are not ogres or tyrants. We are

237

trying to keep peace in Italy, but how can we do it without knowing the facts?'

'But I know nothing!' I burst out. 'How can I tell you what I myself don't know?'

'Because you are lying,' he said coldly. 'My time, and my patience, are limited. You *must* tell us!' He brought his fist down on the table. I started. 'You see, it does not look well,' he said in a gentler voice. 'Your husband's betrayal of us makes us wonder if he was not all the time in league with Byron – a reasonable assumption. And then, you arrive, as he leaves, to carry on his work. You say your timing is a coincidence – perhaps. Perhaps, but I do not think so.'

I shook my head. 'I can only swear my innocence.'

'Ah, yes,' he said quietly. 'But you must not expect me to believe you. I saw a man last week who said the same, but – he changed his mind.'

'You made him change it.'

'Yes, but we were right. Do you know what he had done?' He laughed. 'Swallowed the documents which incriminated him. It was lucky that he remembered the contents. So you see, it is not wise to believe everything one is told. Now, give me the true story. What did Ruthven instruct you to do when you reached Ravenna? Do you know a meeting place, a date, or a list of names?'

'Why won't you accept what I say?' I said wearily. 'I can't help you. I know nothing, except what you yourself have told me. Let me go. I'll return to England if that is what you want.'

'No. You will stay here.' He smiled. 'We will soon make you see how unwise it is to withhold facts. Franz here is very good at obtaining information and, while it would be a shame to damage such pretty, white hands, we have a dangerous insurrection to prevent. When you tell us what we want to know, perhaps we will allow you to leave. It depends.' He leant forward, waiting.

I looked from their granite faces to my threatened hands. I can endure anything but physical pain: the thought of it paralysed me. What to do, what to do . . . there was only one chance, and a slim one. I had to take it. Swaying forward in my chair, I clutched at the edge of the desk. 'Please. I . . .' I held my breath, letting it come up to my throat in slow gasps. 'Air! I can't . . . breathe . . . can't . . .' My head rolled back. Out of the corner of my eye, I saw the quick glance pass between them.

'You'd better take her out,' the commander said.

'And let her escape? I'll get her some water,' Franz said, standing up. Behind me, I heard the door open. I let my body go limp, slid off the chair, twisted convulsively three or four times on the floor and lay still, looking up until only the whites of my eyes showed.

'Christ!' the commander said, crossing himself hurriedly. 'Franz! Franz! Come here!' His boots paused beside me, then he went out of the room.

As soon as he had gone, I leaped to my feet, seized my purse off the desk and threw open the window. Then I jumped.

The canal saved my life. Had I dropped on stone, I would have broken my neck. Spitting out a mouthful of stinking water, I clawed my way up on to the narrow pavement, scraping my knees and arms raw on the rough stones. I had no idea where I was, or what to do, but I had sense enough left to press myself back into the dark cleft between the houses. Seconds later, they leaned out of the window. A flickering beam of light moved over the water, then I heard the commander speak to Franz, an order the nature of which I could imagine. The window blacked out.

I squeezed as much water as I could out of the dripping skirt which would have left a clear trail behind me, and started to run down the street. My heart thudded at my ribs and my breath came in harsh gasps as I panted through the empty piazzas, always taking a new direction, but I did not dare to stop for a moment. The city was on my side. Even the most determined pursuer would be hard put to find his prey in the network of narrow alleys and side-streets and, barefooted, there was no treacherous echo to give me away. But the Austrians wore spurred boots. More than once, I heard them behind me and crouched, trembling in the shadows of an arched walk until they had gone past.

At last, I lost them. The only sound was of water parting in front of the gondolas as I came out on to the deserted front facing the Lido. In the pale moonlight, the grey stone shone white, cracked with deep rifts where the shadows lay still. It looked like a lost city. A thin cat mewed and arched from the gutter at an old woman, head bent, hobbling away down a side street. I chased after her and caught her by the arm. Please, the boats, the boats out of Venice?'

She stared at me, puckering her face strangely, then jerked her head back. 'There, further down, but you'll find none at this hour.'

But already I had started to run again, and I did not stop until the black outlines of rigging rose ahead. Hurrying down the wooden platform, I saw no sign of life. My spirits sank.

'Hello! Hello! Is anybody there?' I waited, shivering as the cold wind swept over the water, but no answer came back.

The boats were anchored as close together as cargo in a ship's hold, and after a moment's hesitation I began to walk across them, peering down the empty decks in the hope that somewhere I might find a sailor or a fisherman, sleeping. And then, in the darkness, I saw a glimmer of light from the cabin of one of the larger boats, a three-masted sloop with a high cruel prow jutting high above its neighbours. Hardened by fear, I jumped the three-foot gap without a qualm and landed neatly on the deck. Nobody came out to halt me, and after a moment's hesitation, I rapped at the cabin door. There was a noise of scuffling and whispering in the cabin, then I heard the bolts being drawn back. I clenched my hands.

'Ye-es. . . . Who is it?' a voice murmured in a soft, southern accent as the door opened, not wide enough to put my foot through.

'Please, I need help, desperately,' I said huskily, in my best Italian. 'I want a passage out of Venice, tonight.'

'A lady!' The door opened a little wider and a dark, raffish face looked down at me. 'And a mermaid, to boot. You'd be better swimming the Adriatic, my dear.'

'Don't send me away!' I cried as he made to shut the door. 'The Austrian police are after me! I'll give you everything I have, I'll ask no questions, I'll do anything . . .'

'Tch, don't offer everything at once, or I'll take you at your word,' he grinned.

I stopped, abashed, as he stroked his pointed beard and

looked me up and down. 'Those damned Austrians again, eh? Well, I'd like to put a spoke in that efficient wheel of theirs, but . . . Come in, and we'll talk it over.'

I followed him timidly, conscious of his friends' hostile faces. I suppose I can't have looked an appetizing prospect as a shipmate, with my hair straggling down my back, my dress clinging to my body in wet folds and my feet not only bare, but black with mud.

'Who in God's name is this, Enrico?' asked one of the men, a tall, dark fellow in a red waistcoat and loose-sleeved shirt.

'Don't you know a lady when you see one?' He lit a long cigar off one of the chandelier candles and leaned back against the wall, inhaling it placidly. As he suddenly turned to me, I was caught off guard by his quick, black eyes. 'So . . .?'

'Miss Lampton.' I curtsied.

'Miss Lampton, what will you offer for your passage?'

I pulled the turquoise earrings out of my ears and tipped the last of my money on the table. One of the men laughed. 'It's all I have,' I said.

'You're mad, Enrico!' The man in the red waistcoat picked up the earrings and threw them across the table in disgust. They're not worth the gold on one of your buttons!'

'Remember that you elected me to be your captain, Roberto.' the other said softly. 'The final choice is mine. We'll take her with us as far as Bari, and she'll sleep in my room. If one of you lays a finger on her, you answer to me. Understood?'

A short, grizzle-haired man came forward, brushing past me without so much as a glance. 'Enrico, listen to me. We've travelled many seas together, you and I, and you know that my advice has never been wrong.'

'Once,' the captain said gently. 'I don't forget.'

'Once, then, in eight years. My captain, it's no good to have women around at sea. They make trouble, they talk, they get in the way. They can't fight like a man. Put her back on the shore.'

Enrico laughed and clapped him on the back. 'Giorgio, my old misogynist, you never change. You're still the staunchest of them all. Listen, I'll give you a reason. Remember the brush we had with the Austrians? It was near to being the rope for all of us, and we lost the profits of a hard voyage.'

They nodded glumly.

'Well, it seems they need Miss . . . Lampton for some reason. I think it would amuse you as well as me to let them be deprived. . . . Agreed?' He didn't wait for an answer, but ground his cigar into the floor with his heel and turned to Giorgio. 'We're moving out. Now. If those damned Austrians come searching the boat, the girl's the least of our problems. Miss Lampton, you will go through that door into the rear cabin and stay there. Gratitude will keep.' He softened the words with a sudden smile and put his hand under my chin, tilting my face towards the swaying lamp. 'We can discuss how you're to pay for the voyage later. It's been a long time since I last had the . . . honour of a lady's company on the *Volpone*.'

His inflection left me in no doubt as to the form my payment was to take. I was to be the price.

I went down the steps to his cabin.

14

I sat by the porthole, watching the slow retreat of the spires and domes beneath the waves, as the sloop dipped gravely across the lagoon. The last rim of lights sank down: I heard the creak of rigging as the night wind billowed out the sails. Above me, the men moved to and fro, shouting over the roar of wind and the slap of water on the sides of the ship.

Bari, he had said. I didn't even know where that was. It hardly mattered. Not now. With a sigh, I lay back, pillowing my head with my arms, wondering whether I should be thankful or sorry to have escaped the Austrians. A pirate ship – and I was certain that it was one – was unlikely to offer me a safe passage. My only hope lay in the Captain, and his friendship came at a price. I shrugged and then began to laugh. That my journey should end with my becoming a pirate's mistress. . . . I was still smiling when the Captain came through the door.

'I'm in your debt,' I said. 'I've never been more thankful to leave a city.'

'You took quite a risk, Miss Lampton,' he said gravely. 'Do you know what sort of ship I sail?' I nodded. 'You aren't afraid?'

'As yet, I've seen no cause for fear,' I said, looking up at him under my lashes.

He laughed and dropped his jacket on the bed. 'I like a woman with courage. We're going to get along very well, if you ask no questions and obey instructions. Don't worry if the crew grumble.' He tapped the mass of black curls on his forehead. 'Enrico Rovere decides how this ship is to be run and nobody contradicts him. Not even a pretty woman, Miss Lampton.'

'You're very kind.'

'Calculating, not kind,' he said, and grinned. 'I always had a weakness for English girls.'

There was something very disarming in his honesty. I found myself smiling back and when he sat beside me and took my hand in his, I made no protest. He turned it over, studying the lines of my palm, then looked up at my face. 'You have a long way to travel before you find what you seek, Miss Lampton,' he said. 'You will, I think be defeated when you find it.'

I drew back my hand. 'Palmistry. . . . It's a charlatan's game. There's no truth that can be seen in a hand.'

'Whom do you seek?' He caressed the nape of my neck.

'Whom *did* I seek,' I said, and turned away my head. 'You wouldn't know him. His name was Byron.'

'Byron! I wouldn't know him! Oh, that's good, that's exquisite!' His face creased with laughter. 'Miss Lampton, you and I were destined to meet. Come, look at this!'

He reached under the cushions of the bed and pulled out a brown leather volume, pointing to the title. 'You see what it says – *The Corsair* by Lord Byron! It's the only book I take on every voyage – you could say it was my bible. Byron's the one man I always wanted to meet, and now I find you!'

I did not want to talk of Byron. It hurt too much. 'And you modelled yourself on the hero?' I asked.

'I? I was buccaneering before Lord Byron began to write.'

'And what were you before then, Signor Rovere?' I asked as he closed the book and lay back, looking at me.

He shrugged lazily. 'What was I? Well, my mother told me that I was the bastard of a duke or a cardinal, but she could never make up her mind which sounded the best. All I know for certain is that no father hurried to claim me for his heir. I was left to make my own way in the world – hence this glorious career.' He paused. 'Sometimes I wish – but there's no use in regretting what I never had. And you, Miss Lampton, what is your real name? You hesitated too long in saying it.'

I leant forward, my hair spilling over his hands. 'Later, perhaps, I'll tell you. Not now.'

'No. Not now,' he repeated softly, and his mouth came down to meet mine.

I would not have given way to him so readily had not the thought of Byron and his Italian contessa been at the back of my mind. If he could be so conscienceless, why should I be virtuous?

I looked for no love, nor expected it, in this affair. It was a matter of convenience being met by obligation. All I knew of pirates had led me to believe that they held women to be whores and treated them accordingly, discarding them as soon as they had served their purpose. Enrico Rovere defied such simple scepticism.

He was, I discovered, held to be an eccentric by the crew. They were embarrassed by their captain's fondness for books and his evident preference for drawing-room reminiscences to stories of past lootings. Yet, I knew from Giorgio that they respected him. He could cut down with a voice like a steel blade any man who questioned his commands: I heard that he fought like the very devil when there was gold to be gained by it. That was another Enrico, not the man I knew.

When we met in the evenings, he came dressed like a lord of my grandfather's time – breeched in velvet, collared in Spanish lace – to talk of the London he had never seen, to question me about Wellington, the Prince Regent, to listen to the gossip of people he had never known about, events which must have been long since resolved. The picture which I attempted to paint for him must have sounded as unreal and alluring as was the pirate's life to me. I listened to stories of Ali Pasha, whose ships were the scourge of the Ionian seas, of Enrico's one strange meeting with an English pirate, Trelawny, so like the *Corsair* that he thought a ghost had risen – and I thought I would gladly exchange all my knowledge of London for a year of the buccaneer's life.

We never spoke of love. There's no use in talking of it when you can see the end of an affair. Enrico was wedded to his ship. The *Volpone* would always come before a woman – and I knew it. And I? How was I to forget Byron, when every night the pirate's curiosity forced me to remember? He wanted to know everything about his hero, and although at first I used to try to change the subject, he looked so downcast that I swallowed my bitterness and told my stories. He would sit with his legs crossed under him on the bed, absorbed as a child, while I recalled it all, all except for Ruthven.

'You give up too easily, you know,' he said one night, when I broke off my memories in mid-sentence and hid my face. 'What makes you think he'll stay with the Contessa for the rest of his life?'

'He loves her.'

'Tch!' He snapped his fingers. 'I think I begin to understand your Byron very well. He is a man to love, but not to be loved by. I think he is a man for causes, not for loves. He'll get bored of domesticity, feel that his life is being wasted. If you go back to England, Lucy, you'll never see him again. You know that.'

I spread my hands hopelessly. 'What else can I do?'

'Live!' He shouted. 'Do what you want to do, not what you think you should do. What will happen if you do go back? I'll tell you. You'll marry a man you don't love and you'll have a child every year and you'll buy yourself dresses which won't fit you any more when you've lived in the country for ten years with nothing to do but eat and breed, breed and eat. God! Do you think I haven't seen what frustration does to women? It's terrible! Terrible. They make themselves repulsive to spite the man they never had, they count the rolls of fat against the beds they never got in, they . . .' He stopped as I began to weep and put his arms round me. 'I'm sorry, Lucy. I can't bear to see anyone submitting so easily to circumstances. Submission's for bed, not a way of life. Not when you've come so far.'

'I know,' I said, 'but I sometimes wonder why I came.'

He kissed my eyelids. 'You stay with me on the *Volpone*, and wait to see where Byron goes next. I'll help you to find him.' He paused smiling. 'On one condition – that as my mistress and my companion, you'll stay with me until then.'

'Your crew will hate me for it. They do, already.'

'Does that matter? Will you?'

'Perhaps,' I said. 'Perhaps.'

But the ship was his true mistress, not I, and when two weeks had passed and never a sight of a ship worth plundering, Enrico gave the orders to head east for Albania. In vain, did I remind him of his promises. He was not prepared to listen. We were bound for Ruthven's territory and there was nothing I could do to prevent it.

I leant over the rail at Enrico's side as the *Volpone* glided into the dark reflections of the mountains of Albania. Cruel and barren, they looked a fit home for Ruthven. Dully, I listened as Enrico talked of the day ahead of us at the port of Butrinto.

'Would you object to my staying on the boat?' I asked in nervous hope. 'I – I doubt if an Albanian port can offer much diversion, and I know you will be occupied.'

He put his arm round my waist. 'Lucy, Lucy, what is this? First you complained that you saw nothing but sea and now you want to stay on the boat? I won't hear of it. Listen: Giorgio can handle the selling of the gold, there's no need for my presence. We'll take two horses and ride up into the mountains . . .'

'No!' I cried, panic-stricken. Enrico shrugged, but I could see that my objections were making him all the more determined. He was not a man who liked to be crossed.

'Then we'll amuse ourselves in the town,' he said, and his white teeth gleamed in his beard as my head drooped. 'Come, don't look so mournful. Go and look in the chest in my cabin and see if you can't find yourself a more suitable costume. You can't go into a provincial port like Butrinto with your face uncovered. They'd take you for a street-walker.'

'Indeed?' I said thoughtfully, wondering if I dared to risk it. With a veil over my face, would he know me? It had, after all, been over four years since I last saw him. What reason had he to think I would set foot in Albania? I put my hand on Enrico's arm. 'I'll make myself as convincing as any Albanian lady.'

But I did not trust a veil alone to hide me from him. I was only satisfied when three heavy shawls were pinned over the bright silk of my dress and another of dark gauze was drawn over my hair and face. I doubted if Ruthven would recognize me now: I saw that Enrico did not. He looked at me blankly for a moment, then pulled aside the veil.

'I hardly expected you to take my suggestion this far,' he said. 'Who are you hiding from, my love?'

247

'What? No . . . nobody,' I stammered. 'I only followed your instructions.'

He gave me a strange look. 'Perhaps I should have said, what are you hiding from me, Lucy? You've been as nervous and uneasy as a hunted animal all day. Why don't you tell me what it is?'

I wished I could. Mistaking the cause of my unhappy face, he took my hands in his and held them to his lips. 'I haven't forgotten,' he said gently. 'I promised my crew this port of call. When we leave Butrinto, the *Volpone* will be sailing west. We'll find your Byron for you.'

Tears formed in the corners of my eyes. I never knew a man so worthy of being loved as Enrico. Heaven knows what odd twist of fate had given him the career of a pirate. 'I don't need Byron when I have you to love,' I said, looking down.

He shook his head. 'Don't offer me lies from kindness. You're not very good at pretending, Lucy my love.'

There was nothing more I could say.

Shifting purple shadows cooled the narrow streets of Butrinto as I walked along at Enrico's side. The fierce blue sky had been washed away by a veil of rose clouds which hung in dreaming stillness above us. By trying to absorb everything I saw, I only achieved a string of unthreaded impressions: the twisting stepped alleys led us in and out of the town in a bewildering maze, past arched plaster doorways where black-robed women sat spinning, not with a distaff but a twig of wood which twirled like a spinning top in their deft fingers. Sometimes we came across a group of Skipetars, arguing the evening hours away under the plane trees which shaded the broader streets, their shaggy white cloaks spread at their sides, their hands never far from the silver pistols thrust through the broad sashes round their waists. And always in the background there were the sounds of bells jangling plaintively, ringing the faithful into the delicate mosques, and music, be it the singsong monotone sadness of a flute, or the high crying note of a woman's chanting which echoed after us.

The bazaar spread its tattered and inviting sleeves round a dark, dirty little square in the centre of the town. Fruit seller and cripples sat outside the tented stalls: carved pipes and crumbling fragments of at least thirty holy trees, saints or shrines were pressed into my hand, unrequested. Without words, I discovered at my cost that a shake of my head meant a keen interest in buying. Hemmed in as a result by a horde of expectant vendors, I could see Enrico's dark head moving steadily away from me. My first moment of panic passed. The square was small: I would easily find him again.

The crowd dispersed, cheated of the little money I had and I was free again to wander in and out of the dark rooms behind the stalls, turning a chased silver goblet over in my hand, laughing at a carved wooden elephant which bore a ridiculous resemblance to an English cow, wondering if Enrico would buy me an ivory handled bell with a pretty silvery tone in its ring. And then I saw it: a narrow belt of woven silver, clasped by a butterfly with jewel studded wings. I had never seen anything which I wanted with such immediacy. I stretched out my hand.

'Is already bought,' the stallholder said in faulty Italian. 'The gentleman.' I looked round for my rival.

A slender boy of quite extraordinary beauty stood behind me, dressed in a blouse and loose trousers of white silk, his hand clasped round the dagger in his red silk sash. His blond hair curled over the girlishly narrow shoulders, framing the face of a fallen angel, both innocent and corrupt. The full red lips glistened, the black lashes drooped, veiling his eyes. He was Byron when I first knew him. His face had turned deathly pale as he looked at me. 'I *know* your eyes,' he said. 'Let me see your face.'

My veil was drawn back before I could prevent him, and I saw him shudder. 'Go from here now, for God's sake,' he said urgently. 'You must not stay. He is here, in the town. He said you would come.'

'*My* Orlando?' I whispered disbelievingly as his beautiful, empty eyes looked into mine.

'His Orlando,' he said with a terrible smile. 'Please. Do as I say if you want to save yourself.'

But terror rooted me to the ground. I had already seen the black figure with the face of a poisoned lily who sauntered towards us, ignoring the crowd who parted before him. It was strange: at that moment I realized I had known this would happen. Fate would never have let me escape. Acceptance gave me courage: I was able to hold my hand out to him with a calm smile on my mouth. He looked shockingly ill, hollow cheeked with his black eyebrows seeming to cut into the drained pallor of his skin.

'So you came at last,' he said, 'and in disguise. Did you think I would not find you out behind a veil?' His eyes had lost none of their power. I drooped in weakness before them. I could hear Enrico calling and I lacked the strength to answer. It was as if a wall cut me off from the noisy square.

He reached my side, his swarthy face looking almost indecently healthy by Ruthven's pallor. 'Lucy, I lost you in the crowd. We should go back. . . .' He looked from the silent figure in black to the sulking beauty of Orlando, then back at me with hot incomprehension in his eyes. His hand fingered the silver hilt of his cutlass. Ruthven gave a faint smile.

'I am the lady's husband. I'm afraid she can only offer you farewells. I'm taking her with me.'

Enrico laughed in frank disbelief and put his arm through mine.

'I mean it,' Ruthven said gently, raising his eyes to Enrico's. 'I don't wish to harm you. I imagine I'm in your debt for bringing her to me.'

'It was not my intention,' he said in a strangled voice. I could not meet his eyes as he looked at me. 'And Byron, was that all a dream, a fantasy?' He winced as I hesitated. 'I would . . . prefer to know.'

Ruthven was watching me like a hawk, avid for news. 'Which Byron do you speak of, his or mine?' I said. 'His is the dream. I did not lie to you, Enrico. Believe me . . .' I turned away from the unhappiness of his face, unable to bear its accusations.

'Your presence is distressing my wife,' Ruthven murmured. 'I think you should go. Orlando, give me my purse. We must reward the gentleman.'

'To hell with you and your money. I loved her,' Enrico said, and he walked away through the crowd, never looking back.

*　　*　　*

Ruthven had gone to find an extra horse for me, leaving me alone with Orlando. He sat in a chair opposite me under one of the plane trees, playing with the butterfly clasp of the silver belt. I stared at him through blurred eyes, trying to discover a vestige of the child I had once loved. 'Did you think to find me with him?' he asked without looking up.

I swallowed. 'I heard . . . something of you in Venice. Were they true, the rumours?'

'Do you really want an answer?' He smiled sadly. 'It was a pity you came so late. I've had no one to guide me but him, you see, and you know the price of his friendship.'

'The price?' I stammered.

He spoke so quietly that I had to lean forward to hear. 'The right to be an individual. You see in me what he would make of Byron. Do you understand? It isn't admiration or love that my father desires.'

'Stop! I don't want to hear!'

'But you must,' he said. 'If I don't make you see the truth, he'll find a way through *you* to bring Byron to him. You must not do it. Ruthven is incapable of love as you know it, as I used to know it. His passion demands a total surrender of will, the possession of . . .' He hesitated. 'The soul,' he said flatly. 'That is why Byron determined never to meet him again, while I . . .' His long curls hid his face as he bent to study the clasp. His shoulders shook as he tried to control himself. 'Please don't believe him,' he said in a muffled voice. 'I know how easy it is to be persuaded by his promises. They all come to nothing.'

'Perhaps we should leave Lucy to make her own decisions.' We started guiltily as Ruthven looked down on us, his hand stretched out to caress the boy's blond hair. I looked for anger in his thin face, and found only a smile. That distressed me more. It was less natural.

It was too late to make the journey that night. We left at dawn, riding the narrow valley paths which wound through the gorse-splashed mountains with a breeze blowing elusive scents of jasmine and broom in our faces. Ruthven was at his most charming, breaking from stories of the places we were passing to tell me that Byron had gone to Pisa with the Shelleys. He laughed at my expression.

'You think I still care for him? You've been listening to Orlando. Certainly, I talk of him: a solitary life always provokes a little nostalgia. My dear Lucy, I realized in Venice that it was hopeless. A foolish passion which I had carried too far. I am quite cured, I assure you.' He turned to Orlando with a smile. 'After all, I have my substitute. Isn't the likeness extraordinary?'

'Remarkable. And if you do not want Byron, what purpose do I serve?'

He lent over to touch my cheek. 'You should not underrate yourself so. I had another mission in mind which will amuse you and help me. And the boy is lonely with only a dissatisfied old hermit for company. Isn't that true, Orlando?'

The boy smiled and said nothing.

'And you will not keep me from Byron?' I asked, with a poor attempt at composure.

'Why should I? I know where your heart lies better than you do yourself. I think you could help him.'

'Oh?'

'Write to him,' Ruthven said gently. 'You'd do better not to go there until the Guccioli's gone. Tell him to come and fight with us. It's a good cause.'

'Is it yours?'

'It's convenient to the location,' Ruthven smiled. 'Don't look so anxious. I promise I have Byron's good at heart. I know how deep his dissatisfaction goes. To write of heroes and have to live with the terrible creeping boredom of the expatriate who is growing old. . . . He needs a cause, as I do. What else is worth living for? But we'll talk of that again.

'And what do you think of your new home?' he said gaily a few moments later. I looked up at the sheer wall of rock. High above us, square on the ragged skyline, I saw a bleak fortress, inaccessible as an eagle's nest. '*That* is your castle?'

Ruthven laughed. 'It depresses you? Come now, I wouldn't want you to escape too easily. We've been patient for so long.'

'And if I agree to perform this mission for you?'

'Never try to force a man's hand, Lucy,' Ruthven murmured, sounding so like Byron that I turned to stare into his face. He smiled and led the way into another path, bordering on a yawning ravine.

'Is this Ali Pasha's territory?' I asked.

'It was. I assume you have heard of the events here?'

'No.'

'You will. Kurschid will explain it.'

'Kurschid?'

'The Grand Vizier. Head of the Sultan's army against Ali Pasha. Look down there.' Ruthven pulled in his reins and pointed with his whip. I followed his gaze. Under the snow-capped Pindus mountains by a long black lake, lay the ruins of a city. The wreckage still had vestiges of beauty. A burned-out mosque stalked like a skeleton over the crumbled stones, the thick fortified walls surrounding the town had withstood the worst of the fire. The only remaining stronghold was a citadel perched on the rocky peninsula which towered above the lake.

'That was Jannina,' Ruthven said. 'And the fortress you see is the Castro where our gallant Pasha is still holding out with a mere hundred men.'

'And who ruined the town?'

'The Pasha. He preferred to destroy it himself rather than let the Turks loot it. He's a remarkable man . . . but the Sultan wants his head.' He turned to me and patted my arm. 'And that, my dear, is what we shall discuss with Kurschid. A messenger is needed, an innocent party whom the Pasha will not suspect. If you do your work well, I may decide to let you go. If not . . .' He smiled. 'I doubt if one could find a more efficient prison.'

*　　*　　*

I dipped my fingers in the bowl of rose-scented water and leaned back from the long dining table. Kurschid, a small dark man with a proud, jutting hawk of a nose, turned to Ruthven. 'I *like* your custom of seating women at the table. Here, it is not customary.'

Ruthven smiled at him. 'You must know how well acquainted I am with your customs by now.'

'Ah yes,' Kurschid replied, turning to me. 'Your husband's name is written in the legends of our country. . . .'

'My family's name,' Ruthven intercepted the words with a sideways glance at Kurschid.

'That was my meaning,' he said smoothly. 'Your husband tells me you might persuade Lord Byron to assist us.'

I looked down at the table.

'Byron is a rich man now,' Ruthven said. 'The sale of his estates brought in an impressive sum and, by now, he may be in a mood to be persuaded. But Lucy can perform a more immediate service for us, Kurschid. She can carry the message.'

'Perhaps she should first know the situation,' I said dryly.

Kurschid looked at me in surprise. 'You know nothing? Well, to put it simply, the Pasha of Jannina has made a gross misuse of his power. The Sultan has officially deposed his family and it is . . . necessary that he should be brought to justice. He has been gaining the sympathy of Greek guerillas like Odysseus, ravaging this land, Turkish land, and causing a feeling of hatred against us in Greece. Now, what you are to do is . . .'

* * *

I walked behind the small, bowed figure of Veli, the Pasha's interpreter, through the deserted rooms of the Castro. Under the shadowed arches and by the stone walls, the Pasha's possessions were piled with no sense of order: old carriage wheels lay on *boule* tables, a silver dressing-case lay wrapped in a Persian carpet, a Sèvres tea service still reposed in the packing box which had brought it. It was the collection of a miser or a madman.

'The Pasha has discarded nothing, ever,' the interpreter stated calmly, seeing my startled face. 'It is a wise man who keeps his life in front of him.'

'Oh, an excellent principle,' I hastily approved.

He inclined his head as we passed under a low arch into a simply furnished octagonal room. 'There he is,' he said in a low voice. 'Follow me.'

The Pasha was very thin and very old. The glory of his presence lay chiefly in his costume, a robe of yellow silk embroidered in gold thread. He gave me a hostile glance and spoke rapidly to Veli.

'I am deeply sorry. The Pasha does not . . .'

'Tell him that I know Lord Byron well,' I said. I saw that Kurschid's advice had been good. The Pasha's face altered as he heard the name. 'Byron? He is your friend?' he asked in thick, but very correct French.

I nodded to Veli to draw back, thankful to be able to dispense with his services. 'He told me often of meeting you,' I said. 'I know the admiration he had for you, and for the beauty of your palaces.'

'Ah!' The Pasha sighed as he lowered himself on to his cushion. 'What would he say now, now they are all gone, and Ali is besieged and penniless? It is tragic, tragic.'

He bent his head but I saw his eyes, sharp as jet fragments, scrutinizing me over his sleeve. 'Byron is a rich man and I, alas, am poor. Life is cruel. But you bring tidings of hope from him. He remembers me when I need him. I have always respected the English.'

'I come from Kurschid,' I said quietly.

The Pasha's eyes flashed. 'That traitor! That creature! I will not have his name mentioned in my presence!'

'He has your pardon from the Sultan.'

'I do not need it, nor desire it,' he said coldly. 'Come. I will show you something.' He limped to the window, and gestured through it with his thin brown hand. 'All this was mine, the making of it and the destroying of it. I made Jannina a great city, and my word was its law, was it not, Veli?'

'Sire, you were its sun and its moon.'

The Pasha grinned. 'They fear me still enough to call me that,' he whispered. 'Your kings should have come to me for lessons, you know. You English do not know how to rule. Byron told me that King George is not allowed to cut heads off. Is that still so?'

'Mercifully, yes,' I said.

Ali shook his head and his little eyes twinkled. 'Mercy is not a necessary virtue in a king, my dear. It should be displayed, but not practised. Force is the essence of ruling.'

A principle which he proceeded to demonstrate with zest. I sat at his feet, listening as he recalled the glories of his past, the victories he had achieved through hiding treachery behind a smiling face. I found it very hard to believe all that he told me, but Veli the interpreter bowed and smiled confirmation at the end of every saga. Sweet sherbert glued a smile to my face as my stomach curled with nausea. The brutality of his rule lost nothing in the telling.

'And now you say you come to give me the Sultan's pardon,' Ali Pasha said, leaning down to me. 'Kurschid is very persistent. I wonder why. You are not the first to have come on his behalf, although your face is prettier than the last one.'

It was in my interest to persuade him. My own freedom depended on it. 'He will present it to you on the island in the lake,' I said. 'Parga will be restored to you, and all the coastal towns.'

'You hear, Veli!' he said softly. 'Parga.' He lingered on the name.

Veli came forward, a smile cracking his cheeks. 'I bask in the reflection of the happiness that you must feel, Sire.'

'Fool!' the Pasha said, waving him away with a disgusted look. 'It's a trick. They'll trap me there, like a rat.' His cunning eyes contemplated me. 'Perhaps we'll keep the girl here as a hostage, and see how many men go with Kurschid to the island tomorrow.'

'I'm a worthless hostage, I'm afraid,' I said with a cool smile. 'Kurschid has no need of me. That's why I was sent.'

'But he is a chivalrous man.'

I inclined my head. 'Like you, Sire, he is only merciful when it is expedient. My death will make no difference. I have told you the truth.'

Veli plucked at Ali's sleeve. 'Sire, I beg of you to trust her. Provisions and arms are running short. We can only hope to last for another twelve days.'

The Pasha turned away restlessly, his thin neck working with emotion, his eyes shut. 'There must be another way, if only I could think of it,' he muttered.

'There is none,' Veli answered quietly. Ali grasped him with unexpected strength, shaking him until the old man begged for mercy. 'Did I ask you?' Ali shouted. '*I* am still the ruler of Jannina. The choice is mine, and mine alone! Go, before I destroy you!'

The interpreter shuffled out, his head bent over his clasped hands.

'The old fool,' Ali said scornfully. 'Now, tell me why I should place myself in Kurschid's hands.'

'Trust me,' I said, lifting up my eyes. 'I would not betray you. My word is my bond.'

'Your bond.' Ali chuckled richly in his beard. 'Oh, the English honour! And you will take offence if I doubt it?'

'Naturally,' I smiled.

There was a long pause. 'Very well,' the Pasha said slowly. 'I accept. I will meet Kurschid. And when my position is restored, you will visit me and we will talk more of Byron. . . . You know that his enemy lives here.'

'Ruthven?' I stammered.

'You are his wife,' the Pasha stated and laughed at my dismay. 'Oh yes, I know many things. But I do not know how much *you* know.'

'Then tell me,' I said softly, 'what I should know.'

'His family is much hated here,' the Pasha murmured. 'People do not like what they do not understand. We have our superstitions. Have you seen how the women cringe when you admire their babies? To them, the praise of a stranger puts the mark of the devil on the child. Your husband's family is not . . . recorded. Simple people say that the Ruthvens do not die, that they cannot unless . . .'

'Yes,' I said as he paused. 'Unless what, Sire?'

'They can find a man of similar, what can one say, *psyche*, to take their place,' he said quietly. 'But that is the talk of the mountain villages. Perhaps it means nothing.'

'Then why do you tell me of it?' I knew I had turned deathly pale. Oh, it made sense of that hideous pursuit of Byron, but it also told me what I had longed not to believe, that nothing had changed. This was not the mission which Ruthven had chosen for me. He knew I would not refuse the other, if I could lie in Byron's arms again. And I would, knowing the price.

'I myself was reared in the village of Tebeleni,' Ali said. 'I grew up with the legend, and I believe in it. I tell it to you only as a warning, because I am about to die.' He patted my hand. 'I know what Kurschid's promise is worth, but I have to take it.

257

Here, there is no hope left, except for a peaceful death. I give you a phrase to consider. He who seeks the absolute good, or evil, with uncompromising zeal, can find it only in sensation. Perhaps that is the key to your husband's way of life.'

*　　*　　*

Ali went to the island in the lake to keep his tryst. There was no pardon, only assurances. They persuaded him to send back the string of amber beads which were the signal to give up the Castro to the Turks, and they promised that the pardon would be brought that evening. But it never came. They shot him in the groin and then they slashed off his head. It was taken to the Sultan in Constantinople and eventually buried beside the heads of his sons outside the city gates.

Kurschid received two and a half million piastres.

I lost my freedom.

Too late, I knew what a fool I had been to trust Ruthven. Nothing had changed. A week after Ali's death, he broke off his alliance with the Turks and added his weight to the Greeks in their fight for independence. No reasons were given. I was no longer in a position to ask for them.

15

A year had passed. Slowly. I had everything I could wish for, except what I wanted. The pretence of freedom made the reality more painful. Every afternoon I studied Greek and wrote my journal. Every morning, I was allowed to ride out with Orlando within a prescribed area, followed by two guards. He and I were drawn together by a bond to which he would not admit. He knew as well as I what Ruthven had done to him, but now he would not speak of it.

We rode over towards Trikkala one summer's day. The mountain-sides were soft with flowers and the sky was that pale, piercing blue which the Greek gods gave as their legacy.

'Byron has landed in Cephalonia,' Orlando said suddenly. 'He decided to join the Greek fight for independence. Ruthven told me last night.' He glanced at me under his long lashes as I swayed forward and clutched the horse's mane.

'Cephalonia. . . . How far is that from here?'

He laughed wickedly. 'You look quite pale. It's not *so* far from here. Anyway . . .' He flicked his whip lightly across his skeetering Arab mare. 'You'll find out soon enough. I think Ruthven's planning to send you there as his envoy.'

'I can think of no message from him that would be welcome to Byron,' I said with an attempt at lightness.

'I think love must be confusing your brain, my dear.' He turned back in the saddle as he trotted ahead of me up the hill. 'Think. Byron will be desperate for troops, and who can supply them better than Ruthven? All the Greek guerilla leaders stand in fear of him, even Odysseus. Don't you wonder what he'll ask from Byron in return? But I shouldn't be telling you this. We're both summoned to dinner tonight.'

259

'Both of us! That's something of an occasion.'

'Well,' he said softly, 'can you think of another which would involve him more? Listen, if you go . . .'

'Yes?' I was only half listening. I had already begun the journey in my mind. It was easy to still my conscience. There was no need to return, nor to bring him back. Nothing could force me.

Orlando's face was strained as he watched me. 'Remember that if you do not bring him back, I am the one who will pay the price,' he said. 'You brought me up as your own child. You could not betray me.'

'But you have paid it already,' I said. 'Orlando, my Orlando is dead. I owe *you* nothing.'

He stared at me, his almond eyes hurt and bewildered, his lips trembling. 'And I thought you kind . . .'

'Women in love are never kind. And why should I be kind to you? Tell me that. You helped to murder innocent children, and for no purpose. For no purpose, except to gratify his whim.'

Orlando's face was waxen. He pulled back my reins as I tried to ride on, forcing me to hear him. 'You *must* bring him!' he said in a shaking, hysterical voice. 'Don't you understand what he means when he says I am Byron's substitute? Don't you *yet* understand what he will do?'

I turned to look at him. 'I understand. But I have made my choice. You cannot change it.'

No, it was not Orlando but his master who succeeded in swaying my mind.

*   *   *

A week later, I set off by boat from Igoumenitsa to Cephalonia with a Suliote crew. They were almost the last of their tribe left in Albania and some of them had families exiled on the island for which we were bound. The journey took several days and I passed the time in listening to their stories.

The Suliotes had been in Albania long before Ali became Pasha of Jannina. Suli consisted of a thread of villages set on the top of a high plateau in an almost impregnable position, and its inhabitants lived by brigandage. I had heard before that they were the bravest of all the guerilla fighters and my crew hoped to be employed by Byron in that capacity.

In the evenings, I sat with them while they sang ballads to the wailing strains of a hollow three-stringed instrument, but the words were hard to follow and their captain, Photo, asked if he could translate for me. I was eager for him to do so.

'They are the songs in memory of our sisters and brothers who died through the treachery of the Pasha,' he murmured. 'Tzara is telling of when the Pasha had promised us our freedom and we were on our way to exile.'

'You were there?'

'I was one of the few to escape,' he said quietly. 'The other party reached Parga safely and crossed over to the Ionian Islands. Some made their new homes in Corfu, others in Cephalonia. But we had taken sanctuary for the night in a monastery on top of a mountain. The Pasha did not keep his word. When we were sleeping, his troops burst open the gates and a terrible massacre began. They would have murdered us all like pigs, the women and children, too. But in our women lay our strength. In the midst of the horror, we heard their voices raised in the old songs of our people as the soldiers of the Pasha forced them out towards the precipice.' He raised his dark face, smiling at the memory. 'And they defied him. They triumphed. That is why we sing to them.'

'But how did they escape?'

Photo looked at me. 'By death, lady. They threw themselves to their death. Sixty women and children. And we, holding a child in one hand and a sabre in the other, hacked our way to freedom. A few, like myself, live to tell the story. Yes, we have good reason to join the Greeks. Our people were driven like sheep off the land by the Turks and Skipetars. We shall be honoured to fight for Lord Byron.' He paused. 'Your husband has been very generous to the cause. Our cargo's weight slows down our progress.'

'And in the end, I doubt if it will be accepted.'

He looked at me curiously. 'And why should Lord Byron not take it?'

I laughed. 'Like all my husband's gifts, it comes at a price, Photo.'

261

'There is no . . . love between you and him, is there?' he said gently. 'Will you return?'

I shut my eyes against the memory of Ruthven's face as he held his dagger to Orlando's throat, the look in the boy's eyes. 'I must. And . . . I am to take Byron with me.'

'Will he go, do you think?'

I looked down at my hands. 'It depends on his need.'

The mountains of the Morea rose before us like pale wraiths from the morning sea and the mist blew past in trailing clouds as we floated into the harbour of Cephalonia. The white houses of a small town wound up the side of the hill through vineyards and olive groves: on the quayside, I saw a throng of people gathered round a man on a horse, a striking-looking Tartar in a silver helmet fashioned after the ancient Homeric style. The heat was stifling after the cool sea wind, but my faintness was from a terror of finding, as in Venice, that Byron had already gone.

We landed and I hesitated before joining the crowd around the horseman, but I did not know where else to ask. Pushing my way through, I plucked at the Tartar's sleeve. 'Sir, can you tell me where I may find Lord Byron?'

Flicking his whip gently over the Cephalonia throng, he guided his horse out into the open. I followed him.

'I'll take you there,' he said, giving me his arm and swinging me into the saddle behind him. He dug his spurs in, hard. I laughed in delight as the wind whipped past my face, and I clung to him, bending my head under the lanced silver cobweb of olive branches. Soon, the little town lay far behind us and still we galloped on, hooves thundering on the springy turf, until we came down to a cove of the palest, softest yellow sand I ever saw, curling in shadowed bands into the caves and rocks. Some three hundred yards out, a graceful sailing boat lay at anchor, her white sails fluttering, the Greek flag streaming from the mast.

The tall Tartar lifted me out of the saddle and swung me down against him, laughing as I struggled helplessly.

'I came to see Lord Byron,' I said through my teeth, as he

put his arms round my waist. 'I bring men . . . and money. Now, will you please let me go?'

He dropped his arms and lifted the helmet off, revealing a dark, sunburned face and a mass of untidy hair. I was pleased to see that he looked very embarrassed as I acknowledged his bow with a curt nod.

'Edward Trelawny at your service, Ma'am. You have to forgive the rough manners of a seafaring man.'

'I've met others with more respect for a lady, one of your admirers among them,' I said coldly, and relented to his hang-dog look. 'You are *the* Trelawny, I suppose, the bold buccaneer?'

Whatever qualities Mr Trelawny had, a sense of humour about himself was not among them. He scowled at the sand without answering. 'Come,' I said, smiling. 'I know you were at Pisa and that you're a loyal friend to both Byron and Shelley. That's good enough for me. Will you be kind enough to take me on board to see him?'

'You know him well?' he asked suspiciously.

'Well enough.' I was not going to elaborate, and he realized it. 'What a beautiful boat she is,' I said.

'It should have been of my choosing,' he said, leading me down to a shallow side-cove where a rowing boat was drawn up on the sand. 'Byron's got no more eye for a good craft than poor Shelley had for sailing one.'

'Poor Shelley?' I asked as he dropped his voice. 'Why? Is he ill?'

'He's dead.' Trelawny bent over the boat, his hair falling forward over his face as he pushed it out into the water. I heard the tremor in his voice. 'The greatest poet and the most remarkable man I ever knew.'

I stared at him in horrified disbelief. 'Shelley dead! It's not possible!'

'He took the sailing boat out when a storm was brewing,' he said quietly. 'Let me help you in. Sit there in the prow, if you will. There were but three of them. Shelley, Williams and the boy, Vivian. It was more than two weeks before the bodies were washed up on the shore. We knew Shelley by the books of poetry he still carried in his jacket. It was all we had to know him by.'

I covered my face with my hands. 'God, how vile!'

'Was it?' Trelawny said slowly. 'I've thought of it so often since then and in a strange way, it seemed as if he chose his own fate. You know he couldn't swim? I tried to teach him once and he sank to the bottom of the pool and just lay there. It was a while before I realized that he wasn't making any effort to come up, so I jumped in and fished him out. He didn't thank me for it. Said he was looking for Truth at the bottom of the Well. Poor Shelley.'

'You buried him there, I suppose?'

He pulled back strongly against the current, his muscular arms flexed and glowing in the sun. 'We buried him my way. On a funeral pyre, sprinkled with essences, burning straight up to heaven until the whole sky quivered with heat. But his brave heart never burned.'

'And what of Mary? And Claire, of course.'

'Mary's at Genoa. I doubt if she'll go back to England now. The loss hardened her. She's a strange woman. Can't say I like her much.'

'How, strange?'

'Oh, rather conventional, you know. Easily shocked.'

I shook my head. 'It doesn't sound at all like the Mary I knew.'

He nodded. 'I think she's decided to sacrifice her ideals to the approval of society. You can't have both. Whereas Claire . . .' His face softened. 'What an admirable woman she is!'

I stiffened. 'I can't think what you find in her to admire.'

'Yes, I can see that other women would envy her,' he said, infuriating me to such a pitch that I could hardly speak. 'Claire has everything a man could ask for. Courage, beauty, and womanliness. Byron treated her abominably. The most in-human behaviour I ever heard of.'

I wanted to ask what he was doing here when his dislike of Byron positively sparked out of his eyes, but it was too late. We had reached the boat. I followed him out in silence.

The deck was swarming with Suliotes, held at bay by a huge, black-haired man who stood spread against the cabin door. 'Tita, what the hell are these jackals after?' Trelawny shouted, springing down on the deck and elbowing his way through them. 'Do you want help?'

'They want what they always want,' Tita answered, grinning and delivering a vicious kick at one who was more persistent than his fellows. 'But I'm not letting them in this time.'

'I'll deal with them!' Trelawny glared and flourished his sabre at them. 'Go on! Back on the shore with you! Milord can't see you now. Get back, damn you!'

He was an imposing figure and the Suliotes fell back in front of him, muttering to each other. I watched Tita and Trelawny herding them down the ladder to the boat, then I slipped past them into the cabin.

Byron lay stretched on the narrow bed, his head in the cushions. I looked down wonderingly. His hair was completely grey. I was suddenly terrified of seeing his face. I wanted to escape before he lifted his head.

'You were right, Tre,' he murmured in the sweet soft voice which I had never forgotten. 'They're no better than vultures. It's not how I remembered them in Albania.'

'What do they have to think of in exile but money to return?' He lay still. I knelt by the bed. 'Oh Byron, do you forget so easily?' He raised his head and I smiled in relief. There was no change that would not be forgotten in the discovery of what was familiar. He was still the Byron I remembered. His long eyelashes fluttered up and he looked at me incredulously, put his hand out towards me. 'Lucy? Is it you? Or is it one of Ruthven's tricks?'

I caught his hand and pressed it to my mouth. 'Real?'

'I don't believe it.' He burst out laughing. 'How in heaven's name did you find me here?'

I smiled and deliberately unbuttoned my silk jacket. 'Don't ask questions now, my love. I found you again. That's all I care about.'

'Well . . .' He put his hand against my breast. 'Apparition or not, I wouldn't resist your invitation for the world.' He stretched up to pull the curtains closed and drew me down to him. His body had grown strong and lean, brown as a nut. I trembled as he drew his fingers slowly down my skin, circling, caressing. My breath came quickly as his violet eyes stared down into mine, his legs enclosed mine, his arms bound mine and as I arched up, he came into me. I twisted my hands in his hair, straining towards him, then it was on us together, the quick dark urgency which makes love a struggle from yourself to yourself, out of being into more until you are neither, nothing and for a moment, you are two become a single white hot one.

I lay in his arms, held as tenderly as a child, shaking with the slow ebb of passion. He stroked my hair, curling it round his fingers. 'Darling Lucy, I waited for you, and you never came. I thought never to see you again.'

I touched his soft lips with my finger. 'I came to Venice, but you were gone . . . with her.' He laughed at the venom in my voice.

'You don't need to be jealous now. Teresa's in Italy, and it's over. She would have made a good Italian husband of me, and I wasn't ready.' He looked at me reflectively. 'God knows how I'm going to explain your presence to Pietro. He'll have to get used to it sometime, I suppose. Sorry. Pietro's her brother, a sweet boy. In other circumstances, you might like him. He's on shore at the moment.'

'You won't send me away? I couldn't bear it, Byron. I . . . I can't live without you.'

He held me close to him. 'No, my darling, you have me now, for what I'm worth. Not much, I'm afraid, by the time this damned war's over.'

'Disillusioned already?'

'Somewhat.' He sighed. 'I sometimes feel I'm financing the whole damned thing myself, and to no purpose.'

'Why don't you just refuse?' I stood up, hastily pulling on my clothes. I had only just realized that the door had no lock.

'Oh . . .' He shrugged. 'They need it. And I need more. We just don't have sufficient men or money to act. And that idiot Tre thinks we should plunge in, now!'

I swallowed. 'Byron, what would you do for men or money?'

We turned like guilty conspirators as the door flew open. 'You found him then,' Trelawny said, sauntering in and leaning over the wooden centre table. 'I've got good news for you, Byron. Your pious parson's following hard on my heels.'

266

'Kennedy! Oh God!' Byron groaned. 'Can't you get rid of him, Tre? I'm not in the mood to be converted.'

'Can't be done, old fellow.' Trelawny clapped him on the back, and looked down at the rumpled bed. Byron moved his twisted foot under a cushion as Trelawny's inquisitive eyes sought it out. 'Showing a leg in front of the lady, eh?'

I winced. Byron's hand flew up instinctively, then he let it drop back. 'Your jokes are in execrable taste as usual, my dear Tre. The lady and I know each other very well.'

'Ho!' Trelawny said wittily, giving me a knowing look. 'I take the point. Yes, indeed.' Byron's face darkened, but he said nothing. Trelawny sat down and looked up at me. 'I heard you asking Byron what he'd do for men and money. We need both. He'll do a lot, won't you, old fellow?'

'It depends on who she's come from,' Byron said slowly. 'I can think of only one likely source. You'd better tell us, Lucy.'

I looked down at my feet. The last thing I wanted was to discuss it with Trelawny. 'I came from Ruthven,' I said finally. 'He's living near Jannina. He sent me with a boatful of gold and a promise that he'll organize all the guerilla leaders of the north into helping the cause.'

Trelawny whistled softly. 'Quite an offer. You'll not refuse that, Byron?'

But Byron looked past him at me. 'And in return?'

'I have to take you back with me.'

'Of course. The final trump card. Well, I'm sorry, Tre, but I'm not taking it.'

'Not taking it!' Trelawny stared at him, open-mouthed. 'For God's sake, man, why not? It's the answer to all our problems. We can get out of this damned island and into some action. You want to fight, don't you?'

'Of course I do,' Byron said angrily. 'But how do you expect me to fight if I'm sitting in Ruthven's castle? I'm not going, and that's final. She knows why.'

Trelawny drummed his fingers on the table. 'Look,' he said. 'Don't take me badly about this, but you aren't built to fight, Byron. You're better out of it. Nobody's going to forget how much you've given of yourself to this war. You don't have to worry about that.'

'You have no idea what this offer involves,' Byron said wearily. 'I've tried to explain about Ruthven to you before, and you have shown yourself incapable of understanding. Now, be a good fellow and leave us alone until Kennedy comes. Lucy and I have a great deal to discuss.' He opened the door and pushed the protesting Trelawny through it. After a little struggle, he went like a lamb. I think, for all his bluster, he was a little afraid of Byron.

I took a step back as Byron shut the door and turned round, his face white with rage. 'What the hell do you mean by this, Lucy? You, of all people, who knew why I had to leave London, how persecuted I was. . . . And I thought you came for love!' He flung himself down on the bed, his face to the wall.

'I did, I do love you more than anyone on earth,' I said painfully. 'Don't you understand, it was the only chance I had of seeing you? I had to take the risk of your reaction. If you knew what I've gone through to find you. . . .' The tears welled up in my eyes. He looked at me coldly, folding his arms across his chest.

'Tell me, and then I'll judge.'

I told him everything, even of my affair with Enrico Rovere. He listened intently, the anger slowly dying out of his face as I described my last year with Ruthven.

'And now, in exchange for the gold and men, I am to give myself up to him?'

'It's all he has to offer.'

'Nothing he could give me would be enough. I know the price,' Byron said. 'I'm sorry, Lucy. I was cruel to damn you so quickly.' He crushed his hands together until the knuckles showed white. 'Shall I never be rid of him! Everywhere I go – everywhere. It's like a dreadful creeping madness. His face overhangs my dreams, I hear his voice when I'm alone. Even here, I haven't escaped it. At Pisa, too, there was your friend Mary Shelley. She used to come into my room and urge me to talk of him to her, for my good. I suppose you told her about him.'

I sat beside him, taking his hands in mine. 'Would it have done any harm?'

'She didn't understand,' he muttered. 'Nobody does. Not

even you.' He put his arms round me, pulling me towards him. 'But who knows, perhaps you'll drive away my dreams.'

'What dreams, my darling?'

He shrugged. 'Tre says they're fits. I hope to God you never see one of them. Everything clouds over, I don't know what I'm doing or saying, and I can feel him, as if he were as close as you are now. "Hell is here, nor am I out of it." Did you ever read Doctor Faustus, Lucy?'

I nodded. 'But long ago.'

'You remember how Mephistopheles became the doctor's servant in exchange for his soul? How Faustus yearned to break his bond and could not. Do you understand?'

I turned away, but he held me, burying his face between my breasts. 'Don't leave me, Lucy.'

I shook my hair forward to hide the tears raining down my cheeks. 'I have to go back.'

'No!' He hesitated. 'I'll marry you even, if that's what you want.'

'You forget,' I said drearily. 'I'm still married to him. Listen. If I don't return, he's going to kill Orlando. He swore he would with a dagger at the boy's throat. And I have to bring a promise that you'll follow.'

We looked at each other in silence. Byron took the glass decanter from the table and poured out two glasses of wine with his back towards me. 'Would he do it, do you think?'

'I'm sure of it.'

'Byron! Kennedy's here. I'll send him in, shall I?' Trelawny called through the door.

'Oh, to hell with him,' Byron muttered, and whether he was damning Kennedy or Ruthven I did not know. 'Come in, Doctor!'

Kennedy was a prim, spare Scot, neatly dressed, grey-headed. I looked at the bible under his arm and decided it was time for my departure. In any case, Byron was always better conversing alone. Company made an actor of him.

The sun was setting behind the distant mountains when I came out on deck, and a path of crimson stretched towards the horizon of the still, wine-dark sea. Against the glowing sky, I saw the silhouettes of Trelawny and another man, leaning against the rail, looking towards the shore. I walked across to join them.

Trelawny looked at me curiously. 'Well, did you persuade him?'

'Persuade him of what?' The other, a good-looking young man, soft-faced, weak in the mouth, turned to me questioningly. 'Pietro Gamba, madam. And you are . . .?'

'Lucy Ruthven.' I watched as he started, then he leaned back against the rail with an assumption of calmness.

'Yes, I have heard your name,' he said slowly. 'Lord Byron spoke of you once to my sister, Teresa.'

'Your sister's beauty is spoken of,' I offered as an olive branch.

'With justice. Perhaps you were not aware of the attachment between her and Lord Byron?'

Trelawny spluttered and put his arm round the younger man. 'Pietro, don't be such an innocent. There's no harm in a little flirtation out of sight.'

'How dare you!' I turned on him in fury. 'You know nothing of this situation!'

He stared at me, perplexed. 'What on earth have I said now? I was only trying to smooth over what's frankly, a bit of an awkward meeting.'

'Awkward!' Pietro exploded, glaring at me. 'What about my sister? I must protect her honour, if you understand the meaning of the word.'

'She did damned little about it before,' I retorted sharply. 'Living in the same house with a husband and a lover is no way to protect it. You didn't object then, I suppose.'

'Tre! What's going on?' Byron stood in the cabin doorway, his hand on his hip.

Gamba looked at him accusingly. 'She, this woman! Why did she come here? What am I to say to Teresa who believes you love her? Byron, you have sullied the name of Gamba! I must demand satisfaction.'

'Pietro, Pietro,' Byron limped across the deck. 'I told you before and you would not believe me, that I am not, I never have been a man to rest with one woman. Teresa knows that in her heart.' He put his arm round my shoulders. 'Lucy and I lost each other long ago, before I ever knew your sister. She has gone through more hardship than Teresa knows the existence of, to find me again. Would you ask us to part, now?'

'Are you asking f-for my approval?' Pietro stammered. 'B-Byron, I love you like my own flesh and blood, but how can I c-condone this?'

'I don't ask you to condone. You're too young to understand,' Byron said quietly. 'But please, keep it out of your letters to your sister. I may never see her again. Her memories should not be bitter.'

'Aye, that's fair enough,' Trelawny added.

Pietro looked at us, his soft eyes glistening. 'I give you my word that she shall not hear of it from me,' he said and vaulted over the deck rail on to the boat ladder. 'I'll go down to Argostoli tonight and sleep at the resident's house.'

Byron clapped him on the shoulder. 'My dear friend! Don't forget the trip to Ithaca tomorrow. We start early.'

* * *

Byron was already dressed when I woke up, peering into the small looking glass in the corner. 'God, I look old!' He turned it to face the wall. 'Are you going to chase the wrinkles off my face, Lucy?'

I stretched lazily. 'I can't see any. What are you talking about?'

'Liar!' He threw a cushion at me. 'Out of bed with you. We'll be late.'

I slid down under the covers. 'I'm not coming. Let Pietro cool his heels for a couple of days without seeing me. It's too small a boat for enmity.'

'Oh!' His face fell. 'Do you really think so? I so wanted you to come.'

I reached out to him. 'Byron, if you knew how much I love you.'

'Sweet Lucy.' He sat by me on the bed. 'I'll miss you. Will you meet us at the monastery on Samos in two days' time? Trelawny can find you a horse. It's a pretty route.'

I put my arms round his neck. 'Come back to bed and love me now.'

'I can't, sweetheart,' he said regretfully. 'I promised to collect Pietro and the doctor at ten.'

'Doctor?' I drew back.

'Silly girl, only little Doctor Bruno who wouldn't hurt a fly. Don't worry so.'

'I'm sorry.' I smiled at him tenderly. 'In two days, then.'

* * *

It was night when I reached the monastery. The arched windows shone out of the darkness and I could hear the soft, monotone chant of the monks at prayer as I rode up the winding track. The air was very still. It smelt of honeysuckle and burning wood, and the fireflies danced in front of me, among the olive trees. I nudged the little mule up the last path to the gate and left him there, munching the grass.

The iron gate was open and I wandered through into the cloisters, then paused at the sound of raised voices. Someone screamed. I caught my breath. It sounded like Byron. A tall monk came out of the shadows, his brown robe swinging heavily from side to side as he hurried towards me.

'What is it?' I looked at him anxiously. 'Someone is ill?'

'Please, come this way.'

I caught his arm. 'Tell me what it is.'

'Very bad. Milord is . . .' He touched his head and shook it significantly. 'We are praying for him.'

He pushed open a low wooden door and beckoned me to follow him. By the bed, a candle sputtered in its socket, casting the shadows of the figures round the room up on the wall and across the ceiling. Byron lay sprawled back, his head rolling from side to side, his eyes open and staring. By his side knelt Gamba, wiping his forehead with a piece of cloth while the doctor tried to pin down the flailing arms. Trelawny leant against the wall, staring down.

Byron screamed suddenly and pushed them back. 'There, at the window! Look! You must see him!' He pointed into the darkness with a shaking hand. 'There!'

They shook their heads despairingly. I hurried forward. 'There's nothing you can do,' Gamba said hopelessly. 'We've tried everything. All we can do is wait until it passes.'

'When did it begin?'

'As soon as we entered the monastery,' he murmured. 'About four hours ago. Doctor Bruno has given him some pills, but they had no effect.'

'And now I try bleeding,' Bruno added. 'It is impure blood which causes the fever. We will weaken it and bring him a little peace!'

'No!' Byron clutched at his arm. 'No . . . bleeding. It will . . . pass.'

'But it is better for you, my lord. It will soothe you.'

'Nothing can soothe me,' Byron muttered. 'No! No!' He strained back, his eyes starting from his head, as if some unseen person leaned over him.

'Please, let me,' I said quickly, moving past Gamba. 'Leave me with him.'

They stared at me. 'Alone? But my dear lady, what can *you* do?' Bruno asked, smiling.

'Just for five minutes. Please.'

He shrugged. 'Well, it will make no difference.' He walked out of the room and after a moment, Gamba and Trelawny followed him.

'Byron.' I knelt beside him. 'Is Ruthven here? Is that what you see?'

He nodded, a strange expression crossing his face. 'To take immortality – would it be – or to be a part of – what? Too high a price, my friend – I would not – better to die than –'

'Than what, my love?' But he did not hear me. I sat holding his hand while he rambled on. The time crept past. My head drooped with weariness, but when Bruno tried to come in, I pushed him back in the passage, ignoring his protests. A cock crowed down in the valley. My muscles ached and my eyes were like two pincushions.

'Lucy.' His voice was clear and true. I leant forward, fatigue forgotten.

'My love?'

He smiled and his eyes were clear as they looked up into mine. 'Nothing you can do is of any use, not now.' His lids closed. 'I'd like to sleep, please,' he murmured. 'Let me rest.'

I kissed his forehead and crept out of the room. They were all gathered outside, waiting.

'Well?'

'I think he'll sleep now.'

Pietro drew me aside, his face eager. 'You knew. What was it? They say he's mad, and I know that's a lie. What did he see out there?'

'What he could become,' I answered quietly.

'I don't understand.' He clasped my hand. 'But I owe you an apology.'

I pushed my hair back wearily. 'For what? I'm sorry, I'm so exhausted.'

'I mistook your nature,' he said. 'If you can help him, it is good that you stay.'

'Pietro!' He turned back towards me. 'If it is of any use to you, I'll tell you the truth,' I said. 'He belongs to no woman, neither to me nor to your sister, Teresa. Where there is no possession, there should be no jealousy. That's all I can say to comfort you.'

* * *

August passed into September, the September when I had given Ruthven my word that I would return. We passed the days as best we could, waiting for the summons to fight which never came. Botzaris, the Suliote captain who had written asking Byron to join him at Missolonghi, was dead. The demands for money accelerated. They came almost every day now, and there was precious little left to pay them with. The Greek Committee in London sent what they could, but it was never enough. And in the harbour, the *Lara* lay at anchor with her cargo of gold untouched.

The green hills of Cephalonia were blistered brown and each day less was achieved with more effort. Only Byron accepted our enforced lethargy, almost too gracefully. At first, I had refused to listen to Trelawny's complaints, but I, too, was beginning to wonder whether Byron lacked the final courage to fight. It was not enough now to have him to myself. The criticism of others was beginning to affect our relationship. I found myself repeating Trelawny's jibes to him in the hope

274

of jarring him into action, but he took them all with an indulgent smile. I was, he said, his beloved mistress, not his counsellor. Byron listened to no one. So they judged him for his arrogance.

There had been another quarrel between him and Trelawny that day, more violent than usual, and our volatile buccaneer had gone off with Tita and Gamba to cool his rage in drink or a brawl on the island. Byron and I were alone on the boat.

I lay awake beside him, hating myself for comparing his languor, his air of amused tolerance to the fiery restlessness of Trelawny, longing for Byron to do something, anything to reassure us all.

The soft splashing of oars disturbed my thoughts.

Raising myself on one arm, I drew up the cloth blind which covered the window above the bed. Peering into the darkness, I saw the black lines of a fleet of small boats thrusting towards us over the moon-dipped sea. It was the quietness of their approach which disturbed me. I turned to Byron, peaceful in his dreams, his hands locked on his chest. I ran my hand over his face.

'What *now*?' His voice was weary.

'There, outside the window,' I said softly. 'What does it mean? Who are they?'

He looked out and I saw his mouth tighten. 'God rot their souls!' he whispered. 'And they're your men. Ruthven's Suliotes. Is that how they would repay me for defending them?' He pushed me to one side. 'Move out of my way, or I'll be too late.'

I clutched his arm in terror, my hair tumbling over my face as I knelt towards him from the edge of the bed. 'Too late for what? Don't go, Byron. They mean some harm to you. How can *you* fight them?' Without answering, he drew on his breeches and knotted a shirt round his waist, before reaching for his sword and the three double-barrelled silver pistols which were always left in ostentatious solitude on the card table. Two were thrust in his sash. The third he kept in his right hand. 'Byron, don't be such a fool! What can you do, alone? Oh God, if only Trelawny was here . . .' He pushed me back on the bed and slapped me, hard, across the mouth.

275

'Now will you be quiet! Or shall I do that again?' His voice was cold with rage. 'To be attracted by that blustering liar and think I did not know what you were thinking. . . . You despise me, do you? Well, we will see now who can fight!' Before I could move, he had rushed out of the cabin.

They were on the decks already. I could hear soft footfalls on the creaking planks. Peering through the window, I saw the glint of cutlasses in their hands, the glaring light in their deep-set eyes as they came at Byron like a pack of wolves. Admiration and terror fought in my mind for the heroic lonely figure, standing on the moonlit deck five yards away from their shining blades. And I had thought him cowardly!

'Well, what brings you here, my valiant friends? I am, as you see, quite alone. You can put down your cutlasses without fear.' His voice was clear and joyful as if he saw death in the dress of a spring morning. And so he does, I thought suddenly. His cause is not the liberty of Greece, but the freeing of himself. But the thought gave me no consolation. I gripped the window ledge in terror as Photo, the Suliote leader, came forward, his arm raised, the curved sword scything the stars. 'Put it down,' Byron said quietly. 'I can shoot remarkably fast when necessary. Your master taught me, which may give you an idea of my ability.'

They stood in a half-circle round him now, mesmerized by his air of cool assurance. 'Observe!' he cried and they huddled back in fright as the shot rang out. The bright flag tumbled from its broken string, down to Photo's feet. 'I merely demonstrate,' Byron said.

Photo made an angry gesture at his alarmed followers who sheepishly returned to their places. He walked forward. There was less than a foot between him and Byron. 'We want the cargo of the *Lara*, the gold,' he said. 'That, and more from your London friends. We are tired of waiting, my lord.'

Byron laughed. 'Neither are mine to give, my friends. There's your answer. Come, what sort of warriors are you? There's no greater admirer of Suliote courage than myself – did I not choose your men for my own bodyguard? – but I cannot credit you with much foresight. How are we to fight wars without money? I cannot give it to you. There's your answer.'

'Then here is ours,' Photo said and his cutlass flashed down. I shut my eyes.

When I opened them at the scream of pain, I saw enough to know what kind of man I loved. Photo lay face down, dead, blood running out from under his body. Byron was pursuing the others with his pistols cracking and flashing like spitfires over their heads. And the gang of valiant Suliotes were running, like a frightened flock of sheep, backwards across the deck, stumbling, tripping and cursing as though the devil himself was after them. They scrambled over each other's bodies in the fight to reach their boats, tumbling over the rails like water barrels. Byron stood back with a great shout of joyous laughter, picked the dead man up, whirled the limp body twice round his head and hurled it down into the nearest of the fleeing craft.

'Next time, perhaps, you'll ask more gracefully!' A furious splashing of oars was his only answer.

I flung myself into his arms as he came through the door, his eyes still blazing, sweat matting his curls. 'You will not call me coward now!' He threw down the pistols and sprawled back into a chair, pulling me down with him.

I covered his glistening face with kisses. 'Byron, I never saw anything more heroic! Oh, how I adore you . . .'

He looked down at me with a twisted grin. 'You adore me now, my lovely, and yet at dinner . . .' And I thought he had not noticed how I hung on Trelawny's words. I had been a fool. 'Trelawny . . .' I snapped my fingers. 'That's what Trelawny is worth. He could never deal with the Suliotes like that.'

Byron sighed. 'I wish it could have been without blood. They're fine men: their greed is a very petty fault compared to their courage.'

'Courage!'

'Pistols are a low trick to employ on tribal swordsmen. I should not have fired.'

'But it was so brave!' I cried. 'I thought they would kill you. They *would* have killed you.'

He gave me a strange, rather sad look. 'Does only the shedding of blood make a hero, then?'

I did not have time to answer. Trelawny bounded into the cabin, snorting and shouting like a stupid bear. I was furious

277

with myself for having been so mistaken in him. Now, I only saw how brash and noisy he seemed next to Byron. All show.

'It's quite all right, Tre. I dealt with them,' Byron said calmly. 'Don't bother to look. You won't find a Suliote under the table.'

'*You* dealt with them?' Trelawny roared with laughter, although his face was corded with rage. 'You?'

'It's perfectly true,' I said. 'There were about thirty of them.' I leant against Byron's side. 'He did it all, alone.'

'Byron wouldn't be capable of it, not with his . . . affliction.' Trelawny said it with premeditated cruelty. His eyes shone with an almost fanatical look of hatred. 'We know that Byron's only capable of torturing women who can't defend themselves.'

Byron was very pale, but his voice was mild and soft as ever. 'I take it you mean Claire? Really, Tre, I hardly think that your having missed the chance of a fight warrants a personal attack.'

'I always wondered,' Trelawny said, 'how a man who prided himself so much on being an aristocrat could behave in such a way. You were never worthy of her.'

Byron yawned. 'If you love her so much, why don't you go after her? Claire would part her pretty little legs for anyone who . . .' I screamed as Trelawny struck him in the face.

'A little unnecessary, my dear fellow,' Byron said and his fist flew from his side like an arrow before Trelawny could draw back. He went down like a ball of butter. I put my hand across my mouth before the laughter could escape. Byron looked immensely pleased as he gave Trelawny his hand. 'I used to be accounted rather a good boxer. It's good to know I haven't lost the touch.'

Slowly, Trelawny stood up and brushed the floor dust off his jacket. His mouth opened and shut in search of a dramatic finale. When it came, it was bathetically lame. 'That finishes it. I'm leaving,' he said. 'I'll find somebody who knows that war is more than a schoolboy's outing on a sailing boat.'

Byron smiled. 'Go, by all means. The town taverns will be desolated, I don't doubt.'

Trelawny left without answering. We watched him go. Byron's face was sad. 'Damned if I shan't miss the old pirate all

278

the same,' he said. 'I'm too old to make distinctions any more between a poor friend and a good enemy. Hatred's a better stimulant, in the end. At least there always have to be two of you involved.'

'Are you so lonely?' I waited, but he went outside without answering.

Trelawny kept his word.

He left in September and we heard that he had joined the guerilla leader, Odysseus.

'Odysseus – he was one of the leaders Ruthven promised to raise,' I said, turning over in the bed and looking at the letter which Byron held.

'From what I've heard of him, he'd need no raising,' he said sleepily, then laughed. 'Perhaps we'll get the help we need without Ruthven's assistance. You'll not go back now, will you? Well, will you?' he repeated anxiously as I lay back in silence. He leaned over me. 'Lucy, if you leave, the likelihood is that we'll never see each other again.'

'Why do you keep saying that?'

'Oh, I had my fortune told long ago. The woman said I'd die in my thirty-seventh year.'

I kissed him. 'Don't be such a fatalist. I'm not going to let you die.'

'Then stay.'

There was a gentle knock at the door. 'Byron,' Gamba called through. 'There's a man from the London Committee here to see you.'

He pulled on his trousers and shirt, knotting it round his waist. 'I'm coming! Take him out in the garden. Lucy, come and join us when you're ready.'

I dressed slowly and went out on to the narrow wooden balcony, combing my hair. After Trelawny's departure, we had moved to a pretty villa in the small town of Metaxata. It stood on the lower reaches of a barren mountain, where the rock sloped gently into vineyards and olive trees. I looked out towards the soft green island of Zante and the mountains of the Morea mainland. Below me, in the narrow street winding up the hill, Byron's own Suliotes were waiting sullenly in the street, eyeing the barred door where Tita stood, implacable. 'Money again?' I called down to him as I twisted my hair up on my neck. He looked up with a broad grin.

'Tell Milord not to worry. I'll hold them off. They met their match in Tita.' He flourished his cudgel. I laughed.

'Bless you! I'll tell him.'

Humming under my breath, I went down the clattering stairs to the garden and stopped dead as I looked through the window. It couldn't be the same man! I pressed my face to the glass, staring at him. Byron turned round, smiling, and beckoned to me.

'Lucy! Come and meet the Doctor.'

I went out, stopped dead as I saw the man's face. Byron took my cold hand and led me forward. 'Doctor, may I introduce you to Lady Ruthven.'

'We've already met,' I said, withdrawing my hand.

Doctor Millingen smiled. 'I don't believe so.'

'But you must remember!' I stared into his eyes, willing him to admit it. He gave me a blank look of incomprehension and shook his head. He knew of the time he had bled me to the point of death under Ruthven's orders. He *knew*.

'I have an excellent memory for faces,' he said. 'We have never met before.'

Byron laughed easily. 'It was probably a chance meeting in a crowd.'

'Please, if you will excuse me.' I turned and fled back into the house before he could stop me. In the little ante-room, I collapsed, my hands clasped in my lap. Pietro came in, whistling, and stopped dead as he saw me.

'Lucy, is anything the matter? What can I do?'

My teeth were chattering, I could hardly get the words out. 'That man, Pietro, the man from London.'

'What of him?' He sat down opposite me. 'You look so ill!'

'I feel it. He nearly killed me once. He's an evil man, Pietro.'

'You're joking! He looks so harmless.'

I smiled wryly. 'So does a scorpion, until it stings you. Listen, I'll tell you . . .'

He listened carefully, stopping me occasionally to question a point. 'So, your husband is with us again,' he said finally.

'Teresa's was bad enough. I think Byron is not lucky with husbands.'

'It's not a joke. You know how terrified Byron is of being bled. Millingen would bleed a man to death, given the chance. If Byron has another of his fits . . .'

He nodded sombrely. 'Ye-es. I follow you. But you are assuming that the little doctor will stay.'

'Why shouldn't he stay?' Byron stormed. 'I like him. I'm sorry to doubt your word, but he has categorically denied meeting you, and I can't see why he should lie.'

'I told you why.'

'But he's never even heard of Ruthven!'

'So he says.' I folded my silk dress and laid it in my trunk.

'I will not let you go for such a ridiculous reason,' he said. 'Take out your clothes and I'll have the horse sent back. Please.'

I closed the trunk firmly and turned to face him. 'You don't realize that your friend Millingen nearly killed me. Do you think that I am going to stay and let him do the same to you?'

'But Bruno . . .'

'Is young and weak. He's easily led. You know that. Byron, I have to go anyway, for Orlando's sake. I can't let the boy die.'

'It's only a threat.'

'Perhaps, but I don't want it on my conscience. If your little Ada was dying, would you stay here?'

He hesitated. 'No. But she's my daughter.'

'And he's all I have. The other who died in Venice was never mine.'

'Lucy.' He put his arms round me, and laid his hand gently on my forehead. 'You're in no state to travel. I suspect you have a fever.'

'No!' I pushed his arm back. 'I *must* go, don't you understand! I'll come back.'

'If he lets you.' He paced up and down the room, then sat down at the desk and scribbled a few lines. 'Here. Give him this. I don't want to lose you.'

I read it, aloud: '*My friend, you can keep your gold and your men, but let her return or I'll break the bond and be damned to the consequences.*' But you signed no bond, Byron. What use is this?'

He laughed bitterly. 'In blood, my dear, long before I knew what the "consequences" were. When I first knew him at Newstead, he said we should bind our souls in brotherly love. Ask him to show it to you.'

I took it in silence. 'Where shall I find you?'

'At Missolonghi. With luck, we leave next week. Mavrocordartos and the Greek fleet have sailed down there. I'll be waiting for you, Lucy my love.'

I looked at him once, then turned and hurried down the stairs before he could see my tears.

I reached Arta before the fever brought me down. I tried to mount my horse and could not. My mouth was parched. My head burned. Dimly, as I collapsed on the ground, I saw the two Suliotes who had ridden with me, whispering and crossing themselves. They were afraid to come near me. I beckoned to them and they looked up guiltily. I knew it was in their minds to leave me there.

'Find somewhere I can rest,' I whispered. 'I can't go any further. Are we near to a village, perhaps?'

They nodded.

'Tell them to fetch me. I'll reward them – and you.'

They went out of my sight behind a rock. I heard them arguing together, then the sound of hooves receding into the distance. I lay back on the turf, fighting to keep conscious.

Night came, and did not bring them back. Dizzy and weak with nausea, I lay still, staring at the cold stars as they swooped down, closing in on me. I could almost touch them, but they danced out of reach and lay like glittering eyes in the long grass. I heard wolves howling, tried to move. After an agonizing hour, I had only covered a few feet of ground. Tears trickled down my hot cheeks as I realized that the Suliotes were not going to return. Too tired to fight any more, I closed my eyes against the spinning darkness.

*   *   *

The smell of coffee. A skirt, rustling. An aching back. I blinked against the light. I lay beneath the windows of a small, whitewashed room on a straw pallet. An icon faced me, a long-eyed Madonna, with a chipped golden halo. In the corner of the room, an old woman crouched, watching me with an impassive stare. I raised myself on my arms and looked at her. 'You found me, then?'

She nodded.

'How long have I been here?'

'Two months, three . . . I don't remember. You should not have been travelling. It was a bad fever.'

I laughed shakily. 'I thought I was going to die.'

'You would have if my goat had not wandered out of her usual pasture.' She turned as a bell rang out a slow funeral toll, echoing sombrely up the hill. 'All day, they ring it, in every village.'

'Who is dead? Have you heard?'

She shook her head gravely. 'I see nobody. I do not know. You would like some coffee now?' She came towards me with a brimming cup, so strong and sweet that I nearly choked on it. She grinned.

'I think you are well now.'

'Well enough to travel, do you think?'

'If you have to, yes. I brought your horse down to the field. Where do you go?'

I looked down at the cup, twisting it in my hands. She laughed. 'You read it?'

'When I have a choice to make. What do you see?'

She took it from me and studied it carefully. 'A flower, burning. A road, south. Water. A lake, perhaps a sea to cross. So, where does the cup tell you to go?' She gave me a hand to help me up.

'The cup says south. South, then, to Missolonghi.'

'A long way, lady.'

I looked into her wise, cracked face. 'There is no other.'

She sighed gently and patted my cheek. 'I'll fetch in your mare. Wait here.' Her face was sad. 'I will pray that you find what you seek, my dear.'

I reined in at the top of the hill and looked back. She stood in the doorway, a small figure in black, her hand raised. From the lower valley rose the sound of the church bell tolling, tolling. I turned in the saddle and set my face towards Missolonghi.